Wolf Tales 12

BOOKS BY KATE DOUGLAS

Wolf Tales 12

KATE DOUGLAS

APHRODISIA

KENSINGTON PUBLISHING CORP.

Kensington Publishing Corp.
119 West 40th Street
New York, NY 10018

All Kensington titles, imprints, and distributed lines are available at special quantity discounts for bulk purchases for sales promotion, premiums, fund-raising, and educational, or institutional use.

Aphrodisia and the A logo Reg. U.S. Pat. & TM Off.

ISBN-13: 978-1-61129-729-4

Printed in the United States of America

This final book in the series is dedicated, with much love, to all of you—the wonderful readers who make writing so much fun. Thank you for your thoughtful, encouraging notes, for allowing my Chanku—and me—to be part of your lives, and for asking such interesting questions about my sexy shapeshifters.

You have no idea how inspirational your questions are!

To Yahaira Huertas, a very special thanks for your fascinating observations. Your questions and comments about the effect of nutrients on Chanku babies gave this final story a twist I hadn't even imagined!

Acknowledgments

I've said all along that it takes a village to produce a book, and I've been blessed with a most amazing village from the very beginning of the Wolf Tales series—my sincere thanks to Camille Anthony, Lena Austin, Dakota Cassidy, Sheri Ross Fogarty, Treva Harte, Ann Jacobs, Willa Okati, Devyn Quinn, Jan Takane, Rose Toubbeh, Karen "MT" Williams, Rhonda Wilson, and Karen Woods for their eagle eyes, pithy comments, and advice over the years. I could not have done this without your help, nor would I want to.

I also want to thank Mischa Parris for the wonderful Chanku family tree she created for the series. This final effort was a labor of love, and I can't thank her enough.

Many thanks also to my agent, Jessica Faust, of Book-Ends LLC, for managing my career, an involved process that also includes occasional hand-holding and therapy sessions; to my editor, Audrey LaFehr, for seeing the potential in a series of short stories that refused to follow any rules, and then giving me the freedom to continue breaking those rules; and to Assistant Editor Martin Biro, for doing what it takes to keep me somewhat organized.

You can't help but notice I've been blessed by the cover art gods, thanks to the amazing and multitalented Kristine Mills-Noble—I doubt you'll find a series anywhere with more beautiful covers, though I have to admit, I'd really have appreciated an invitation to at least one photo session. (Anyone listening?) Thanks also to the production staff, those talented folks behind the scenes who somehow make sense of my scribbled editorial comments and then turn them into a real book.

Most of all, my deep appreciation to Kensington Publishing for taking a chance on stories that really didn't fit anywhere in particular.

Somehow you made it fit.

To Margaret and Bill Riley, owners of Changeling Press—the birthplace of the Chanku—my sincere thanks for setting my shapeshifters free to roam. (Anton thanks you, too.)

And to my husband, who has managed to keep the homestead in order while putting up with me on a daily basis through deadlines and stalled plots and characters who take charge and won't pay attention . . . there really are no words, and for a writer, that's quite an admission.

Last but not least, my thanks to you, the readers—those who have faithfully followed my Chanku from the very beginning, and those of you only now discovering life on the wild side. Your willingness to open your hearts and minds to the world of Wolf Tales has made this a most amazing journey.

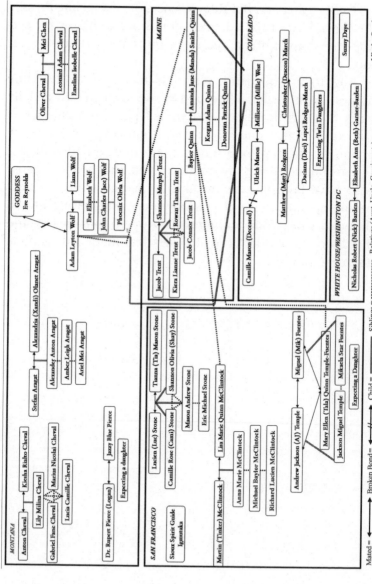

MONTANA

Anton Cheval
Lily Milina Cheval
Kiesha Rialto Cheval
Gabriel Fane Cheval ··· Marius Nicolai Cheval
Lucia Camille Cheval

Stefan Aragat
Alexander Anton Aragat
Amber Leigh Aragat
Ariel Mei Aragat

Alexandria (Xandi) Olanet Aragat

Oliver Cheval — Mei Chen
Leonard Adam Cheval
Emeline Isobelle Cheval

GODDESS
Eve Reynolds

Adam Leyton Wolf
Liana Wolf
Eve Elizabeth Wolf
John Charles (Jace) Wolf
Phoenix Olivia Wolf

Dr. Rupert Pierce (Logan)
Jazzy Blue Pierce
Expecting a daughter

MAINE

Jacob Trent
Kiera Lianne Trent
Shannon Murphy Trent
Rowan Tianna Trent
Jacob Connor Trent

Baylor Quinn

Amanda Jane (Manda) Smith- Quinn
Keegan Adam Quinn
Donovan Patrick Quinn

COLORADO

Camille Mason (Deceased)

Ulrich Mason

Millicent (Millie) West

Christopher (Deacon) March

Matthew (Matt) Rodgers
Daciana (Daci) Lupei Rodgers-March
Expecting Twin Daughters

WHITE HOUSE/WASHINGTON DC

Nicholas Robert (Nick) Barden — Elizabeth Ann (Beth) Garner-Barden

Sunny Daye

Mischa Parris

SAN FRANCISCO

Lucien (Luc) Stone
Camille Rose (Cami) Stone ··· Tianna (Tia) Mason Stone
Shannon Olivia (Shay) Stone
Mason Andrew Stone
Eric Michael Stone

Lisa Marie Quinn McClintock

Martin (Tinker) McClintock
Anna Marie McClintock
Michael Baylor McClintock
Richard Lucien McClintock

Sioux Spirit Guide
Igmutaka

Andrew Jackson (AJ) Temple

Mary Ellen (Tila) Quinn Temple-Fuentes

Miguel (Mik) Fuentes

Jackson Miguel Temple
Mikaela Star Fuentes
Expecting a Daughter

Mated = ⟷ — Broken Bond = ⟷ — Child = ↕ — Siblings = ═══ — Relatives (Aunt, Uncle, Cousins, etc) = ─··─··─··─

Chapter 1

Montana, early August

He paused, raised his muzzle to the dark sky, and sniffed the subtle currents on the night air. The scent was there—faint, but still calling to him, even as the silent night, the gentle breeze, the resinous scent of pine and fir called.

His eyes narrowed and his ears pricked forward. Using all his senses—those of the wolf, those of the man within, and those amazing Chanku senses—he tested the world around him.

This was where he belonged, in this wild, unforgiving place. This was home—the only home he wanted. The only place where he could truly be free.

But what good was freedom without his mate? What was the point? She didn't run with him tonight. She hadn't run with him for much too long.

A low whine sounded from the thick tangle of willows. Cautiously he sniffed the air again. The scent was stronger. Not his mate. No, but someone every bit as important. Someone he sought here in the forest, in the ripe hours balanced on the knife's edge between darkness and dawning. Those perfect hours when all about him slept.

Even the skitter of mice in the long grass, the squeak of

bats overhead, the soft hoot of owls . . . even those sounds had faded away as all the woodland creatures went off to sleep, to hide, to mate . . . to celebrate another night of life before the rising of the sun.

But he was awake, and so was this other, the one who was his friend, his brother, his closest male companion. The one he loved above all other men. The one who called to him now.

Quite literally, in fact.

"Anton? Over here."

Anton Cheval slowly turned in the direction of the soft call and blinked as Stefan Aragat rose to two feet. Despite the darkness, Anton saw his smile. Thank the Goddess for a man who smiled, even when all about them seemed so . . . what? How could it be, that he felt so dissatisfied?

Life was good. All was well, and yet . . .

Shifting, standing as a man beside his lover, Anton chuckled. "You couldn't sleep, either?"

Stefan shook his head, ran long fingers through dark hair threaded with silver, and sighed dramatically. "Teething is the bane of parenthood." His familiar dry sense of humor eased some of the odd tension stringing Anton tight as a bow.

"I did my fatherly duty," Stef said, placing his right hand over his heart. "I spelled Xandi the first half of the night, but it's her turn. She's on kid duty now, praise the Goddess!"

Anton flashed him an understanding grin as he stepped over the low-growing willows. "Lucia was fussing, too. I waited until she fell asleep. Unfortunately, Keisha was nursing her when they both drifted off. There wasn't much room left in the bed."

"There was always plenty of room for four adults." Stefan laughed and hooked his arm around Anton's neck. "How is it a single woman and a three-month-old can take up the entire bed?"

Silence stretched between them for a long count as Anton thought about the statement Stefan had made in jest. "So much has changed," he said, unsure if it was a good or bad thing. He leaned into Stef's casual embrace and stared toward the east, searching for the coming dawn. Was that a faint glow between the trees? No. Not yet. He glanced at Stef. "It's all good, I think. All these changes, but . . ."

Stefan's amber eyes twinkled. "But you're dissatisfied. I can feel it. What's wrong, my friend? Everything is as it should be. The pack is growing. Our children are strong and healthy. We've gone a full five years without an attack, a kidnapping, an assault of any kind against any one of us. . . ."

"Not since the assassination attempt." Anton shoved his tangled hair back from his eyes, remembering. Those hectic months following the attempt on the president's life had ended with lengthy prison sentences meted out to their worst enemies. There were still plenty of bad guys out there, but at least none were focused on controlling or destroying Chanku.

Their secret was still safe. With Nick and Beth Barden continuing as private security for the First Family—at least until the president's second term ended—they certainly had powerful friends in high places.

"So, what's the problem? It's not like you to go searching for trouble." Stefan planted both hands on Anton's shoulders and stared solemnly at him. There was no teasing now, no sense of humor. Merely concern. Loving concern.

Feeling a little foolish, Anton slowly shook his head. "I don't know." He shrugged. "Maybe things are too good, too settled. I have a strong sense of change in the air, as if something is going to happen. No reason for it. We're all healthy, our children are growing." He smiled. "Our numbers are growing, that's for sure. I never once imagined myself as a husband, much less a father of four."

"You're not the only one. I never thought of myself as a father. At least Xandi's content with our three. I hope."

Anton raised an eyebrow. "I believe Ariel counts as two."

"That's sort of what Xandi and I think. Ariel's made Alex look like the world's easiest baby." Stefan chuckled. "So why the dissatisfaction? Our once cozy foursome of known Chanku, counting Eve, even though she's our goddess, now numbers fifty-five, a number that will be growing quickly with Liana, Jazzy, Tala, and Daci expecting. No one's tried to kill us in the past five years." He raised one expressive eyebrow. "In case you're wondering, that's a good thing. You've completed the purchase of over half a million acres adjoining this property, the economy's strong, and our business ventures are all showing a profit. Anton, my friend, only you could find something wrong with so much that's good."

Again Anton shrugged. He wished the sense of foreboding would leave him, but he'd learned to listen to his premonitions. Still, he hated to worry Stefan. He wasn't about to let Keisha in on his fears, either, not until or unless they actually proved valid.

"You know me," he said, feeling just a little bit foolish. "I'm never happy unless I'm worried about something." He laughed. "I imagine it has to do with control issues. If I can't identify it, I can't be in charge."

Stefan chuckled, but he kept his comments to himself. That alone got him a raised eyebrow from Anton. Damn. He hated a sense of something waiting when he didn't know what to expect. "It's odd. Nothing I can put a finger on, but I have the strangest sense that things are about to change. I can't explain it, but I'm afraid to ignore it."

Stefan leaned his forehead against Anton's. "Aren't you the one who told me change is good?"

"I may have said something stupid like that at some point. I don't know, Stef. . . ." Anton took a deep breath, inhaling Stefan's scent, feeling the warmth from his body, sensing as much as hearing the rush of blood in his veins, the steady beat of his heart. He tangled his fingers in the thick fall of hair at Stefan's nape, angled his head just right, and kissed him.

This at least he understood. This he could control.

There was no hesitation in Stefan's response. His lips were firm. Cool at first from the night air, and then warming as they pressed close to Anton's, as they parted beneath the gentle probing of his tongue.

Heads tilting for easier access, tongues tangling, they stood perfectly still as they kissed—longtime lovers and friends, as familiar to one another as the face in the mirror, as emotionally linked as if they were bonded mates.

As they explored the intimate recesses of one another's mouths, their hearts found their perfect rhythm and fell into a synchronicity never explained, yet never doubted or questioned.

Some things, my friend, are better because they don't change. Because they're familiar and beloved. Anton ended the kiss and leaned back enough to peer into Stef's dark amber eyes.

Stef nodded. *This is true. C'mon. Follow me.* He took Anton's hand and tugged lightly.

Smiling, Anton allowed himself to be led, following the narrow trail through the tangled willows until there was nothing but soft, dry grass beneath his bare feet, and the musical notes of water dancing in the shadows.

He tilted his head, listening to the soothing sound of the small waterfall. "I'm surprised the water's still falling this late in the season. Most years it's barely a trickle by now."

Stef's low chuckle sent a wave of gooseflesh down his arms, across his chest. "Why are you whispering, oh exalted leader?"

Anton laughed out loud. "Not sure. Habit, I guess. Afraid of waking the babies?"

"They can't hear us here, and personally, I fully intend to make a lot of noise." Stef plopped down on a blanket he'd obviously laid out in advance. Again, he tugged Anton's hand. "You coming?"

"I certainly hope to." He'd grown hard from the first touch of Stefan's lips against his, but now, knowing what his friend had planned, Anton's heart raced and the breath strained his lungs. He stretched out on the soft blanket beside Stefan, trying to look calmer than he actually felt. It had been a long time since they'd done this. *Too damned long*. He ran his fingers across the sharp ridge of Stef's collarbone. "How did you know I'd follow you?"

"When have you not?" Stefan's voice sounded hoarse, as if it were an effort to form the words, but it was obvious he had other things on his mind. He ran his hand over Anton's shoulder, followed the muscular curve of his arm, trailed across the sharp jut of hipbone, and then cupped the rounded curve of his butt.

Anton's buttocks clenched involuntarily, tightening around Stefan's fingers as they slipped along the valley between his cheeks and paused over his puckered sphincter. He groaned and forced his muscles to relax. Stefan never said a word. With his eyes focused on Anton's, he stroked intimately and probed lightly—not enough pressure to penetrate, but more than enough to tease.

Damn, but he'd missed this. What had once occurred nightly was now too rare—this intimate time alone. Time to explore one another's bodies, to wallow in the pure sensuality of taste and scent and touch, of fucking until their legs trembled and their overwhelming Chanku sex drives were—for the moment, at least—sated.

When had their lives grown so complicated that their time together had almost disappeared? Was this what was missing? These private moments? Did this alone explain

Anton's absurd dissatisfaction with what should otherwise be a perfect life?

Stefan leaned close and caught Anton's left nipple between the sharp edges of his teeth and bit down. Hard.

Holy hell! Anton groaned a soft expletive. "Oh, shit. Stef." The curse felt like a prayer, escaping on a hiss of pleasure. He'd worry about all his dissatisfaction crap later. For now there were better things to occupy his mind—and his body. At this moment, in this place, Stefan Aragat was quickly becoming the center of his world. Stefan and the soft breezes and seductive scents of man and sweat and arousal, of forest and night and the two of them.

Just the two of them.

Anton sat up and countered Stefan's painful nip, running his fingers through dark hair laced with silver on Stef's chest, trailing slowly down and down farther, through the silky strands. Stefan stretched out on his side and propped himself up on one elbow, moving slowly while Anton paused to twirl a fingertip in the dip of his navel. He moaned softly when Anton spread his fingers wide to push through the thick hair covering Stef's groin.

So perfect, that smooth, sleek feel of hair that had, at one time, been coarse and curly. Shifting had changed that. Years of shifting from human to wolf and back again, until the coarse curls had eventually relaxed and now lay sleek and smooth like the fine undercoat of a wolf. Even his beloved Keisha's once tightly kinked hair—long the bane of her existence—now fell past her shoulders in shimmering waves of midnight silk.

So many changes over the years to both bodies and lives, but the best change of all was this—this amazing sexual need that always culminated in such exquisite pleasure, such absolute fulfillment. When Anton clasped the thick root of Stefan's erection, both of them groaned. The sensation of that hot length of hard flesh sliding across his palm made a connection like nothing else. He squeezed tighter. Stef groaned again and arched into his grasp.

Anton nudged Stef's shoulder with his forehead, toppling him from his side to his back. He sat there for a long moment, studying the perfect body, the powerful stretch and pull of taut muscle and sleek flesh. Anton's breath caught in his throat and his entire body thrummed with arousal.

Straddling Stef's legs, he leaned over and, cupping Stef's heavy sac in one hand and the thick length of his cock in the other, drew damp circles around the crown of his erection with the tip of his tongue.

He spent long minutes exploring. Licking, tasting, nipping at the silky skin covering such hard, quivering muscle. He sucked the rounded glans between his lips and found the narrow slit, sucking first, and then dipping his tongue into it, tasting the first salty, bittersweet drops of semen that appeared as Stef's arousal grew. He circled Stef's growing erection, using his tongue and lips, nibbling with the sharp edges of his teeth as he worked his way up and then down the thick shaft.

Opening his thoughts to Stefan's swirling impressions, he felt the hot press of his own tongue, the sharp nips, the exquisite pressure when he locked his lips around the broad crown and sucked hard, when he stretched the small opening with the tip of his tongue, forcing entry to the point of pain.

But not beyond. Sharing the sensations, reacting to Stefan's internal barometer of what worked, what didn't, he knew exactly how to please his lover. Anton's own erection felt hot and heavy, rising slowly to press against his taut belly, and he shared that with Stefan, that sense of hot blood throbbing along his length, accompanied by the perfect ache of arousal. His balls tightened up close between his legs, muscles hardened in response to taste and touch, blood rushed into his cock until he was fully engorged.

And ready. He was so ready to take it further, but delaying satisfaction, teasing . . . the slow build of sensation was a luxury neither of them had indulged in for much too long.

Scent rich with pheromones drifted with the gentle air currents, teasing.

Arousing.

Stef bucked his hips, raising Anton slightly. His breath was choppy and fast, his lips parted on a tight, feral grin. "You gonna play all night, my friend? Or do you know where you're going with this?"

"Oh, I know, all right." Anton swept his tongue over Stefan's leaking crown and once again caught a tiny bubble of cream. The sharp taste stirred his senses. He inhaled, filling his lungs with Stef's musky scent. His breath hitched in his throat as he wrapped his fist around his lover's erection and gave him a few hard, fast strokes. "I merely wanted to make sure we're in agreement. No argument. You're mine tonight, Stef. All mine, in all ways."

Stefan's amber eyes blazed in the pale light of dawn as he nodded. Short, sharp—almost frantic—jerks of his chin. When had the day begun to grow light? How long had they lain here, the two of them touching and tasting?

Keisha might be wondering where he'd gone. Anton pulled his mind out of the moment and sent a brief thought her way, finding only the resting mind of his beloved mate. His wife slept, her body wrapped close around their slumbering three-month-old daughter. He searched wider and found the twins, Gabe and Mac. Almost four now, they sprawled loose-limbed and dreaming in their bunk beds. Then on to the next room where Lily slept peacefully, practically lost among stuffed toys and dolls. He paused a moment, curious about her dreams, but her powerful mind was closed to him. Moving on, he left her dreaming alone in her princess bed with the pink canopy draped all about.

Someday he'd have to ask Lily what she dreamed. He'd

loved the way her mind would take him on amazing journeys when she was tiny. Now, though, as she grew older, she wrapped her privacy about her like a warm cloak.

Much as Anton had learned to do. Still, she amazed him, this perfect daughter he and Keisha had created. Already she showed signs of holding more magical power than Anton had ever imagined, even for himself, but that was a worry for another time. For now, all of those he loved were where they belonged.

All of them were safe.

Relieved, Anton crawled off Stef's legs, shoved them apart, and knelt between them. He sat there a moment, feeling the warmth of Stef's thighs against his calves, admiring the perfect body lying before him. Goddess, how he loved this man!

So many years now, so much history between them. They'd wasted some, and they'd put each other through hell. But they'd not only survived, they'd come through all of it stronger than ever. Strong enough to withstand anything the Fates might throw at them.

At least Stefan appeared to have given up on arguing that point—he no longer insisted all that had happened was mere coincidence. Happenstance had nothing to do with a love as powerful as theirs—one born of so very many mixed emotions, so many terrible mistakes.

Anton sighed. He really had to quit worrying, but he bit back a grin as his mind whirled with the myriad changes he'd gone through since discovering he wasn't just a man at all—he was, instead, a powerful shapeshifter who'd barely tapped his magical powers.

Stefan watched him with a small grin on his face. "I'm in your mind, my friend. Stop thinking. We don't have a lot of time. I insist on being the focus of your attention. You can worry about how we got to this point later."

Anton laughed. Then he palmed Stef's knees and pressed them back. Stefan's amber eyes drifted closed and he sighed his pleasure as Anton slowly bent his legs until they folded tightly against his chest. He ran his palm over Stef's muscular flank, trailed across his taut buttock, and found the crease between his cheeks. Sliding his fingers slowly along the warm valley, he stroked and circled the tight ring guarding entrance. Using his fingertips and saliva, Anton rubbed lightly over the puckered muscle.

Stefan groaned and raised his hips to Anton's slight pressure. One finger. Just one, pressing harder until he forced entry. Then two, and it was easier now as he sawed in and out with total concentration. He added a third, drawing a soft curse from Stefan, stretching the tight muscle, preparing him. Stef's groans turned to sighs as Anton pushed his middle finger deep inside to rub gently over Stef's small, hard prostate. This time Anton forced a whimper of pleasure from his lover's lips.

"Shit." Stefan groaned and reached for Anton's wrist, grabbing him. Stopping him. "I'm too close for that."

Anton laughed. "I told you, you're mine. Let go." He slipped his finger in and then out again. "I'll just have to make you come more than once. It's good for you, old man."

"Cut the old-man crap. Just fuck me." Stefan clutched his knees and flashed a grin at Anton. "I was wondering what you were planning. Thought maybe you were the one getting too old for this."

"Never." Grinning ferociously, Anton clasped his cock in his fist and rubbed the broad crown over Stefan's anus. Stef groaned and held his knees closer to his chest as Anton eased forward, breaching the taut entrance, filling him, slowly pushing deep inside, and deeper still until Stef's tight hole clasped the base of Anton's thick erection, flexing and squeezing him almost painfully.

They held there a long, silent moment, both of them panting, straining for control. Anton's mind drifted to their teasing. They'd hassled each other about age for years. Hell, he was fifty-eight and Stef eight years younger. They'd just celebrated his fiftieth birthday.

Yet both of them could easily pass for men in their early thirties. In fact, Stefan, with silver lacing his thick, dark hair, actually looked a bit older than Anton, though both of them appeared younger now than they had when they'd first met over fifteen years ago.

One more miracle of embracing their Chanku heritage. In the beginning, they'd all wondered if they aged like normal humans. Liana, Adam's mate—and once their Goddess—had explained that Chanku, while not immortal, were almost ageless. Their bodies, if they were born into their heritage and always lived as Chanku, reached their prime age and stayed there for untold years.

If, like Anton and Stefan and the others, they didn't find out about their heritage, didn't get the nutrients to enable their Chanku abilities until they were older, their bodies slowly but surely returned to that perfect age. It seemed to take longer for men than for women—Millie West had been close to sixty before she had started taking the nutrients that brought her shapeshifting abilities to life. Within a couple of years she'd looked like a young woman in her twenties with a body once again able to bear children— which would only happen when hell froze over, according to Millie.

With four grandchildren and one on the way, she preferred being a grandmother. It had something to do with being able to spoil the kids rotten and then give them back to their parents.

On occasion, when the baby fussed or the boys were making them crazy, Anton figured she definitely had the right idea. It was all a mystery, though. No one really knew just how long their lives might be.

Already it was growing difficult to explain his ageless appearance to business associates. One more thing they'd have to address at some point, but not now.

No, now he intended to fuck Stefan Aragat until his eyes crossed. Anton slowly withdrew from the clasping heat of Stefan's tight passage, absorbing each sensation, each ripple and clench of powerful muscles. He paused with the head of his cock almost pulling free of the dark, damp clasp that held it. He grabbed Stef's flanks with both hands while the thick crown of his cock stretched Stefan's taut sphincter. Felt the throb of blood, whether his pulse or Stefan's he couldn't tell, but it pulsed in time with his breathing, with Stefan's deep breaths, with the thundering rhythm of both their hearts.

He held there for one heartbeat after the next. Until his body trembled. Until Stefan's legs quivered and his skin rippled beneath Anton's palms.

Then he tilted his hips forward and drove deep.

Stef groaned. The sharply defined muscles across his belly rippled. He tilted his head back and arched into Anton's powerful thrust. Again Anton speared him hard and deep, and again, harder and faster, until the forest seemed to spin around them and Anton's heart raced to keep up with the demands of his muscles, with the growing coil of desire spiraling from his spine to his belly to his balls.

He wrapped his fingers around Stef's cock, clasping tightly, stroking him in time with his powerful thrusts. Creamy trails of pre-cum covered the back of his hand, spread over his fingers, and filled the early-morning meadow with the rich scent of sex and arousal.

With his left hand, Anton palmed Stef's heavy sac, holding Stefan's testicles down against the length of his own cock as he thrust in and out of that hot, wet channel. Anton opened his thoughts again and linked with Stefan in time to feel the tight clenching of muscles at Stef's spine, the hot rush of semen from balls to cock to freedom.

Stefan cried out. His body went rigid, his cock jerked in Anton's grasp as his climax exploded, splashing both of them with thick streams of ejaculate. The sight of the creamy fluid erupting from Stefan's cock, the rich scent and the hot flow as it covered his hand and spilled between his fingers took Anton over the edge.

He hammered hard and deep, emptying his balls in a series of hard, fast jerks, of clenching muscles and mind-blowing images. His mind linked tightly to Stefan's and threw the emotions and physical sensations of two orgasms shared into a loop, so that each man felt what the other experienced, each knew the love and the need and the overwhelming sense of family that held them forever linked, forever bonded as packmates.

As lovers.

Over and over and over again. Climax shared. Need shared. And love. Always that deep, abiding love.

As the involuntary pulsing of his orgasm slowed, Anton leaned forward, supporting himself over Stefan's chest, but Stef wrapped his arms around Anton and pulled him close. Still firmly locked within his lover's body, Anton hugged him tightly, kissed the beard-roughened cheek, and sighed with the sense of completion that always followed love-making with this man.

It was good. So damned good, but the sun was rising and the day moving forward, and so must they. It took Anton a moment before he had the energy to separate from Stef, but finally he slipped his softening penis free and practically crawled the few short steps to the woodland pool and the gently falling water.

Stefan was right behind them. Together, laughing like a couple of kids, they tumbled into the cold water and played like children while the sun rose over the forest.

Chapter 2

Late August

Keisha stood in the doorway and smiled at Anton. They'd run as wolves and grabbed quick showers. The baby was sleeping, the older kids watching a movie, and they were alone. For now. He waited impatiently in their bed as she leaned against the door frame and stretched one arm overhead, brushing her free hand down over her thigh, parting the shimmering fabric to display one long, dark, sleek leg.

Immediately his body hardened and he was ready for her as he was always ready, wanting her with a need that was almost painful in its intensity.

Then she blew it.

Keisha managed to hold the seductive pose for a good five seconds before bursting into giggles. "Sex queens are us. C'mon, Anton. You're supposed to be impressed. Not bad for forty-two, eh, big guy?"

"Not even bad for twenty-five." Stefan grabbed Keisha from behind and whispered, "Happy birthday, Keish!" She squealed with surprise and laughter as he planted a sloppy, wet kiss on the back of her neck. His mate, Xandi, slipped past them and flopped down on the bed beside Anton.

"Happy birthday, sweetie." Xandi held up a bottle of chilled wine.

"What's this?" Keisha glanced over her shoulder at Stef's twinkling eyes and then sauntered across the floor to the bed. "Where are your kids?"

"With yours." Laughing, Xandi punched Anton lightly on the shoulder. "You didn't tell her, did you? I'm impressed! You actually kept our secret. We got Jazzy and Mei to watch the babies while Oliver and Logan take the big kids to the new Disney movie and then out for ice cream."

"After which," Stefan added, sounding awfully smug for a guy who hadn't made any of the arrangements himself, "they are camping out in the back yard in a tent. We will, of course, owe them child care for the next twenty years."

Keisha glanced at Anton. "You knew this and didn't tell me? How'd you ever manage that?"

He shrugged, almost embarrassed to admit how much he wanted this time for all of them—how much he wanted Keisha to understand how he'd missed this. As he spoke, he opened his mind to her, showed her how much he loved her, how much he needed this night where all of them could step back to what they'd once had. "I wanted it to be a surprise, and I didn't want you fretting over details." He reached for her hands, took both of them in his, and gently squeezed. "It's been a long time since we all got together without rug rats underfoot. I've missed time with you. With all of us together."

The interlude in the forest with Stefan had reminded him of what they'd so easily taken for granted for so many years. Maybe this was all that was missing. Time as adults. He could only hope. Keisha's smile spread so wide he thought he'd burst with the sense of having chosen correctly, at least as far as birthday gifts went.

"It has been too long. And I'm not wasting a second."

WOLF TALES 12 / 17

She slipped the silky fabric over her shoulders and let it fall to the floor in a puddle of teal blue silk. In spite of her bravado, he sensed her worry, that her body might not be quite as firm after her fourth child, that the others might not find her as appealing.

"You're wrong, you know." The words slipped out before he even considered the fact he'd invaded her private thoughts. "You're more beautiful now than ever before."

She blinked rapidly, and he hoped he hadn't made her cry. That wasn't what he wanted at all. Then she slid across the smooth sheets, reached Anton first, and kissed him soundly. Before he could deepen the kiss further, she turned and gave Stefan a quick kiss, but she saved the last for Xandi.

He savored her joy in this long, deep kiss with the woman she loved. Heard her thoughts, open to all of them now. It had been much too long since they'd kissed one another with passion in mind. Too long since either of them had been together without a baby slung on one hip.

He noticed Xandi had braided her hair—dozens of tiny braids falling in auburn perfection, each one tipped with a colored glass or wooden bead, and it reminded him of an earlier time, when they'd all been new to this now-familiar reality, new to the world of Chanku.

The memories were fresh in Keisha's eyes as she lifted a handful of Xandi's braids in her palm. They clattered softly, beads bouncing off one another, sparking old and treasured memories that she shared with both men.

Arousing, sensual memories with graphic images filled all their thoughts, images so clear they were almost tactile.

"Remember our first time?" she asked, and while she spoke directly to Xandi, the words were obviously meant for both Anton and Stefan. "Remember when I was so damned scared, so afraid to be touched, and you made love to me? Your hair was braided, just like this." She ran her fingers through the tiny braids. "I remember thinking those beads felt like dozens of tiny fingers trailing across my skin. When you swept your hair across my breasts, I almost came, just from that alone. It was such an amazing time. The first time in my entire life that I had sex with a woman, that I climaxed with a woman. That experience took away so much of my fear."

"Do I remember? Are you kidding? You spanked me!" Xandi laughed. "How could I forget that? You tied me to the bed and spanked my butt and you got me so turned on I was practically screaming." Muttering in mock outrage, she added, "Telling me I had to address you as the alpha bitch. You wouldn't let me come for the longest time."

"Yeah, but when I did, I did you right." Keisha wrapped her fingers around the back of Xandi's neck and pulled her close for another kiss.

Anton tapped her shoulder. "Whoa, ladies. Wait a minute. I want more details. Did you ever tell us about tying Xandi to the bed? Why don't I recall that part of the story?" He glanced over his shoulder at Stefan. "Why is it, with these two, you and I are always the ones in restraints?"

Stefan shook his head. "I'm not sure, but don't you think we need to do something about that terribly unfair and sexist dynamic?"

Anton nodded. "I do." He glanced again at Stefan, carefully keeping his mind shuttered and his thoughts hidden from Keisha. He knew she was still wondering about those shielded thoughts when he pounced. She'd barely let out a shriek when he flattened her to the bed, holding her down with the weight of his body.

She squirmed beneath him and his body surged. Stefan nailed Xandi at the same time, though, and they had work to do. Within seconds, in spite of the screaming and cursing and giggles, despite the twisting and turning of two well-toned female bodies, both women were tightly restrained on their bellies, with hands and feet tied to the four posts on the bed.

Stefan sat back to admire their handiwork. Then he laughed and high-fived Anton while Keisha and Xandi twisted and tugged, struggling against the restraints. If they really wanted free, all they had to do was shift. Obviously neither woman wanted to be anywhere other than where they were.

This was, after all, a game, and from the scent of arousal in the air, it was one all of them were more than ready to play. Keisha glanced at Xandi and winked. Xandi pursed her lips in a quick air kiss. Then Stefan began shoving pillows beneath Keisha's belly, raising her hips in the air. Anton slipped off the bed and grabbed the box of sex toys off the top shelf in the closet.

One more change in their lives—moving grown-up toys out of the way of curious little ones.

But the little ones were with their packmates for the night, and it was just the four of them, the way it used to be. The way it had been before children, before the babies had all come along.

Keisha caught Anton's eye, grinned, and made a half-hearted attempt to break free. She twisted and tugged at the restraints holding her wrists and ankles, but it was all for show.

Stefan glanced at Anton, silently requesting permission before he knelt behind Keisha, settling himself comfortably between her knees. His erection rested hot and heavy against her buttocks. The sight of his lover and his wife together had Anton's breath hitching in his throat.

So beautiful, that long, thick cock, dark with pulsing blood, yet it looked pale against Keisha's beautiful bittersweet chocolate skin. The visual was more than Anton could handle, so he turned his attention back to the box of toys they'd collected under Mei Chen's influence.

There was a lot to be said for the younger generation and their fixation with all things electronic. He finally pulled a vibrator out of the box that looked like it could hang between the legs of Babe the Blue Ox.

Chuckling softly, he twisted the base. The low hum had Keisha and Xandi slowly turning to see what he'd selected. Xandi groaned. Keisha's eyes went wide, and Stefan raised one very expressive brow.

Anton dragged the vibrator across Xandi's bottom and left her giggling and writhing against the restraints. Then he teased Keisha for just a moment longer. Stefan laughed and put a restraining hand over Anton's. "This woman's mine right now. I think Xandi really needs to spend some quality time with Babe."

Anton leaned over and kissed Keisha's shoulder. Then he turned his attention to Xandi and did exactly as Stefan suggested.

Anton awoke in darkness. Body sated, mind moderately relaxed, he lay in the tangle of arms and legs and ran a silent inventory of what body parts belonged to which of his lovers.

Xandi's arms were wrapped around his lower legs and Keisha's cheek rested on his thigh. That had to be Stefan's head on his belly—he recognized the stubble from a day's growth of beard. Anton lay quietly, thinking of the night past, of the joy they'd all taken in this very special time with one another.

Still, the restlessness remained. He couldn't attribute the subtle sense of something undone, of change looming, to anything in particular. He'd wondered if he might be frustrated by the changes in their lives with so many children—Keisha certainly hadn't planned on twins, but Gabe and Mac were identical, and that single egg had split all on its own. Lucia had come along when Keisha had suddenly realized her boys were no longer babies, that Lily—already an old soul—was growing up faster than she'd expected.

Anton hoped she no longer felt guilty about her unplanned pregnancy with Lucia. She'd released an egg without actually discussing it with him, thank goodness. Lucia was already proving to be a treasure, one they might not have had if he'd allowed his practical nature to interfere with Keisha's powerful need to mother.

Still, four children meant so little time alone together.

So little time like this past evening, making love. Playing grown-up games as if they had all the time in the world.

Keisha stretched and shifted her position until she lay alongside him. She ran her fingers through his tangled hair. *Thank you for last night. This feels so good, just lying here without anyone depending on us. Without anyone needing anything.*

It does. He nuzzled his cheek against her breasts, now swollen with milk, and sighed. She'd need to leave soon and feed Lucia. He'd heard her get up once during the night, but already it was time again.

Something troubles you, my love. What is it? Everything is so good right now. What can possibly be worrying you?

Her question interrupted his convoluted thoughts, but for some reason, knowing Keisha worried helped him focus his concerns, and it came to him then, so clearly he couldn't believe he'd not realized before what was wrong with their lives. What they were all missing.

Don't laugh when I tell you. It's the fact that everything is so good. He rolled his head to one side and smiled sheepishly at her. *I worry that we've grown complacent, that we've adjusted so completely to our lives as Chanku that we've settled into a routine. Routines frighten me. Complacency is dangerous.*

Stefan rolled slowly to a sitting position. "Sorry," he said, stretching. "I was eavesdropping without shame."

Xandi sat up and leaned against the headboard. "Sweetheart, your middle name is shameless. So what's this about complacency, and why are we all awake? It's barely dawn."

Anton sat up and crossed his legs. He pulled Keisha into his lap and grinned at Stef and Xandi. All of them awake and sitting on the big, rumpled bed, hair in disarray, bodies damp from sweat and hours of sex. It reminded him of those first early months before Lily and Alex were born, when they'd made love every night, when all of this had been so fresh and new.

"Stef and I talked about this a while back," he said. "The fact we're all healthy, the children are healthy. We've gone five years now without an attack or any threats to our safety. Our lives are as close to perfect as I'd ever imagined, but this perfection reminds me that we've forgotten something important."

He wrapped his fingers around Keisha's hand and squeezed. "What if I hadn't found you? What if Stef hadn't rescued Xandi, or Oliver hadn't found Adam walking along that road? If Mik and AJ hadn't stopped in that little bar in New Mexico and saved Tala, or Baylor hadn't gone in search of the wolf girl and ended up with Manda? Stef? Remember how we used to argue about coincidence versus fate? I still believe in fate, but I think we need to help it along, not wait complacently for fate to happen to us. I've been thinking of all the others, the Chanku out there who don't know who or what they are. The desperation in their lives. The unfulfilled destinies of people just like us, who don't know they're like us. Who haven't got a clue what their lives could be."

Stefan grabbed Xandi's hand and lifted her fingers to his lips for a quick kiss. "I would have no life without Alexandria Olanet as my mate, as my wife. None at all." He turned to her and rested his palms on her shoulders, touched his forehead to hers. "Anton's right. We've grown much too comfortable; our lives are fairly well cocooned. But how do we find them? It's not like we can run an ad or spike the water supply with Tibetan grasses."

"No." Anton chuckled. "Though I hadn't thought of the water-supply angle. I'm actually thinking more along the lines of talking to Liana, maybe even reaching out to Eve. As an ex-goddess, Liana might be able to help. As our current Goddess, Eve could possibly steer us in the right direction."

He raised his head. "All the packs are planning to come for the birth of Adam and Liana's baby next month. Let's see if anyone's got any ideas. We can't be the only ones." He shook his head and tightened his grasp around Keisha's waist. "There are others out there. They have no idea who or what they are. We have to find them."

Keisha squeezed Anton's hand, and he stared into her beautiful amber eyes. They were filled with tears—tears that sparkled on her dark lashes.

"I agree with you, my love. I know we should be look-ing, but it makes me afraid, too." She sighed. One of those errant tears ran down her cheek and trembled against her lips. With a brusque swipe of her fingers, she wiped it away. "I'm sorry, but I keep thinking of that old saying, something about borrowing trouble." She shook her head. "Why do I have a horrible feeling that's exactly what you might be doing?"

A shiver raced over Anton's spine. Without a word, he tightened his hold on Keisha and held her even closer.

Chapter 3

"Lily? Do you want to help? Alex, Stefan, and I are going into the cave to check supplies."

Lily glanced up from her book, and it was obvious she didn't want to be interrupted, but Harry Potter could wait awhile. If he didn't occasionally drag her away from her reading, Anton feared she'd never leave her beloved books.

"If you need me, Daddy." She sighed. "But I'm in a really good part."

Anton grabbed her hand and pulled her out of his big leather recliner. "It's Harry Potter, Lily. They're all good parts."

She carefully set the big hardback aside. "It's all about magicians. Did you know Alex said magicians aren't real? I told him you were a magician, and he said you weren't a real one."

"Does it matter if Alex believes you or not?" They'd had this conversation before. No matter what Lily said, Alex tried his best to prove her wrong. Unfortunately for Alex, Lily was generally right.

Lily shrugged. "Not really. Not about stuff that's not important, but what if it is something important? What if I'm right and he's wrong and it's something dangerous?"

"Hopefully we won't be faced with anything dangerous, but if that happens, you call for a grown-up."

"He'll say I'm a tattletale."

Anton stopped at the doorway leading from the kitchen to the caverns beneath the house and knelt down to Lily's height. She was already so beautiful she took his breath; to think that he'd had a part in creating a creature this perfect—and one who never, ever ran out of questions. "Lily. Think of what you're saying. What's more important? Being called a silly name, or keeping someone safe from harm?"

"Keeping someone safe." She planted her hands on her hips. "But if he calls me names, I'm gonna sock him."

"You do that. But don't tell Uncle Stef I said you could."

"Don't tell Uncle Stef what?"

Anton whirled around as Stefan opened the door behind him and stepped into the kitchen from the cellar. Alex was right behind him. Both of them had their hands filled with bags. "Nothing important. Merely a discussion about name calling."

"Ah." Stef glanced over his shoulder at Alex, who stared at his shoes with rapt fascination. "I see."

"What's all that?" Anton peered at the bags in Stef's arms.

"We were checking the big pantry in the main cavern and discovered mice and cereal and an open door make a rather messy combination." He stepped past Anton and headed toward the back door to dispose of the trash. "We need to tell Xandi to pick up traps next time she's in town."

"One more thing to add to the list. It was a lot easier for everyone to gather here before there were so many of us."

Stefan grunted as he and Alex went out the door. Anton and Lily headed down the stairs, through the cellar, and into the caves. The air was warm in this first level, surprisingly so for a cavern, but the water flowing into the large pool at one end originated in an underground hot spring.

Stefan returned a few minutes later. Anton gave Lily and Alex bags to check for any trash that might have been left after the last gathering, and then went to work on their inventory.

After a while, Lily's voice rang out from the far side of the pond. "Daddy? Did you know someone wrote on the wall?"

Anton peered into the shadows. Alex and Lily were standing beneath an area where Mik Fuentes had spotted what he called cave art years ago. Anton hadn't even thought of it since then.

"I think it's cave art, Lily. Something Native Americans might have written ages ago."

"Oh."

He heard her talking to Alex and went back to his inventory. It was so peaceful here in the caverns. There was an almost otherworldly sense—as if people had walked here for ages and left nothing but memories.

And a few fascinating drawings on the wall, if Lily's interest was any indication. He shook his head. They really needed to do a big shopping. Between the mice and the healthy appetites, stores were sorely depleted.

"Mommy, did you know there's a picture book on the walls in the cave?"

Keisha looked up from the book she was reading. "A picture book?" She shot a quick glance at Anton.

He shrugged. "Remember the cave drawings Mik found all those years ago? Lily and Alex were looking at them today."

She nodded and focused on Lily. "Did they say anything interesting? Can you read what they mean?"

Lily grinned. "Of course I can. I can read anything."

She held up her Harry Potter book. At six and a half, she was already finishing the fourth book in the series.

"So, what's the writing say?"

"It's a story about us. About the Chanku and where we came from and how we're related to spirit guides and other kinds of shapeshifters."

Anton frowned. Where the hell did she come up with all that stuff? Then he glanced at her Harry Potter book—lately the source of all fantasies—and relaxed. Lily's imagination knew no bounds, and there was no lack of inspiration. He caught Keisha's curious glance and shrugged, but Lily was still chattering away.

"There are some words I don't understand, but I think if I ask Eve, she can tell me."

"Eve?" Keisha flashed another confused glance at Anton. "Eve's just learning to read. She's only four."

"No, Mommy. Not little Eve Elizabeth. Sparkly Eve. I bet she can read the stories."

Anton set his newspaper in his lap. "Sparkly Eve? Who is Sparkly Eve?"

"Daddy." A huge sigh followed. "Sparkly Eve is the one who lives in the pretty place between worlds. The lady with the swirly eyes."

"The Goddess Eve?"

Lily smiled. "Yeah. That Eve. She can tell me what it says?"

"Lily, how do you know where Sparkly Eve lives?"

Lily suddenly took great interest in her pink ballet shoes. "I dunno." Then she glanced up with a big grin. "Is Sparkly Eve a grown-up?"

"Yes, Lily." He let out an impatient breath. "She's a grown-up. Now look at me. How do you know where Sparkly Eve lives?"

Lily sighed dramatically, as only a six- going on sixteen-year-old can. " 'Cause I go see her sometimes. At night. When you and Mommy are sleeping."

A shiver raced along Anton's spine. Very calmly, he said, "You do? And how do you go to the place between worlds?"

"You know, Daddy. You're the one who told me how. You just dream yourself there. You lie down and think of Sparkly Eve and how pretty her world is, and then you fall asleep and go there."

Unexpected relief washed through Anton. Knowing what he did of Lily's abilities, he'd been afraid she was talking a bit more literally about traveling on the astral plane. At least dreaming herself there sounded harmless enough.

"I think that's a great idea, Lily. I'm sure Sparkly Eve can answer any of your questions," he said, going back to his newspaper. "Why don't you try it tonight when you go to bed?"

"She really had me going there for a while." Anton slipped out of his pants and tossed them on the bed beside Keisha's clothing. "I had images of hunting our daughter down like a fugitive on the astral plane."

"Don't even make jokes about it." Keisha slipped the back door open and gazed into the star-filled night. "That little girl's so filled with magic she practically glows in the dark. There's no telling what she could do if she put her head to it."

"She's magic because her mother's magic." He leaned close to kiss his mate. Keisha turned away, laughing, so that his lips caught the silk of her cheek.

"Uh-uh," she said, wagging her finger under his nose. "I'm not taking the blame for that one. Lily's definitely her daddy's girl and all the magic comes from you. Not my fault, buster."

He chuckled. No point in denying the truth. "Come on. We can argue that point while we run." Tonight Xandi and Stefan were watching the kids so he and Keisha could have a couple of hours alone together. They'd best make the most of it.

Keisha cast him a sly glance. "You want to talk? An evening by ourselves and the man wants to talk? Give me a break!"

She shifted in the midst of her laughter, hit the deck lightly on all four paws, and leapt over the railing with her plume of a tail held high. Anton followed right behind her.

The night was warm, the air currents shifting before them as they followed the now-familiar path through the woods. With Lucia's feeding schedule, they wouldn't have long to run, or the time to go very far.

No matter. Now, with children needing them close, every opportunity to run as wolves was a gift, each time they shifted a special occasion. Unfortunately, gratification of the sexual rush after running was often delayed by circumstances—generally in the shape of one or more of the kids needing something *now*.

Dry grass and twigs crackled beneath their feet; the night was clear and stars sparkled overhead. Anton quickly lost himself in the myriad sensations of running as a wolf in the dark forest, following the ripe and seductive scent of his bonded mate, of the woman he'd taken to wife. No matter how often they sped down this same path, how many times he followed his female, it was always new, her allure as powerful as if he chased her for the first time.

As familiar as it was to him, the path they followed was always filled with surprises along the way; the sensations he filtered through his Chanku eyes and ears, inhaled with each breath, always exciting. He knew he would never grow tired of seeing, smelling, and hearing the natural world—his world—through the senses of a predator.

He couldn't help but wonder if their children would appreciate this same sense of disbelief, the same thrill. They should all begin to shift once they reached puberty—for their generation, it was going to be a normal part of growing up. Would it still be as special?

All the kids had known of their amazing legacy from the beginning. Already even the littlest ones were aware that grown-ups turned into wolves or leopards. The kids knew that when they got bigger, they'd shift, too. They also knew it was a very big secret, and so far, they'd honored their parents' trust.

Still, what an amazing thing, not to be alone with this. Always accepted for who and what they were—perfectly normal, not like outcasts as so many of the adults had been.

He heard bats soaring overhead, and cocked an ear to catch their high-pitched cries. The soft chatter and squeak of their voices reminded him of the hours he'd spent in the cave today. Lily had kept Alex entertained the entire time, making up her long, drawn-out story about the beginnings of Chanku history and spirit guides and such.

Her imagination was boundless, as unfettered and free as it could possibly be. She spoke with such authority that Anton and Stefan had joked about poor Alex growing up with an entire history lesson fabricated from a few scratches on the cave wall.

Thank goodness the pack had the ability to homeschool the kids. The Montana school system was not ready for Lily Cheval and her merry band of shapeshifters-to-be. He didn't even want to think of what it was going to be like when the kids actually started shifting.

How did you deal with a teenaged shapeshifter's hormones and the increased libido following a shift? That was something they'd have to figure out sooner rather than later. Hopefully not too soon, though none of them knew how long it might be before the older kids gained the ability to become wolves.

Mei was the one who'd asked the question none of them had considered—since the adults all still occasionally took the supplement, didn't that mean the babies got it from mother's milk? They'd been exposed to the nutrients in the Tibetan grasses through their mothers from the time of conception to birth. Had that already enabled development of the tiny gland near the hypothalamus that made them Chanku?

Logan had run some tests, but he had nothing to compare the kids to, no control group to study. For all they knew, Lily and Alex could shift at any time.

Anton admitted he most definitely was not ready for that.

Anton? What are you worrying about now? We're here, and you didn't even notice we'd arrived!

Blinking stupidly, Anton gazed about him and realized they'd reached the small meadow where he'd made love to Keisha so many times before. Where the boys had been conceived one cold February night, a few months after the assassination attempt.

There was no way to answer Keisha. She was right. He'd run on instinct alone, his mind twisting around problems without answers, things he'd just have to accept and deal with when the time came.

I wish I had your ability to compartmentalize and put aside those worries I can't do a thing about. He stepped close and rubbed his muzzle through the thick ruff of fur at her throat. *You are so much more than me, my love. So perfect in every way.*

Laughter bubbled in his thoughts. *Damn, but you're a smooth talker.* She plopped her butt down and sat on her haunches. Her ears pricked forward and her teeth shimmered in the darkness.

I am, aren't I? He bumped her shoulder, surprising her, bowling her over beneath his larger weight. She yipped and scrambled out from beneath him, tail wagging, tongue lolling, ready for a tumble.

He stalked her this time, head low, his dark tail waving slowly behind him. She took a step backward, and then another. He leapt and she shifted direction just in time, scampering out of the way. A startled rabbit jumped straight up from beneath her and scrambled into the weeds growing along the creek.

Keisha twisted and pounced. She missed the rabbit entirely and landed in the creek. Water flew, splashing Anton, soaking the front of him. This time when he leapt he caught the loose skin at her neck in his powerful jaws and, without breaking the skin or hurting her, managed to drag her back to dry ground. She rolled to her back in total submission. Then she faked him out and rolled aside to get away—but he was there.

He was always there. He was her mate. He would be there for her forever—and with the knowledge of their extended life expectancy, that promise was truer than he'd ever realized.

Anton stood over Keisha, sides heaving, ears forward as she submitted to him. With absolute grace she rolled to her belly and rose to her feet. Then she stood perfectly still as he mounted her.

Power surged through him—the power of the wolf, of his own magic, of the love he felt for the woman who had saved him in so many ways. Locking his front legs about her body, he thrust unerringly into her welcoming sex. She was hot and slick inside, her body tightening around him as he quickly filled her in the manner of wolves. His penis pierced her channel, sliding deep, swelling, locking the two of them together.

Her vaginal muscles clamped down and held him close. The knot at the base of his penis fit her perfectly.

There was something magical about their mating. It

was always this way, yet always different. The sense of something primeval, an act greater than both of them, of a history none of them truly understood culminating in the two of them here, in the dark forest, mating beneath a starry sky as wolves.

Thrusting hard and fast, he reveled in the sensation, the unbelievable bliss of Keisha's tight muscles clasping him, holding him like a hot fist. Her sheath rippled over his length, tighter, closer, until their climax caught both of them in its powerful rush.

Crying out in a voice trapped between a growl and a whimper, Anton collapsed beside Keisha. With his mind still linked to hers, his cock still tied deep inside her heat, he took a moment to catch his breath. Then he licked her shoulder and rested his muzzle on the thick fur.

I love you, he said. Such simple words. Could she possibly understand just how powerful they were, how much they affected him whenever he thought them, felt them? Said them?

Of course I know. I'm here with you. Our bodies are one. Our minds are one. We are one. Together always. She gazed at him with those fathomless amber eyes, the woman who was all things to him. Mate, wife, the mother of his children. The best friend he'd ever had in his life.

He slipped out of her thoughts, content to experience the physical sharing alone. Then he sensed her silent laughter and raised his head. *What?*

I don't know why, but I was just thinking of our wedding. Me pregnant with the twins and looking like a beached whale, Lily like a little princess as the flower girl, Alex in his tux with the ring. They did a wonderful job, but I was still in shock over the fact you were actually marrying me. It was such a wonderful surprise when you proposed. You had seemed content with our bonding.

He snorted, which always felt like the wolven equivalent to laughter. *You'd already given birth to our daughter and you were pregnant with twins. It was time to make an honest woman of you.*

I'm glad. I never realized how much the simple ceremony of marriage would mean to me. It will always be a perfect memory. Just like tonight will be a perfect memory. Her eyes sparkled. *Now, though, we need to go back. My breasts are full and that means Lucia will be waking.*

Reluctantly, Anton shifted. Their bodies separated and he rose to two feet. He tugged Keisha to her feet as well.

"Why'd we shift?" She looped her arms around his neck and kissed him.

He cupped her full breasts in his palms, leaned close, and planted a kiss on each turgid nipple. Then he sighed. "These. I just wanted one good look before I have to share." He kissed her breasts again.

Laughing, she shifted and took off running. He followed close behind and chased her all the way back to the house, nipping at her heels, knowing he was the luckiest man on earth.

After a quick shower, Keisha went in to feed Lucia. Anton checked on the twins. Both boys slept soundly. Beautiful little boys sprawled as usual in their bunk beds, Gabe on the top one, Mac below. They made him smile—angelic in sleep, they could be holy terrors when awake. He stepped out of their room and reached for Lily's door when Stefan sauntered down the hallway with a brandy snifter of what looked like cognac in each hand. One could only hope. . . .

"Brought you something." Stef held out a glass.

Anton took it, smiling. "Thanks. You always seem to know what I need. How were the kids?"

"Not a sound. Lucia's been asleep the whole time and the boys were out like lights as soon as they had their baths."

He glanced at Lily's door. "How about the princess?"

"She said Alex was being a poop, so she went to bed early with her Harry Potter book."

"Nothing new there. She sure bosses your son around. Poor Alex is going to grow up with issues." Anton wrapped his hand around the doorknob. "Meet me in the study. I need to go tell her good night."

"Will do. And, Anton . . . don't hold it against Lily. She's just practicing for her alpha bitch role."

Stefan touched the rim of his glass to Anton's. Both of them took a swallow of their cognac. The rich bite of the liquor took Anton back in time. How many glasses had he and Stefan shared over the years, how many life-altering events?

He was probably better off not knowing.

Quite true, my friend. Stefan shot him a quick grin, raised his glass in salute, and headed back down the hall. Anton stepped into Lily's room.

Lily's *empty* room.

"Lily? Where are you?" The light was on, the bed still made up, and while the pillows were piled against the headboard and her Harry Potter book lay on the covers, there was no sign of Lily. He checked the small bathroom, all the while casting out mentally for his daughter's signal.

Keisha? Is Lily with you?

No. I'm in the nursery feeding Lucia. Isn't she in her room?

No. Her book is here, and . . . He checked the closet. *She must be wearing her new nightgown. It's not on the hook. I can't imagine her going outside in her gown, but I can't pick up her mental signal anywhere.*

Lucia's almost asleep. I'll be right there.

Anton put out an open call, reaching for Adam and Liana, for Oliver, Mei, Logan, and Jazzy. He included Keisha, Xandi, and Stefan. *Have any of you seen Lily? She's not in her room. There's nothing out of place, but I can't read her mind. She's not answering. Do any of you have any idea where she might be?*

He sent his thoughts out again, a powerful burst from a most powerful mind, calling Lily. Begging her to answer him. Ordering her to respond. There was nothing. Nothing but a great silence where his daughter's unique mental voice should be.

Chapter 4

She didn't usually block Daddy's voice, especially when he sounded this upset. Lily paused, caught between wanting to do what her father wanted and answer him, and wanting to do what she knew was right.

She was probably going to get a time-out, no matter what she chose, but sometimes she honestly felt as if she knew better. She might be only six years old, but even Mommy said she was an old soul. Older than Daddy?

Lily sighed and tightened the barriers in her mind. She'd figure out a way to explain this later, when he'd had some time to cool down. Besides, he was the one who'd told her to go see Sparkly Eve, wasn't he? And after reading the story in the cavern, and knowing how worried Daddy was about all the Chanku who had never been found, it made perfect sense to follow the map carved right here, right in the middle of the wall.

It was easier than trying to think her way there. This way, she wouldn't be just a ghost on the astral—she'd be herself. That would be much nicer.

Sparkly Eve always wore her pretty gown, and the best Lily had was her new princess nightgown with the silver sparkles all around the hem. She felt beautiful when she wore it, and even Mommy said that feeling good about yourself made you brave.

It must be working. Usually when Daddy used his angry voice, she did exactly what he said the minute he said it. She'd never blocked him before when he'd actually ordered her to do something. She stared at the cavern wall, thinking.

She'd done it now, and there was no way to avoid getting in trouble, so she might as well go through with it. He'd be proud of her when she showed him, though. He always was. She still remembered the time when Daddy's smile had been trapped in Uncle AJ and she'd been the only one who could fix things.

That's how she felt now—as if she was the only one who could help find those poor people who didn't know they were Chanku. It was important to all of them, but if Lily didn't do something about it, they'd just stay lost forever.

She couldn't let that happen, and she was almost positive Daddy would agree. She held the flashlight with both hands and read the instructions carved into the cavern wall again. It was in that different language, the one Sparkly Eve had helped her with, but she was still learning, so it took her a little longer to figure it out. There were so many new things to learn. Some days her head almost hurt, like it was way too full of stuff.

Stuff she didn't even tell Mommy and Daddy. Like a lot of the stuff that was in this story on the wall. She'd told them a little bit tonight, but she knew they thought she was making it up. That was the problem with grown-ups. They had a hard time believing when kids knew what they were talking about.

At least Alex believed her, even though he had to argue about everything.

She frowned at the words on the wall. Then, all of a sudden, the instructions made perfect sense. She set the flashlight down—no point in carrying it with her, since the sun was always shining where Sparkly Eve lived—stood on her toes so she could reach high enough, and flattened her palms against the two handprints on the wall.

Then she thought about Sparkly Eve and the beautiful pond with all the bubbles, and it happened! Just the way it was supposed to, the wall began to shimmer and glow and her hands slipped through into sunshine and a beautiful meadow surrounded by a dark green forest.

Daddy was probably still calling her. Lily glanced over her shoulder before stepping through the gateway, but she didn't plan to be gone long. She might get into trouble, but she hoped not. Still, she'd been keeping a lot of secrets from Daddy lately, things he just wasn't ready to deal with.

He worried about so many things, and not just about finding all the Chanku who were still lost, though she knew that was really bothering him now. She'd heard the stories about how Uncle Stef found Aunt Xandi and how Oliver found Adam just walking down a road, but what her daddy said was right. It was sad there were probably a lot more out there who didn't know who they were, and he felt responsible.

Lily was certain she knew how to help him find them. She'd do anything she could to make things easier for Daddy, and for Mommy, too. It must be awfully hard to have so many people counting on you. Her daddy was an important man. He had business people and all the Chanku in the different packs, and little Lucia who cried a lot, and Gabe and Mac who were both holy terriers. That's what Mommy called them, which kind of made sense because terriers were dogs and her little brothers did act like puppies sometimes.

At least Lily thought it made sense. She glanced over her shoulder once again at the dark cavern, which was really kind of spooky when you were down here all alone late at night, but Sparkly Eve would be waiting and sunlight glowed through the doorway she'd just opened.

With her mental shields tightly in place, Lily stepped through the shimmering gateway. Walking from the dark cavern beneath her father's Montana home, she entered the astral plane.

Three small steps that carried her out of this world, into the magic of the Goddess's special *where* and *when*.

Anton glanced out the window of his study, stared blindly at the pale strip of violet rimming the eastern horizon, and rubbed his burning eyes. They'd searched all night and found nothing. Nothing at all. The only answer he refused to acknowledge, the only possibility he had for the lack of mental connection with his daughter was one he dared not voice.

If Lily were dead, he didn't know if he could go on. She was young and perfect and had such a wonderful future ahead of her. She had saved his life on more than one occasion—what if he couldn't save hers?

Keisha and Lucia slept alone in their big bed. Keisha was exhausted from worry, but she trusted him to find Lily.

What if he failed her? Failed Lily. The boys would be waking soon. What could he say to Gabe and Mac? They idolized their big sister.

"You need to get some sleep, my friend." Stef sat down on the sofa beside him and looped an arm around Anton's shoulders. "She'll turn up. She can't just disappear."

"I can't find her mind." Anton ran his hands through hair tangled from the long night of fruitless searching. "Her thoughts are always there, fluttering in the background like a tiny moth, bursting forward when she wants to connect, but always there. Where the fuck is she?"

He jerked his head around and caught Stefan's sympathetic gaze. "Where, Stef?"

Stefan shook his head. "I don't know." He sighed. "When you and Keisha left, she was with us. After the kids had their baths, Xandi said she walked Lily to her room, fluffed her pillows, and left her reading her book. It was early enough that she didn't think you'd mind if Lily stayed up a bit past her normal bedtime. You and Keisha were home less than half an hour later." He let out a huge puff of air, as if their frustrating search had him holding his breath. Then he cocked his head to one side and stared at Anton. "Anton . . . has Lily ever consciously blocked you?"

Had she? He honestly didn't know, though he'd not ever given it much thought. Slowly, Anton shook his head. "I don't know for certain. She's terribly powerful. Sometimes at night when I check on her before bed, I can't read her, but I've never pushed to see if she's actually blocking, or if it's just her natural shield. I sense she might be. I imagine she could if she wanted to. But why?"

Sighing, Stefan rubbed Anton's shoulders. "I've been thinking about when I was putting Alex to bed last night. He was rattling on about the storybook in the cavern, the one Lily was supposedly reading to him yesterday."

Frowning, Anton stared at Stef. "Those old scratches on the walls? She told us some of it last night. It was obviously all fantasy. She was just fabricating a story for Alex's benefit."

"Was she?" Stefan stood and held out a hand. "I think we should go down and take a look at Lily's storybook. The tale Alex told me was pretty outlandish. In fact, it was so far over the top, I'm inclined to wonder if Lily was making it up . . . or if, just maybe, she really was reading it."

There was a fresh pot of coffee going in the kitchen, but the room was empty. Anton and Stefan each grabbed a cup before going down the stairs to the cellar. At the last moment, Anton stuffed a small flashlight in his pocket.

They'd left the cabinet that usually hid the cave entrance shoved to one side, so it was easy enough to enter the doorway and follow the narrow tunnel leading to the main cavern.

The electric lights they'd installed a couple of years earlier lit the tunnel with an eerie blue glow, casting dark shadows off the rough walls. After a short hike, Stefan led the way through a narrow fissure into the huge cavern beyond. He flipped a switch and light filled the area, reflecting off the pool at one end, the water spilling into it from an upper level, and the tiny crystals that sparkled across much of the ceiling.

The air was still, smelling of damp earth and fungus, and . . . Anton's heart thundered in his chest. Wasn't that . . . ? He jerked his head up, sucking in a deep breath, pulling all his Chanku instincts to the fore. "I can smell Lil—"

Stef interrupted. "Alex, too. Remember, they were here with us all afternoon yesterday."

Anton felt as if someone had pulled his plug, as if all the energy that had kept him going throughout the long night had finally disappeared. He sighed and closed his eyes against the sting of tears. "I wasn't thinking."

Stef gave him a quick hug. "No. You're thinking too much. C'mon. Let's check out Lily's storybook."

They circled the pool. It was darker against this side of the cavern, out of the direct beams of light, but the series of carvings and drawings on the wall were still visible. Anton pulled out his small flashlight to study them closer. "I can't believe we've never pursued this. The detail is fascinating. There's a lot more here than I realized."

Stefan ran his fingers over some of the etched symbols. "Alex said Lily can read what it says. She told him someone named Sparkly Eve told her how."

"Lily was talking about Sparkly Eve last night. That's her name for the Goddess Eve."

"Our Goddess?" Stef raised one eyebrow.

"The same. She said she visits Eve in the pretty place between worlds."

"The astral?" This time Stefan straightened up and stared at Anton. "Lily's traveled on the astral? Shit, man. She's only six years old!"

"Tell me something I don't know." He ran his fingers through his hair and let out a frustrated breath. Had he been in denial, treating some of Lily's stories as childish fantasy merely because it was easier? Less terrifying?

"But if she's on the astral . . ." Stefan shook his head. "Time is so different there. She'd have no idea how long she was gone, how far from home she really is."

"I know, and I'm wondering . . ." Anton felt as if he anchored himself to the odd symbols covering the cave. He had to—his mind was flying in a million directions at once. "Could she have actually gone there? I mean, physically gone there? You and I have done it a couple of times, at least while Liana was Goddess, but generally when you visit Eve, it's more a psychic visit. The corporeal body remains behind."

"For most people it would. For any other child it would. We're talking about Lily. This is the little girl who talked you out of taking that final journey to follow the light when she was still an infant. Not your average kid."

Smiling for the first time in hours, Anton merely shook his head. No, Lily was far from an average kid. She was amazing, and suddenly, she didn't feel nearly as far away. He peered at the drawings. There were pictures and obvious hieroglyphs, but smaller symbols as well that could have been letters, though in a language that made no sense at all to Anton.

"What's it mean?" He gazed at Stefan. "Do you have any idea what it says?"

"No, but I'll bet Alex could tell you. I wasn't paying close enough attention to him last night, but he couldn't stop talking about Lily's storybook. Something about a spaceship comes to mind."

"Did you say spaceship?" He had a little trouble wrapping his mind around that one.

Stefan nodded. "I did." He glanced at his watch. "Alex will be up in another hour. Let's you and me get cleaned up. It's been a long night, and I have a feeling it will be an even longer day. Let's shower, have some breakfast . . . what d'ya say?"

Anton nodded, only partially paying attention. He was following the etchings and paintings, surprised to see that the hieroglyphs appeared to be carved into the walls while the smaller symbols were drawn with what might have been charcoal. Done at a later date, maybe? It was hard to tell, but he could see that there was an actual format to the tale, if that's what it was. And one of the drawings did look like a child's rendition of a spaceship, or, more precisely, a flying saucer.

Or maybe it was a large serving plate. He almost laughed at the myriad routes his imagination was taking, but it was obvious there was a story here. He just wished he knew what it was.

Something clattered at his feet. He glanced at the ground to see what he'd kicked. It was a little flashlight covered in cartoon characters, the one Lily kept beside her bed. As he reached down to pick it up, he noticed footprints. Small, perfect little prints that looked exactly like the ballet slippers Lily insisted on wearing much of the time.

They were, after all, what princesses wore. She'd been adamant about that. The prints suddenly blurred, and Anton realized his eyes had filled with tears. Yesterday, when Lily and Alex were down here, both kids had been wearing tennis shoes. These prints were different. They'd been made since then. She had to have been here last night. The prints were fresh, her scent was fresh, so it hadn't been all that long ago.

"What've you got?"

Stefan knelt beside him. Anton hadn't even realized he'd fallen to his knees. "Lily's prints. Look. Look where they go." He pointed, and then he turned and looked directly into Stefan's amber eyes.

"That can't be right. How could she possibly walk into a wall of solid stone?"

"Shit." Anton cleared his throat. "Last night when Keisha and I were with Lily, she was talking about Sparkly Eve. How she liked to visit the Goddess in her dreams. I suggested she go and see Eve when she went to bed. You don't think . . ." He planted his hands on his knees and bowed his head.

"I think Lily understands more of what's written on this wall than we're giving her credit for. And I'm wondering if there might be instructions for traveling on the astral plane. Instructions she came down here to follow."

Anton stood up and shoved Lily's flashlight into his pocket. "I know if I call on Eve she'll answer, but I'm exhausted right now, and I don't want to make any mistakes. We need to talk to Alex first, but I don't want to get him up this early. Let's use the shower in one of the guest rooms so we don't wake anyone. It was a long night, but there's no way I can sleep now. I have no doubt we're on the right track. I also have no doubt I know a little girl who's going to end up grounded until she's eighty."

Laughing, Stefan followed him out of the caverns. "I so do not envy your life when that girl hits puberty."

Neither did he. "Not funny, Stef. Not funny at all."

But at least he knew Lily was alive. Alive and safe. She'd gone to see Eve, and there was no way Eve would let anything or anyone harm his daughter. He thought again about going after her now, but something held him back.

Lily had shown, time and again, that she was not a typical child. If she had crossed over to the astral, there had to be a reason. A very good one to make her take such a risk without first telling her mother or father.

Lily had saved him on more than one occasion. He had to respect the fact she was intelligent beyond measure and much more talented than the average child.

More than most adults. He chuckled at that thought. She'd already demonstrated she was a lot smarter than her father.

A dark shroud slowly peeled away from his heart and mind. Lily would be fine. He had to trust her instincts as well as his own. Then he had to find her and bring her home.

And ground that kid until she was ninety. At least.

Chapter 5

Anton felt unaccountably lighthearted as they left the cellar and climbed the stairs to the kitchen. After a night of unrelenting fear, of imagining the worst, finding that little flashlight lying in the sand, seeing her footsteps disappearing into the solid wall of stone were the most reassurance he'd had since first learning that Lily was missing.

If she was with the Goddess, he had to believe she was fine. Eve would watch over her, and while she might not take the initiative to let Anton know she had his daughter, Lily would be safe.

Eve, after all, existed in a totally different element of time. What could feel like seconds for her could be hours here, and vice versa.

Which meant they'd better find Lily quickly, before she grew up on the astral plane. Of course, if that were to happen, he'd avoid puberty altogether. . . .

He chuckled softly, following Stefan toward one of the empty guest rooms.

Stefan paused in front of the doorway. "What's so funny?"

"Thinking about the time anomaly, the way time runs at a different rate on the astral. If we could figure out how to work this right, maybe we could get Lily when she's all grown-up. You know, avoid those teen years altogether?"

"You're a sick man, Anton Cheval." Stefan chuckled. "But if you figure it out, I want the details. Amber and Ariel won't be little forever."

"None of them will." The thought left him uncomfortably rattled as he followed Stefan into the bathroom. The adults kept getting younger while the children grew up and out of their childhood. Such a strange thing to consider, how their Chanku bodies developed and aged—or didn't. Fascinating, and allowing his thoughts to meander achieved an extra bonus—at least he was no longer as worried about Lily.

She was with Eve and she was safe. He had to believe that. He couldn't accept anything else. Couldn't allow himself to consider an alternative. He reached for Keisha, caught her sleepy thoughts, and told her what they'd discovered.

You're going after her?

As soon as Stefan and I talk to Alex. I'm unable to read the carvings, and we want to know what Lily told him. Go back to sleep. With any luck, I'll have her home by the time you awaken.

Be careful, my love. Just bring our baby home.

There was no question of showering alone. Stefan sensed Anton's need this morning—a need so powerful it frightened him. Did he have what Anton required? For a man always in control, one often able to control the very elements around him, having no control over events right now had to be tearing him apart.

His calm acceptance of Lily's disappearance made Stefan nervous. The man should be frantic with worry—begging Eve for help, dragging Alex out of bed and demanding the information he needed. Instead, he was carefully, almost methodically removing his clothing, folding his pants neatly, and doing the same with his shirt. Waiting patiently on Stefan and then following him into the big bathroom with the spray heads at each end of the huge shower.

Calm. Controlled. Too controlled. This was wrong. Wrong and potentially dangerous if that control were to slip at the wrong time, in the wrong place. He glanced to his right and caught their reflection in the big mirror—two tall, lean men who still, even after all these years, looked enough alike to be brothers.

Yet could any two men be more different? Anton's intensity was almost a third entity in the room. Stefan wished he could see auras—he wondered what shades of color were spiking forth from Anton right now.

Their eyes met in the mirror, a brief connection Anton quickly ended. What was he really thinking right now? What was he honestly feeling? His thoughts were blocked, his emotions hidden behind a mask of unconcern and the reality of exhaustion.

Stefan looked away, his emotions in turmoil as he turned on both sprayers and stepped into the tile enclosure. The water was hot, coming out with enough force to sting, but he stood beneath the spray and washed the hours of sweat and worry off his tired body. Neither he nor Anton had slept, and the day ahead would probably be a long one.

If they managed to get through the morning.

He opened his eyes and felt Anton watching him, but when Stef tried to link, the barrier protecting his friend's mind was still impenetrable. This time, when he turned and gazed at the man, the look in Anton's eyes was one of desperation, as if he feared losing the control that was so terribly important to him.

Is that what you need, my friend? To have that iron control taken from you by one who loves you? The thought was silent, private and not shared, but somehow,

Stefan knew he was right. Without hesitation, Stef went to his knees in front of Anton, cupped his heavy sac in his palm, and took his flaccid penis in his mouth.

"No. Stef . . . please. . . ."

Anton crying? Stef ignored the broken plea and sucked him deep. He felt the heat and pulse of blood as Anton's cock surged to life, wrapped one arm across his firm buttocks, and held him close, sucking and licking, taking him quickly to the peak without any finesse at all.

The tile was hard beneath his knees, hot water beating against his back and shoulders, but he focused all his senses on pulling Anton out of his dark pit and dragging him over the top. Somehow, he sensed he would have to force the man to feel, to acknowledge his fears for Lily.

He had to break that iron control. Stef rolled Anton's balls between his fingers, concentrating on the hard orbs sliding within the soft pouch. With his other hand, he gently stroked and then penetrated Anton's taut sphincter.

It took Stef only a couple of minutes to take him to the edge. First one finger, then two, pumping in and out in time with the movement of lips over smooth skin, with the slow slide of tongue and teeth over Anton's now fully erect cock. Sucking and tonguing the thick veins along the surface while cupping his balls, rolling and massaging the hard balls inside his scrotal sac, sliding his fingers deep inside his tight channel.

Anton groaned, his body stiffened, and Stef tasted the bittersweet ejaculate as his dearest friend finally gave in to the overwhelming stimulation.

There was no sense of pleasure for either man. This was something Stefan needed to do for Anton. It was something Anton merely needed.

But as Stef rose, Anton shuttered his expression, turned away without looking at him, and leaned against the shower wall. Resting his forehead on his folded arms, he said, *I need more, Stef. Please.*

Are you sure?

Anton merely nodded. His shoulders were bowed, his body submissive as he leaned forward with the water sluicing off his back and buttocks. Stef was hard. He'd planned to jerk off to ease the pressure, not ask Anton to help him. He'd certainly not planned to take him like this. Not now, but there was no doubt in his mind this was what Anton wanted.

Instead of asking why, he merely used soap to ease the way without any preliminaries at all. He'd do this the way he sensed Anton wanted him—hard and fast, the same way he'd sucked him off. Stef rubbed the bar of soap across Anton's taut sphincter and then took his cock in his hand. He brushed the broad head through the soap and then pressed forward.

Anton adjusted his stance. Stefan filled him, fascinated as always by the way the thick head of his cock reformed and stretched Anton's tightly puckered ass as he entered. Slowly at first, he breached the taut ring of muscle, slipping the broad head through, easing his entire length inside until he was buried balls deep. His pubic hair brushed Anton's buttocks. He felt the slight tickle when his balls brushed against Anton's.

Stef held still for a moment, giving Anton time to adjust to this sensual invasion. He was big and hard, and they'd not done this for quite some time, not with Stef topping Anton. Usually, when they were together, Anton took the dominant role.

It was only right—he would always be the dominant male in Stef's life. Even now, Stef knew that he merely did as Anton wished. His status within the pack wasn't something Stefan ever questioned. He didn't doubt his inner resolve, his alpha qualities, or his position as Anton's second. He would always be there for the man he loved, no matter what Anton asked of him.

It was what it was, accepted and honored.

Just as all of them accepted and honored the changes in their lives. Parenthood had been the biggest. It had enriched them, yet it had also stolen so many freedoms they'd once taken for granted. For creatures ruled by an unforgiving libido, by the need to shift and run as wolves, the new restraints of parenthood had been a major adjustment.

Their lives were now filled with give and take, with compromise and sharing of child care amongst themselves in order to give each bonded pair the time they needed on their own, and yet Stefan knew none of them would change the way their lives were now. Parenthood was a two-edged sword—it made them stronger, better people, but it also made them vulnerable.

Love worked that way. Strengthened them, even as it came with its own baggage, its own set of rules. Yet Stef freely admitted that in spite of the fears for his children's future, his worries over their day-to-day lives, his life was richer, fuller because of their love.

Even in times like this, when fear overrode the joy, when everything seemed to be spinning out of control.

Well . . . not entirely. After a few seconds, Anton nodded that he could go on. Even taking Stef up his ass, the man was still the über alpha, still in charge.

Thank the Goddess, some things never changed.

Smiling to himself, Stefan planted his hands on the wall above Anton's shoulders, braced beneath the shower's spray, and began to move. His hips rocked forward with each hard thrust. He held nothing back. Not this time.

He heard Anton's soft grunts as he plowed into him, penetrating deep, using all the strength in his back and hips, in the practiced buck and sway of one man dominating another. Their bodies slapped together in an ever-increasing rhythm. Stefan picked up speed, going deep, and deeper still.

He opened his thoughts, not sure if Anton would join

him, but the link was there, strong and solid, bursting with energy.

Deeper. Harder, Stef. More. I need more. Deeper!

I should have known. You're giving orders even when you bottom.

Anton's harsh bark of laughter turned into a long, low groan as Stefan grabbed his hips and pulled him back against his groin. He grabbed Anton's erection, amazed by its hard strength so quickly after coming. The mere sensation of wrapping his fingers around that familiar length, the feeling of heat and life in his palm, was all it took.

A hot coil of energy burned from the small of his back, through his bowels and belly. His balls tightened and his cock jerked. Stef groaned and slammed forward, burying himself deeper still, filling Anton with the hot pulsing waves of his ejaculate.

At the same time, Anton's knees buckled. All that held him upright were Stef's tight grip around his cock and his hand planted firmly against Anton's belly. Slowly, both of them sank to their knees on the floor of the shower. Others in the house must be up and showering now, because the water was turning cold, but Stef didn't have the energy to move.

He doubted Anton could, either. He leaned against Anton's back and rubbed his chin across his shoulder. "I didn't hurt you, did I? I didn't mean to go so deep."

Without warning, Anton cursed. He tried to stand, but Stef's weight and the full length of his cock still planted deeply inside held him down.

Laughing, he glared ferociously over his shoulder at Stef. "Get off me, you oaf."

Confused, Stef pulled free and turned to rinse off under the cooling water. "What's so funny?"

"Deeper. They were deeper in front." Anton washed himself as if he were totally oblivious to the fact the water was growing unbearably cold. "She stood on her toes."

Shivering from the aftermath of orgasm, from the hard sting of water barely above freezing, Stefan shut off the tap. "You lost me. What are you talking about?" He grabbed a towel for himself and threw one to Anton.

"I still want to talk to Alex, but I knew there was something I wasn't seeing, and it's been driving me nuts. Lily's footprints. Right there in front of the wall, I showed you the set of prints where she stood with her feet together. Perfect little prints, and then you can see where she stepped forward and disappeared into the wall. Remember?"

"I saw them. So?"

"The prints that were parallel, the ones where her feet were together, had deeper impressions in front. Her toes had pressed almost an inch deeper into the sand than her heels. She stood on her toes to reach something. Do you recall what's on the wall at that point?"

Stef thought about the drawings, the writing, the . . . "Handprints. There were handprints. They were different because they were chiseled into the rock and then the impression had been painted, as well. Up high. . . ."

Anton nodded. "High enough for you or me to comfortably place our hands in them at chest level. Lily would have to stand on her toes to reach them."

Anton was right. He could see them now—the two prints placed side by side at the very end of the artwork on the wall. Stefan grabbed his wristwatch off the counter and slipped it on. It was almost seven, and though he'd gone the night without sleep, he was wide awake. Adrenaline rushed through his veins; his mind was crystal clear.

He wrapped the towel around his waist and grabbed his dirty clothes off the bed. Anton did the same, and they left the room together. "I'm going to grab some fresh clothes. I'll meet you in Alex's room. Let's get him up and see what he remembers of Lily's story." Stef paused, shivering. "And while I think of it, we need to add another hot water heater to this wing."

Laughing, Anton flipped him off and headed toward his suite of rooms.

Alex reminded Anton of a miniature version of his father—already growing tall and lanky with amber eyes too big for his face and a thick mop of dark hair that resisted whatever attempts Xandi made to tame it. He had Stef's boundless good humor and his mother's zest for life.

He was smart and funny, and idolized Lily—a little too much, in Anton's estimation. Even he knew his daughter was far from perfect. No, she had a bit too much of her father in her, and way too much influence on Alex.

Liana had accompanied them into the caverns. She'd heard about the cave drawings and tagged along in case the language was still familiar to her. As their Goddess, she had known every language the Chanku had ever used, but much of that information had been given to Eve, deleted forever from Liana's memories.

Munching on a breakfast bar, Alex stood in front of the cavern wall with Stefan on one side and Anton on the other, and pointed out the various characters in "Lily's storybook." Liana stood off to one side, quietly watching.

"Lily told me this part is about the mountains where they lived when they first came here, in a place they called the frozen wilderness. The ones who wrote the story left their home when it got really cold there. They came here to find their brothers, who were called spirit guides. See this?"

He pointed to marks that looked like smoke. "This is how they got here. They traveled on the magic."

Stefan flashed a questioning glance at Anton. "On the magic?"

Anton shrugged. "Another name for the astral plane? Maybe the word 'magic' is merely Lily's interpretation."

"I think that might be it." Liana stepped forward, shaking her head. "I used to know this. I've got bits of memories, but they're faint." She pointed to the circular shape. "This is the ship they arrived in. I'd forgotten all about these early stories, but the drawings are jogging some old memories loose, I guess."

She glanced at Anton. "Our ancient ancestors left a dying world and immigrated here, long before there were any modern humans. They settled in what is now the Tibetan steppe before the plateau was as high and the climate as cold as it is now." She shrugged. "Many millions of years ago. I don't know for sure. Time passes. . . ."

As her voice faded, Anton merely nodded. Time passed differently on the astral plane. Even now, Liana often had trouble keeping track of time, as if her internal clock had never been locked into a particular set of seconds, minutes, or hours.

"Anyway . . ." Alex interrupted, obviously reaching for the spotlight again. "This is the story of how we got here, and Lily said she thought it might be a door that went to the place where the Goddess lives." He crossed his arms on his chest, obviously more than a little perturbed. "We were going to look for it today. Together." He pouted and glared at Anton. "She didn't wait. She went all by herself and didn't take me. Lily just thinks she's so special because she's older."

Anton folded his arms and stared very seriously at Alex. "Lily is going to be in a lot of trouble for going away without telling us. Be thankful you didn't go with her."

Stefan ruffled Alex's hair. "Anton's right, sport. If you'd gone with Lily, you'd be in big trouble, too. C'mon. Let's go talk Mom into some real breakfast."

"Pancakes?" Alex's eyes lit up.

"Works for me." *Anton, I'm going to get him out of here before you cross over. The last thing this kid needs is to see how to get to the astral. Liana? Can you stay and help Anton?*

Liana nodded and Stef herded his six-year-old out of the cave. When they were gone, Anton placed his hands in the carved prints on the wall. "I can feel magic here. I don't understand why I never noticed it before. It's thrumming just beneath the surface, as if the barrier between worlds is quite thin."

"Lily may have enabled an ancient power. It's been lying dormant for a long time or I would have sensed it before now." She shook her head, laughing softly. "Oh, Anton! That little girl is really going to keep you on your toes."

"Don't I know it." He felt the warmth in the rock, the slight vibration as if the stone lived. "I think I know how this works. Once my hands are in position, I need to picture where I want to go. This should open a gateway into that particular place. Is that correct?"

"It is. I believe Eve still exists in the same domain where I once lived, though if you think of Eve, you should be transported to wherever and whenever she is. Do you want me to come with you?"

Anton stepped back from the wall and placed his hands on Liana's shoulders. Her belly was round with the child she carried. This would be the third for her and Adam—a second daughter—due in just over a month. She was breathtakingly beautiful. Strong and calm and the perfect mate for Adam Wolf.

"I would love to have you beside me, but you are going back to your husband and your children, and I'm going after my wayward daughter by myself. Thank you, Liana. For more than you will ever know." He kissed her, marveling at how warm and alive she felt. Nothing at all like the cold goddess who had once held him captive as nothing more than a sex slave to her needs.

They definitely had history between them, one Anton wouldn't change for anything. Once Liana had been self-serving and even cruel, but she was the link, the one who had sent him on his original quest to discover his lost heritage.

And now he was off on another quest, this time in search of his future. *Lily.* She was unbelievably special, and in so many ways represented all that he hoped for, all that he wanted for every one of them.

She truly was touched by the Goddess, but no matter.

She was still a little girl. Still his.

Anton turned away from Liana and again placed his palms against the stone. He slipped his fingers into the perfectly carved indentations, and thought of Eve. Thought of the woman who had once been Adam Wolf's mate, the woman who had been there for all of them in so many ways before she'd died her untimely death.

He thought of Eve and put his fears for Lily out of his mind. He felt the stone grow warm beneath his palms, blinked at the brilliant colors of the world that opened to him as the dark cavern beneath his Montana home faded from view.

And without a backward glance, Anton stepped through the gateway, into the shimmering light and timeless beauty of the astral plane.

Chapter 6

"What do you mean, you don't know where she is? You're the goddess, Eve. Damn it! You're supposed to know everything!" Anton glared at the woman who stared at him out of those damned swirling eyes as if he was the one who was crazy. Gray to green to amber, her irises spun in a mesmerizing pattern guaranteed to make him nuts.

Calm as a damned stone statue with just as much compassion, she merely smiled at him and sighed. "Lily is on a quest, one critical to all Chanku—those we know and those yet to be found. She is fated to do so much, Anton. You must accept that she is a special child."

Anton clenched his hands and tried not to snarl. "Eve. Lily is six years old. She's still a baby. She has no business going on a quest. She's not even allowed to leave the fucking meadow without her parents' permission."

When Eve continued smiling, Anton had to forcibly hold himself back from taking a swing at her. Her quiet reply had him shaking with rage.

"Lily Milina is an old soul, and I mean that in a very literal way. Her body may be that of a child, but she has the mental strength of an adult. She carries the hopes and dreams of the Ancient Ones—the monks you met years ago—within her soul." Eve's smile disappeared in the beat of his heart. Now her look was one of frustration, as if he was the helpless child, not Lily.

"I know you're going to have a hard time accepting this, Anton, but her magical abilities are already far beyond yours."

"What magical abilities?" He swung away and paced a few steps, turned and glared at Eve. "She's good at mindtalking and I have a feeling she can block me, but . . ."

"But you have absolutely no idea your daughter is reading your thoughts during much of the day, and quite often at night." In a rapid-fire monologue, Eve interrupted Anton and set his mind reeling. "Did you know that she is a beautiful black wolf with golden highlights when she shifts? That she has taught herself to read the ancient language? That she communicates with the unborn babies within the pack? Did you know your daughter worries about you, about your responsibilities as their leader, and wants to do what she can to ease your stress? Did you—"

"Stop. Please . . ." He held up his right hand. Pleading? Begging for her to stop, because . . . Anton's legs suddenly gave out and he found himself sitting in the grass with his head between his knees and Eve standing over him, laughing softly.

"I'm sorry, Anton, but you of all people cannot afford to keep your head buried in the sand. Your denial of reality helps no one, least of all your daughter. Lily is an unusual child."

"I knew she was special, but I had no idea. . . ."

"But you should. You need to know what your daughter is capable of. There is much to that child even I don't understand, but she is good. She is pure of heart and soul, and all she wants to do is make you proud, to ease your life, to be a good daughter. Right now, being a good daughter means she has undertaken a quest that will change the lives of all of you, including the hundreds of Chanku who are still lost."

He raised his head, blinking. "Hundreds? Shouldn't there be more? By now, I would imagine thousands, if not millions of our kind across the globe."

Eve shook her head and sat beside him on the soft grass. She took Anton's left hand and turned it over, running her fingertip over the lifeline on his palm. Over and over again, as if the subtle repetition soothed her thoughts.

"You're right. There should be millions, but very few survive. Chanku have been hunted throughout the ages, destroyed by those who fear their amazing abilities. Those first star-voyagers who settled on a primitive Earth tried to blend in, but their differences made that impossible. They did not want to be seen as gods—they merely wanted to be left alone to go on with lives that had been upended when their world died. They felt they would be safer in small groups, so they spread out across the earth, using various gates that allowed them to travel on the astral.

"Some were the original Gypsies, the Rom. Others came to the North American continent and became spirit guides to indigenous peoples. Wherever legends of shape-shifters abound, Chanku are generally the source, but not all of those early travelers survived. Cut off from their packs, their lines died out. History and circumstance have not been kind to Chanku."

Eve paused, her expression pensive. "The diaspora that Liana knew of was the second migration, and it was really quite small. Only a few survived the long march from their Tibetan home. They had lost access to the nutrients their bodies needed to shift, and they'd forgotten about the gates, the pathways that gave them easy access to the astral plane, and thus to other parts of the earth."

"The gateway Lily found in the cavern beneath my home?"

Eve nodded. "The same. They were established millions of years ago to give the first Chanku access to different parts of the world via the astral, but through cataclysm and pure happenstance, their locations were lost. Your friend Igmutaka? He is the child of shapeshifters who were part of the very earliest migration out of Tibet, Chanku who chose to stay in their animal form. He was born a cougar and tapped by the Mother as a spirit guide, but without any knowledge of his human self. He knew only the animal and the ethereal. When he discovered his human form, his history finally became known to me." She chuckled. "I wish I knew his future. I look forward to his trials with Tala and Mik's little Star."

"But he's her spirit guide." Anton's mind was reeling, and he focused on the simplest part of the information Eve shared . . . none of which appeared to be at all related to bringing his daughter home. "Why would a spirit guide have trials with the one he watches over? Star seems like a wonderful child."

Eve burst into laughter. Her amusement was so honest, so unexpected, that Anton found himself laughing alongside her. "What?" he asked.

"Igmutaka recognized Star as his future mate at the moment of her birth. He has no idea how he's going to make that leap from spirit guide to suitor, and I don't see her making it easy for him. I look forward to watching the hoops she makes him jump through. Think about it! With Tala as her mother, and . . ."

Anton laughed. "No need to say another word. You're right. The man deserves our sympathies, but this doesn't help me get my daughter back. Where is she, Eve? What can I do?"

She covered his hand with hers. "Nothing right now. This is something Lily must do on her own. I told her how to find that which she seeks. I am watching over her and I promise to do my best to keep her safe. You must find the strength to give Lily the freedom she needs to complete her quest. It won't be easy for you, but you have to let her finish what she has begun. Lives hang in the balance. Chanku lives."

"Can I see her? Talk to her? Reassure myself she's safe?" His heart felt like a huge block of ice in his chest. What kind of father was he? He should be demanding her return. Going after her, no matter where she'd gone. She was his daughter, his baby . . . she was, and would always be, his heart.

But she was also Chanku, an alpha by nature, amazingly intelligent. Her magic was undeniably strong. He had to learn to trust his child's instincts. And, as Eve said, accept the fact her magic was even more powerful than his.

Accept the fact his daughter was already shifting. That alone terrified him. Was he ready for that? Were any of them?

"I can let you see her, but not speak to her, and only if you promise me you will not try to go after her. I know you will recognize the place she's gone—it's where you yourself went in search of answers. If you can't promise me, I won't be able to give you even this much."

He closed his eyes and searched himself. Could he truly promise not to try to rescue his daughter? He would have to. For all her youth, Lily was no fool. He'd always known she would test him—he just hadn't thought it would start so soon.

Solemnly, with a mind filled with doubt, Anton nodded. "I promise, Eve, though you have to know this is the most difficult thing you've ever asked of me."

She smiled and squeezed his hand. "I hope you realize it probably won't be the last. She's an amazing child, Anton. Your child, with your strengths and your magic, and Keisha's beauty, style"—she laughed—"and attitude. Don't expect it to be easy, to be blessed with a child like Lily. She is a tremendous responsibility."

He laughed but at the same time closed his eyes against the sting of unshed tears. "Blessed? Or cursed, perhaps?"

"It's up to you whether you see her as a blessing or a curse. I don't have any doubt in your ability to realize just how blessed you and Keisha are. Now look, but keep your thoughts to yourself. We must not let her know we're watching."

She waved her hand, and where it passed through the air, a shimmer of light followed. The shimmer spread, took on form and substance, and slowly, like the aperture of an old-fashioned camera lens, brought a most amazing scene into focus.

Lily sat at a long stone table in what appeared to be a large underground cavern. She was surrounded by men wearing robes the color of red dirt. Anton shoved his palm across his lips to keep from crying out.

Tibet? How the hell did six-year-old Lily find her way to Tibet, to the cavern with the monks and the secret scrolls of the Chanku? He blinked, unable to stem the flow of tears. They fell freely as he heard Lily's clear, childish voice, asking for the monks' help to find the missing Chanku.

The men listened reverently, nodding and talking quietly among themselves. Anton didn't understand their language, but it was obvious Lily could. She replied in English, and they answered in their unknown tongue, yet there appeared to be no language barrier as they conversed.

He wanted to reach for Lily, to call out how much he loved her, but Anton fought the impulse and held his silence. Eve was right. Lily was obviously in no danger. She'd somehow managed to unlock an ancient mystery and travel halfway around the world. And now she sat with this group of ancient, learned men, and she held them in the palm of her hand. It was more than obvious that

each and every one of them was enthralled by her innocence, her intelligence, her very presence.

And it came to him then, how truly special she was.
This child of his loins, this perfect creature who had taken
all the best he and Keisha had to offer and turned it into
magic.

Lily was magic. More powerful than anything Anton
had ever aspired to, yet for her the magic was as natural as
breathing, as easy as the smile that so rarely left her face.

He couldn't see her anymore. He wasn't sure when the
blur of his tears had been eclipsed by the closure of Eve's
window into Lily's experience, but he sat beside the Goddess with his face buried in his hands and cried. Great,
gulping sobs of relief and fear that Lily's journey had
taken her so far away, that the innocent child he loved
would so quickly surpass her parents.

He felt Eve's arms around him, her warm hug a comfort
he hadn't expected. "She's going to be all right, Anton.
She's an amazing child, and I believe she'll find answers no
one else has been able to discover."

He grabbed a clean handkerchief out of his pocket and
wiped his eyes, blew his nose, reached for whatever sense
of composure he had left. "Who are those men? The
monks? Why do they hold our history? I recognize one of
them. He's not changed since I was there, so many years
ago."

Eve's eyes swirled in that mystical blend of gray to
green to amber. "They are the last of the first. The only
survivors of that long-ago journey from a dying world.
They are the keepers of the records, the ones who hold the
knowledge of an entire civilization. They are your ancestors, Anton. Ancient beyond belief, immortals protected
by the Mother. The Ancient Ones will watch over Lily. The
Mother has sworn to me they will keep your daughter
safe. She will return to you when her quest has ended."

"When? I can't go back to Keisha and tell her our daughter is alive and well in Tibet, but we can't bring her home." He shook his head slowly. Physically and emotionally drained, he had no idea how to face his mate, his beloved wife.

Not without Lily.

Eve's fingers brushed his shoulder. "It won't be long, even by my time. Keisha loves you and trusts you. She also has a mother's understanding of her daughter. I believe it is easier for Keisha to accept Lily's abilities than it is for you."

Smiling, she leaned close and kissed him. "Be patient, my friend. When Lily has the knowledge she seeks, she'll return to you through the gateway to the cavern. Tell Keisha I give my word not only as the Goddess, but as friend and lover to both of you."

It was the best he could hope for. He'd seen Lily, sitting at that same stone table where he and Oliver had been, holding court as if royal blood coursed through her veins. She wore her princess nightgown with the silver sparkles and her pink satin ballet slippers, and her dark curls cascaded over her shoulders in soft ringlets that fell to her waist. She was beautiful beyond belief, and it was more than obvious, by the look of pure bliss on the faces of the men around her, that Lily held their hearts and souls in her hands.

It was only right they should adore her. His little girl knew exactly how a princess should behave. Pushing himself to his feet, Anton slowly looked about him. He was in the meadow, the one he and Stefan had gone to in search of Matt Rodgers when he'd been kidnapped by the goddess Liana, but this place felt different, now. Warmer, more natural. As if Liana's loneliness and anger had been swept away by Eve's loving nature.

He smiled warmly at Eve. "Liana and Adam are expecting their third child. A girl. They're going to call her Olivia."

"After Oliver?" Eve smiled. "I knew Liana was pregnant. Eve Elizabeth talks to me sometimes. I feel as if she's my own child." She laughed this time. "Motherhood without the swollen ankles and stretch marks—or diapers."

Anton noted Eve's broad smile and gazed steadily into her mesmerizing eyes. "Are you truly happy, Eve? Living here, apart from all of us? Apart from the real world? Don't you miss love?"

"Oh, Anton. I have love." She took his hands in hers and held them tightly. "It's hard to explain, but the love you feel for your family, your friends—I feel that same love. When Adam and Liana find time away from the children and make love to one another, I feel every touch, every kiss. I see every smile, feel each caress. It's like that with all of you, as if I am every one of you and more. I feel the connection to the Mother of us all, to the world, to the astral plane and all who move upon it.

"I feel your magic." She laughed, and the sound was musical in Anton's ears. "I really feel Lily's! Don't ever pity me, Anton. I have more than any woman alive. I have what all of you have and more."

She kissed him quickly, stepped back, and linked her hands over her flat belly. "Go now. Before too many hours pass. Keisha grows worried and you are exhausted. Lily will come home to you soon, when her quest has ended. I promise to return her safely to her mother and father, her brothers and her beautiful sister."

He bowed his head, a quick acknowledgment of Eve's power, of her generosity in always responding to their requests. She'd never held herself apart from her people, though there were times, like now, where her help wasn't exactly what Anton wanted.

"One more thing." Her fingers circled his forearm.

Anton's entire body jerked from the powerful shock of her touch, but she was smiling and shaking her head. "I'm sorry. I almost forgot there was something I need to tell you, and I did forget to tone down my power. Anton, there is something I want you to consider. Have you thought of calling all the packs home to Montana? Not just for a visit, but permanently?"

He cocked his head and stared at her. He and Keisha had discussed it off and on over the years, the fact that they were so much stronger when they were all together, that they missed the ones who were not with them. He nodded. "Keisha and I have talked of it, but we've never pursued the idea. The packs are all strong and healthy. I fear they might not want to live in a single community."

"You fear battles for dominance, don't you?"

He nodded again. Though their human nature proved to be the stronger, the occasional feral posturing when they were in wolf form had once been a problem. He hated to risk bringing that behavior back by living too close. "I think I'm afraid of change more than anything. What's the saying? If it ain't broke, don't fix it?"

Eve laughed. "The benefits would outweigh the problems. Think about it. Ask them how they feel about living together. You've increased your holdings, so overcrowding wouldn't be an issue. You're all going to gather when Liana gives birth, aren't you? Ask them. See what they say. It's not a frivolous suggestion on my part, my friend. Change is coming. Changes I want all of you prepared to face. You're stronger together."

"I will." He turned away quickly, his mind spinning with her enigmatic comment. Change? He'd sensed change for the past few weeks, but he also knew Eve wouldn't say anything else. Not until it was time.

He had to go now, before he found more reasons to question Eve, to beg for Lily's return. He wanted to question her reasons for suggesting all the packs combine, to come to Montana and make this beautiful country their home. Why would she ask him now? When Lily was missing and he had failed in his quest to bring his daughter home?

It was the most difficult thing he'd done today, but he thought of the cavern and blinked, and Eve and the meadow were gone. He stepped out onto the dry, sandy floor of the cave. The lights still burned. Oliver sat nearby, leaning against the curved wall, smiling at him. "About time you got back," he said. Then he frowned. "Where's Lily? Is she okay?" He stood up and strode toward Anton, his dark face creased with concern.

"How long has it been? When did she disappear?"

Oliver shook his head. "Not long. Last night sometime. You've only been gone a short time. Stefan asked me to come down and wait in case you needed help." He held up his book. "I only read a couple of pages."

"Good. I was afraid . . ." He shrugged. "You know how time is on the astral."

"Lily?" Oliver raised one eyebrow.

Anton didn't think he could tell this story more than once without falling apart. "Let's go up. I want to tell it once. I hardly believe this myself." He slung an arm around Oliver's shoulders. "Remember that cavern in Tibet where we sat at the long stone table and looked through the ancient scrolls?"

Oliver nodded.

"Picture this—my six-year-old daughter is currently sitting at that same table, holding court with half a dozen immortal monks, learning how to find the lost Chanku."

After a moment of stunned silence, Oliver chuckled. Then he burst out laughing. He was still giggling as they headed through the cellar and up the stairs to the kitchen. He paused at the doorway, turned, and grinned at Anton.

"This, my friend, is a story I think we all need to hear. Why is it, though, that I doubt any of us will find it hard to believe?"

He raised one eyebrow. "We're talking about my firstborn, Oliver. Need I say more?"

"Nope. Not at all."

Oliver led him into a kitchen filled with their packmates. Many of the adults, a few of the older children—everyone waiting to hear word of his daughter. He sensed their concern, their anxiety and love, but most of all, Anton felt the connection—almost visible links holding all of them together.

This was his pack. His family. It was Lily's family.

All of them here, waiting for word of the one who was lost. Eve was wrong. She didn't have more love. They all shared it—that same connection that bound them tighter than chains, bound them more fiercely than anything Anton had ever imagined. They were family—linked by DNA, but even more, connected by love.

Was that why Eve had made her suggestion that he bring the rest of the packs together? Was it time to reunite a people who had been splintered for eons, time to bring together the ones they knew? Later. He'd have to weigh the pros and cons, consider the logistics of adding so many people to his Montana holdings.

They'd need to build more housing, an infrastructure to serve so many more Chanku, but the children would grow up with others like them, the adults would have the support of more packmates. He'd talk to Keisha. To Stefan and Xandi. Oliver . . . He bit back a smile. This was a decision for the entire pack to make. Later. After Lily was home.

He walked through the silent group, knelt down, and hugged Gabe and Mac. His sons clung to him, then to their mother's legs, unsure of what had happened to their sister, but knowing enough to be afraid. Anton stood and, careful of his infant daughter asleep in Keisha's arms, gently hugged his wife. *Don't worry, my love. Our daughter is safe and well. She won't be home right away, but she is having a most amazing adventure.*

Keisha's trust humbled him. There were no tears. She didn't rail at him for failing to bring Lily home. No, she merely smiled, leaned her head against his chest, and waited for Anton to tell all of them what was going on.

With his arm wrapped tightly around Lily's mother, Anton faced his pack. "I've been to see the Goddess," he said. "I've seen Lily. She is safe. And I've heard an unbelievable story."

While everyone listened in rapt fascination, he told them of Lily's amazing adventure and the ancient history of their kind—and the answer to a question most of them had long wondered—the fact they were not originally of this world.

His control broke and he wept as he spoke, but it wasn't fear for Lily that unmanned him. No, even more powerful than the love of a father for his child was the love beyond measure in this room—the love of his packmates and his wife, of the Goddess who watched over them, and the magic that surrounded them all.

Eve was right. They were stronger when they were together, and if her warning was correct, that they were facing great change, they would need that strength. More and more he felt it was time to gather the rest of the Chanku, to create a community where they could live without fear, with the support and love of the entire pack.

There was so much power in this room, the house seemed to vibrate with its strength. He tried to imagine what it would be like if all of them lived here—if every single one of the Chanku could share this sense of connection, could draw on the power of their love.

They had gathered before, time after time, whenever there was a need. What would it be like to coexist as a single pack, constantly sharing the amazing connection that made each of them stronger when they were together, so much more than when one tried to stand alone?

Maybe it was time. He drew their love to him and felt stronger. Felt the trust and love of his little boys, Keisha's love and steadfast support, the connection from every Chanku—young and old—in the room. He took a deep breath and gazed about at the familiar faces, and he knew there was nothing, nothing in or beyond this world more powerful than what existed here in this country kitchen in Montana.

Enough power to give him hope, enough love to conquer fear. Then he imagined what it would be like if all of them were here—together, connected in the way of their kind—and the reality of what could be left him feeling both stunned and humbled.

When the time was right, he had no doubt—there would be more power than needed to bring Lily safely home where she belonged.

And when the time was right, he would invite them all, each and every single one, to make this beautiful mountain property their home.

When the time was right. There was no need to rush such huge decisions, asking others to pack up their lives and relocate to his isolated mountain home.

They had plenty of time for that.

Chapter 7

Colorado, late August

"Millie, m'love? Are you sure you want to do this?"

Millie West turned an exasperated, eyebrow-raised glare on her mate and huffed out what she hoped was enough hot air to tell him exactly what she thought of his question. Of course she was sure. She never did a damned thing she wasn't sure about.

Not anymore. At least not very often.

Ulrich laughed and planted a quick kiss on her pursed lips. "Don't give me that look, Millicent West. I know you better than you know yourself. The wolf sanctuary has been your life for over twenty years. I can't imagine you just packing up and walking away from this place without a second glance."

He ran his fingers through her hair and this time kissed her soundly. "I don't want you to make any decisions you'll regret, and I know you're going to miss this life if we go. I don't ever want you unhappy, m'love. Never."

She sighed. Well, she'd have to give him that much. In some ways he was right to be concerned, and he was in her thoughts, after all, no matter how much she tried to block him. He'd probably picked up on her basic insecurities, though she'd been keeping her shields up more often than not over the past few weeks.

It was going to be hard for her to leave, but she'd come to the conclusion it would kill her to stay. She'd lived with the nightmares long enough, had given away too many years of her life to a past she couldn't escape. Not while she stayed here, where so many terrible things had occurred. Where memories haunted every tree, every rock, every part of her life.

It was time to move on. Time to give up a past that was threatening to choke her. She dipped her head and gazed at her toes. She couldn't meet his eyes, couldn't look into the honesty in those amber depths and admit she was living a lie.

Ric brushed the hair away from her face, lifted her chin, and smiled so gently she thought her heart would break. He didn't know who she really was. He couldn't, or he would have been gone long ago.

"What is it, sweetheart? You've been blocking me for days now. You know I don't want to pry, but I'm picking up so much stress and misery from you that I'm worried." His callused fingers stroked the line of her jaw.

Her lips trembled. She would not cry. She'd done enough crying already. It was time to move on. She shook her head and smiled brightly. Her entire face felt brittle, as if it might crack and shatter into a thousand shards like broken glass.

"No need to worry. I'll be fine. We have grandchildren we hardly know. We're at an age where we should be free to travel, to see and do things we've talked about doing but never followed through on. I want to see more of Manda and Adam, and . . ."

"And you're making excuses to avoid the truth."

His soft accusation stopped her in mid-sentence, left her with her mouth hanging open. She pressed her lips together.

The truth? What was the truth, other than the fact she'd been forever damaged as a child—damage no one could repair? She'd talked about life with her uncle on very few occasions, but she'd never told the whole story. Not to anyone. Ulrich had seen a lot of it when they'd bonded and her childhood had opened to him, but he hadn't seen it all. He couldn't have, or he would have been long gone.

Millie knew she'd never return to that time in her life on purpose, not ever. But the nightmare of her childhood had invaded her life anyway. Returned with a vengeance, for some ungodly reason. Why? She didn't want to go back!

Not to those filthy, disgusting memories she'd tried so hard to block. Why now? Why, for whatever reason, had they returned? After so many years, she'd thought she'd finally come to terms with them, but they haunted her now, to the point her nights were no longer her own. Instead, the hours between dusk and dawn were filled with the horror of the perverted lusts that had defined her formative years.

Perversions in which she'd been a willing participant.

Ulrich cupped her face in his big hands and stared solemnly into her eyes, forcing her to meet his gaze. Dear Goddess, how she loved this man! The thought of possibly losing him, of feeling his disgust for her, was more than she could bear.

"Millie? I know you're having bad dreams at night, I know something is bothering you, but if you don't share, we'll never figure out how to beat it. There's nothing we can't beat when we're together, m'love. You know that." He drew her carefully into his embrace, and there was something about the steady beat of his heart, the rise and fall of his broad chest as he drew each breath, that comforted her.

Comforted her, and reminded her she was no longer the

same as she'd once been. No longer a defenseless victim. Still, his steadfast support made her feel foolish. He was right—why was it always so hard for her to realize she wasn't alone?

Not anymore. She was no longer that helpless little girl trembling before her uncle, wondering with a confusing sense of both fear and anticipation what horrible punishment lay in store for her next. Not the frightened, confused teenager, terrified of the way her body would betray her, afraid of the pain and yet wanting it, relishing it.

Becoming aroused by it. No. It was wrong, it was sick, and she didn't want to remember. She wanted the memories to go away, but they were back, stronger, more graphic, more tempting than ever before.

How could that be? She was grown now, an alpha bitch with a mate who loved her, two younger men who desired her, a young woman who took as much delight in Millie's body as Millie did in hers. How could she be tempted by the darkness of her past—tempted to the point where her fantasies now carried her into those disgusting memories and left her shivering with unwanted, unwholesome needs?

She took a few calming breaths and tried to take control of the fear that simmered just below the surface. She couldn't go on like this. She wouldn't. She raised her head and looked directly into his eyes, and made her decision.

For better or for worse, she had to accept the fact that maybe Ric was right. It was time to stand strong and face her ghosts before they destroyed her. She had no doubt Ric truly loved her. As long as her past didn't disgust him to the point where he wanted to leave, maybe, just maybe, he could help her understand and fight the horror that wouldn't stay buried.

Obviously my ostrich-with-her-head-buried-in-the-sand approach isn't working. Millie tilted her head just enough to plant a light kiss on Ric's mouth, but before he could part her lips and deepen the kiss, she pulled back and ran a fingertip across his full lower lip. He couldn't possibly know she was shaking like a leaf inside, but if she didn't do this now, she'd chicken out.

It was now or never, but she couldn't live with this, couldn't take it any longer.

Taking a deep breath, she tried to control her trembling limbs. "Will you run with me tonight? There's something I have to do, but I want you with me. I need to take you somewhere. Show you something."

The love and understanding on that rugged face was almost her undoing. He didn't question her, didn't look at her like she was losing it, even though Millie suspected she very well might be. He didn't even try to invade her tightly blocked thoughts. No, all he did was smile gently and answer, "Anything, m'love. Anything you want."

Daci stared at her profile in the mirror and wanted to cry. How could the guys love her like this? She was fat and ugly and awkward, and her once smooth and perfect skin was marred with deep striations marching across her expanding belly. Liana said the stretch marks would go away after the babies came and she was shifting and running again, but right now it was hard to believe she'd ever look even remotely normal. Not ever again.

Much less, even remotely attractive to her two absolutely gorgeous guys. What if they hated the way she looked? Did her big belly and swollen ankles gross them out? What about later? After the babies came? Would they still want her?

She wished Liana didn't live so far away. They'd hit it off so well the first time they met, and Daci missed girl talk. She missed Logan and Jazzy, and Mei and Oliver and all the other Chanku—especially the ones who were pregnant. The ones who understood what she was going through.

Millie was really wonderful, but she'd never raised her

own babies and didn't know all that much about kids—
and her unintended pregnancy with Adam and Manda
had, for all intents and purposes, been an absolute nightmare.

Daci already loved the two little girls she carried—she
couldn't imagine having them taken from her the way Millie had lost hers. It was a nightmare she couldn't allow
herself to imagine, the horror of giving birth and never
seeing her babies. It had been hard enough to make the decision to get pregnant in the first place. Now that she was,
she knew she would protect these little ones with everything that was in her.

If only the whole process wasn't doing such a crappy
job on her self-esteem. She hated feeling ugly. Hated wondering what the guys really thought.

Matt opened the door to the bathroom and caught her
staring at herself. He grinned and did what he and Deacon
seemed to take such great pleasure in—cupped her belly
with his big hands, leaned close, and kissed the taut surface.

"How can you stand me like this?" She sniffed, grabbed
a tissue, and blew her nose.

"You're kidding, right?" He stared at her like she'd
grown two heads. "Good Goddess, Daci. You're gorgeous. I've never seen you so beautiful. Your skin glows
and your breasts are . . . I mean. Wow." He let out a rever-
ent sigh. "Your breasts are magnificent. They're so perfect
I can't even begin to . . ."

"They're huge. My belly's huge and my breasts look
like two big cantaloupes sitting on top of a giant water-
melon."

Deacon stuck his head through the open door. "She at it
again? Makin' with the food analogies?" He laughed and
Daci wanted to hit him, except it was so neat to hear Deacon's laughter. He'd always been such a dour sort, but for
some reason her pregnancy had changed him.

In good ways. Not like her. He certainly hadn't gained forty extra pounds, even though it wouldn't hurt him a bit if he did, and he didn't have to worry about having to pee every five minutes. No, his smile came more often now, and he'd relaxed in so many ways. It was as if Deacon finally realized that the life they had wasn't going to be taken away. That the three of them had something permanent, something that worked.

So why couldn't she feel that way? Because she wasn't sure, that's why. What if babies changed everything? What if adding twins to their small but perfect family altered the dynamic to the point where it didn't work at all?

"Yeah, we're into cantaloupes and watermelons today. She's in here telling me how ugly she is." Matt grinned at Deacon. "Can you believe that line of crap?"

Deacon squeezed into the tiny bathroom and sat on the counter, effectively blocking Daci's view of herself in the mirror. "I think she's looking for attention," he said, flashing a big wink at Daci. "I mean . . . look at this woman. She's tall and gorgeous and she's carrying our babies."

The moment the words left his mouth, Deacon blinked rapidly. He turned to Matt, and his voice was so low, the emotions behind his words so intense, Daci had to watch his lips to understand what he said.

"Now, that's the part I'm having trouble with. Our babies, Matt. Did you ever, in your wildest dreams, imagine finding the perfect woman who would love you enough to carry your child? Who would put up with the changes in her body and the hormones and all that crap, to give you something as special as this?"

When he turned to look at her, his eyes sparkled with unshed tears. He palmed her belly with his big hands and Matt shifted his stance and did the same. They stood there a moment, the three of them together, Daci and both her guys, connected through the warmth in their hands against her huge belly, holding Daci, protecting their babies.

Reassuring her that all her worries were for naught. Reminding her they were in this for the long run. The three of them plus whatever babies they were lucky enough to have, together. Forever.

And at that moment, one of the girls kicked, or maybe it was an elbow. Whatever. It landed squarely on her bladder.

Moment ended . . . but what a perfect moment it had been.

Grumbling to herself, Daci ran the guys out of the bathroom so she could pee. Still feeling like a beached whale, she eased herself down on the pot, but she couldn't stop grinning.

They weren't just saying they loved her, that they loved the way she looked. She could tell by the heartfelt emotion in their eyes, the gentleness in their touch, that both her guys really meant what they said. She knew they loved her, and wasn't Ric always saying that with love, anything was possible? Maybe she was worried about nothing. Maybe the changes coming to their family would be good for all of them.

What was she so worried about? They were a pack—they were family. She wished they were closer to more of their kind, but since they weren't, then she, Daciana Lupei Rodgers-March was doing her part by adding two brand-new members.

All she needed to do was get through the next couple of months.

October couldn't come soon enough.

They'd shifted once the sun dropped below the mountains, and now it was just the two of them, trotting along a narrow path with Millie in the lead. Ric had no idea where she was leading him. This was something that had been building over the past few weeks, and as much as he'd wanted to pry, he knew that Millie needed to work through whatever it was at her own speed.

She was such a loving woman. A strong, loving, good-hearted woman who had suffered too much, lost too much, and been forced to endure too many horrors. Whatever she needed, he would do his best to fulfill. All he hoped was to make her future brighter than her past had been.

He knew more than Millie wanted him to know, but Ric made a point of never referring to her past—not unless she brought it up. He was well aware she just wanted it to go away, even though he knew that wasn't going to happen.

All he could do was be there for her.

The first time he'd shared her memories, Ric had felt physically ill. Seeing what this lovely woman had been through sickened him. She'd been raised by her uncle, a pedophile who excused his perversions under the guise of his religious fanaticism. He was a terrible example of a man with Chanku genes and the accompanying libido, who had never known of his true heritage—though Ric wondered if even knowing who and what he was would have helped.

He'd been a sick and twisted man who used his innocent niece for his own perverted pleasure. He'd raised her with equally twisted religious beliefs that defied everything the Good Book taught. Millie'd gotten pregnant—not by him, thank the Goddess, but by a young cowboy who, Millie didn't learn until years later, had been killed shortly after they met.

When her twins were born, Millie had no one in her life except for her uncle, who told her the babies died at birth. She had no idea her babies had actually survived—they'd been taken away, separated, and sold in black-market adoptions.

For all Millie knew at the time, she'd been abandoned by her lover, and after hours of labor she'd been left with nothing but a broken heart. She'd wanted her babies more than anything, but she'd gone back alone to a home where she was hated and mistreated and eventually disowned.

There'd been so much sadness in her life. Ric was glad he'd been the one who helped Millie reconnect with her children, now grown. Both Chanku, Adam and Manda were now in loving relationships with healthy, well-adjusted children of their own.

Yet Millie still carried the guilt, both from her sexual abuse and the twisted quasi-religious teachings that had been drilled into her from such a young age. She'd suffered years of pain she'd never truly escaped. Somehow, he would help her through this. Now that he knew their lives were practically immortal, he wasn't about to allow her to live forever with the unearned guilt of a tormented childhood.

This was probably the biggest mistake she'd ever made. Ric was going to be so disgusted by her. He'd never be able to look her in the eye after tonight, but she had to try. Somehow Millie knew she had to explain what was going on in her head, why she could barely look at her reflection in the mirror anymore.

It wasn't fair to Ric, making life-altering decisions without explaining why she knew she had to escape the shadows of her past. She'd never be whole if she didn't leave the place where it had all happened. She'd miss the wild wolves and she'd really miss Daci and the boys, but she had a feeling they were growing restless, too.

Daci had mentioned how isolated she often felt, especially now that she was pregnant. She needed other women around her to share this time—young women with a lot better experience at pregnancy than Millie—but all she had, other than the guys, were Millie and Ric, two folks old enough to be her parents. Millie often felt that Daci really wanted to be back in Montana, closer to their friends. Maybe this would give her the freedom to choose.

Ric trotted along behind her. His steady, loving presence was the only reason she'd come this far. She would find the strength to tell him.

She had to.

They reached the foundation of her uncle's old home long before Millie was ready. The house was gone, burned to the ground in a fire years ago, but the foundation remained.

Concrete piers, burned timbers, a few pieces of twisted metal and old pipe cast bizarre shadows in the soft glow of the new moon. A porcelain bathtub, stained and filthy with one side caved in, reflected silver light.

Millie paused in a dark swath of shadow beneath a big cedar and shifted. Ric shifted and stood beside her. Quietly he wrapped his arm around her waist as he studied the refuse scattered about—all that was left of the home where she'd spent the first years of her life.

She couldn't look at Ric, but at least she managed to get the words out, even though she felt compelled to whisper for fear of disturbing ghosts she hoped were long gone. "Did you know I come back here sometimes, all by myself? Just to reassure myself it's really gone. That he's really gone."

Ric remained silent, but his presence, the warmth of that strong arm around her body, gave Millie the courage to go on. "I've told you what it was like with my uncle. How he enjoyed punishing me, spanking me on my bare butt well into my teens."

Her skin went hot and cold all over, merely from saying the words out loud. She stepped away from Ric. He didn't try to hold her, but she heard his soft footsteps as he followed close behind. Walking carefully on bare feet through the thick grass, Millie paused at what was left of the front steps.

"What I haven't told you . . ." She took a shuddering breath. "What I haven't wanted you to know is how much I grew to anticipate the punishment. How I looked forward to his spankings. To the way he touched me."

She turned and gazed solemnly at Ric, blinking back tears. "I hated him, but I think I hated myself more. I knew what he did was wrong. I tried to deny it, but when I was old enough to understand, I was well aware he took sexual gratification from punishing me, from the things he did to me. What I haven't had the courage to tell you was how much I enjoyed it." She coughed and cleared her throat. "I didn't want you to know I was as bad as he was."

"Not true, m'love. There's nothing bad about you. Nothing at all."

Ric's arms slipped around her waist and he rested his chin on her head. She felt the steady beat of his heart and wished she could feel as calm. "But there is, Ric. When I knew I was going to get a spanking, I had my clothes off so fast it wasn't even funny. I learned to tease him with my body. I'd rub my breasts against his arm and make it look like an accident. I'd position myself on his lap so that I trapped his erection between my thighs."

"Was he naked when he beat you?"

Ric's soft question was so matter-of-fact, Millie didn't even hesitate to answer. "No. Not entirely, though at some point he'd unzip his pants and free himself. He was always erect when he beat me." She swallowed back the gorge rising in her throat. "I learned to rub him against me so that I'd climax during the spanking. He would, too. Then he would curse and call me a slut, and beat me harder, because obviously that was evil, and it was my fault. I would come again, just from the pain alone. He made me like it, Ric. I didn't fight the pleasure, and it was wrong."

"What he did was wrong, sweetheart. Your reaction was perfectly normal." He took her face in his big, callused hands and forced her to look at him. "It's called survival. Don't you know by now . . . that's the way pedophiles work. They groom their victims. They twist everything around so that you feel as if you owe them your compliance. He turned his punishment of your childhood infractions into an excuse to molest you, but I bet he also made certain to touch you enough that you felt physical pleasure even when you were little. And think about this—he raised you from the time you were a toddler. He taught you. There was no one telling you it was wrong. His sick reality was all you knew."

Once again he wrapped his arms around her and held her close. Protected by his strength, Millie opened herself to the memories she'd tried so hard to deny. They rushed into her mind, dark and viscous, covering her with filth. He had touched her, even when she was tiny. He'd taught her to touch him as well. How could she have forgotten? He'd rewarded her with attention when she did as he ordered.

Sick and perverted, but it was still attention. Without a mother, without anyone else, she had craved attention.

You're a slut, Millicent. Just like your mother.

But I didn't know what he meant. It sounded bad, but I had no idea what a slut was.

Touch me, Millicent. Use your mouth, too, you little slut. This is what sluts and whores do. This is what they're good for. It's all you'll ever be good for.

Ric's deep voice drowned the sound of her ghosts. "It's okay, m'love. It's over. It all happened a long time ago, but he's dead and he can't touch you anymore. That brave little girl won. She was stronger and smarter and she won."

Millie didn't know how or when she ended up sitting in Ric's lap on the dirty top step, but somehow she was no longer standing. He held her close, hugging her as she cried, telling her it was over, she was fine, her past was behind her.

But he was wrong and she wasn't sure how to tell him. It wasn't over and she wasn't fine. Not by a long shot.

Chapter 8

They trotted slowly back to the cabin. The moon had disappeared behind the mountains and the night was still and dark. Millie followed Ric along the familiar trail, but instead of feeling empowered by her confession, she was hot and edgy and more confused than ever. She'd confessed everything—the dark desires she'd felt as a kid, the fact her celibacy for so many years was as much a lack of opportunity as it was self-inflicted punishment. Saying the words out loud had felt strange, as if someone else confessed to all the disgusting things, but she'd said them.

And Ric had listened. Nonjudgmental and loving, he'd listened intently to everything she'd said. Listened and not said a word. In fact, he'd not reacted at all.

She'd expected to feel . . . different. Admitting she still fantasized about her own abuse seemed even more perverse than her uncle's behavior, but somehow, she figured once she opened up to Ric and put voice to her disgusting thoughts, the way she still remembered and replayed the arousal she'd experienced when her uncle beat her, that she'd somehow be free.

She wasn't. She was twitchy and aroused and uncomfortably empty inside, like a container that needed to be filled before it caved in on itself and imploded. Ric still hadn't said a word. She'd tried linking, but he was miles away, his mind locked down tight, his thoughts a complete mystery.

Did he hate her? Was he as disgusted by Millie as she was by herself? Had she ruined everything by her selfish— and it was selfish—confession? She hadn't shared those awful things for Ric's benefit. No, it was entirely for herself. To make Millie West feel better.

So why the hell didn't she?

They reached the cabin. She glanced toward the small one where the kids lived, but the windows were dark, and even with her Chanku hearing she couldn't pick up any sound. Maybe they'd run tonight as well. She envied them their contentment, the love they had for one another— love that was free of the shadows she'd always known.

That's not true, you know.

Ric's soft admonishment brought her up short. *What do you mean?*

Daci's the illegitimate daughter of the man who made your daughter's life a living hell, a witness to much of Manda's mistreatment. She has to live with that legacy of hate and cruelty. Matt grew up in a totally dysfunctional home and ended up prostituting himself merely to survive. Deacon's mother was a prostitute. He's been on the streets since he was fourteen, and his experience was even worse than Matt's. All of us, in one way or another, are damaged. No better, no worse than anyone else.

She jerked her head back as if he'd slapped her. Her entire body flushed with mortification. She wanted to crawl in a hole and hide. Dear Goddess, of course he was right. She was bitching and moaning and complaining about something that wasn't any more horrible than what others had gone through—and survived. It was over and done. So why couldn't she get past it?

You can, and you will. I'm going to help you, but you'll have to trust me.

Ric didn't wait for her. He reached the deck, shifted, and walked inside the cabin. Millie followed him, head down, still embarrassed but curious, too. *How?*

He stopped and turned, and his expression was deadly serious. "Millie, you know I love you. I love you more than anyone or anything, but I've handled you with kid gloves from the time I first met you. I've treated you as damaged goods. My mistake. That ends here. Now. Tonight."

She couldn't meet his gaze. Instead, retreating to an instinctive pose of submission, she lowered her head, but when she looked down, all she could see was his huge cock, erect and glistening. A smear of white spread across the broad crown. She fought the impossible lure, the powerful desire to fall to her knees and take him in her mouth.

She couldn't do it. Not now, not when he seemed so distant. Not when she felt unclean.

It wasn't easy, holding on to the threads of control. She was always so damned aroused after a run—tonight Millie felt like she was going to explode.

She wasn't alone.

It appeared Ric was in the same shape.

But he hadn't mentioned sex. Hadn't reached for her the way he always did the moment they slipped through the door. In fact, he'd not reached for her at all tonight. She hadn't realized it until now—he'd not mounted her during their run, either. Always they had sex at least once, but she'd been so caught up in her own drama tonight that—

"Are you coming?"

Her head snapped up. Ric stood in the doorway to their bedroom, almost military straight with his hands planted on his hips. Naked and hard from their run, he was without a doubt the most beautiful man she'd ever seen, but tonight there was something about his stance that sent shivers down her spine.

Something that seemed to feed the very nightmares she'd been trying to work out of her head. This wasn't Ric—not the Ric she knew and loved. He looked angry, and he reminded Millie of her uncle, the way he'd stood and waited for her to follow him when it was time for her punishment.

The tilt of his head, the glare in his eyes, the way he'd planted his hands on his lean hips—though Ric looked nothing at all like that man, everything about his stance and his attitude was so similar, the visual almost brought her to her knees.

Millie shivered, but at the same time her womb clenched with the stirrings of her arousal. Her nipples tightened, puckering into hard points. Ric raised his eyebrow, telling her with that simple expression he was fully aware of her growing desire. It was exactly the way her uncle used to look at her before he spanked her, as if he could read her mind and he knew she wanted exactly what he planned to do to her.

The similarity infuriated her.

How could Ric do this? Why would he duplicate the very nightmare she was trying to erase? And how did he know how to stand, how to look? It was almost as if he were bringing that bastard back to life. Why, damn it? Breathing hard, she clenched her fists, angry with Ric, angry with herself.

Her body thrummed, and the edginess, the sense of her skin wanting to crawl off the bones, the unbelievable arousal from their run, the heavy emotions of the night, the memories . . . all of it was just too much. Too damned much.

Not nearly enough.

She dug deep and found the alpha bitch cowering inside, pulled her out, and put her to work. Wearing her attitude like a cloak of armor, Millie held her head high and stalked past Ric, leading him into their room. Damn him! How could he do this?

He was telling her she was okay and then treating her like a kid about to be punished. What the hell was he up to? She clenched her jaw tight to keep from asking him anything. She wasn't going to fold, and she was not about to give him the pleasure of watching her break.

She hadn't done anything wrong. She never did. Why did he always punish her for every little thing? She was just being a kid. She didn't know how else to act.

Except she wanted this, didn't she? Wanted him to punish her. To pull down her panties and spank her bottom as hard as he could. She wanted it so much she could almost hear the sound of his palm hitting her smooth cheeks, feel the warmth as each slap reddened her skin. And the whole time her butt was stinging and getting hotter and hotter, his prick was getting just as hot.

Standing up, high and hard enough for her to trap him between her legs. Ride him and use him as much as she wanted. It was like a game now. He thought he was in charge, but Millie knew better. Uncle might be the one hitting her, but she was the one in control, she was the one using him to get rid of that horrible need that seemed to get stronger every day.

She hated being needy. Hated needing him. Hated him.

He grabbed her arm. Not as roughly as she recalled, the way he always had in the past, but his firm grasp was so tight she couldn't break free. She glared at him, but he didn't say a thing. He merely dragged her over to the edge of the bed, sat down, and pulled her over his knees.

He wasn't wearing his jeans, and that was different, but she felt the rough hair on his legs rubbing against her belly as he slid her into the familiar position, felt the bulge of his penis beneath her. At first that big part of him had disgusted her, but not anymore. Now she split her legs, her adjustment so subtle he wouldn't notice, separating them just enough to allow that hard thing to rise between her thighs. The moment she felt the heat against her pussy, she closed her legs and trapped him. Held him up close against her sex where he could do her some good.

She remembered the first time she did that. The first time when, instead of treating his erection like a big lump pressing against her belly, she'd taken control and held him with the strength of her thighs. He'd moaned the moment she caught him, and she remembered him cursing her, cursing himself. Cursing God.

She'd loved that, the fact she'd thrown him off enough that he'd curse the very god he claimed told him to hit her. It served him right. But then he'd spanked her hard and she'd bucked against his hand, careful to slide up and down that stiff rod of his until her pussy was slick and wet and he'd suddenly stopped hitting her. He'd cried out and cursed again and his body had gone rigid. She remembered the hot splash of something slimy and wet hitting her buttocks.

He'd shoved her away and she'd tumbled to the floor. He'd screamed at her. Called her every filthy name he could think of, but Millie had taken it without comment, because she knew then that she'd won. And she would continue to win—as long as she took control.

Now he brushed her buttocks with his palm and she trembled as arousal spiked from the soft touch of his hand to that needy spot between her legs. His cock flexed against her thigh muscles, and she loved the fact he was as turned on as she was. Loved that, even though he might hurt her, she still had that control, that power over him.

He'd never been this large before. This aroused. She couldn't remember enjoying it this much, either—this prelude to a beating—the skin-prickly awareness of the rough hair on his thighs against her tender skin, or the pulse of his cock between her thighs.

There was no warning when the flat of his hand connected with her bottom. The sharp crack of flesh on flesh resounded in the small room. She jumped at the contact, but she didn't cry out. That was giving up, giving in, letting him win. She wasn't going to do that. Never again.

As long as she treated it like a game, there was a good chance she'd win. He swatted her again, just as hard. The sharp slap sent a shiver of excitement from her bottom to her clit to the hard points of her erect nipples. And again, and again, each measured slap heating her flesh, heating her entire body.

He rubbed her sore bottom after a few slaps, almost as if he wanted to soothe away the pain. That was new, but she liked it. Liked the soothing touch of his palm on her fiery butt, but as soon as he rubbed the sting away, he hit her again.

She realized she was rocking in time with his blows, rising to meet the palm of his hand, grasping his cock between her thighs so the hard length of it rode across her clit on every slide. They were in this together, the two of them doing this dark and sensual dance. She was so wet, her feminine lips soft, almost buttery with arousal. Her entire body was so sensitized that every touch was magnified, every slap resounded in more wet heat between her legs.

The sound of flesh connecting with flesh would reach her ears a split second before the pain registered, but she couldn't really even call it pain. No, not when it felt this good, not when her body tightened in anticipation before each blow, not when her fluids soaked the tangle of his pubic hair beneath her and eased the slick girth of his cock over her engorged and sensitive labia, across her swollen clit.

Riding him, her muscles quivering, her sex contracting and pulsing with need, his hand connecting in that almost dreamlike rhythm, took her into another level of sensation, another state of being.

She wasn't afraid and she wasn't a slut. She was a woman—an alpha bitch with a powerful mind and a libido as strong as her mate's. She had needs that only he could meet.

Just as he met them now.

His hand came down hard, again and again, and she realized she was grinning, anticipating the climax hovering so close she trembled, but the spanking wasn't enough. No, not with this man, not with the one she loved. The one who understood what it was to need, to desire and want something that seemed so wrong, and yet, between two who loved, could only be right.

Fully aware and in the moment, Millie pushed herself up and off Ric's knees, spun around in a tangle of arms and legs, and straddled him. Laughing now, with tears falling and her sex weeping her need, she impaled herself on that thick length and took him deep.

The absolute fullness, the sense she'd come home after wandering for far too long, swept through Millie the moment the broad crown of his penis slipped through her tight channel and touched the mouth of her womb. She locked her knees against his hips and arched her back, forcing him deep. Her vaginal muscles contracted, tightening along Ric's full length, rippling over skin like silk, practically squeezing the climax out of him.

Ric laughed and held her. He bucked his hips and lifted Millie as orgasm claimed him, claimed Millie, took them both higher and harder than ever before. And this time, when she came down from the heights, she was laughing with Ric, kissing his face, his throat, his chest. Holding him close and wondering how he could possibly have known exactly what she'd needed, but had been too ashamed to request.

* * *

Without even thinking, Ric snapped Millie's red bottom with the towel when she got out of the shower. She flipped him off—a perfect bird right under his nose. "Watch it, buster. I'm a little tender down there."

"Oh, crap. I'm sorry!" He grabbed her shoulders and spun her around, knelt behind her, and planted a kiss on the fiery skin. "I wasn't thinking. I didn't mean to hurt you, m'love. You know that."

She turned around and cupped his face in her hands. "What you did was perfect. Probably a bit perverted, but absolutely perfect." She leaned over and kissed him. "But how did you know? Even I had no idea."

"I asked Logan. I contacted him while we were running home after we'd gone up to your uncle's old place."

"Logan? Why would you ask him?"

"He's a doctor, Millie. A damned good doctor, and you obviously had a problem I didn't know how to deal with."

"Oh."

She sat on the edge of the bed. Ric sat beside her and wrapped an arm around her shoulders. "He said you needed to experience punishment without the perversion, something that would take you back to what happened when you were young, but still give you complete control."

She sighed and leaned against his shoulder. "You were standing just like him. You even had the same expression on your face. It was eerie. All of a sudden I was a child again."

"I picked his image out of your memories. You've been blocking me for weeks, but when you stood in front of that burned-out house, your mind was wide open, almost like you invited me in."

"Maybe I did. You know, Ric . . . you're the first man I've ever felt safe with. Safe enough to share my memories with. I'm sorry I blocked you, but I was embarrassed."

She turned and wrapped her arms around Ric. He

hugged her close and inhaled the sweet smell of her hair, the scent of her skin. He thought about what it felt like, spanking her—how her fair skin had glowed a deep red after only a few swats, how the scent of her arousal and the sharp sound of his hand hitting her bottom had him so hard he hurt.

He'd never imagined striking a woman. Never pictured himself doing anything like they'd done tonight—or dreamed how much it would turn him on. Thinking about it had blood rushing to his groin, his cock swelling and growing hard again. He wanted her. Now.

"Then we'll have to do it again, won't we?" Millie laughed at his raised eyebrows. "You're broadcasting, love. Quite clearly, actually." She wrapped her fingers around his erection and stroked it. The damned thing was already standing tall and ready between them. The soft clasp of her fingers made him even harder. When she rubbed her thumb over the sensitive crown, he groaned and thrust his hips forward, pushing his cock through her warm, tightly clasped hand.

She looked up at him with a twinkle in her beautiful amber eyes. "Of course, even if I weren't reading your thoughts, I'd know something was going on." She gave him a playful squeeze.

He rolled her to the bed and held her down. "I never could hide anything from you, could I?"

She snorted. "Not that thing, anyway." Millie was still laughing when he filled her once again.

Chapter 9

Colorado, first week of September

"Do you think I'm crazy because I still want to move away, Ric?" Millie glanced up from the mail she was sorting. "I think your, um . . ." She cleared her throat and flashed him a big smile. "Your therapy has worked wonders, but I'm still ready for something else. My motivation for wanting a change isn't the same, but the desire is still there. I've got the foundation ready to take over the sanctuary, so that's under control. There's really nothing holding us here any longer that can't be dealt with, so my only concern is the kids. What about you?"

Ric leaned against the kitchen counter with a cup of coffee in his hand and gazed out the window at the towering pines and cedars surrounding their cabin. He didn't miss life in San Francisco a bit. He loved it here, but he understood Millie's desire for a change. She'd never lived anywhere else, and in spite of the fact she was handling her memories a lot better, he knew she'd be happier in a new place—somewhere fresh. "Don't think about the kids right now. Think about Millie West and what she wants. Do you have any idea where you'd like to go?"

She shrugged. "I don't really know. We've got grandbabies on both coasts, but for some reason I keep thinking of Montana. Anton's got a lot of room. He and Keisha have invited us more than once to live there. I worry, though—you're so used to the alpha role after all those years with Pack Dynamics and now here. Would you be happy with Anton as the undisputed leader? And face it"— she laughed—"there's no disputing Anton."

Ric hadn't really thought about that part of the move. Would he miss the role he'd held his entire adult life? He'd always admired Anton and had never felt a need to challenge him, though as wolves they'd learned to give one another a wide berth when their feral instincts were engaged.

Then he thought of Matt and how the young man had been slowly moving into a stronger role within their small group, occasionally taking over from Ric—not only in the day-to-day decisions around the sanctuary, but even in the bedroom. Matt topped him now more often than not, but Ric hadn't ever felt threatened. He'd never felt a need to challenge Matt—he was too proud of how far the kid had come. Obviously Ric's human nature was stronger than his wolf when it came to pack dynamics.

He gazed squarely at Millie. "I don't think it's a problem. Anton and I have always gotten on without any dominance issues. He carries his leadership well. He's intelligent and his magical abilities put him on another level altogether. Even when the guy screws up, he does it with panache."

"True." Millie grinned. "Still, it's a big decision to make. And we really do have to think about the kids, what our moving away will mean to them. Daci's babies are due the end of next month, and I hate to leave when I know they'll need help."

"Speak of the devil." Ric heard the sound of laughter a moment before Daci, Deacon, and Matt climbed the steps to the deck. He opened the door and held it wide. "C'mon in. We were just talking about you."

"That can't be good." Matt stepped into the kitchen ahead of the others, pulled a chair out for Daci, and helped her sit. He flashed a grin at Deacon. "I swear we're innocent."

"Yeah, right." Deacon flipped a chair around and straddled it. "I'll speak for myself, but you, my friend, weren't even born innocent."

"Behave, boys." Daci grinned at Ric. "See, Millie? Look what I have to put up with all the time."

"It's got to be tough, dealing with not one, but two drop-dead-gorgeous young men." Millie rolled her eyes dramatically and pressed a hand to her chest. "My heart bleeds for you."

"What'd I tell ya?" Matt sat beside Daci and nudged her shoulder. "Millie thinks we're gorgeous. See how lucky you are? We could be butt-ugly, but we're not, so quit picking on us."

Daci nipped his shoulder. "Pick, pick, pick," she said. Then she giggled when he groaned.

Ric could stand there all day and listen to the teasing. He thought of Millie's desire to move away and realized how much he'd miss these three. They were like his own children—and not.

They were friends, but they were also his lovers. He'd never allowed himself that same familiarity with any of the people who worked under him at Pack Dynamics, but here, with Millie and these three, he'd been able to let down his guard in ways he'd never done before.

"So what's up?" he asked. "You guys want coffee? Anything to eat?"

"Not for me, thanks. We just had breakfast." Daci glanced from Matt to Deacon and then back at Matt. He'd grown into a formidable young man—it was hard for Ric to even remember him as the young beta he'd first met. Now Matt was the undisputed leader in his small family.

"Anton called this morning," Matt said. "Our conversation sort of solidified some things the three of us have been talking about for a while."

Ric shot a quick glance at Millie, then returned his attention to Matt.

"A couple of things have happened over the past few days that he felt we should be aware of—he's contacting all the Chanku who either have children or are expecting them." Matt gazed softly at Daci. "Calling to warn us."

Deacon interrupted with a shrug of one broad shoulder. "It appears some of the older kids are manifesting their Chanku abilities a lot earlier than anyone expected."

"How so? I haven't heard from Anton for at least a month." Ric folded his arms and tried to imagine what would have Anton upset enough to pick up a phone. He generally just invaded the minds of the ones he wanted to talk to.

"Well, Lily's disappeared. She's okay," Daci added at the sound of Millie's soft gasp. "Considering she went for a walk on the astral plane and ended up in Tibet."

"Holy shit." Ric set his coffee cup down before he dropped the damned thing. "She's what? Six?"

"Six and a half." Matt shook his head. "It seems she figured out how to read the hieroglyphs carved on the wall in that cavern under Anton's house. No one had any idea they gave explicit instructions for crossing through onto the astral. Once he realized she was missing, Anton followed her. He met up with Eve, who told him Lily was on a quest, that she'd already gone on to Tibet."

"I don't get it." Millie looked a little shell-shocked. "Why Tibet?"

"Remember? That's where Anton and Oliver went years ago when they were searching for more about Chanku history. Anton said that's where the Chanku started out," Daci said. "It's where our history is kept, with a bunch of monks he called the Ancient Ones. They're in a temple somewhere at the foot of the Himalayas, though he said he suspects it's not really Tibet as we know it, but maybe Tibet as it exists on the astral."

"But even then, it's not where we actually originated." Deacon interrupted Daci. "It's so cool. Anton said our ancestors actually came from another planet, long before modern humans had evolved here at all. We've always suspected it, but now we know for sure we really aren't human."

"Not even close," Daci said, laughing. She winked at Matt. "Why does that not surprise me? Anyway, Lily decided she wanted to help Anton find all the missing Chanku. That led to her reading the directions on the cavern wall, crossing over to the astral, and traveling on it to wherever it is that these guys called the Ancient Ones and their temple are. She's there now."

"And Anton's letting her stay?" Millie looked utterly shocked. "She's hardly more than a baby. I find it hard to believe that he would leave her there, knowing where she is."

"I know, and the poor guy sounds like it's killing him not to go after her, but he said Eve told him he had to let Lily do this on her own, that she has an old soul." Daci rubbed her belly. "I'm with you, Millie. I don't know how he and Keisha are handling this. I can't imagine letting one of my children do something so scary. Of course, Lily's always been precocious."

"I think this is taking precocious to an entirely unacceptable level." Millie's dry comment had everyone laughing.

"The point is," Matt said, "Eve told Anton Lily isn't merely capable of traveling on the astral plane—she's already shifting, too. He had no idea she'd learned to shift, because she's able to block his mind."

Ric shook his head in disbelief. "I didn't think anyone could block Anton."

"I know." Daci shrugged. "No one but Lily. Eve said

Lily didn't want to worry him, which is why she hasn't said anything."

"She's six and she's shifting?" Millie glanced at Ric. "Cami and Shay aren't that much younger."

"Exactly." Matt sighed and shook his head. "We all thought we had years before we'd have to worry about our kids shifting, but it's already happening. That's why Anton called—to suggest we think about moving to Montana. We'd be closer to more parents with little ones. We'd have the support of the pack when it's time for us to deal with this. There's a huge worry about our secret getting out. What if a kid shifts in public?"

"Exactly. The thing is"—Daci clasped Deacon's hand in one of hers and Matt's in the other—"we hate to leave you with the sanctuary and all this responsibility. At the same time, I really want to raise our kids with others who are like them. I think it's going to be a lot harder than we ever imagined, but we don't want to make a decision this big without talking to you about it."

Ric moved to stand behind Millie and rested his hands on her shoulders. "Thank you. We appreciate that, and I think Anton's right, it makes sense for you to be around other young parents dealing with the same issues. It's an excellent idea."

He leaned over and kissed Millie's cheek. "We're talking about a change, too. Millie has actually got things rolling for the foundation to take over running the sanctuary. They're going to make it part of the university's threatened species reintroduction program. It's set up so that there will still be places for you to stay on, should you want to, but from what you're saying, living closer to the main pack sounds like something you really need to consider. I want to know more, though. Lily's always been a step ahead of the rest of the kids. How does Anton think this will affect the other children?"

Deacon shook his head. "It's not only Lily. She was just

the first." He glanced at the others before continuing. "Last night, Stefan went out to get the kids in for their baths. They'd been playing in the meadow. His two oldest, Amber and Alex, were flying a kite with Oliver and Mei's little guy, Leo."

"The kite got caught in the branches of an oak," Daci added. "It was up higher than anyone could reach, but it was getting late and Stefan told them to leave it, that he'd figure out how to get it down in the morning."

Matt laughed. "I guess Alex didn't agree with his dad. He threw a typical Alex fit, stripped off his clothes, shifted into an eagle, and flew up to the branch. Then he turned back into a little boy, untangled the line and dropped the kite, shifted back, flew back to the ground, and landed in front of Stefan."

Ric reached for a chair and sat down, hard. "An eagle? Alex? But how . . . ?"

"So far," Matt said, "Alex and Lily are the only two who can shift. Alex admitted they've been doing it for a couple of months, but since they figured it was grown-up stuff, they didn't want to get into trouble, so they haven't said anything."

"What I think is even scarier than the fact they're already shifting," Daci added, "is that both kids are capable of hiding this kind of info from their parents. Their minds are already that strong, their abilities that refined."

Matt interrupted. "As far as the how of it, Anton said that Logan thinks it's the exposure of the developing fetus to the nutrients. None of us take the pills all the time anymore, but Daci has craved them throughout her entire pregnancy. So did Keisha and Xandi, and the others, as far as we know."

"And the nutrients are in our breast milk, too," Daci said. "All the babies have been breast-fed, including Shannon's triplets. None of our generation or yours were exposed from conception except for Keisha, but she had no idea her mother was a shifter, so she had no example to follow. Plus, she doesn't think she was breast-fed, and would have missed out on the nutrients through mother's milk."

She shook her head, tossing her dark brown curls over her shoulders, looking both exasperated and excited at the same time. "It's scary and exciting to think about, but our babies have been exposed from the very beginning to the nutrients. They'll continue that exposure later, through lactation. Anton said Logan is convinced the gland for making us Chanku is developing the way it was designed to, from conception on. Our children probably won't need the pills to become Chanku—it will be a normal part of their development, but that puts us all in the position of raising children with the ability to shapeshift long before they can understand the need for secrecy. It puts all of us at risk."

She focused on Ric. "Your granddaughters aren't that much younger than Alex and Lily. Luc and Tia could be faced with shapeshifting kids one of these days in downtown San Francisco. Try keeping that a secret."

Ric's head wouldn't stop spinning. He kept thinking of Luc and Tia and those two beautiful little girls—plus, their boys were already three. What of AJ and Mik and Tala and their two kids, and Tinker and Lisa with their three? Anna Marie was almost five. So were Tala's twins. And Daci was right—Cami and Shay were five and a half. The thought of those two shifting at this age was mind-boggling, to say the least.

Ric's head snapped up. He focused on Matt. "You said Alex became an eagle. How can that be? We're wolves or, in Mei's case, snow leopards. How the hell did he learn to be an eagle?"

Matt shook his head, more serious now as all of them considered the implications. "I asked Anton. He's not sure, but he thinks that we all became wolves because that's either our primary beast or maybe just the creature we were first exposed to. Like with Deacon's and my small group. Our first exposure to shapeshifting happened when we saw Nick turn into a wolf to protect Tala. This was before any of us knew we were shifters, but maybe a wolf was a natural creature to protect a helpless woman."

Millie snorted. Everyone turned to look at her. "Sorry," she said, choking back laughter. "I'm just trying to wrap my mind around the words 'helpless woman' in reference to Tala."

Ric patted her hand, chuckling. "You're forgiven, m'dear."

"Point being," Matt said, obviously trying not to laugh, "we were essentially all preconditioned to become wolves. Mei was the only one who was seriously not a wolf, though she can become one now, which means the leopard might have been her primary beast." He shrugged. "A different branch of the Chanku family tree? Who knows. But when I asked about Alex, Anton said no one has ever told Alex he can't be an eagle."

"I don't think anyone tells Alex anything. Even if you did, he'd do it anyway to prove you were wrong." Ric chuckled. "I can see why Anton wants all of you close. This could be dangerous until we can teach the children the importance of secrecy."

Daci stared directly into Ric's eyes. There was more than a new mother-to-be's worry in those amber depths. "What if we can't teach them? What if our secret gets out? What then?"

Ric sighed and reached across the table to cover her hand with his. "I don't know, sweetie. But I think we all need to consider making a move to Montana, at least until we figure out exactly what these little ones are going to be capable of. At least then if our story becomes public, we'll be together. I should probably say *when* our story becomes public. The more of us there are, the greater the risk that we'll be discovered. We really need to be prepared for any contingency, but we already know there's strength in numbers."

Deacon covered Ric's hand. Millie put hers over Deacon's, and Matt covered them all with his big hand.

It felt to Ric as if they sealed a pact among themselves, a promise made without words, yet a promise all the same.

Matt made eye contact with each of them, and the sense of destiny hit Ric even more powerfully. "We're all planning to go to Montana for Liana's delivery," Matt said. "I think that's as good a time as any to make plans for a move, don't you?"

He grinned at Millie, then he focused on Ric. "What about you two? Have you thought about living in Big Sky Country?"

Ric nodded. He felt a sense of things coming together, of life and all its twists and turns taking a sudden and unexpected—yet strangely synchronized—jog in a new direction. It wasn't an uncomfortable feeling, but certainly none of this had been in his plans when he'd made love to Millie this morning.

Of course, he really hadn't had any plans this morning, other than making love to Millie. As long as he had his woman beside him, Ric figured he was up for just about anything, even if it meant a move to Montana.

It appeared change was coming, ready or not.

Chapter 10

Maine, early September

Baylor Quinn jerked awake at the sound of the bedroom door opening. Not yet entirely alert, he listened, expecting Keegan's clear, childish voice.

Instead, Jacob Trent's silent laughter floated through his sleep-addled brain. *The kids are asleep. All of them. It's almost five, but if we're real quiet . . .*

Bay opened his eyes and tried to focus, but the room was still dark. He lay there in bed, grinning—his brain might still be half asleep, but it was obvious part of him was ready to wake up. Blinking owlishly, he leaned over, nuzzled his way through the thick strands of Manda's long, blond hair, kissed her bare shoulder and again beneath her ear. "We have visitors."

"Hmmm?" His mate—now his beloved wife—groaned and stretched. "Is the baby awake?"

"Good Goddess, I hope not." Jake slipped in beside Bay with Shannon right behind him.

Still not entirely awake, Manda scooted over to make room. "What are you guys doing here?"

"What do you think?" Shannon leaned over and kissed her. "Wake up, sweetie. Quietly. This reminds me of when

I was in high school, sneaking into my boyfriend's bedroom."

"Ooh . . ." Manda sighed dramatically. "I want details."

"No. You don't." Jake slid over Bay and rolled to Manda's other side. "There are some things we don't need to know."

"Silly. You already know all the details." Shannon snuggled between Bay and Manda and whispered, "He was kind of a dork, but damn, the boy could—"

"That's enough, my dear, sweet wife." Jake leaned over Manda and kissed Shannon. "Our companions don't need to know he was hung like a bull moose and could screw all night. He was a teenager. That's what they do best."

"I see." Manda winked at Bay and opened her thoughts to him. He was in her mind when she wrapped her fingers around Jake's growing erection and stroked his full, hot length. "And what is it you do best?"

Jake sighed. "Whatever . . ."

"Did you lock the door?" Bay glanced over his shoulder. It had been ages since they'd risked anything like this, but with four four-year-olds in the house, there'd been more than a few changes.

"I did," Shannon said. "And we probably don't have long, but damn, guys. I've missed this."

She rubbed her butt over Bay's growing erection, but her focus appeared to be on Manda's breasts. Since Manda was still nursing six-month-old Donovan, they were full and firm at this time of morning. The baby would be awake before too long.

Shannon fastened her lips around one turgid nipple. Manda groaned. "You're killing me here. If you're not careful, you're going to get a mouthful."

"Control, sweetie." But Manda whimpered and Shannon turned her loose with a quick kiss to her mouth. "Spoilsport." When Manda tried to kiss her back, Shannon backed out of reach.

Moving slowly and with much contact, she slid down between Manda's legs, kissing and sucking her way over belly and groin, teasing and nipping until Manda whimpered again.

Bay loved the sounds she made, the sweet little whimpers and needy cries. He loved watching Shannon's silly seduction, teasing, tasting, and giggling until Manda was writhing beneath Shannon's practiced mouth, her lips and tongue, her busy and oh so talented fingers.

He glanced up and caught Jake's eye. Jake winked. Bay knew he was thinking exactly the same thing—how the hell did two guys get so damned lucky? Beautiful Shannon with her lush curves, sexy green eyes, and thick head of dark auburn hair, and his amazing Manda, all long, lean woman with her broad-shouldered swimmer's build, tiny waist and hips, and that mass of long blond hair he loved to get lost in.

Both women so much fun, so smart and loving and much more patient than either Bay or Jake deserved.

Jake flashed him a grin. *I'm listening . . . block it, buddy! Don't you dare tell them what we both know, that they could have done a hell of a lot better than the two of us.*

I promise. Laughing softly, he moved out of the way when Manda twisted out of Shannon's grasp and turned beneath her.

Bay's arousal grew, thrumming inside him with an insistent beat of need as Manda quickly buried her face between Shannon's thighs. Watching the two women pleasure one another, hearing the wet sounds and soft moans, and scenting the subtle perfume of their arousal captured him on a visceral level like nothing else, pulling him into the cauldron of their passion.

Manda opened her mind. With barriers nonexistent, shamelessly she shared her thoughts and impressions—the tastes and feelings, Shannon's rich, familiar scent that spiked her growing need, the sharp, shivering desire building with every touch, every lick and kiss and stroke.

Dazed by the sensual overload, Bay reached for his swollen cock, but Jake was there, pressing along his back, slipping one arm around him and wrapping his long fingers around Bay's shaft. Carefully, Jake slipped Bay's foreskin up and over the smooth crown, sliding and pulling, working the soft cowl, stretching the skin almost to the point of pain.

Bay arched into his touch, well aware that Jake's other hand was exploring the tight crease between his cheeks, circling that sensitive ring of muscle, pressing . . . pressing slowly and steadily until he suddenly breached the opening and slipped inside. One finger, then two, all the while keeping up the steady slide and pull on Bay's cock.

Bay tried to concentrate on the women, on their shared pleasure, but Jake's middle finger stroked him deep. A sharp jolt of pleasure was all the warning Bay got that Jake had found his prostate. Groaning, he fought the need to let go, to embrace the climax surging for release.

Jake pulled his fingers free and released Bay's cock. His thick member rose against his belly, suddenly bereft without Jake's stroking fingers. Bay went perfectly still, but the sound of foil tearing and the sharp pressure against his ass once again had him flexing his legs, adjusting for Jake's entry.

It had been too damned long. They'd all expected the major adjustments to their lives once they had children, although none of them realized entirely what life after babies would be like. Especially Jake and Shannon.

They certainly hadn't planned on triplets.

Those first weeks had been crazy, and if Ric and Millie hadn't come to help out, Bay wasn't sure they would have made it, but the triplets—daughters Kiera and Rowan and son Connor—and his and Manda's little Keegan were all four now. Four was, unfortunately, old enough to question parents all sleeping in the same bed.

There were some discussions Bay really didn't want to have. Not yet, anyway. It was hard enough, hiding the fact they could shift, but no one was quite certain how to handle their Chanku shapeshifting abilities or their open sexuality around children too young to understand the need to keep serious secrets from the unsuspecting townfolk.

He knew the Montana pack openly shifted in front of their kids. He wished they felt confident enough with their five to do the same, but sometimes this little group just felt so isolated here, as if their small pack had to hide everything in order to stay safe.

Bay hated secrets. He'd worked for the government long enough to abhor the power that secrets gave to those who found them out. Damn. He shoved his fears aside as worries for later.

Now the kids were asleep and Jake was stroking Bay's cock, pressing his fingers once again against the tight ring of his ass. Bay almost whimpered with pleasure when the slick lube eased the way. He definitely groaned as Jake's fingers were replaced by the broad, sheathed head of his cock, and groaned again when the pressure verged on pain as Jake pressed forward.

Breathing hard and fast, Bay forced his body to relax despite the sharp sting as Jake stretched his anal ring far enough to finally allow entrance—pain that quickly turned to burning pleasure when the fat crown passed through.

He visualized the slow entrance, the way his sphincter muscle tightened around Jake's shaft. His entire body clenched in painful arousal and he clamped down hard on Jake's cock.

Both men held still for a moment, giving Bay time to adjust to the fullness. Then Jake pressed closer, slowly slipping deep inside Bay, sliding in until his groin pressed up against Bay's butt and their balls barely touched between them.

Bay's lungs pumped like a bellows and he couldn't seem to get enough air. Jake's fingers tightened around his cock, stroking from tip to root and back up again. At the same time, he tilted his hips away, withdrawing almost entirely from Baylor's tight channel. Bay gasped, startled by the sense of loss as Jake withdrew, the sudden pressure as he rammed forward, driving deep, thrusting hard.

Jake stroked Bay's cock with one hand in perfect counterpoint to each driving beat. Pleasurable strokes, the pain of deep penetration. Pain that burned and ached in a most seductive manner. He cradled Bay's balls with his other hand, holding them in place so that their testicles rubbed together with every rock and sway of his hips.

Bay lost himself to sensation, to the sounds and scents of their women, to the harsh breaths in his ear as Jake took him higher, drove deeper, held him tighter. In what seemed like mere seconds, both of them hovered on the edge of orgasm.

Jake squeezed and stroked the length of Bay's shaft. He tightened his grasp painfully around Bay's sac.

It took only a few deep thrusts before—body trembling, heart pounding—Bay flew over the top. Jake squeezed his cock and balls, using the thick streams of ejaculate to lube his steady strokes. Bay's climax lasted forever. He knew he'd never run out of seed, never lose the sense of pleasure bordering on pain as his cock jerked within Jake's fist.

Manda's ecstatic cries and Shannon's muffled curse announced their simultaneous orgasm. Bay's muscles clutched at Jake's cock and trapped him deep inside, holding him in a viselike grip. He felt the throb and surge of Jake's climax, the ripple and pulse of his lover's thick cock filling him.

Bay's muscles clamped down even tighter on Jake's surging cock, and their bodies jerked and spasmed in the fierce power of their orgasm. Then, with a final, heartfelt groan, Bay's rigid muscles went lax, his lungs filled with air, his heart thudded against the walls of his chest.

They lay there in the big bed in a tangle of arms and legs, covered in sweat and semen and saliva, laughing at the mess they'd made, laughing over the fact they'd managed to find this small bit of time to be together in the way of their kind.

Once Bay's breathing slowed and his heart began to beat its usual steady tattoo, he cast his thoughts out, searching the children's rooms for signs of activity.

He found them all deep in slumber, their thoughts peaceful and their bodies at rest. He kissed Shannon first, then Manda. Then he turned and planted a deep, soul-searing kiss on Jake.

Thanks for thinking of this. I've missed it. Missed you.

Me too, bro. Me, too. I know you're just down the hall, but sometimes it feels like a million miles.

Bay chuckled. *That's because the path is guarded by crafty four-year-olds.*

Laughing softly, Jake slipped free of Bay's body and carefully removed the condom. "Ain't that the truth." He planted a kiss on Bay's shoulder and held a hand out for Shannon. "C'mon, love. Party's over. Time for all good little boys and girls to hit the shower."

Groaning, Shannon crawled off Manda, kissed her quickly, and then followed Jake out of the bedroom.

Bay turned to gaze at Manda. She caught his eye. Her lips twitched. She tried biting them, but that didn't work a bit. She burst into laughter just before Baylor tackled her.

Even the pines looked wilted, unusual in this normally lush valley in Maine. The sun beat down on the grassy front yard, which was the only patch of green in the entire meadow. Jake had put up a shade over the area where the kids played in the water in their little plastic pool to keep

114 / Kate Douglas

their fair skin from burning, but it didn't do much to cut the heat.

Even though two of the four oldest were girls, Jake and Bay still referred to the kids as the little Irishmen. Bay's six-month-old Donovan was going to look just like the others, with his pink cheeks and strawberry blond hair.

Bay leaned back in his lawn chair with his feet in the kiddy pool and reached for the cold beer Jake handed to him, but he was obviously keeping a close watch on his four-year-old son, Keegan, who splashed with true abandon in the foot of water filling the pool. He and Jake's son Connor were doing their best to irritate the girls, but Kiera and Rowan had already learned how to drive the boys nuts.

They ignored them.

"D'ya think they'll ever figure it out?" Jake took the chair beside Bay and stuck his feet in the water. It felt absolutely wonderful.

"What? That the girls are playing them?"

"Exactly." Jake took a sip of his beer and glanced at the driveway. "Poor guys haven't got a clue or a prayer. Which reminds me—wonder when Shannon and Manda will be back?"

Bay laughed. "This clueless male figures it shouldn't be too much longer. The baby'll be waking up any time now. Manda's going to be more than ready to feed the ravening beast."

"I checked on him." Jake glared at Connor just as he prepared to dunk Kiera. Flashing his daddy an innocent *Who? Me?* look, Connor poured the bucket of water over his own head. Jake bit back a grin and hid it in another swallow of cold beer.

Raising triplets certainly hadn't been on the radar the night of the attempted presidential assassination, when he and Shannon had finally managed to conceive. Now he could barely remember what life had been like before the babies were born.

They'd just turned four a little over a month ago—two beautiful little girls and one wild little boy who, as Shannon often reminded Jake, was very much his father's son.

Bay and Manda had Keegan, just a week older than Jake and Shannon's three, and little Donovan who, at six months, was the spitting image of Manda's twin brother, his uncle Adam. Everyone joked about their growing herd of Irishmen, but life was good. Hectic, but good.

Especially when they were able to start the morning off the way they had today. Watching Shannon and Manda was something Jake knew he'd never grow tired of. As the image of his beautiful wife pleasuring her lover filled his senses, Shannon's voice was suddenly in his head. Jake sat up and glanced at Baylor. Bay's attention was riveted on the long driveway leading to the main road.

We've got poachers on the property. Two men, heavily armed, wearing camo. They're parked off the road a couple hundred yards north of the main gate. We just got a glimpse of them going under the fence where it cuts across the creek bed.

The kids are in the pool. Donovan's still asleep. We'll get rid of the bastards as soon as you're here.

Two more minutes.

"Did you get all that?" Jake glanced at Bay, speaking in a low voice so the kids wouldn't hear.

Bay nodded. "Should we call it in?"

"Yeah, but it won't do any good. The sheriff's department is so understaffed, I doubt we'd get a deputy out here in time—unless we catch them first."

"Wanna go for a run?" Baylor's grin suggested he was thinking of more than mere exercise.

Jake laughed. "And then what? Accost them naked?"

"Why not? It'd definitely get their attention." Bay shook

his head. "We've got enough clothing cached around the property that I'm sure we can find something to wear before we detain the bastards. I'm getting damned tired of this. We've had what? Six poachers in the past couple of weeks? Idiots shooting their high-caliber guns and they don't even think of the fact we've got little ones here."

"We need to do something, that's for sure. I think the sheriff's department is getting tired of the calls, too, but they sure haven't offered any suggestions. There're the girls." Jake pointed toward the oncoming SUV and splashed his feet in the water to get the kids' attention. "Hey, guys! Looks like the mommies are home."

Baylor trotted behind Jake, following a narrow trail that ran along a sharp ridge. They'd heard the men talking and knew exactly where they were set up, in a sheltered grove of trees near a small, spring-fed pond.

Obviously they'd been here before if they knew the area this well, which made him even angrier. He and Jake had fenced the entire property and posted it heavily with no trespassing and no hunting signs, but sometimes Bay felt as if the damned signs acted more as an invitation than a deterrent.

The truth was, this whole area had grown crowded over the past couple of years and they'd had to deal with more trespassers than ever before. Where they'd once been miles from the closest neighbor, they now had homes almost within hailing distance. Jake's piece of property was huge, but obviously not big enough for the kind of privacy they needed.

Wolves needed a lot of room to run.

And if what Anton said was true, they were going to have a good-sized pack long before they'd ever imagined if their kids were only a couple of years away from shifting. How crowded would their country retreat be by then? How dangerous?

Anton Cheval's suggestion that they consider a move to his huge Montana spread was beginning to look more inviting all the time.

In the meantime, the two bozos drinking beer and smoking cigarettes in the dry grass were breaking the law—they were trespassing where they didn't belong, carrying guns in an area marked as no hunting. Bay imagined all sorts of things he'd love to do with them—things involving his sharp canines and the predatory instincts that hovered much too close beneath his civilized veneer, but he'd have to maintain control. This was, after all, Jake's land.

Therefore, it would have to be Jake's decision. Bay could handle that—they were always on the same page with decisions and they'd never had any of the alpha male issues Anton had warned them about. At least, not since Bay had turned away from his undercover work for the government and given his loyalty to Jake and the rest of the Chanku.

His loyalty, his heart, and if it were ever necessary, his life. All forfeit without fear to keep the pack and his family safe. Carefully controlling the anger beating at the feral part of his mind, Baylor quietly deferred to his lover.

Chapter 11

You wanna play the pissed-off human or should I?

Jake snorted at Bay's offhand comment. Obviously, the situation wasn't at all funny, but they'd both reached the point where if they didn't look for the humor, they'd rip into these two jerks and then have to deal with the fallout once the sheriff's deputy arrived.

Finding humor in trespassers coming onto their property with guns didn't entirely control the anger, but explaining two idiots killed by the wolves Baylor and Jake were known to keep as guard animals would raise more red flags than Jake was ready to deal with. Still, anger boiled hot and ripe through his blood. It felt so good to let it roll free for a while. Felt good to imagine the way the hot blood would taste were he to sink his teeth into that big guy's throat and just rip away.

What it would feel like if he latched onto the smaller guy and did some serious chewing, if . . . oh shit. He was drooling all over himself.

Bay head-butted him. *Why don't you play the big, bad wolf? You're slobbering. It makes you look rabid. Personally, I think it's very effective.*

Smart-ass. Jake licked his muzzle and found a shady spot where he could watch the two men unobserved, raised his head, and stared at Bay. *Go for it. Jeans and sandals in the cache.*

Bay trotted straight to a long-ago fallen tree and dug in the soft dirt beneath it. After a moment he stuck his nose in the hole and came out with a waterproof duffel bag. As soon as he'd dragged it free, he shifted, unzipped the bag, and pulled out a pair of worn jeans and comfortable sandals.

Moments later, Baylor looked like any other local guy out walking his land, comfortably clad yet shirtless in the warm afternoon sun. Well, not entirely like any other, Jake thought, studying the tall, darkly beautiful man he loved. There was no one else quite like Bay, all lean, dangerous lines and piercing eyes—and a heart as pure and loving as any he'd ever known.

"You ready?" Bay glanced at Jake. There was an unmistakable grimness to the line of his jaw, the tension in his lean body. It didn't bode well for the trespassers. They were a threat to his family, to his beloved wife, to his pack.

Jake understood. He felt exactly the same way. And now, standing beside Bay, who remained in his human form, Jake let his feral instincts come to the surface. He glanced in the direction of the trespassers and snarled.

Then he rose and trotted alongside Bay. Taking a deep, calming breath, Jake inhaled the scent of Bay's anger, an acrid odor almost hidden in the rich blend of man and clean sweat and hot sex he wore like an aura. The guy had a body like a god, his sensuality so much a part of him that Jake had to force his mind away from sex and back to the problem at hand.

With Bay taking point, they crept quietly along a trail leading to a spot directly above the two men. Bay waited until Jake was beside him. *You disarm the little guy on the right. I'll take the big guy. Be careful. No teeth marks.*

The men sat on small folding chairs in a homemade blind about five feet below the rock shelf Bay and Jake stood upon. Their chosen perch gave them a perfect vantage of the small pond that was a popular watering hole for the wildlife in the area.

The men's voices carried clearly, and already the ground was littered with empty beer cans, cigarette butts, and other trash. It was obvious from the mess and their conversation they'd hunted here before, which explained the fresh deer carcass Manda and Shannon had found a couple of days ago. These jerks hadn't even taken the time to track the wounded doe. She'd bled to death, not far from the house.

Jake had to consciously suppress the snarl that fought for release. No teeth marks? He wasn't going to promise. He sniffed the air and immediately recognized the rich scent of natural prey. *We need to move now. Smells like a doe with at least one fawn coming to the water. I don't want them to shoot her.*

Baylor nodded. *Now!*

Jake leapt from the rocky ledge and hit the smaller man in the middle of his back. The rifle went flying, the folding chair collapsed, and the man went down, screaming. Bay jumped at the same time and landed on the big guy. Jake heard his muffled curse as the man's chair folded beneath him and he hit the ground hard. Bay rolled away and came up with the man's rifle in his hands.

Jake snarled and lunged at the smaller man, who screamed again and tried to hide behind his friend. The big guy stumbled to his feet, shaking his head like an angry bear.

"What the fuck do you think you—"

"Shut up." Bay pointed the barrel of the Remington .30-06 at the man's rather large belly. "You're trespassing. Can't you idiots read? This is private property."

Jake snarled and flattened his ears to his skull. Both men stared at him, wide-eyed. "I've called the sheriff," Bay said. He waved the barrel of the gun toward the trail.

"I'd suggest you start back toward your car. We don't want the deputy to have to come hunting for you."

The smaller man leaned over to retrieve his weapon.

Jake growled and snapped at his hand. He jerked it back and almost fell over, backpedaling out of the reach of all those teeth. "Leave it," Bay said. "Now move."

"Leave it? Are you crazy? That's an expensive weapon. I paid good money for—"

"Move." Bay stood with feet spread, holding the big rifle rock-steady in one hand at hip level without any visible effort. Sweat glistened off his broad chest and the worn jeans clung to his muscular legs. Not only was he taller than the bigger of the two men, he was broader and obviously much more powerful.

And there wasn't an ounce of fat on that impressive body.

Jake felt an immense swelling of pride as he watched his lover take control. Unarmed, Baylor was deadly. Armed, Baylor Quinn was an unstoppable foe. Neither of these jerks had any idea who they were dealing with—an ex–government agent who, not so many years ago, hadn't hesitated to kill. He had been—and for all Jake knew, still was—a man capable of killing without remorse. A man who'd helped Jake dispose of the bodies of agents he'd probably shared coffee with mere hours before they died.

Men who had died by Jake and Shannon's hands—and teeth. But on that day, Baylor had made a choice. He'd given his loyalties to the pack, just as he'd eventually given them his love.

It finally appeared to sink in to the idiots that Baylor wasn't kidding. Cursing and complaining and threatening legal action, the two men left behind their ice chest and the ruined chairs where they'd hidden behind their makeshift blind. All of it evidence, Jake figured. For what good it would do.

Even with evidence, they'd merely pay a fine and get off

with a slap on the wrist. This was an issue that wasn't going to go away. Not as long as civilization continued to encroach on their once-private home.

It was only going to grow worse and the problem more threatening. With four children nearing an age where they'd be shifting and running as wolves along the trails that covered this beautiful part of what had once been Maine wilderness, Jake knew they needed to find a solution.

He'd once thought this land was paradise. He'd planned to live out the rest of his life here, content with Shannon, Baylor and Manda, and their kids. Now it was beginning to feel like a damned subdivision. Plus, their situation had changed, now that they knew their lives had the potential to last much longer than previously assumed. So much for plans. . . .

He glanced at Baylor, recognized sadness in his beautiful amber eyes, and knew he was thinking the same thing. They both loved it here. Loved the work they'd been able to do for Pack Dynamics on the East Coast. Close enough to Washington and the intrigue that kept Nick and Beth Barden guarding the First Family in the capital, they'd been able to satisfy their testosterone-driven need for the occasional adrenaline rush while still being close to their families.

It appeared it was all coming to an end. Jake loved this land. Loved the home he and the others shared, the harsh winters, the glorious autumns, the unbelievable beauty of spring and summer, but it felt as if all of it was slipping out of his grasp.

He knew Manda and Shannon were okay with the idea of moving. They missed being around the other moms, missed seeing the children and spending time with the other Chanku women—the only ones who truly understood this reality that had become their lives. He missed the others, too, but he'd found peace here. Peace and the love of a woman who was more perfect for him than he'd ever dreamed.

Shannon was everything to him—adding Baylor and Manda to the mix made their lives so close to perfect it scared the crap out of him.

He'd never had so much to lose before.

He and Baylor had talked about the possibility of selling this place and moving to Montana. They'd weighed the plusses and minuses, but it hadn't felt like something that had to be decided right at this moment.

Of course, the latest phone call from Anton had definitely added some pressure.

He still couldn't believe Lily and Alex were capable of shifting. They were hardly more than babies. The thought of Lily traveling on the astral was totally beyond his comprehension. He wondered how Anton was coping. Wondered how he'd cope, if one of his three suddenly decided to take a journey into another realm.

Everything had been moving along so beautifully—now all of a sudden, it felt like his world was being rearranged without his permission.

Change wasn't necessarily bad, as long as it was change he was ready for. He really wasn't ready for any of this, and yet Jake sensed a need to make a decision, and make it soon.

He knew how he would vote. It wasn't just about his own needs or wants. Not anymore. What he wanted for himself really didn't even enter the equation. He couldn't risk his children and he couldn't risk his wife. His own life was worthless compared to theirs. Always had been, but now he had something worth protecting. A family to love, who, for whatever reason, loved him in return.

He heard the deputy talking on his radio and glanced at Baylor. Bay nodded, and Jake slipped off into the brush.

There was no need to show himself. As far as the deputy needed to know, Bay had sent his well-trained wolf back to the house.

It helped that local law enforcement agencies were well acquainted with Pack Dynamics. Lucien Stone had made a special trip out shortly after the attempted presidential assassination. He'd introduced Baylor Quinn and Jacob Trent, along with two of their wolves used, among other things, in search and rescue and the occasional hunt for escaped felons. Shannon and Manda had been more than happy to play the four-legged roles, though both had been pregnant at the time.

Since then, Bay and Jake had aided the sheriff's department on more than one operation under the guise of Pack Dynamics. They'd earned the locals' respect for their professionalism and dedication to getting the job done, especially since they'd done the work pro bono.

For the eternally cash-strapped agencies, Pack Dynamics's professional assistance had earned a lot of points.

Now, as he waited in the shadows, Jake heard Baylor greet the deputy, a man they both knew well. He waited while Baylor turned over the weapon he'd confiscated and the two trespassers were cuffed and secured in the backseat. Then he followed discreetly while Bay took the deputy back to retrieve the second rifle. A few minutes later, the cruiser pulled away with the prisoners in the back.

Jake met Baylor back at the fallen tree.

Bay stood there, staring off in the direction of their home. After a moment, he sighed. "Will it never end, Jake? Will we ever have lives where we don't have to worry about some idiot discovering who we are? What we are?"

Bay blinked rapidly before he turned away and began to undress. When Jake tried to see what was going on in his mind, the shields to his thoughts were high and tight.

Obviously Bay didn't expect an answer to a question that had no answers.

It took him only a moment to change and stash the clothes beneath the log once again, less than a heartbeat to lose any semblance of humanity before two wolves turned and trotted back toward the house. Each kept his thoughts to himself, though Jake realized this incident today had, in many ways, been a good thing—a catalyst of sorts. It had been all he'd needed to convince him Anton's offer made sense.

Whether he liked it or not, it was their only choice.

There were no longer any doubts in his mind. He'd wait until they were all together at the house and see how the others felt. Today's incident had been persuasive. He had a feeling they were going to spend the next few days packing.

Bay couldn't get Manda out of his mind as he and Jake loped back to the house. Her years of captivity were a nightmare that she still occasionally revisited, especially after an event like today's. Any time there was a threat to their lives, to their children's lives, Manda was once again entangled in the memories of those terrible years of life in a cage—twenty-five years as a lab experiment had done a job on her, and he knew she'd never totally escape the fears that lurked below the surface of her conscious mind.

Now that they had children, it was even worse. She knew of the terrible deeds evil men could do to innocent children. Telling Manda not to worry, that he would always be there to care for her, to protect her and their babies, was never going to convince her they were entirely safe.

And who could blame her? They'd had more than their share of scares over the years. This latest problem was merely a reminder that things were getting worse, not better.

The sky was a robin's-egg blue and the meadow a soft, golden brown as he and Jake rounded a curve in the drive and the house came into view. He loved it here. Loved the life they'd built for themselves and their children.

But he no longer felt safe. No longer knew if he could truly protect them. What if the kids decided to shift when there were strangers lurking? What if someone saw them? The risks grew by the day as more people moved into the area, and now, knowing that Lily and Alex were already shifting . . .

The idea scared the crap out of him.

Jake nipped his shoulder. *Race ya.*

You're on.

Jake immediately took the lead. The silver tips of his dark gray coat rippled like quicksilver in the sunlight. Ears back, tail stretched out behind him, he ran hard and fast, his belly low to the ground, his big paws tearing up clumps of earth.

Baylor felt the pull and bunch of his muscles as he built up speed. Within seconds he was gaining on Jake, then catching up to him. The house was only a couple of hundred yards away. He saw Manda and Shannon in the front yard sitting beneath the shade while the kids splashed in the plastic pool.

They looked up and waved as he passed Jake with a cocky nip to his shoulder. The sounds of the children laughing, the joy on Manda's face, and the laughter in her eyes had him pushing harder, running faster, all thought of the race with Jake lost in the sense of homecoming he felt whenever he saw his mate.

Then, without warning, without any sense of contact, a single word filled his head. A name, screamed into his mind with such pain, such unimaginable horror, it sent him rolling and tumbling across the dried grass.

In the distance he heard Manda's cry, Shannon's curse, and the terrified shrieks of the children. Jake lay nearby, whimpering, his body twitching, eyes glazed from shock and pain.

Slowly, Bay struggled to get his front legs under him, to find the strength in his hindquarters to stand. It took him a couple of tries before he felt confident enough to take a few steps, to actually move at a lurching gait toward his family.

Jake was slowly coming around. Bay went on ahead, aiming directly for Manda.

She was still in her chair, doubled over and holding the baby protectively in her lap. As his head cleared, Bay heard Donovan's cries and broke into a run. His gait was awkward, his head still reeling. Keegan had crawled out of the pool and was clinging to Manda's legs. Shannon was sitting in the water fully dressed, holding all three of her children in a tight embrace.

All the kids were crying, but Donovan's wails were the loudest. Jake caught up to Bay, wobbling as he raced to Shannon. Baylor reached Manda at the same time and shifted. He wrapped a towel around his hips and knelt beside her, running his hands over Keegan's narrow spine, planting a kiss on Donovan's fuzzy head.

Shannon glanced up as Jake knelt beside her in the water and embraced his entire family. "Call Anton," she said. "Find out what's happened. We're okay, but . . ."

Bay rose slowly to his feet. Keegan was no longer crying and Donovan's screams had turned to whimpers. The baby clung to Manda with his fist jammed in his mouth and gazed up at Baylor with tear-filled eyes. Sighing, Bay kissed his son. "Stay here, Jake. I'll call Anton," he said.

Jake's three were still crying. "Thanks, bro. It can't be good."

Bay kissed Manda. She nodded in response to his unspoken question.

"We're fine," she said. "They were more startled than hurt, but something terrible has happened. It must have, to cause Anton such pain. Now I can't feel him in my thoughts at all."

"Me, either." With a last stroke over Keegan's narrow back, a final kiss to Donovan's head, and another for Manda, Bay turned away. He hated leaving them, but even more, he hated what he might learn. Still, he walked quickly into the house and prayed it wasn't what he feared. There'd been no question when that scream had seared his mind. No question at all that Anton had been lost in grief.

That single word, that one name, was burned in his mind.

Lily.

Anton's cry still reverberated in Bay's mind—a cry filled with unbelievable pain, with a father's love compounded by fear. Then all had gone silent. His mental cry in Montana had practically deafened all of them here in Maine.

What in the name of the Goddess had happened to Anton's beautiful little girl? What would have wrenched such a horrible cry from her father?

She couldn't be dead. That was totally unacceptable. If anything happened to Lily, Keisha and Anton would never get past the pain.

None of them would. She was the first of the next generation. A beautiful child with all her mother's sass and style, her brilliance and her warmth, her father's amazing mind and magic, and a unique aura that was pure Lily.

Unique, irreplaceable, unimaginably pure. She had to be okay. With trembling fingers, Bay reached for the phone and hit the key for Anton's number in Montana.

Chapter 12

Washington DC—early September

Nick Barden glanced across the crowded room and made eye contact with his mate. Beth flashed him a quick smile, but her concentration, as always, was focused on the two teenaged girls they'd been assigned to watch over throughout the event.

The press was thick and kids from twelve to twenty filled the building. Problem was, Nick thought, it was hard to tell, just looking, if all those older kids were really kids.

Security was tight and the place was swarming with Secret Service and uniformed guards, but that didn't take the edge off his typical case of nerves. After five years as personal security for the First Family, Nick had long ago realized he'd never be able to relax.

Thank the Goddess he'd learned to tune out the constant chatter in his earpiece, because Beth's mental voice suddenly came through loud and clear.

Nick, something's off. My senses are firing like crazy right now. Someone is here under false pretenses. What about you? Do you feel anything wrong?

Nothing here, but you're always better at picking up on stuff than I am.

Beth's laughter sounded a bit more strained than usual. *I am woman. I am strong.*

I've heard that one before.

I can also tell when some bastard is lying through his teeth, and someone in this room is lying about something big.

I'm on it. Nick scanned the throng of kids, all of them anxious for a chance to hopefully meet the president's daughters. So far, everything felt fine to him, but he'd learned to trust his mate's instincts.

There was a surge from the back of the crowd, a subtle parting of tightly packed bodies as a young man carefully pushed a wheelchair through the group.

These were all good kids—young people here to be honored for their work with the homeless across the country—and they politely moved aside to allow the chair through.

Something drew Nick's attention to the girl in the chair. She was pretty, about thirteen or so. Spiky blond hair, slight build. Her legs were strapped to the chair, thin and obviously useless. Her spine appeared to be somewhat twisted, but her eyes . . . her eyes watched him with a look of utter desperation.

Amber eyes, so eerily familiar they twisted his heart and stopped the breath in his lungs.

Without considering the consequences, he projected his thoughts, including Beth in the silent conversation. *Why are you frightened? What's happening that has you afraid?*

She blinked rapidly, focused intently on Nick's face. And, as clear as if she spoke aloud, her words filled Nick's mind.

The man pushing me. He's evil. He wants to kill us all. He's put a bomb in the pack on the back of my chair. It's set to go off in under four minutes. I'm unable to speak. I've been paralyzed since I was little. Help me. Please!

Beth? Did you get that?

I did. I'm moving the girls to safety.

Contact the Red and Blue teams. Nick was already pushing through the crowd, moving at a normal pace so that he wouldn't draw attention to himself. *Have Blue clear the room. Tell Red to make sure they get this guy. I'll take care of the backpack. It doesn't appear to be attached to any kind of fail-safe device.*

He focused on the young girl. *What is your name?*

Sunny. My name is Sunny.

Act like you know me, Sunny. I'm going to stop and chat with you like we're old friends, okay?

Okay. But I can't talk. They've disabled my computer.

Do you know if there's anything connecting the bomb to the man, any type of trigger?

Just a timing device in the pack. It's set to coincide with an alarm on my wristwatch, but there's no way to turn off the alarm. It's got a huge range—a couple hundred yards at least. I heard them talking. They figured I wouldn't be able to tell anyone anything, but I was paying attention. Hurry! It's less than three minutes now.

Smiling broadly, waving as if he'd known Sunny forever, Nick planted himself in front of her wheelchair, forcing the one pushing her to come to a quick halt. "Sunny! I didn't know you were going to be here." He knelt in front of the chair, flashed a quick, innocent grin at the young man, and turned his full attention on the girl. She smiled, but it was more of a grimace.

"What happened to your computer? Isn't it working?" He looked once again at the young man, who was beginning to fidget. "Usually Sunny talks to me with the computer. What's wrong?"

The man shrugged. "How should I know? I was just asked to move her chair to a spot near the podium. They've opened up access for the kids in wheelchairs. Look, man. I gotta hurry. There's more kids. Outta my way."

Nick stood up. "I think not." He gestured to the Secret

Service members who had carefully taken up position on either side. "Take him." He grabbed the pack as the young man turned to flee. Three large men leapt forward and restrained him. A woman took control of the wheelchair.

"Hurry." Nick grabbed the pack. "Get her to safety."

If Sunny was right, he had less than two minutes to get far enough away from people to dispose of the case. Already the crowd of kids was moving away, obviously aware of a problem.

The press, unfortunately, was moving closer with cameras trained on Nick.

Nick! Shift. It's the only way you can get far enough in time!

Nick kicked off his shoes and tugged at his tie. He yelled at one of the men guarding the doorway that led outside. "Open the door," he shouted, holding the blue backpack high. He threw his shirt to the ground as people scattered.

Then he kicked off his pants and shifted, making the change from man to wolf so quickly he hoped it might actually go unnoticed.

Small chance of that with the media here. He grabbed up the pack in his jaws and raced for the door, all too aware of the screams and gasps in the room behind him. Running for all he was worth, scrambling on the hardwood floor, he charged through the open door, raced across the wide, covered walkway in front of the event center, and leapt over an iron railing. With the backpack clenched tightly in his teeth, he hit the grassy slope almost twelve feet below at a full run.

His Chanku senses picked up the acrid scent of explosive material, the subtle hum of electronic gear as the timer clicked away the seconds.

He had no idea how many of those precious seconds were left, no idea if he'd have time to lose the crowds, dump the bomb, and still get far enough from the thing to keep from blowing himself up.

No time at all to think of what he'd just done. He might have saved a room full of kids, but he'd most likely condemned the entire race of Chanku shapeshifters to persecution, possibly imprisonment and death.

He spotted a large concrete wall on the far side of the grassy area. That would have to do. There was nowhere else he could leave the damned bag that wouldn't risk harming someone. He had no idea how large an explosive it contained, only the certain knowledge that he was running out of time.

Skidding in the soft turf, he dropped the bag against the solid base. He turned, lost traction, and almost fell as he spun away from the bomb, but he managed to scramble and keep his balance, plant his hind feet, and get moving in the right direction.

Bunching his powerful hindquarters, he lunged away from the innocuous backpack. He'd gone only a few steps when he heard the soft click and felt the concussion, the almost gentle *whump* as the bomb exploded.

Followed by a deafening roar.

The blast caught him in mid-leap, tumbling him across the soft grass like a rag doll. He was aware of heat and pressure, of the thunderous noise as sound reached his sensitive ears. Flames, chunks of sod, and something sharp beat at him, tore through his thick, wolven coat, pierced his skin and then, almost miraculously, stopped.

In one sharp moment, one instant so precise he knew he would never forget it as long as he lived, Nick sensed death.

He thought of Beth. Only Beth. Of how much he loved her, of all they'd shared. All they still planned to do. The children they'd talked of. The lives they wanted, some day, to live.

Then darkness descended and his dreams winked out.

*   *   *

Concussion from an explosion rocked the entire building. At the same time, Beth was almost certain she heard Anton call out, but why? It made no sense, and she couldn't worry about Anton now. She didn't miss a step when the bomb blew, though she was sure her heart was breaking. She knew all eyes were on her as she took a last look around to make sure all was under control, and then she spun away and raced after Nick.

The girls were safely away with two trusted security guards, and the children attending the event were being herded into a separate room. She knew the tables there were already laden with enough food to keep them occupied while the chief of security sorted things out.

It was chaos, but controlled chaos, and no one had been injured. Except Nick. She'd been in his head, and then he was gone. Dear Goddess, where was he?

She planted one hand on the iron railing and vaulted smoothly, but she was only human and landed hard on the ground below. Immediately she was up and running, slower on two feet than she might have been on four, but Nick was going to need her human help.

She focused on the concrete wall on the far end of the lawn area. Security was everywhere, but most were racing toward the building where the event was being held. A few men ran toward the plume of black smoke rising in front of the wall.

Her mind was spinning. How in the hell had that man gotten a bomb through the detectors? Everything was scanned, and they had dogs working the perimeter. Security was tight as could be.

Damn. Heads would roll after this. At least she and Nick had done the job they were paid to do—they'd kept the kids safe and prevented a horrible disaster.

Everything had worked like clockwork—everything except Nick's unplanned shift from man to wolf. Dear Goddess, she hoped he was all right. Frantic, continuing to search for his beloved mental voice, she raced toward the plume of black smoke.

How could he possibly have gotten so far in such a short period of time?

Unless he ran until the bomb exploded.

"Nick!"

Vaguely aware of a small group of reporters following her, Beth ran for all she was worth. There . . . mere yards from a huge crater in the green, green grass . . . something. Something dark, stretched out amid the ripped sod and the bits and pieces of whatever had exploded.

"Oh, Nick." Whispering his name, she fell to her knees beside the bleeding wolf. Slowly stroking her hand over his dark brown fur, she pressed her palm to his chest. The slow, steady thud of his heart had her sobbing without shame.

A paramedic knelt beside her. "He . . . shit. They said he was a man and then he was a wolf. What happened?"

Beth took a deep breath. Exhaled and knew there was no escaping the truth. "We're called Chanku. We're shapeshifters. He can't shift back until he's conscious." She bit back a cry and choked back her tears. "Unless he dies. Help him. Please?"

A news reporter shoved a microphone under her nose. Beth turned and snarled at him, an alpha bitch defending her mate. "Get the fuck out of my way."

The man backed away. The cameraman continued filming. More security forces reached them. Nick was loaded onto a stretcher while Beth spoke into her com unit, checking in with the rest of the team. Then she crawled into the ambulance behind Nick.

No one questioned her right to be there. They'd put an oxygen mask over Nick's muzzle and one of the men held a stethoscope pressed to his chest. There was no talking in the back of the ambulance—everyone went about their jobs, treating Nick as if he were human.

Beth grabbed her cell phone and dialed Anton's number. Damn. The man had more than enough on his plate right now with Lily wandering the astral plane, but she had to let him know what had happened. She had to warn him. She had no idea how they were going to manage this mess, but somehow they needed to figure out damage control.

Their secret was out. Nick was seriously injured, his shift from man to wolf had been captured by dozens of cameras, and there was no way they could deny what so many had witnessed.

The packs were at risk, and she had no idea what to do.

Praise the Goddess, Nicky was himself again, as long and lean and gorgeous as any man could possibly be while covered from head to foot with shrapnel wounds.

"Beth?" Blinking slowly, he reached for her hand. She was beside him in a heartbeat. "What . . ." He closed his eyes, but his grasp on her hand was firm. "Are the girls okay?"

"They are. You're a hero, sweetheart. You saved all those kids, the president's daughters, everyone in that room. They all owe you their lives."

"I shifted. Everyone knows."

"It's okay. Our secret is out, but it's out in the best of ways. You saved lives today. Think about that."

"What about the girl? Sunny? Is she okay?"

Beth leaned close and kissed him. "She's better than okay. She's Chanku. Baylor and Manda are flying down as soon as they can to get her. They'll take her on to Montana with them. Hopefully Adam and Logan can help with her paralysis. She's an orphan. No family at all. She's spent her life in foster care as a ward of the state. Now she's in a group home."

"I saw her eyes. She was so afraid."

"Not anymore. But, Nick . . . sweetheart, there's something you need to know. I called Anton. I wanted him to know you'd shifted in front of the press, that you'd probably end up on the six o'clock news."

"Oh, crap. He's gonna kill me."

Beth slowly shook her head. "He's got bigger worries. About the time the bomb exploded, he discovered Lily's disappeared. Again. Even the Goddess has lost her."

"Shit. How? What happened? Help me sit up." Nick shoved at the hard mattress but Beth hit the controls and slowly raised the bed. Then she sat on the edge and grabbed Nicky's hands.

"She was still on the astral plane, still under Eve's protection. When Eve went after her to send her back home, she was gone. The monks, Anton's calling them Ancient Ones, would only say she wasn't yet through with her quest, but they refused to tell Eve where she is. Anton's beside himself. He's absolutely frantic. In fact, I heard his cry all the way here. He's searching for her now."

"Is there any way we can help?" He squeezed her hands. "Goddess, Beth. I can't imagine what he and Keisha are going through. I mean, we don't have kids, but losing someone you love is . . ." He shook his head, leaned back against the pillows, and closed his eyes.

"I know. I almost lost you. Oh, Nicky. . . ." She touched his dark hair and blinked back tears. Red slashes marred the dark bronze of his chest. Bloody cuts peppered his cheeks, and one large slash across his throat had stitches holding it closed. She'd seen him naked right after his shift. One whole side of his body was covered with shrapnel wounds.

He was a mess, and more concerned about Anton and

Keisha's child than his own life. Beth bit her lips to keep from crying. "I've never been so afraid in my life. The bomb was filled with nails. It was designed to do as much damage as possible. When I got to you, you were unconscious and bleeding everywhere. You were full of shrapnel."

Nick frowned, as if trying to recall those final, frantic moments. "I was a wolf. How'd I shift?"

"I linked with you in the surgery, before the doctors operated. When I explained that anything foreign to your body would most likely come out, they wanted me to try that first. Once I was able to find a thread of consciousness, I linked with you and made you shift."

He quirked an eyebrow at her. "Did it work?"

She almost giggled. Relief did strange things to a person. "Bits and pieces of metal all over the place. Made me think of your Jacob's Ladder."

This time he laughed out loud. "Ya know, sweetheart, I knew I was in love with you when you said you'd put all those little barbells back in my dick after my first shift. Not just any girl would have offered."

Beth felt herself beginning to relax. They'd been through so much together. Somehow they'd weather this as well. "I was already in love with you." She leaned close and kissed him, amazed, as she always was, that this beautiful and caring man loved her. "Anyway, the doctors were impressed when a second scan showed that all the shrapnel was gone. I think they wanted to see you shift even more than they wanted to stitch up all your injuries. The entire operating room was filled."

"Well, I guess our secret's definitely out, then. Did you talk to Anton?"

She shook her head. "No. Adam took the call. Anton's gone into the astral in search of Lily. Eve's helping him, so Adam and Stefan are holding down the fort. It sounds like everyone's preparing to move back to Montana because of the new info about the kids shifting way ahead of what we expected. Even Jake's pack is planning to move."

"What's going to happen now? Now that our secret is out?"

Beth shook her head. "I don't know." She leaned close and kissed him again. "And do you want to know the honest truth? I don't really care. You're alive. That's all that matters."

"Actually, that's not all that matters."

Beth whirled around. The president stood in the doorway, flanked by two burly members of the Secret Service.

He stepped into the room and stood beside the bed. "I can never thank you enough, Nick. You and Beth have been there for us for the past five years without any thought to your own safety. My wife and I don't want to lose your service, which could happen if public opinion were to go against you. We've got people working on a campaign to out you, so to speak, in an entirely positive manner."

Beth stared at the closed door long after the president was gone. Finally she sighed and turned to face Nick. "Do you think it'll work? Putting a spin on things so people will accept us?"

Nick brushed her dark hair back from her eyes. "It can't hurt. We all know the power of a good marketing campaign. What time is it?"

Beth glanced at her watch. "Time for the news."

Nick scooted to one side and Beth snuggled up beside him on the bed. She flipped the controls and found one of the major networks.

Today's attack wasn't the lead story. No, it was only a small part of the coverage. The main story was the film of Nick throwing off his clothing and turning into a wolf on camera—that was what had obviously caught the world's attention. It was Beth racing across the grass with the press on her heels, the torn and bleeding wolf lying near a huge crater in the otherwise pristine lawn.

And then it was the president's press secretary, standing at the familiar podium in the East Room of the White House, explaining that Nick and Beth were both part of an ancient race of shapeshifters, long known to certain members of government, their identity kept secret in order to make their protection of the president and his family more effective.

A secret Nick had bravely given up to the world to keep a room filled with innocent young people safe from a terrorist's bomb. He painted Nick as a hero, which made Nick feel like squirming under the covers and going into hiding. "I wish he'd just shut up."

Beth laughed. "Be quiet. I want to hear the rest of this."

"I don't. Crap. I can't believe we made the nightly news, not after being so careful for so many years. I wish there'd been a better way to handle it."

Beth patted his hand. "Don't worry. The White House is working on it, plus I'm sure Anton will think of something."

"I don't even want to go there. Besides, Anton's not going to be thinking about anything but his daughter." He leaned his head against Beth's. "Any word of Lily?"

"No. Nothing. Luc and the rest of the pack from San Francisco are on their way to Montana. They're probably there by now. Ric and his group arrived last night. I told you Bay and Manda and their kids are coming here to get Sunny and then flying directly to Montana with her. Stefan's arranged for a private plane that can handle her wheelchair. Jake and Shannon and their three kids left this afternoon."

"What about Sunny? You said she's Chanku." Nick thought of the beautiful young girl trapped in such a horribly disabled body. "Is there anything Adam or Logan can do for her?"

Beth shook her head. "I don't know. She's been paralyzed since she was a toddler. She came from an abusive home, but I don't know exactly what happened to her."

"Her mind is sharp as a tack. She didn't even hesitate when I contacted her telepathically. She's what . . . twelve? Thirteen?"

"Nineteen. Her growth was stunted by her injury."

Nick stared at Beth for a moment. She tried to reach him, but his thoughts were blocked. Then he reached for the buzzer to call the nurse.

"What are you doing?"

"Getting out of here. Beth, there's too much going on right now. I imagine we can take some time off. Get in touch with the White House, tell them I need time to recover. Anton needs us. Sunny will, too. I keep thinking of what her life has been like. What hell she's gone through." He took a deep breath, replaying those last seconds when he was sure he wasn't going to live.

At that moment, all his priorities had made a major shift.

His first thoughts when he'd raced away with that damned bomb between his jaws had been about his job and nothing more—he had to get it away from the innocent kids, away from that little girl in the wheelchair—away from Beth. But when he dropped the backpack and ran, he wasn't thinking like a hero—he was thinking like a man who finally realized what was really important in his life.

Then, in those final seconds after the damned thing blew, when he knew he was too close, all he'd thought of was Beth. That he wouldn't hold her in his arms again, wouldn't watch the laughter in her eyes, wouldn't run with her in the deep woods.

Wouldn't see their child in her arms.

Those were the things that counted. The only things. Not the job, not their careers in Washington. Only Beth and the life they should have together. He wrapped an arm around her and held her close. Resting his chin atop her dark hair, he realized he was blinking back tears. He never cried. Not ever.

"Beth? I learned something important today. You know I love you, but I don't think I've ever thought of not being here with you. Not holding you. I know now how very much I need you."

He took a deep breath and rubbed his chin against her dark hair. "I want to take some time for the two of us. Just you and me, without any responsibilities other than to each other and our pack. It's time to go home to Montana. Time to get out of Washington for a while. This place can be toxic. Let's just go. We can wait for all the publicity to die down and then figure out what comes next."

Beth tilted her head and kissed his chin, then his lips. After a long moment, she pulled away and smiled. "I know what I'd like to come next. How and with whom . . ."

Just then the door swung open and a nurse entered the room. Both Nick and Beth broke into laughter.

She glanced their way and began unhooking the IVs and monitors. "I take it you're feeling well enough to go home."

Nick grinned. "How'd you know?"

She flashed him a knowing smile. "I've been watching the heart rate monitor at the nurse's station. I knew your wife was in here with you." She raised an eyebrow. "Do you really want me to spell it out?"

Laughing, Beth jumped off the bed so the nurse could unhook her husband.

Chapter 13

Montana

Stefan clicked off the power and the big screen TV went dark. He shot a quick glance at Adam and then faced the room filled with so many of their friends and family.

Doc Logan and Jazzy Blue sat with Oliver and Mei on one of the sofas, AJ, Mik, and Tala filled up one half of the sectional couch with Luc and Tia, Lisa and Tinker on the other end. Liana, looking uncomfortably pregnant, rocked slowly in the bentwood rocker. Jake sat in one of the recliners with Shannon in his lap, both of them exhausted from the quick flight across the country with triplets, and the whole group from Colorado took up a cluster of chairs by the window.

Keisha and Xandi had offered to stay with the children so the parents could all be here. One member was conspicuously absent—Anton was still somewhere on the astral, searching for Lily. Stefan couldn't let himself think about that. Not now—not with so many other things to worry about.

Like the fact Nick, Beth, Manda, and Baylor weren't here, for good reason. Of course, they'd all just gotten a better view of Nick—on national news—than any of them could have imagined. Stefan sighed. They'd worked so hard at keeping their existence secret, but poor Nick hadn't had a choice. He'd done what he had to do. All of them knew this day was coming, but Stefan never expected they'd be outed in such a spectacular manner.

At least the White House press secretary was on top of things. "They're being proactive," he said. "They're calling Nick a hero, which he is. The country always needs more heroes." Stef glanced at Adam. He trusted the man's judgment and the sense of calm he always managed to project.

Adam casually leaned against the wall behind Liana with his arms crossed over his chest. "The fact they're talking as if the government has been aware of our existence for years is good. It makes us less threatening to people. They didn't mention our numbers or any of our locations. . . ."

Oliver laughed. "I'm glad they didn't mention we're aliens. I can see all of us packed up and herded off to Area 51."

Jazzy shook her head. "Takes immigration policies to a whole new level, doesn't it?" There wasn't much humor in her laugh. "Don't even go there. Personally, I'm glad they didn't mention the mindtalking. The fact we can read each other's minds and sometimes even people who aren't Chanku."

"Jazzy's right." Stefan sat on the arm of the sofa. "If they only know about the shapeshifting, we're not quite as threatening. We can't let them know anything about Anton's abilities, the fact he's currently trotting around the astral with a goddess."

"Try putting a spin on that one." Mik glanced at Stefan. He was smiling, but Stef could feel the big man's concern. "How is Anton? Any word?"

Stef shook his head. "No. I've thought of trying to contact him, but he's only been gone for a few hours. On the astral, that could feel like minutes or days. I'm not going to worry about Anton. He'll find Lily. He's got Eve helping him, and his little girl's too sharp to let anything bad happen. Right now we need to think about ourselves and our kids—how we're going to deal with this news getting out, with our location becoming public. You know it will. There are no secrets anymore."

"I'm amazed we've stayed under the radar as long as we have." Logan glanced at his mate. Jazzy smiled sadly and rested her head on his shoulder. She was pregnant with their first child, and Stefan knew exactly what she was thinking without even looking into her thoughts.

She was worried for their daughter's future. Wondering if any of their children would ever know safety, would ever have a chance at even remotely normal lives.

As if a shapeshifting child's life could ever be considered normal.

Adam grinned at him. "It's the new normal, Stef." When Stefan raised his eyebrows, Adam merely shrugged. "You're broadcasting, but I can assure you, our children will be safe. Each and every one of us here will ensure that they are."

Ric stood up and stretched. He still carried an air of authority about him, even though Luc had been managing Pack Dynamics for years.

"Before Lily went missing," he said, "Anton issued an invitation to everyone to move to Montana. Millie and I had already decided it was time to leave Colorado. Daci and her boys"—he shot a teasing grin at Matt and Deacon—"have decided to move here, and Millie and I intend to do the same. There's strength in numbers. Whatever's coming, I think we can handle it better if we're together."

Luc nodded. He glanced at Tia and then looked directly at Stefan. "We've talked about it as well. San Francisco is a better, more centralized location for Pack Dynamics, but the reality is, we can work from anywhere. Now that Tinker's flying the chopper, we've got a mobility we lacked before. Anton's got terrific facilities here. The landing pad is great and the hangar he's planning to build will be plenty big enough for both the helicopter and any other aircraft he might want to add."

"Weather's an issue in winter," Mik added, "but it can be just as bad in the Bay Area due to the fog and winds. It's a trade-off we're willing to make to have our kids grow up with a forest around them instead of high-rises and concrete."

Tala nodded. "A forest, and others like them. We all know what it was like growing up, feeling so different and not knowing why. I want it better for our kids. I want the chance to do it right for them. We can do that here."

Shannon raised her hand. "I'm a credentialed teacher. So is Tia, and Mei's just waiting on the paperwork, though how she managed to get her degree with Leo and Emeline I'll never understand." She grinned at Mei, who'd worked her tail off for the college education she'd always wanted. "I imagine there are others here as well who can teach, and definitely more than enough kids to start our own school."

Jake patted her flat stomach. "Goddess knows, we've done our part."

Laughing, she swatted his hand away. "You'll notice we stopped at three," she said.

Jake rolled his eyes and drawled, "But didja have ta do them all at once?"

Laughter followed, and soon ideas were flowing, along with talk about where so many new families would live. Stefan glanced at Adam and tuned out the noise. *Baylor and Manda decided to go to DC today instead of waiting until morning. They've already got Sunny's paperwork squared away. Nick's out of the hospital, but everyone's exhausted. Bay says they'll get a hotel room tonight, pick up Sunny tomorrow as soon as she's ready, and fly out in the morning.*

They've already got her paperwork? How'd that happen?

Folks at the White House expedited everything. They agreed that, given the fact she's probably Chanku, it's a good idea to get her far from Washington before anyone figures it out. Poor kid . . . Manda said all her belongings fit in a single bag. I hope you and Logan can help her.

We'll do our best. Right now, though, I'm more concerned about Anton and Lily.

Stef nodded and sent a quick thought to Xandi. Keisha was holding on, barely. First Lily, now Anton. As always, Keisha was the one left to hold down the fort and keep it all together while Anton went off to save the world. If he didn't love Anton Cheval so much, Stef figured he probably would have murdered the bastard long ago.

Did Anton have any idea how hard it was on those who loved him when he put himself at risk?

Stef answered his own question. Of course he did, because Anton didn't take risks without a very good reason. A six-year-old child lost on the astral certainly fit that description.

It took every bit of self-control he could muster to hang on to the threads of his temper. Anton stared at Eve, at the fear in her eyes, and wished he were the one she feared.

He wasn't scaring her at all. No, she was worried sick about Lily. "How'd this happen, Eve? You promised me she'd be safe. You said they would protect her. You didn't tell me they'd send a six-year-old girl on a journey to Goddess—knows—where by herself."

She wrung her hands, but she didn't look away. He'd give her credit for that. "Oh, Anton . . . I wish I had answers. I've asked the Mother. She merely tells me to have patience. I've asked the Ancient Ones and they look at me as if I'm crazy to wonder where their princess has gone."

She bowed her head and her shoulders were shaking. That sign of vulnerability was Anton's undoing. He shed his anger, even some of his fear, and wrapped his arms around the woman who had once been a member of his pack, the one who had helped care for the children, who'd been mated to Adam.

A woman who was now a goddess. The one he'd charged with protecting his daughter. She'd failed him. Dear Goddess, how she'd failed him, but she came into his arms and laid her cheek against his chest. She was warm and alive and, like Anton, worried sick over Lily's disappearance.

"What can we do to search for her? Do you have any idea where to look?" He rested his chin on top of her head.

After a moment she pulled out of his embrace and took a deep breath. "I've asked the elements—the wind, the trees, the creatures that inhabit this time and place. None have seen her. The Mother tells me not to worry, but I can't help myself. I do worry, and I hate that I've failed you."

"I want to go to Tibet. Speak to the Ancient Ones. Even if they won't tell me where she's gone, we might be able to get some clues from what they say. Will you take me there?"

Eve stared at him for a moment. Her eyes swirled in that mesmerizing shift from green to gray to brilliant amber that he always found so unsettling. Finally she nodded. "The Mother will allow it. Come."

The Mother? She's involving herself in this? He found himself glancing over his shoulder, watching for Her presence, some sense that the One Over All had suddenly appeared.

But there was nothing beyond the pristine meadow, the blue, blue sky, and the perfect forest. The pond bubbled with its natural effervescence. The air maintained a perfect temperature.

If he hadn't known better, Anton would think that all was well in paradise. But it wasn't. His daughter was missing, and the Goddess who was supposed to keep her safe had failed miserably at her job.

Once again, the one watching over the Chanku had proved to have feet of clay.

With that thought in mind, Anton followed Eve through a shimmering doorway that opened with the wave of her hand. Together they stepped out of the perfect meadow onto a rocky promontory high on a mountainside in the rugged Himalayas.

The air was bitter cold, whistling around the high cliffs and sending dirt and dust into the air. Anton remembered this place, the cold and bitter land, the narrow trail cut into the side of the cliff. He'd walked this way with Oliver, so many years ago. They'd come here searching for answers to questions neither of them knew to ask.

This time was different. This time he searched for his daughter, and he'd be damned if he'd leave without her.

"We're almost a mile from the monastery, if I remember correctly." He glanced at Eve's flowing gown, at the way the layers of sheer fabric wrapped around her legs and clung to her arms. "You're not dressed for this kind of cold weather. Will you be okay?"

She nodded. He held out a hand to help her along the trail. Her sandals were thin, lightweight things. Definitely not designed for such rocky ground. At least he'd been dressed as he usually was around the compound—jeans, a flannel shirt, and work boots.

"I don't feel the cold. Not the heat, not any of the dis-

150 / Kate Douglas

comforts of the living." She smiled sadly at him and his heart almost stopped in his chest. It was so easy to forget her reality when he held her warm, vital hand in his.

"I am, after all, dead," she reminded him. "At least as far as the world of the living is concerned."

Eve would always be alive to him. Even more so, now that she was their Goddess. She'd taken a more active role with the pack after her mortal death than she ever had when she lived among them. Then she'd been quiet and unassuming, appearing to take pleasure as Adam's mate but rarely doing anything to make herself stand out in the group.

"I find that hard to believe," he said, squeezing her fingers. "You still look pretty lifelike to me." He helped her over an area where the trail had crumbled, leaving little more than a narrow ledge.

He couldn't help himself and made the mistake of glancing down. The valley far, far below was lost in the swirling mists. His stomach lurched. "Holy crap. Probably shouldn't have done that." He leaned against the face of the cliff, pressing his back to the solid stone until the vertigo passed.

"Come." Eve tugged his hand and he realized she'd somehow moved ahead of him. "You've done this before, when you traveled this way with Oliver."

Anton shook his head, cleared his mind and nodded. "I was a lot younger then." Following carefully behind her, he wondered how Eve could know what he and Oliver had done. She'd not been here then.

"I have Liana's memories." She smiled at him. "Know that your thoughts are always open to me, Anton. Even your anger with me, your disappointment in my abilities. Your knowledge of my failure is not an easy burden to bear, but it's one I will carry. You're right. I have failed you badly. I bear the weight of the memories and the guilt of

Liana's failings as well. I am she, for all intents and pur-poses. When I took her memories and her knowledge, I took her guilt as well."

Carefully, Anton placed one foot in front of the other along the slippery, narrow path. "Sounds like a pretty good deal for Liana. She got your man, she got your life, you got the guilt. What's in this for you?"

Eve's laughter surprised him. "You have no idea, Anton Cheval. No idea at all. I would not trade this existence for anything, and you, a man who treasures knowledge above all else, should be the first to understand."

He didn't answer her. There was no need, not if she could read his mind. But Anton knew there was something he treasured even more than knowledge. Something— some *ones*—who meant more than anything else. More, even, than his life.

His mate. His children, and the daughter he searched for now. Without them, there was nothing. Even knowl-edge couldn't compare.

Eve's grasp on his hand tightened. A small gesture of re-assurance, but one he would hold on to.

"We're here," she said.

He'd lost track of time, which wasn't all that unusual on the astral, though he'd thought he was physically on the Tibetan steppe. Maybe not? No matter . . . yet he had somehow traversed the narrow path and now stood on a broad trail that ended in front of the familiar gates of the monastery. The dirt beneath his feet was red, the moun-tains loomed high above, and the desolation of the rugged steppe stretched as far as the eye could see.

He'd stood in this same place with Oliver so many years ago, and as the huge gates slowly swung opened, he experienced an overwhelming sense of déjà vu.

A monk wearing a robe the same deep red as the dirt and the stone walls around them gestured for Anton and

Eve to follow. Was this man perhaps one of the Ancient Ones? He wondered again if they were still on the astral or if this place existed in the real world.

"We're in a place between," Eve said, which made absolutely no sense to him at all. They followed the silent monk down a long tunnel leading beneath the monastery. "Here and yet not," she added. "These men are not of the earth. They're the last of the original Chanku, the ones who made the journey here from a dying world eons ago. Too long ago to have lived so long in the mortal world. They've chosen existence here, where time moves at a different pace."

"Why?" Anton gazed about at the unadorned cold stone walls as they wound deeper into the ground. "Why would anyone choose to live such an ascetic life?"

Eve paused and turned to stare at him. Her eyes spun more quickly than ever before. "For knowledge, Anton. This is what happens when the desire for knowledge outweighs the need for emotion, for the connection that humanity offers. When the mind overpowers the body's need for love, this is what is left."

He studied those swirling eyes while the monk stood silently by, waiting on them. Was this a reproach? His constant search for knowledge had often gotten him in trouble. He'd made some foolish and selfish choices over the years. Choices that, in the long run, had worked out, but they'd put his life and his pack at risk.

He gazed at the silent monk and caught the man looking at him. He'd not noticed before that the man's eyes were darkest amber. Eve had said he was Chanku. Did that mean he was a shapeshifter? Did they still run as wolves or snow leopards?

Slowly, the monk shook his head and sighed. Images blossomed in Anton's mind. Images of a life the monk had lived millennia ago beneath a brilliant teal blue sky surrounded by unusual plants and brighter-than-life colors.

Surrounded by a loving family, by children. A woman's image filled Anton's mind. A beautiful woman with a look of utter sadness in her eyes. Of desperation.

A huge flash in the night sky—a sun gone nova? A world destroyed in the blink of an eye.

Was this the world this Ancient One had escaped? Had that woman, those children survived? Or were they lost in the rubble, the detritus and dust of history?

The man slowly nodded and turned away. Anton was left with a sense of desolation, of grief so powerful he fought the rush of tears that threatened to spill.

Knowledge spilled into his mind—knowledge he'd not thought to seek, information he wasn't certain how to use or understand. This monk and the others like him had stayed on in this desolate place, clinging to the remnants of life and sanity in the hope they might one day pass their knowledge on to their descendants.

This small handful of survivors had stayed in the hope that their history—their beginnings and their knowledge of that life so long ago—would not be lost.

Lily was the key to their final rest. His darling Lily was the one who would carry their past into the future.

She alone was becoming the repository. And once she held the secrets of their past, only then could this small group of survivors move on. Only then could they rejoin the ones they'd lost so long ago.

Stunned, Anton followed Eve, followed the silent monk into the bowels of the earth. Deeper, walking the same path he'd walked with Oliver so long ago.

Then he'd come in search of knowledge. This time, he felt as if he knew too much, when all he wanted was his beautiful, brilliant, amazing little girl.

Chapter 14

Bay adjusted Sunny's slight weight in his arms. She'd been thoroughly checked by a doctor the night before, and her medical records had all been e-mailed to Doc Logan. Her paralysis was unusual—her limbs and speech were affected and her growth had been badly stunted, yet she was able to breathe on her own without a problem. Her records showed she'd had very little therapy over the years.

Unfortunately, the foster care system hadn't dealt with anything beyond her most basic needs from the time she was little. Bay wondered how many of her disabilities were due to lack of therapy more than the actual injuries she'd suffered.

They'd know soon, once Adam and Logan had a chance to examine her, but he had to consciously bottle up his anger as he started up the steps to the private jet Stefan had sent for them. This poor kid hadn't had a chance. Not from the very beginning. With any luck, that would change as soon as they got her to Montana.

Thank goodness Nick had been able to communicate with her, or they might never have known Sunny was Chanku. For that matter, thank goodness she and all the other kids who'd been in that room were still alive. Nick's actions had truly been heroic.

Baylor glanced over his shoulder at Nick and Beth.

"You guys going to be okay?"

Nick laughed as he grabbed hold of the railing. "I'm fine, other than feeling like I got run over by a truck. Shit, I didn't hurt this bad yesterday when my ears were still ringing."

"Watch your language." Beth grinned at Sunny, who smiled brightly. "There's a lady present."

"Yes, ma'am." Nick flashed a quick smile at Sunny, too. "Beth means you, Sunny. She's not referring to herself."

"Excuse me?" Beth pretended to kick him. "You are most definitely asking for trouble. You want to carry your own bags?" Beth raised one dark eyebrow and glared at him. She'd looped one heavy bag over her shoulder and had another big carry-on clasped tightly in her hand.

"I'm injured. Can't you tell?" Limping dramatically, Nick followed Bay up the steps with both hands free.

Grumbling with just as much drama, Beth followed.

Bay could feel Sunny's silent laughter as she watched Nick and Beth teasing each other. It amazed him she still had a sense of humor, but it was obvious she was enjoying herself immensely.

Manda'd gone on first, carrying baby Donovan in her arms and helping Keegan maneuver the few steep steps. Baylor ducked his head and turned sideways to get through the door with Sunny.

She was so tiny with her stunted body and shriveled legs that she barely weighed anything at all, but her spirit was amazing and her mental chatter nonstop.

Having spent a life trapped without a voice, suddenly discovering such a simple way to communicate after so many years locked in a body that wouldn't obey had to feel like a miracle to her.

He had to guard his thoughts—the last thing he wanted

this child to hear was pity, but dear Goddess! How could anyone remain this upbeat, this beautiful inside, after the horrible nightmare of a life she'd led?

Then he glanced at Manda, smiling as she teased Keegan about flying in Anton's jet all the way to Montana, and he realized how very strong these women were. All of them. Manda had survived even worse than Sunny, who at least had social services looking out for her.

Manda had had no one, yet she was a healthy, happy, well-adjusted mother of two. After fleeing an abusive home, Beth's life on the streets had been a nightmare. Now she was a personal bodyguard to the First Family.

If they could rise above such awful beginnings, there was just as much hope for Sunny to lead an amazing life one day.

A life as Chanku. Bay had no doubt that Adam and Logan could repair at least some of the damage to Sunny's spine, which meant there was a chance she'd walk again. Once she had the nutrients, she'd be able to shift.

And damn it all, if Oliver could grow a set of balls after his first shift, there was no reason on earth Sunny couldn't be made whole. Bay settled her into a comfortable seat where she could look out the window. Her wheelchair was already stowed in the back and an attendant was bringing the rest of the luggage on board.

Bay checked her belt. "You going to be okay, sweetie?"

She nodded and her eyes sparkled. *I've never been in an airplane before.*

"This one's special. A friend of ours chartered it just for us. You'll meet him when we get to Montana." He patted her shoulder. "Just a few hours and we'll be there. It's a beautiful place, and you're going to love it. You'll be able to talk to everyone the way you can talk to us."

That will be . . . She sighed. *I can't imagine what that will be like. I've never been able to speak to anyone before.*

"You'll probably be wishing for some quiet before long." Bay stroked her spiky, pale blond hair. He wasn't about to tell her what their hopes were, that they all wanted to see her shift and hoped she'd be able to run as a wolf.

But what if she can't? What if she's still paralyzed even after she shifts?

Baylor turned and caught Manda's worried look. *We're not even going to think that. Look what happened when you shifted for the first time. Your body was stunted, twisted like Sunny's. Now you're perfect.*

She smiled at him. *No, I'm not.*

We've had this argument before. I always win. Remember?

Donovan started to fuss. Manda turned her attention to the baby, but Bay didn't miss her very satisfied smile. She was always uncomfortable with praise, but he knew she loved it just the same. Taking the seat across from Sunny, he buckled himself in as the pilot began to taxi away toward the runway. They'd be home in a few more hours.

Home. He'd thought of Maine as his home for over seven years, but suddenly he was looking west when he thought of going home. He turned and smiled at Manda. She was nursing Donovan so the pressure changes as they took off wouldn't bother the baby's ears as much.

She blew Bay a kiss. *Me, too. I'm anxious to get home to Montana. I miss my mom and my brother, our packmates. I can't believe I already miss Shannon and Jake.*

Nick and Beth had the two seats in the back. Nick glanced up and smiled at Bay. *Feels right, doesn't it? I'm really excited about seeing Deacon and Matt and Jazzy and Logan. It's been a while since we've all gotten together.*

It has. Bay turned around in his seat. Nick was right. It had been too long since they'd gathered. After a month-long trip to Montana when Manda gave birth to Donovan on Saint Patrick's Day last March, they'd not been back. They'd missed Lucia's birth at the end of April, but Manda and Bay had been anxious to return to Maine. Nick and Beth had missed both births, as they'd missed many of the others.

Duty with the First Family took priority.

Bay wondered how knowledge of their Chanku heritage might change their work—or if it even would. The news last night had painted Nick as a hero, but only the White House press corps knew any of the facts about them, so it had been totally one-sided.

Once the other networks got hold of more details, Bay didn't expect everything to remain as positive, especially when the cable networks started digging—and making stuff up. There'd be a lot of misinformation over the next few weeks—they had to expect that. Misinformation that would lead to fear, and fear could bring all kinds of unexpected problems.

It was probably a good thing they were leaving for a while. Nick was supposedly recuperating from severe injuries at an *undisclosed* location.

He just hoped they could keep Anton's spread in Montana *undisclosed*. He hated the thought of their privacy being lost, of reporters and curiosity seekers swarming them. Of crazies wanting to hunt them.

They'd discussed all the possible scenarios. Some were good, most weren't, but he didn't want to dwell on those. Nick felt bad enough for outing them, especially after so many successful years in hiding.

Bay tightened his seat belt. He'd concentrate on the good things. On the young woman sitting across the aisle, staring raptly out of the plane window. Sunny Daye was the first newly discovered Chanku in over five years, and he couldn't wait to turn her over to Adam and Logan for treatment.

He'd think of the fact Nick had survived. He'd not only saved hundreds of lives, he'd helped catch a terrorist, stopped a plot that would have had disastrous consequences, and he'd acted with bravery.

Bay turned far enough in his seat that he could make eye contact with Nick and Beth. They had their heads close together and were obviously deep in conversation. Without prying, Bay could almost bet Nick was agonizing over the fact he'd allowed their existence to become public knowledge. The guilt was obviously weighing on both of them.

Interrupting the two, Bay said, "Ya know, Nick, for what it's worth, I think it's a good thing the world knows about us."

Nick's head popped up. He stared intently at Baylor.

"Think about it. It's stressful to keep a secret this big. We've all been worried about one of the kids accidently giving us away, or the wrong people in the government learning of our existence. We've talked about going public for years, but no one's been willing to take the chance. You just solved the problem for us."

Beth laughed and poked Nick's arm. "Yeah, but don't you think he could have found a smaller stage? I mean, making your first public shift is one thing, but to drop your pants in front of the world's top news organizations with all those cameras? I think that's pushing it, even for Nick."

Manda glanced at Bay, and her eyes were twinkling. "Oh, I think Nick just wanted to show off his package to the biggest audience possible." She dipped her head and focused on the baby.

After a moment's stunned silence, all of them laughed.

Even Sunny obviously got the joke, which made Bay feel a bit uncomfortable at first. He had to remind himself that even though she looked like a child, she was almost twenty years old and most definitely an adult.

Still chuckling at Manda's uncharacteristic comment, Bay turned around and focused forward. For someone who was usually so quiet and shy, Manda could—and did, on occasion—throw out a zinger. Laughing was good. They were facing an uncertain future. He had a feeling they were going to need as much laughter as they could possibly get.

Anton stepped through the astral gateway Eve opened for him into the silent cavern beneath his home. He hated the thought of what he had to tell Keisha, that Lily was still not able to return. At least now he knew she was safe. He'd seen her, though he'd not been allowed to speak to her.

She lay as still as death on a soft pallet far beneath the room where the scrolls still gathered dust. She'd not changed a bit, and the Ancient Ones had assured him that, for Lily, only a few hours had passed.

She was almost done. When she left the monastery, she would know all there was to know of their beginnings, their life before they'd fled their home world, and how the first Chanku had settled into this frightening new world.

It was a huge responsibility for such a little girl, but the Ancient Ones assured him she was more than capable. He honestly didn't know whether to burst with pride or crumple to his knees and weep.

She would always be his baby, his first, his favorite. He knew parents weren't supposed to favor one child over another—he loved each of his children unconditionally. The others would never know the special bond he felt with

Lily, but he and his first child had connected almost from the moment of her conception.

She had saved his life, his soul, his laughter.

"Anton? You're back!"

He jerked around at the sound of Keisha's voice. "Keisha? Where are you? What are you doing down here?"

"I've been waiting for you."

He saw her then, sitting in the dust, wearing faded jeans and a tank top. She leaned against the cavern wall with her hands looped over her knees. "How long have you been here?" He walked over, took her hand, and pulled his beloved wife to her feet. She stood and wrapped her arms around him.

"Not long. Only about an hour. You've been gone for so long, but I had a feeling you were coming home today. Where's Lily? Did you find her?"

He nodded. "I did. She'll be home soon. It's a long, amazing story, but Lily is safe. I saw her not an hour ago."

Keisha let out a long sigh of relief. "Good. That's good. I'd rather have her home, but knowing she's safe takes some of the pressure away. Things have happened while you were gone. Stefan's headed to Kalispell to pick up Manda and Bay and their kids. Stefan chartered the corporate jet. I hope that was okay, but Nick and Beth are with them, and a young girl with severe physical disabilities. She's Chanku. Adam and Logan are hoping they can help her."

"Of course it's all right. Chanku? How did they find her?" He leaned back with his arms still hooked around her waist and stared into Keisha's eyes. She smiled at him.

"It's another long story. Maybe one not so good. She was an innocent victim in a terrorist plot. Nick was a hero. He was able to get a bomb out of a room filled with kids, including the girls, before it exploded."

"The president's daughters? Crap. What happened?" He led Keisha to a low stone formation by the pool and tugged her down beside him. "Tell me here, before we go up."

"It sounds so scary. It was really close. Beth sensed something wrong about the same time Nick made a telepathic connection with a young girl in a wheelchair. She was being used to smuggle an explosive device into a room filled with kids. Nick got the backpack with only seconds to spare. But the only way to get it far enough away from everyone . . . the only way . . ." She shook her head. "Oh, love . . . the room was filled with reporters and cameramen, but he had no other choice."

For some reason, Anton suddenly felt like laughing. "He shifted on camera, didn't he? Crap. I bet that got everyone's attention. Poor Nick. He must be tearing himself apart."

Blinking, Keisha stared at him with her mouth open. "You're not upset? Anton, the whole world knows about us. It couldn't have been more public—we got outed on the nightly news—every major network and cable station was there."

He kissed her very quickly, but his mind was spinning. "It was bound to happen sooner or later, with our children reaching an age where they're ready to shift, with cameras everywhere and everyone carrying cell phones with video. Don't you see? This is wonderful. Nick shifted in full view of the public, doing something heroic. He saved lives. . . . He's okay, isn't he? He did get it far enough away, right?"

"He did. He was injured—some shrapnel wounds. The device was filled with nails and would have done horrible damage. Beth went with him to the hospital. He was still in wolf form, still unconscious from the blast. She figured, since their secret was out, if he could shift back to human the doctors wouldn't have to operate because he'd lose the shrapnel. She managed to link with him, helped him shift, and they avoided surgery."

He lost it then. The visual was just too much, especially since he remembered Beth's story of Nick's very first shift, when he'd saved Tala from an attacker. He'd had a Jacob's Ladder piercing—tiny silver barbells running the length of his penis—and all of them had fallen out when he turned into a wolf.

"Anton? Are you okay? Honey?"

He raised his head. Keisha held his face in her hands and he was laughing so hard there were tears running down his cheeks. She stared at him as if he might be crazy. Maybe he was, just a little, but it was a better crazy than he'd felt when he heard Lily was missing.

He'd found his daughter, sort of. Their secret was out, definitely. They'd survived much worse, really. What else could possibly happen? "Ah, Keisha, my love. I'm perfectly okay. Have I told you lately how much I love you?"

She held him close. "Yes, you have. But I never get tired of hearing it. Tell me again."

He kissed her, running his lips over the soft fullness of her mouth, pulling her close enough to fit their bodies together, two pieces of a puzzle that clicked perfectly into place. Where he was hard, she was soft. Where his body dipped, Keisha's curved. They stood up and he tugged her cotton tank top off and unsnapped her jeans.

She helped him. When had she not helped? They were a team, a perfect combination of male and female, of man and wife. He slipped his hand inside her open fly, found her damp curls, her soft feminine lips, and the wet heat of her sex.

She was ready for him—always ready, and she tugged at his jeans, pulling them down over his butt until they tangled around his ankles. His blood surged and he thrust his hips forward, his cock rising hot and hard against his belly.

He wanted to lift her, take her there, standing in the dark cavern, but she went to her knees before he realized what she planned. Her fingers wrapped around the thick root of his cock and she squeezed. Her other hand cupped his sac and forced an unexpected groan out of him. Then her hot mouth drew him deep, her tongue laved the sensitive underside of the flared crown, and he was lost.

He didn't even try to hold back. She sucked him hard, sliding her tongue over the smooth head of his cock, poking the tip into his sensitive slit. Her lips rode up and down the veined surface of his shaft. He felt his climax boiling to the surface only seconds before his body jerked, his balls drew up close and tight within Keisha's grasp, and he filled her mouth with his seed.

She swallowed, taking all of him, sucking and licking while his knees went week and his legs trembled. Finally she released him. His cock slipped free of her mouth with a soft pop.

She'd brought him to his knees in mere minutes. Now she grinned at him with a look of what had to be feminine victory.

"This is not a contest, my love." He leaned close and kissed her, tasting his seed on her lips. The visual of what those lips had just been doing had him surging to life once again, but he gently tackled her and stretched her out in the clean sand beside the pond.

Giggling, she fought him, but he noticed she merely managed to get both their jeans off in the process. He nuzzled the soft curls between her legs while she squirmed, and slowly ran his tongue through her sweet nectar. "You know, I should take you right here, right now, but I don't think that's a good idea."

She stopped struggling and frowned at him. "Why not?"

"Touch me."

Still frowning, she wrapped her fingers around his cock. "Oh, ick. You're covered in sand."

"Exactly." Laughing, he rolled her into the pond. The water was warmed by an underground spring, the smell slightly sulfuric, but he'd always wanted to make love to his wife in its warm depths.

He'd never had the chance, but that was about to change.

Chapter 15

Sunny had, by necessity, become an observer. It was hard to be anything else when your eyes and your brain were about the only things that worked. She'd had to learn not to be frustrated or angry about crap she couldn't change, though it would help if she didn't look like a little kid. People tended to treat her like a helpless baby.

She might be physically helpless, but she was no fucking baby. She was almost twenty years old, an age when most young women had been on dates, experimented with sex, had a boyfriend. That would probably never happen for her.

Gazing around at all the gorgeous people in this room made her ache. If she was going to learn about sex, she definitely wished it could be with someone here. They were amazing, and she'd never felt more at ease with strangers in her life.

No one here, not a single one, felt like a stranger.

Of course, when you could talk to someone—actually communicate without using a stupid computer—they didn't stay strangers for long. Even the little kids could speak telepathically, which was about the coolest thing ever.

All her life she'd been able to understand, but she'd never had a voice. At least, not since she was really tiny, before she got hurt. She thought she could remember talking, but she wasn't sure if it was her imagination or her real voice she recalled.

She wondered sometimes what she'd sound like if she could make sounds, but now that didn't seem as important. Not here in this amazing house in the middle of the biggest mountains she'd ever seen. Everyone was so nice. The men were all gorgeous, the women were beautiful—and all of them could understand her.

She caught a movement in her peripheral vision. A tall, absolutely sexy man with tangled blond hair and a gentle smile was squatting beside her chair. She focused on him. He'd positioned himself perfectly—not too close, but just close enough that she could look directly into his eyes.

He had such beautiful eyes. Warm and kind. And just like every other guy in the room, he made her want what she'd never have. Then another man moved into her field of vision. Tall, like the first guy, but with dark hair. He had the same gorgeous amber-colored eyes. Sighing inside, she watched them.

"Sunny?" The blond guy spoke. "I'm Adam Wolf. This is Doc Logan. We'd like to take a look at you and see if there's a chance we can repair any of the injuries that are causing your paralysis. We won't do anything tonight, and we promise not to do anything that makes you uncomfortable, but do you mind if we take a look? All you have to do is sit really still. We can examine you with our minds, and I promise it won't hurt."

How can you do that? Examine someone with your mind?

The dark-haired guy shrugged and grinned at her. "I haven't got the foggiest idea how it works, but it does. Adam's a healer—he's also a damned good mechanic, so if you've got problems with your carburetor he can fix that, too."

Adam glared at him and Doc Logan laughed. "Sorry.

I'll stick to business. Adam can go inside your body with his mind and actually fix stuff that's broken. He's taught me to do it, too, though I'm also a real doctor."

Adam nudged the doctor with his shoulder. "What? You're saying I'm not a real healer?"

Doc Logan rolled his eyes. "You're a real healer, Adam. I'm the doctor. Why do you think everyone calls me Doc?"

He winked at Sunny and she had a feeling they'd done this routine before. A lot. *Neither one of you looks like any doctor I've ever seen, but if you can fix anything, that would be great. Even something little, like I really want to know what food tastes like. I've had to eat through a tube all my life because I can't swallow very well.*

Adam blinked a lot of times and glanced at Doc. They both nodded. "Then that's one of the things we'll check on first." He stood up. She liked that he knelt down so he was at her level. She hated always looking up at people. "Liana? Sweetie, do you want to help us? Doc and I are going to take a look at Sunny. See if she's got anything we can fix."

Adam's wife smiled and sat carefully on a chair next to Sunny. She was beautiful, too, with long blond hair and the most gorgeous smile, but she was so pregnant she looked like she was ready to explode. She was still more beautiful than any movie star Sunny had ever seen. Everyone was. Even the little kids.

"Hi, Sunny. I'd love to help. Adam, it might be better if she's lying down. Sunny? Do you mind if we put you on the couch?"

No. You can put me wherever you like. It's not like I can go anywhere on my own.

"Maybe not right now," Liana said, "but we have high hopes for you."

Adam had Liana sit on an ottoman in front of the sofa. Logan sat near Sunny's head and he scooted her over enough so Adam could fit on the edge of the cushion beside her withered legs. The girl was so trusting it made him angry to think of all she'd gone through, especially with a spirit as powerful as hers.

He had to get past his anger, though, or he'd never be able to examine her. He took a couple of deep breaths and let it go. All of it, until he was calm and every bit as accepting as the girl. He moved her sweatshirt aside and touched her smooth belly with his fingertips, just beside the little port that had been surgically added to allow her to eat.

Then he slipped free of his corporeal body.

Mindwalking, as Anton called it, never failed to amaze him. To think a once-homeless mechanic could have an ability this magical, this *helpful*. He felt blessed by his ability, though if Anton hadn't pushed him, had never suggested his ability to fix things could be transferred to people, he wouldn't have thought to give it a try.

Not like this. He'd helped Oliver, but that had been a different sort of intervention where he'd used the Chanku ability to link. This was totally unique, becoming nothing more than energy as he moved within someone's body. It felt like a million years ago since that first time he'd gone inside Eve's skull to heal her damaged brain.

Who'd have thought that he, Adam Wolf, would save the life of the woman who would become their Goddess? Amazing. Now, becoming one with the cells in this girl's body, he looked at Sunny from the inside out. He knew that Logan would be studying her brain and neck for damage, while Liana was checking for old injuries to her spine.

His job was less specific—he'd merely look for any anomalies, anything that might need repairs that could be done easily and might make her life more comfortable.

They'd already started her on the nutrients with Sunny's full permission and understanding of what they would do to her. When Jazzy had helped prepare the meal given to Sunny through the feeding tube in her abdomen, she'd added the first of the pills to the mix.

He checked Sunny's legs, the shape of her bones, her joints and tendons. Something was definitely wrong, but he couldn't be sure. Not until he talked to Liana and Logan, but in the meantime, he decided to hold off on trying to fix some of the strange anomalies he saw.

He had no idea how long he'd been exploring the inner workings of Sunny Daye's body, but Adam knew when he'd seen enough. When he was once again inside himself, he sat back and lifted his hands from the girl's motionless body.

She blinked and smiled at him. *Did you see anything weird?*

"No frogs or mice in there. That's good." He grinned at her when she smiled at him.

Well, darn. I was hoping you'd find the rabbit I lost.

She certainly understood teasing. "I saw one, but it got away. Those critters are fast." He chuckled, but his attention was on Liana and Logan. Liana was returning to her body, sitting up and blinking rapidly. She shot a quick glance at Adam but didn't say a word. Logan shook his head and cracked his knuckles.

"Sunny, we're going to get you back in your chair and I will consult with my disreputable associates," he teased. "Back in a flash, okay?"

Okay.

Again, Adam felt angry. What else was the poor kid going to say? Had she ever had a choice in anything?

They met in Anton's study with the door closed. Logan cut right to the point. "I want your first opinion. What did you think when you looked over her bones and joints, Adam?"

"First impression? That she tried to shift at some point, maybe years ago when bones were still fairly soft and unformed. There's evidence of minimal change, but it's enough to stunt her legs and screw up her joints."

Liana nodded. "I see the same thing in her spine. Twisting, some vertebrae out of position. Scarring where the spinal cord is compressed in a couple of places, though that could be from a childhood injury as much as from an aborted shift. What did you see in her brain and neck?"

"The same," Logan said. "Her skull is slightly misshapen. I looked at her medical records, and it's blamed on a blow to the head but there was no other visible sign of trauma. According to her records, when she was first brought to the attention of Child Protective Services at about the age of twenty months, her body was badly bruised, her right arm and a couple of ribs broken. She was unconscious and paralyzed and was eventually diagnosed with severe head and spinal trauma, along with the other injuries."

Once again anger beat at Adam. He folded his arms across his chest and stared at Logan. "So, Doc. What's your diagnosis?"

Logan gazed at Liana and then looked directly at Adam. "I think someone beat the hell out of a toddler. Beat her so badly she would have done anything to get away. Her natural instinct, still totally undeveloped, was to shift, but she was too young and she'd never had the nutrients her body needed. But someone was really hurting her, so her body still tried, and, like Manda, she got caught. The change was minimal, but in a growing child the effects would multiply over time. I think it's caused most of the crippling you see now."

"I can accept that," Liana said. "But what about her inability to talk?"

Logan shook his head and glanced at Adam. "That I don't know. I can't find anything physical that would affect her ability to speak or swallow."

Liana grabbed Adam's hand and squeezed his fingers.

"I have my own theory," she said. "What if that baby girl was punished because she wouldn't stop crying? The records say her mother was a drug addict, which means we can discount the fact she was thinking clearly. She couldn't have been rational, to beat her own child half to death. What if Sunny's reaction to all that pain and fear was not to make any more sound?"

"Psychosomatic?" Logan shrugged. "Possible, but there's no way I know of to fix that, not without psychiatric therapy. I can do some research and see if there's something we can . . ."

"I think I know how to deal with it." Adam shoved his hands in his pockets. "She's already had the nutrients today. Women generally make the shift before men—a matter of days rather than weeks. I think she's going to shift without any problem at all, and I have a feeling, when she does, she'll be a perfectly healthy, mobile wolf. With a voice. If, when she shifts back, she's able to feel her extremities, I imagine she'll also be able to talk. It won't happen overnight, but it should happen."

"Pretty optimistic, don't you think?" Logan laughed softly. "But since I don't have any better ideas, I'll go with your diagnosis, healer. I think we need to hold off on any repairs until Sunny makes her first shift."

Second week of September

The house was really quiet tonight. Jazzy and Logan had put her to bed hours ago, but for some reason Sunny couldn't sleep. She felt wired, like her brain wouldn't stop buzzing, and even though she knew she couldn't have any sensation from her neck down, her arms and legs felt twitchy.

It was driving her nuts. She didn't want to bother anyone, but she couldn't stand it. If she could, she'd be screaming her frustration, but all she could do was lie here and feel awful.

She had no right to complain. Everyone was so nice. Even the man who owned the house. *Anton.* She hadn't seen too much of him, but the others had told her he was really worried because his little girl was gone. She was only six and it was weird, because everyone knew where she was but they couldn't go after her. It didn't make sense at all.

Damn, but her legs itched! How could they? Normally she couldn't feel them, but she wanted to reach down and claw the skin off, they itched so badly.

"Sunny? You okay?"

A shaft of light from the hallway spilled through her door. Adam stood there with one hand on the door. He looked as if he'd just crawled out of bed. His dark blond hair was more tangled than usual, and he was wearing a pair of raggedy old shorts that hung loosely from his narrow hips. Even though he was married, and even though she really loved Liana, Sunny didn't care. She wanted him to touch her. Anywhere. Anything to make this strange itching go away.

I can't sleep. I feel all twitchy.

"I think you're ready to shift."

He yawned and stretched, and she couldn't stop looking at his beautiful flat belly and the dark gold hair that flared across his chest and then narrowed all the way down until it turned into a single line that disappeared beneath the waistband of his shorts. She'd never seen a half-naked man in person before, and it was hard not to stare.

He smiled really big, like he knew what she was thinking, but he didn't seem at all angry, even though her twitching and not-so-silent bitching had obviously just awakened him.

"I've called Logan," he said. "When he gets here, do you want to give it a try? See if you can turn into a wolf?"

She'd watched the others shift throughout the past week. They were beautiful, elegant yet feral creatures. Graceful and scary at the same time. *Do you really think I won't be paralyzed if I shift? Will I be like the rest of you?*

She wanted to be just like them. In her dreams, she'd always been able to run. Her legs were powerful, her senses so sensitive she hated to awaken to the numb existence that was all she'd ever really known in her real life.

"That's our plan." Adam stepped into the room.

Logan followed right behind him, still rubbing his eyes. "Couldn't do this during waking hours, eh, Sunny?" He flipped on the bedroom light and, blinking against the sudden brightness, walked over to her. He stopped beside the bed and grinned at her. Then he brushed his hand over her short, spiky hair and grinned some more.

She'd had to keep it short so it was easier for her caretakers, but if everything worked, if shifting really did help her heal, she wanted to let it grow out. She wanted it long and flowing, just like Liana's. Imagining possibilities, she realized she was smiling as broadly as Logan, even though nothing had happened.

Not yet. But it was going to. There were no doubts in her mind. Not anymore. She blinked and looked into Logan's amber eyes. She knew he was teasing her about waking him—all of them teased her as if she were a normal girl. No one here treated her like a cripple, and they definitely didn't think she was stupid.

She answered his question seriously, even though she knew that wasn't how it was meant. *I don't want to attempt my first shift when there are others around. I don't want to make them sad if it doesn't work. You and Adam . . . you know what I'm like inside. It's different with both of you.*

Logan gazed at her a moment. His teasing grin had become a soft, understanding smile. "I understand. You're a good woman, Sunny. Life's kicked you more times than anyone deserves, but you're still putting others first." He glanced at Adam. "You ready to give it a try?" When Adam nodded, Logan said, "Go ahead and shift. Sunny, you link to Adam. Pay attention to what he's thinking, not to how he looks. You'll have to ignore the fact this ugly guy's going to get naked first. Just see what he does from the inside, and then do the same thing. I'm going to help you out of your nightgown so you don't get tangled in your clothes. Are you okay with that?"

If she could have, she'd be laughing like an idiot. One of the most gorgeous guys she'd ever seen was asking permission to take her clothes off? *Of course I am. Like I said, you've seen me from the inside out. It's hard to feel shy with you guys.*

"That's good to know."

He slipped her gown off and set it aside, and just as quickly, without embarrassing her at all, removed the adult diaper she wore. Then he ran his fingers over the small button on her abdomen where her feeding tube went. "When you shift, this is probably going to fall out. I've got my medical bag with me in case it causes any problems. If you're still paralyzed when you shift back to your human self, I'll have to replace it. You okay with that?"

Okay. For a moment, it was hard to breathe. She'd had the feeding tube for as long as she could remember. What would it be like, to actually be able to eat real food like everyone else?

"Adam? You ready?"

She looked at Adam and immediately forgot about the feeding tube. She couldn't stop staring. She'd never seen him naked, but he'd slipped out of his old shorts and stood beside her bed, unself-conscious and so beautiful she wanted to cry.

She'd read her share of erotic romances. She'd looked at porn on the Internet. She knew how guys were built, and she'd seen some of the men when they'd shifted over the past week, but never any of them up close like this. Never anyone as beautiful as Adam.

"I'm going to shift, Sunny." Adam touched her shoulder and forced her to pay attention. "I want you to get into my mind. See what I do when I change."

She blinked and stared at his eyes. It was hard when all she wanted to do was look at the rest of him. She should probably feel embarrassed—there was no hiding her growing arousal from either man. Even her nipples had tightened, which was just weird, considering her paralysis, but she could actually feel them. She knew they were tight and pointed, something they'd never done before. Thank goodness both men ignored her surging fantasies. Their ease with nudity made her feel even more comfortable.

She linked with Adam and saw herself as he saw her. He thought she was beautiful. His perceptions of her were so shocking she almost forgot to pay attention—the idea that this man, that any man, would see her as beautiful and strong and brave was impossible to accept.

But then he was shifting, and the change was so swift, so simple, she almost missed it. She replayed the steps in her mind. Did exactly as Adam had just done.

Felt her body, the body she'd not felt for almost all of her life, suddenly come to life. Felt the bedding beneath her paws, the air in the room ruffling her thick coat and then . . .

Pain! Unrelenting, unimaginable pain! She opened her mouth to scream, but the only sound that emerged was a shrieking howl, a high-pitched cry that went on and on and . . .

Chapter 16

"How is she?"

Adam glanced up and slowly shook his head. Anton stood in the doorway to the clinic, looking as if he'd aged a million years over the past long days. And now he and Logan, like idiots, had added another layer of worry to Anton's plate.

"We've got her sedated. Crap, Anton. We didn't even think of what it would be like, sending impulses through nerves that haven't experienced sensation for so many years. I can't imagine the pain she was in, whether real or perceived."

"You had no way of knowing." Anton stepped closer to the bed. "She's a beautiful wolf, isn't she? Her coat is unusual. So fair, like rich cream." He ran his hand over her cream-colored shoulder, gently ruffling the thick fur. "When do you plan to bring her out of it?"

Adam sighed. She really was beautiful, and such an innocent. What were the changes going to do to her? Had she ever really experienced sexual need, with a body that couldn't feel?

"We're going to let the drugs wear off naturally. We'll be able to tell before she's fully conscious if she's still experiencing pain. Logan's sleeping right now. He was up all night, monitoring her. I figure she'll be coming out of it in another hour or so."

"Just when we think we know so much."

"Anton? You want to know the truth? We don't know a fucking thing. Logan, Liana, and I go trucking through people's bodies, fixing stuff that looks wrong, without a clue what we're doing. All we can do is pray that we don't make things worse. I keep thinking that maybe Lily will be able to tell us things when she comes back. Maybe she'll learn things from those old guys that she can teach us. Have you had any word from her at all?"

"No. Not yet." Anton glanced toward the window that opened out over the back meadow. The swings and jungle gym were crawling with kids, the sound of laughter and childish voices impossible to ignore.

Lily's voice wasn't among them. Adam wondered how the man handled this, where he found the strength. Even Eve's word that Lily was safe couldn't possibly ease all his worry.

Anton turned slowly away from the window and leaned against the desk. He planted his hands on the smooth surface behind him and stared down for a long, silent moment. Adam watched him, worrying, until Anton took a deep breath, raised his head and, uncharacteristically, seemed to struggle for words.

"You're right, you know." His eyes blinked rapidly, and he took another audible breath. "Not having Lily here is tearing me apart. It's killing Keisha, but the little ones need their mother and she finds her strength for them. Their need helps Keisha focus her attention." He bit back a harsh sound. "Hell, who am I kidding? Keisha's stronger than I'll ever be. She goes to bed at night and cries, then she sleeps, and then she gets up and deals with another day. I can't allow myself the luxury of giving in to fear, because I'd lose it altogether, and if that were to happen, I couldn't get up again. Couldn't go forward. Not the way she does."

He shrugged, so obviously struggling that Adam felt tears welling in his eyes.

"Adam, I have to trust that Lily will be all right. That's the only way I can go on. The only way. As far as Sunny . . . for what it's worth, you and Logan are doing the right thing. We know she's Chanku. She has a voice as a wolf and you said she fought you, that she tried to break away, which means she's not paralyzed, at least in wolf form. We wouldn't have known this otherwise. If she's still paralyzed as a human after she shifts, she can choose life as a wolf, among those of us who will love her and understand her. That's more than she had. Much more."

"I caused her so much pain." Adam stared at the floor, unable to face Anton, unwilling to look at Sunny.

"Is that what you think?" Anton pushed away from the desk and stood in front of Adam. "That it's your fault? Not true, Adam. You and Logan helped this girl find her true nature. What happens next is up to Sunny and the body she should have had all along. I think she'll be fine, once her system adjusts to the changes, to the sensations she's not had for far too long. Keeping her under in wolf form is giving her that chance. Look . . ." He rested his hand on Adam's shoulder. "You're doing everything you know, everything you can to help her. That should be enough, but if you need me for anything, call me."

"Thank you." Adam stood and stretched. His vertebrae made little popping noises as he worked the kinks out. "Where're you going?"

Anton shrugged. "To the caverns. I want to be there when Lily comes home." He started to smile, failed, and turned away.

Adam watched him leave. Anton's shoulders were bowed, his body tired. As he walked away, he looked like a beaten man.

Adam sat down beside Sunny's bed and resumed his vigil.

Something was very, very wrong, and yet, at the same time, amazingly right. Sunny lay on the soft mattress, aware of its softness. She'd never been able to feel her bed before. Then she inhaled and picked up so many different scents she almost sneezed.

She took another breath, fought it for a second, and did sneeze. Blinked. Opened her eyes, and totally freaked.

Everything was different. Colors were off, sound too loud, smells overwhelming. Panic flashed and she rolled to her belly, prepared to flee. She had to run, had to . . .

"Sunny? Sunny, don't be afraid. You're okay."

Fingers burrowed into the soft fur at her shoulder. *Fur?* A familiar voice. *Nick?* She raised her head and looked into Nick's dark eyes. Adam stood beside him, smiling broadly.

Still panting, her heart pounding in terror, Sunny jerked her head around, chasing the scents and sounds of many. Four women sat in chairs along the wall. Jazzy Blue, Beth, Xandi, and Tala held hands and smiled at her.

Nick's grip on her neck tightened.

What? She blinked, snapped her gaze down, and saw her feet. She was looking at what should be her hands, but they were paws. Big, furry paws with long, sharp nails. Experimentally, she flexed first one and then the other. She whimpered before she remembered she was a wolf, not a woman.

Would she be able to speak and move when she shifted back? *I can move. I'm not paralyzed anymore!*

Adam stepped close and stroked her shoulder. "Not as a wolf, at least. Are you feeling any pain? You scared the crap out of Logan and me when you shifted last night. I'm not certain, but I think the pain you felt was mostly from your nerves experiencing sensation after a lifetime without any."

She gazed at him a moment, thinking about that, remembering the sharp pain that had exploded through her body, categorizing it on a level of one to ten. The more she thought about it, the more she realized it had probably frightened her more than it actually hurt.

She couldn't remember what *feeling* felt like! After a moment, she slowly rolled her shoulders and, moving carefully, struggling to coordinate unfamiliar muscles with nerves she'd never used, stood up. Nick stepped aside, but Adam kept his hands on her shoulders, helping to stabilize her. Her legs were sort of rubbery and shaky and she was breathing hard from the effort, but nothing hurt. In fact, she felt sort of numb, the way she imagined an anesthetic would make her feel. Not actually dead, the way her body had always been—just numb.

She glanced again toward the women. *You're doing something to take away the pain, aren't you?*

Tala grinned at her. "Yep. We learned to do this for each other during labor." She glanced at the others. "We link with you and share the pain, though I'm not feeling any with you at all right now. You guys noticing any?"

"Nope," Xandi said. "I think she's good to go, though, Sunny, I can feel your muscles, and they're very weak. You don't want to push it right away. You're going to need to build up strength slowly."

"Good advice." Laughing softly, Logan stepped into the room. "Who needs me? I'm just the doctor. Sheesh . . . I go take a nap and miss all the excitement. How's our patient?"

"She's good," Adam said, still holding on to her.

Then his hands fell away so that Sunny stood on her own. Her legs wobbled, but she didn't fall. Still, she missed Adam's touch. Nick's hands stroking her fur. The physical connection that was so amazing. Sunny almost asked both men to come back and touch her some more. As the thought flitted through her mind, she experienced an unfamiliar coil of heat. She shivered, curious about the sensation. What it meant. What had caused it.

She'd have to figure it out later. Instead, she plopped her butt down on the bed, panting. It was hard work, standing up, keeping her balance. *When I shift back to me, to Sunny, will I still be paralyzed?*

Logan ran his hand over her forehead, down her neck. "I don't think so. I hope not. I have a feeling—and it's a strong feeling—that you're going to be able to move, though you might be too weak to walk at first. You've never used your muscles, and your nerves are going to have to learn to get those messages moving around again. You'll probably need physical therapy."

Adam sat on the edge of the bed beside her. "Are you ready to give it a try? Do you want to shift back now?"

Did she? Sunny looked around at the people who waited with so much hope in their eyes. They wanted her healed every bit as much as she wanted it. She felt sensation gradually returning to her limbs and knew the women had withdrawn their link.

Her muscles twitched, but she didn't actually hurt. It was more a sense of exhaustion, as if holding this body upright was straining muscles long unused. She could handle that.

What she didn't think she could handle was shifting back and discovering that she couldn't move, that she was still paralyzed. *I want to walk outside first. Before I shift back, I want to walk in the grass. I don't know what that feels like. Can we do that?*

"Damn right we can." Adam shot Logan a quick look, and before Sunny could question how she'd get outside, he'd scooped her up in his powerful arms and held her against his chest. "We're moving this show outside, folks." Laughing, he carried her out the door and down the hallway.

Stefan met them by the back sliding door that led to the deck and the children's play area beyond. He slid the heavy glass door open. Sunny looked over Adam's shoulder and saw everyone gathering; all of the Chanku who'd been inside were following them out. The ones who'd been out here with the children waited on the small patch of lawn.

The sun was shining brightly and the day felt really warm as Adam set her down in the damp green grass at the back of the house. This was the only area she'd noticed with actual lawn—a small patch for babies to walk barefoot and the kids to roll and play. It tickled her butt and between her toes. She lifted one paw to sniff, and realized everyone was looking at her.

She suddenly felt terribly self-conscious—at least until Mei and Oliver's little Emeline, who had yet to take her first steps, stood up on her fat little legs and chose that moment to walk. She toddled across the grass with arms outstretched, heading directly for Sunny.

Giggling, she grabbed Sunny's ears and hung on tight, leaned forward, and planted a sloppy kiss on her nose. Sunny slowly sank to her belly and rolled over to her back. The baby rolled with her, still hanging on to her ears.

Laughing, Mei leapt to Sunny's rescue and grabbed her daughter. "Wouldn't you know it—the daughter of a leopard takes her first steps to catch a wolf."

Sunny just lay there in the grass, listening to the laughter, feeling the sun on her belly. Everyone around her laughed and talked and the children chattered, and their voices flowed in and out of her mind like music on the wind.

She'd never known contentment like this. Had never

experienced this sense of family, of connection with any-one, much less an entire pack. For the first time in her life, Sunny belonged. She truly belonged.

Like a warm hug, it hit her.

This is what it's like to be loved.

It couldn't possibly get any better.

Sunny lay in the shade beside the back deck, panting. Her muscles ached, though she'd not left the yard during the hour she'd been out here. A few steps across the grass exhausted her, and she actually envied the babies going in for their naps.

Only Adam and Logan remained. Everyone else had gone off to do whatever they all did when they gathered here at Keisha and Anton's Montana home. Keisha had explained that when the entire pack came together like this, each person took on a chore so that no single one of them would have too much to do.

Stefan and Oliver were handling the day's business, since Anton was holding vigil in the caverns waiting for Lily to return. The others had told her about his daughter and her travels on the astral plane, her search for knowledge of Chanku history. Sunny wondered if she'd ever get used to the way these people discussed impossible things as if they were commonplace—things Sunny had always believed were nothing more than fantasy.

Of course, now that she was a wolf, fantasy had taken on an entirely new meaning, even though the day-to-day living she'd observed was really pretty mundane. Everyone seemed to have a job—some were busy doing laundry, others working on dinner or cleaning house or watching children. Tia, Shannon, and Mei had spent the past few days putting together plans for homeschooling all the children once they got everyone moved here, to Montana.

Sunny had thought they all already lived here. It hadn't

taken her long to learn a gathering had originally been scheduled for the impending birth of Adam and Liana's third child.

Then Lily had gone missing and everyone headed to Montana ahead of schedule. Everything had changed again after the bombing in Washington, after Nick's heroic efforts that saved so many lives gave away the closely guarded secret of the Chanku.

Now Nick, Matt, and Deacon were monitoring news channels, watching for any mention of shapeshifters, while Beth and Tala were spending hours in Anton's study keeping track of everything they could find on the Internet. So far, all the news they'd come across was fairly positive, though rampant curiosity and a desire for more information were growing by the day.

Nick's shift in front of so many cameras had definitely captured the world's interest. Sunny was just relieved they'd overlooked her entirely. No one had asked a thing about the young woman in the wheelchair.

The same young woman now lying on the cool grass, wondering if she'd be able to make the long walk up the stairs, all the way inside and down the hallway to her room.

Adam knelt beside her. "You look beat, Sunny. Ready to go back inside?"

She had to think about that for a minute. Going inside meant shifting back to a girl. If she was still paralyzed, it meant adult diapers or a catheter, replacing the tube in her belly so she could eat, living once again in a wheelchair.

Did she really want that?

Adam was shaking his head and laughing. "No, it doesn't mean that at all, but I'll carry you to the woods so you can pee first, if you want. If you're hungry, you can have some meat while you're still in this form. Sunny, no one's going to make you stay in a wheelchair ever again. If you shift and can't move, you can go back to being a wolf. There's no rule that says you've got to be a disabled human. You're certainly not a disabled wolf."

I can stay a wolf?

"You can do whatever you want. It's your life, Sunny. From here on out, you make your own decisions about how to live it. The main thing is, you have options you didn't have before." He ran his palm over her skull and down her neck and rested his fingers on her shoulders.

"When my first mate unexpectedly died, I didn't deal well with my grief. I shifted and remained a wolf for weeks before I finally got past it. No one forced me to shift back. It was my choice. There's no rule that says you have to be in your human form. None at all."

She hadn't thought of that. Suddenly, going back inside, shifting back to a regular girl, didn't sound nearly as scary. Not if she didn't have to stay that way. *I'm ready to go back,* she said. *I'm really tired. It may take me a while to get there.*

"No, it won't take long at all. Not if I carry you."

Logan stood up and brushed the grass off his pants. "You guys go ahead. If there's a problem when Sunny shifts, call me immediately, but I need to get back to the clinic. I think Liana's getting close, even though she's not due for a couple of weeks. Just a feeling, but I want to make sure everything's ready for her."

"Sounds good. She's gone up to our rooms to take a nap, but I don't sense any contractions. Doesn't hurt to be prepared." Adam slipped his arms beneath Sunny's lean wolven body and lifted her as if she weighed nothing at all. Holding her like a big, four-legged baby, he climbed the stairs to the deck.

But when he reached the door, Adam stopped dead in his tracks. Sunny tilted her head so she could see his expression. Something had him staring through the glass sliding door with a look of wide-eyed shock on his face.

The door slid open. Sunny snapped her head around and found herself looking into eyes that mesmerized her with their stunning beauty, looking at a face that belonged to an angel—a man so absolutely perfect he didn't appear real. She blinked, but he was still there, still perfect, only now he was looking directly at her.

"Adam? Where did you find her?"

Even his voice was gorgeous.

"Shit, Ig. Where the hell have you been? It's been . . . crap, man. It's been years."

Ig whoever he was dipped his chin as if acknowledging Adam's stunned comment. "I've been watching over my charge. Tala and Mik's little Star takes much of my time. It's easier from the spirit world. Much easier than watching over her as a man."

Sunny was still trying to figure out that enigmatic statement when Adam shook himself as if he were coming out of a trance. "Igmutaka, this is Sunny Daye. Nick and Beth found her in Washington, DC. About the same time Nick exposed—literally—the existence of Chanku to the world."

Adam stepped through the door as Igmutaka moved aside.

"I've heard. Very little escapes the spirit world."

Adam carried Sunny down the hall to her room. She watched the big man over his shoulder. He followed close behind, moving so gracefully, so sinuously, he made her think of the big lions she'd seen in the zoo.

Very good, little one. You are perceptive. I am a cougar in my other form. Welcome. I'm here to help you.

How? How can you help me?

Later. When you need me, I will be there. He dipped his head, almost as if showing her respect. Then he turned and grinned at Adam. His entire countenance changed, from ethereal beauty to just another hot, gorgeous guy. "Adam? I hope to see you and Liana later this evening."

Adam stood in the doorway to Sunny's room, still hold-

188 / Kate Douglas

ing her in his arms, but he laughed at Igmutaka's comment. "I hope you realize Liana's due to give birth any day now. You'll have to keep the Louisville Slugger to yourself."

Then the new guy surprised the hell out of Sunny. Igmutaka laughed, leaned close to Adam, and kissed him. It wasn't just a little peck on the cheek, either. It was an open-mouth-insert-tongue kind of kiss, as if Sunny weren't mere inches away.

She knew these guys sometimes got it on together, just from the conversations she'd heard or eavesdropped on, but this was the first time she'd actually seen anything remotely sexual between any of the people here.

The biggest surprise was what it did to her insides. She might be a wolf and they were men, but her reaction was all female. Their kiss sent a lick of heat between her legs, a coil of desire building deep in her middle, feelings so intense she almost shifted in Adam's arms so that Igmutaka would kiss her, instead.

He broke the kiss with Adam, but both men were breathing hard. Sunny wondered if they'd forgotten she was even there. Igmutaka leaned his forehead against Adam's.

"I know of your wife's condition. You, my friend, may still play with my bat. Liana's welcome to watch." He grinned and winked at Sunny. "Invite the little one, if you wish." Then he turned and sauntered out of the room.

Adam let out a huge whoosh of air, shook his head, and gave Sunny a dopey grin. "I've really missed that guy," he said. Then he carried Sunny to her bed and gently set her on the covers.

Chapter 17

What is he? He's not like you and the others. Not exactly.

Sunny's soft question pulled Adam out of the amazing erotic fantasy neither his mind nor his body wanted to abandon. Damn, he'd missed Ig. He and Liana both had, but the spirit guide hadn't made more than a half dozen brief appearances over the past five years, not since Tala and Mik's little Mikaela Star was born—and only when they were all here in Montana.

Igmutaka had gone from being Mik's grandfather's spirit guide, to Mik's, to a powerful, free-roaming cougar protecting the Montana pack. Then he'd appeared one day in his human form and become Adam and Liana's sometime lover.

Then, when Star arrived, Ig disappeared. He'd gone back to his spirit form to better protect Star and her twin brother Jack, who was AJ's son. Adam hadn't expected to miss him as much as he did, though with the babies coming along, he hadn't really had time to think about the gorgeous, androgynous male who'd somehow claimed a piece of his heart.

Seeing the man brought it all back, but how to explain that to a sexually innocent young woman? He looked into Sunny's steady gaze and tried to organize his thoughts.

She snarled. Bared her sharp teeth and actually snarled at him. Adam involuntarily jerked his hand out of reach of her sharp teeth. The snarl turned to a low growl, and her anger came through loud and clear.

I'm listening to what you're thinking, you know. And I'm not all that innocent. I may not have experienced sex, but I've read about it. I've seen porn on the Internet. A lot of it. There's not a whole hell of a lot to do when you're stuck in a wheelchair all day and the only thing you can operate is your computer. I know what naked men look like, and I've got a good idea what you two were talking about when you referred to his Louisville Slugger. Please don't patronize me, and don't try to protect me. I'm not a child. I'm an adult. Do you have any idea how frustrating it is to be at everyone's mercy? To be treated as if I haven't got a mind of my own? Don't you dare do it, too.

"Shit. You're right, Sunny, and I'm sorry." He sat on the bed beside her. "In my own defense, you have to realize you make me feel like a dirty old man. In human form, you look about twelve. I know you're a virgin, Sunny, so I do apologize, but you'll have to forgive me for erring on the side of caution."

He chuckled softly. "But I promise not to treat you like a child. Igmutaka is a spirit guide. He was born a cougar, though we've recently learned he's actually Chanku, like we are. His ancestors were from the first migration from Tibet to the New World. He came to us through Mik, one of Tala's men, and while he was sort of between charges to protect, he became Liana's and my lover."

Both of you?

Her eyes went wide. Adam laughed out loud. "I take it no one's explained the Chanku libido to you. You'll find out about it really fast, now that you're shifting. To put it bluntly, we've got a really powerful sex drive. If all goes according to plan, I imagine you're going to discover exactly what I mean when you shift back to your human self. It's especially strong after we shift and run, more so if we hunt and kill something, so I'm not sure how much it will affect you at this point."

He ran his fingers through her thick coat and she sighed. It felt so good to be touched. Even better to have him sitting here talking to her like she was an adult.

It was about damned time.

"You're aware of the sexual drives of lesbian women, gay men, and heterosexuals. As Chanku, we're all of the above. Even if we have someone we're bonded to—a life-mate, so to speak—we take others within the pack as our lovers. Multiple lovers. I've been sexually involved with all of the men and all of the women you've met, except Manda and Millie, and Millie's mate, Ric."

Why not them?

He smiled. "I thought you knew. Millie may look young enough to be my sister, but she's my mother. Manda's my twin sister. Chanku avoid incestuous relationships. I consider Ric off-limits on general principles." He laughed. "I can't quite get past the fact he's sleeping with my mother."

So that means that if I have sex with any of the adults, no one minds? They don't get jealous?

"No one has so far. No reason to, though we only mate as wolves with our chosen mate. There's a bond that takes place when two wolves mate that's pretty amazing. It truly links us for life, though we've all been known to fool around with one partner in wolf form and the other human."

He chuckled softly and she had a feeling he was remembering something very personal. "The thing is, Sunny, when you can read each other's minds, you know exactly what's going on. You know that if your guy is having sex with someone else, he still loves you, though we honestly do love one another. It's just different with bonded mates.

Stronger. Deeper. We want a strong, healthy pack, a steady, loving environment for our kids. . . . It's a given that we will protect all our children with our lives. We're family, Sunny. You're part of that now. Once you're healthy enough, strong enough to want sex, it's whoever you choose, when you choose. Trust me on that. You'll know when it happens that it's right."

Then he stood up and folded his arms across his chest. "So. You ready to give it a try?"

What? Sex or shifting?

She imagined she sounded a lot cockier than she felt.

Adam raised one eyebrow and grinned at her. "Let's try the shifting first, okay?"

She sighed. It was now or never. She called on that part of her mind, the part that had told her how to shift from girl to wolf. It happened so quickly, she didn't have time to be afraid, though she was just a little bit embarrassed.

She lay on the bed on her belly, completely naked, gazing up at Adam. Her body was sort of twitching, as if there were neurons firing that hadn't been fired in way too long. Nothing really hurt, but she had feeling in a body that had long been dead to her.

And some of those feelings were totally unexpected. Adam hadn't been kidding about the libido. She might never have known sexual arousal before, but she certainly recognized it now.

Adam had a huge grin on his face. He grabbed her hand and squeezed her fingers. She tried to squeeze him back, but wasn't sure how successful she was. Still, she could feel his hand, the rough calluses, what must be a scab on one of his knuckles. The sensation of touch was absolutely fascinating.

"Well? You gonna say something?"

Sunny hung on to his hand. She opened her mouth, but all that came out was a funny croaking sound. She tried again, aware of muscles in her throat working for the first time since she could remember. Feeling her throat move, she tried her toes, but she wasn't quite sure what to do to make them move.

She must have done something right. Adam laughed. "Your toes are wiggling. Slow, but they're definitely moving. I've let Logan know. He's headed this way."

"I'm naked."

He laughed even harder. "That you are. Of all the things you could say for your very first words, 'I'm naked' is the best you can do?"

"I guess. I . . ." She swallowed the unexpected lump in her throat. Her toes were moving. Her fingers. She could feel her arms and legs beginning to jerk and twitch. Muscles that hadn't seen action in a lifetime jumped and shivered and ached as she stretched out her arms, stretched her legs, and tried to roll over and sit up.

The room went blurry. She sniffed and, without thinking, rubbed her eyes against the back of her hand.

She'd not touched her own face since she was hurt. Not since before she was two.

Without any warning at all, the tears came. A veritable flood of them. Adam reached for her and pulled her into his lap, into his arms, and she didn't even think about her nudity or the fact she'd never been held by a man in her life. Not until he held her close and she felt the steady thud of his heart and the warmth of his body through the thin T-shirt he wore. Still, she couldn't stop crying, and when he handed her the clean white handkerchief out of his back pocket, she cried even harder.

Logan's voice barely penetrated. She'd not heard him come into the room. "Sweetie? You okay?"

She nodded her head. It was the best she could do.

"I think it's a bit much for her," Adam said. He rested his chin on the top of her head and held her close. "I can't imagine what it must feel like, to have a body suddenly work the way it's meant to after a lifetime without any function at all."

"F . . . f . . . feels wonderful." She hiccupped. Swallowed and sniffed. "I'm sorry, but . . ."

"You've never heard your own voice before, have you?" Adam chuckled. She felt his chest bounce against her. "Your arms are surprisingly straight. Your legs appear to be, too, though you definitely need to work on those muscles. You're much too thin. I think Liana and I were right with our original diagnosis."

She sniffed. "What diagnosis?"

Logan sat on the bed beside Adam and softly stroked her spiky hair. "We think when you were little, whoever beat you hurt you so badly that you tried to shift. It's a natural instinct for a shapeshifter, to become a wolf and run away from what's hurting you. That or take a bite out of them. You shift, then run or attack. But you were too young. You've been caught in an incomplete shift ever since. It's caused compression on your spine, injuries that couldn't heal because everything was out of place and it kept growing that way. When you shifted, all those muscles, bones, and tendons realigned."

Adam rested his cheek against her head. "That probably explains some of the pain you felt when you shifted for the first time. Once you're stronger, you should be able to do anything you want. For now, I'd suggest you work at building up your strength, work on your coordination. All of your joints, your bones and muscles, are lined up where they belong. You should talk to my sister about it. Manda was caught in the middle of a shift for twenty-five years. You'd never know it, looking at her now, but her body was grotesque, a nightmare."

"But Manda's beautiful." She sniffed. She couldn't imagine her as anything other than she was now—perfect in every way.

Logan stood up and went to the closet. He pulled a dark blue bathrobe off a hanger. "Jazzy and I stayed in this room years ago. I think this robe's been hanging here ever since. Let's see if you can stand up and I'll help you get it on. It'll be a little long for you, but I imagine you'll be more comfortable with something on. Besides, I want to see if the hole for your feeding tube has closed up."

With Adam's help, Sunny stood. She was taller than she thought she'd be, though not too much bigger than Tala. She was definitely too skinny, but no one seemed to mind that her arms and legs looked like sticks. Logan slipped the robe over her shoulders and she managed to get her arms in the sleeves. Her legs felt shaky, but she didn't want to sit down. Not yet.

What if she couldn't get up again? What if this wonderful sense of feeling went away? Logan knelt beside her and checked the opening in her side. She'd had the feeding tube for so long that the skin was puckered and raw, though no longer entirely open. Shifting must have helped it close.

Logan stood up. "Sunny, I want you to lie down so we can close this from the inside out. Then you need to rest a bit before dinner. If you're up to it, come join all of us for dinner tonight. I think your mindtalking is powerful enough to reach one of us to come and get you."

She lay back on the bed while Logan and Adam placed their hands on her side. As the warmth from their healing touch soothed her body, she drifted off, imagining all the possibilities of a life she'd never dared dream.

Anton sat in the dirt on the cavern floor with his legs folded, elbows resting on his bent knees, chin resting on his fingertips. He'd remained in this position, unmoving, for the better part of the day, not quite meditating, not entirely within this space and time.

He wanted to go to Lily. Wanted his daughter home so badly he ached, but he'd given his word. He understood the importance of Lily's quest, no matter her age. Since going after her was out of the question, he waited for the moment when she would walk through the gateway.

Eve had said that as far as Lily was concerned, she'd only feel as if she'd been gone for a few hours. He'd find that hard to believe if he hadn't already experienced the anomaly that was time on the astral plane.

In his case, it had worked in reverse. His thoughts wandered back to that day so many years ago, when Liana had been their goddess, not Adam's very mortal mate. Anton had been a two-bit magician in a two-bit circus, overwintering in Florida when the Goddess snagged him out of his tent between shows.

He'd spent long days with her, making love, experiencing sex unlike anything he'd known before, and then he was back in his tent and only moments had passed—and he'd totally forgotten the woman and the sex.

But when the memories returned—as they did, years later—he realized he'd spent hours, days, maybe even weeks somewhere with a woman who was in truth a goddess, a woman who had gained power from the sex she'd had with him. She had taken him against his will, kept him as her lover, and then returned him to the same place and time where she'd found him. He'd lost no time at all in the real world.

Since then, he'd gone to their Goddess Eve and spent what seemed like hours or days with her while searching for Lily, only to come home and discover no time at all had passed.

Eve assured him it worked both ways. He prayed she was right, but however long it was—for him or for Lily— he wanted his daughter back.

Sunny turned off the shower and wrapped herself in a soft, fluffy towel. She wasn't even short of breath, and she was so gloriously clean. No wonder showers were so highly rated! Not that she hadn't bathed regularly, but the indignity of sitting strapped in a chair while someone hosed your body down and washed your privates with mechanical skill while you couldn't even feel the water, much less their touch—well, there was no comparison to this. None at all.

She'd even used the toilet, which might not be all that momentous an act, but it was the first time for her, and she was really quite proud of herself. So many firsts, and dinner tonight would be another.

Xandi had brought her some lipstick, and Keisha had left a beautiful moss green sarong on her bed. The lipstick wasn't too hard to use, though she messed up the first time and had to wipe everything off and do it over, but wrapping the sarong around her body was like a religious experience.

The cool silk slithered over her skin as if it were alive. It left her shivering and oddly aroused. Adam and Logan hadn't been kidding about the libido thing.

There was a full-length mirror in her room. Sunny stood in front of it and carefully smoothed the silk over breasts that were surprisingly full on such a thin frame, and hips that flared from an actual waist. It took her a few minutes to get the knot right, but she finally got it tied over one shoulder. She'd seen the other women wearing them in dozens of different ways, but this was her favorite.

It was the way Keisha had worn hers this morning.

Once again, Sunny smoothed the pale silk over her hips and stared. The woman in the mirror was a stranger to her, but she wasn't ugly. Not at all, even with her spiky blond hair and eyes too big for her narrow face. Sunny turned and posed, careful not to stumble. She'd never have Keisha's stately presence, but she didn't look bad at all.

The kitchen was at the end of the hallway. The dining room next to that. She'd decided during her shower that she was going to do this on her own. It was time to stop

198 / Kate Douglas

depending on Adam to carry her everywhere—being carried in that gorgeous man's strong arms could become ad-
dictive.

She took a deep breath, opened the door, and started
walking. It was easier than she'd expected. She might have
legs as skinny as matchsticks, but already her gait was
steadier, her strength something she was beginning to
count on. It wasn't hard to find the dining room—all she
had to do was follow the sound of laughter. But when she
stepped into the big room, Sunny was met with stunned silence.

Then Stefan rose and began to applaud. The others followed suit, and damn it, but she didn't want to cry. Adam
hurried out of the kitchen and took her arm. She let him
lead her to an empty chair next to Igmutaka. Moving awk-
wardly, with everyone watching, suddenly she felt horribly
unsure of how to make her arms and legs do what they
were meant to do. At least she managed to sit without
falling on the floor.

Ig leaned close and kissed her cheek. *Soon it will all be
easier for you, sweet one. Before long, these strange move-
ments will feel normal. The feelings in your hands and
feet, the sense of space around you. All will be as if you'd
always walked among men and women as one of us.*

How do you know this? He gazed at her so sincerely,
she was positive he understood what she was feeling.

She knew she'd guessed right when he nodded. *I
walked as a cougar for millennia,* he said. *I had no idea
there was this creature, this human man, inside my cat.
When I manifested for the first time, I didn't know how to
stand on two legs. The ground was much too far from my
eyes. Now it has become my nature to walk on two legs or
four, just as it will quickly become yours.*

Thank you.

He gave her a slight bow of his head. Then he reached
beneath the table and squeezed her hand. *Relax. You're*

among friends. None of us bite. He chuckled softly. *Unless, of course, we're hunting . . . or the sex gets a little rough.*

She was still considering what he meant by that curious little comment when Keisha carried a plate in and set it in front of her. "Enjoy, sweetie. We thought you were still sleeping, but I'm so glad you decided to join us." Keisha took a seat across the table from her.

Sunny picked up her fork.

For the longest time, she sat and stared at the big piece of rare beef on the plate in front of her, fully appreciating, for the first time, the saliva that filled her mouth, the rumble of hunger in her stomach. Then she grabbed her knife, cut into the tender slice of meat, and enjoyed the first solid meal she'd eaten since before she was two.

It was pure ambrosia. She closed her eyes and chewed, savoring the flavor, the texture, the sense of chewing and swallowing. And while she quietly ate, conversation ebbed and flowed about the two long tables that were set side by side. The older children ate at one, helping the little ones still in high chairs, while the adults filled the larger table.

Manners among children and adults were impeccable, but the meal was fun and relaxed. Sunny gazed about at the various faces and shook her head. "How do you do it? The kids are all so well behaved. I've never seen anything like it."

Adam shot a stern glance at three-year-old Jace. The little boy ducked his head and put whatever he was about to throw at his sister back on his plate. Then Adam grinned at Sunny. "It helps when you can read their rotten little minds."

Tia glanced over her shoulder at her two sets of twins and laughed. "You're not kidding. I can't imagine dealing with our four without being able to stay a step ahead all the time."

Conversation went on around her. She ate slowly, loving every minute. The wonderful meal, the sound of laughter, the little bits and pieces of gossip and news. She was focusing on Nick's comments about the latest news on the Chanku going public when a sharp gasp drew all eyes to Keisha.

She stood so quickly she knocked her chair over. "Watch my kids," she said. Then she raced out of the room.

Adam got up and righted Keisha's chair, but instead of sitting down again, he stood there with his hands resting on the back of the wooden chair, staring toward the kitchen. No one made a sound, no one else got up, though everyone had turned in their seats. Even the children were silent. All attention focused on the door leading to the kitchen.

After what felt like hours, a smiling Keisha opened the door and held it wide. Anton stepped through the opening and a loud cheer went up. The eminently unflappable alpha had a smile that practically split his handsome face. His cheeks were streaked with tears, and in his arms he carried the most beautiful little girl Sunny had ever seen.

Looking very much like a younger, lighter-skinned version of Keisha, she was tucked tightly against her daddy's shoulder, peeking out through masses of dark brown hair cascading in shining ringlets past her waist. She wore pink ballet slippers and a slightly dusty pink nightgown with silver sparkles around the hem. Her smile was as big as Anton's, as filled with joy as Keisha's.

It appeared the long-missing Lily had finally come home.

Chapter 18

Sunny scraped the last of the dishes and handed the plate to Ig. "Was it hard, learning to load the dishwasher?"

He laughed and slipped the plate into its slot. "Only because I refused to learn."

When she frowned, he laughed harder. "You must realize, I was a spirit guide, not human. I didn't do menial labor. My first reaction, when I saw Liana cleaning the kitchen, was utter shock. How could a woman once a goddess lower herself to such work? She laughed at me and told me to get over myself."

Sunny squeezed water from the sponge and wiped out the inside of the industrial-sized sink. "Well? Did you?"

He nodded, added just enough detergent to the machine, and shut the door. "Oh, yes. Very quickly. You can't have this many people together without everyone pulling their load. Even Anton and Keisha do dishes and laundry, and housework."

"Not tonight, though. I could feel their joy and relief when they walked into the room. They were both broadcasting it so powerfully." Exhausted, she turned and leaned against the sink, aware in one small part of her mind how natural these moves had already become. "I feel honored to be part of this. Does that makes sense?"

202 / Kate Douglas

"It does. As I feel honored to show you new things. Like washing dishes." He leaned over and kissed her cheek. "Do you feel able to run tonight? I would like to take you into the forest, be with you when you feel the hard ground beneath your feet, when you see the beauty of the night through feral eyes."

She hadn't really thought of the evening ahead. Those with little ones were busy bathing kids and putting them to bed. Others had taken off shortly after dinner, shifting and running into the woods. Stefan and Mei had helped with some of the cleanup, at least until it was obvious Sunny and Ig were capable of finishing the job.

Now, with the two of them the only ones left, and even though she was really tired, it seemed like the perfect time to try an actual run as a wolf. She'd felt stronger as a wolf than she did in her human form, so maybe she'd be okay. She knew she was too keyed up to go to her room, and if they went now, there wouldn't be anyone around to judge her or watch her stumble.

No one will ever judge you, sweet one. We've all had to learn—every last one of us. We all make mistakes. Run with me tonight. I promise not to move too fast or go too far.

She thought about it a moment, about what she assumed was an unintentional double-entendre. There were some things she'd love to take too far, especially with a man like Igmutaka. As much as she'd been drawn to other males among the pack, they were all happily bonded to someone else. For her first time, whether it was running as a wolf or exploring the sexual side of her nature, she wanted it with this man who was quickly becoming her friend, her confidant, and, hopefully, the one who would teach her what it really meant to be Chanku.

I'd like that, she said. Tilting her chin, she realized he'd moved closer and she had to look way up to meet his gaze, to look into dark, mysterious eyes the color of the forest. Eyes that saw everything she felt. *I think I'd like that very much.*

Anton sat beside Lily's bed long after the child had fallen into an exhausted sleep. Keisha stepped into the quiet room and stood beside him with her hands on his shoulders.

"Has she said much about her time with the monks?"

He nodded. "A little. I told her to sleep, that we'd talk tomorrow." He covered Keisha's hands with his. "I hope you don't mind, but I promised her she wouldn't be punished for leaving without permission this time, but if it happened again, the shit was gonna hit the fan."

Keisha's soft laughter had him smiling in return. "Not in those words, I hope."

He chuckled and stood up. "No, I was more circumspect. I did, however, tell her she would regret it for as long as she lived should she venture anywhere without asking us first. I think she got the message." He tugged Keisha's hand and they quietly left Lily's room.

Outside the closed door, Anton looped his arms around her waist and hugged her close. "Damn. I have never been so frightened. This has been the longest two weeks of my entire life."

"Mine, too. I never doubted she would return, but I had visions of a teenaged Lily popping back into our lives."

"It could have easily happened that way. She thought she was only gone for a few hours. I told her the truth, that for us it's been two weeks. When I told her that Gabe and Mac cried themselves to sleep at night because their big sister was gone, I think she got the message. Did you notice how the boys didn't want to turn her loose tonight?"

"I did. They idolize their big sister." She leaned close and kissed his nose. "Have I told you lately how I lust after their father?"

He cupped her face in his hands and kissed her. *Not nearly enough. I think I'd like to hear more.*

Come with me. I'll show you.

She didn't have to make the invitation twice.

Ig waited on the back deck. Sensing his impatience, Sunny still took a moment to watch him through the big sliding glass door. He leaned against the railing, staring off into the darkness with his face in profile, his long nose and full lips cast in stark shadows from the light on the deck.

Though all the Chanku were exceptional, she'd never seen a man as beautiful as Igmutaka. The others had a more masculine appearance—all were handsome, powerful men. Only Nick had that dark, androgynous look similar to Igmutaka's, but even Nick, as gorgeous as he was, paled by comparison.

There was something ethereal about Igmutaka. An unworldly quality that he alone possessed, though she couldn't really point to anything in particular, couldn't actually name what made him so unique.

Her body quivered. Nerves? Arousal? She wasn't sure about that, either. She knew that she wanted, but not what. Knew that she anticipated the evening ahead without any idea what it would entail, and didn't really care. She only knew that standing here, imagining what was coming wasn't nearly as frightening as stepping through the doorway.

She'd been curious her entire life, wondering what things felt like. Wondering was familiar. Actually stepping out, moving forward and doing them was so new it was equal parts terrifying and thrilling. . . .

Ig turned and stared at the window. He must have noticed her, because his mouth turned up in the sweetest, sexiest smile she'd ever seen.

Come, sweet one. I won't hurt you. Don't be afraid.

I'm not. At least I don't think I am. Laughing at herself, she stepped out onto the deck. The night was cool, and a gentle breeze lifted the hem of her sarong and then wrapped it against her legs in a delicious, tickling whisper of sensation. The moon was just rising over the treetops—almost full, glowing brightly.

Sunny crossed the wide deck and stood beside Ig, gazing out into the darkness.

"Once we're away from the lights around the house, the forest will seem bright as day to our feral eyes. The night will be magic. Are you ready for such an adventure?"

She tilted her chin and gazed up at Ig. His eyes sparkled with reflected light and she felt an unexpected coil of heat in her belly. So many changes in such a brief time, but this was the greatest of all, this amazing sexual need, the powerful awareness of her own sensuality continuing to blossom within.

She wanted him to kiss her. Was afraid to ask, but she knew that she wanted to taste those perfect lips, feel the brush of his tongue against her mouth. So many things she'd read about and never experienced, so many needs she was only now beginning to recognize.

This was the greatest one of all. Igmutaka smiled and cupped her shoulders in his big hands. His palms were warm, the solid grasp a steadying, calming anchor to a body that was ready to leap into the air and fly—or at the very least, to run.

Obviously reading her, Ig leaned close and pressed his lips to hers. His touch was gentle at first, a sweet exploration that had her leaning close, silently begging for more. His tongue softly traced the seam between her lips and she felt sort of stupid to think she'd kept them pressed tightly close together.

She'd watched enough movies to know she was supposed to open her mouth and use her tongue as much as her lips.

Not necessarily, sweet one. You should only do what your body tells you is right. Never what you think you should do—only what you want. Sex, arousal—all of desire should be something you want, not something you believe is expected of you.

I want this. I want to know what you taste like. Ig, I want everything!

And you shall have it. He carefully ended the kiss and pressed his forehead close to hers. "But first we run as wolf and cougar. Our beasts are mortal enemies in the wild—you must trust my cat. I promise to protect your wolf."

She nodded, but the taste of him was still on her lips and her heart thudded in her chest as she reached for the knot tied at her shoulder. Slowly she released the silky fabric. Ig caught it up in his hands and draped it over the railing for her.

Before she had time to worry about standing in front of him entirely nude with her skinny arms and legs, he was slipping out of his jeans and hanging them beside the moss green fabric. Sunny got her first look at his Louisville Slugger. She giggled, blushed, and shifted before she could make a total fool of herself, but at least now she knew why Adam had given Ig's package a nickname.

He was truly impressive, even by Internet porn standards. She wondered if he knew that's where she'd gotten her entire sexual education? Or if he even cared. . . .

Ig shifted, and it was amazing to stand here, nose to nose, with a cougar that was bigger than her wolf. Amazing to stare into those gorgeous green eyes and recognize the eyes of the man. He gazed steadily at her. She sensed his voice in her mind.

Can you understand me? A few of the wolves are able to, but not all.

I can. It's like listening to someone with a weird accent, but I understand you.

The big cat slowly blinked. *Good. It will make it easier. Safer if we can communicate without having to shift. Are you ready?* He stared intently at her.

I think so. But would she ever be ready? Was there a way to prepare for something this momentous? This unbelievable?

Without another word, Igmutaka turned and trotted down the stairs. She'd watched on other nights as wolves leapt over the railing and raced across the meadow, but it appeared that Ig was willing to take it easy on her. She relaxed and followed him across the damp grass, trotting along on four feet, heading into the dark forest for the very first time in her life.

The first thing she noticed were the smells. Someone had recently mowed the lawn, and the scent of fresh-cut grass tickled her nostrils. As they crossed into the part of the meadow that wasn't regularly watered, she smelled dry grass and dirt and sun-warmed rocks. Sounds intruded. The whisper she somehow recognized as a snake slithering in the weeds, the tiny squeaks of mice, and what had to be the whoosh of wings through the night air as an owl passed low overhead.

Dry leaves and grass crunched and crackled beneath her paws. When they passed through the shrubbery growing between the meadow and the thick woods, she felt the brush of twigs against her coat, smelled the pungent leaves from some unfamiliar plant, and recognized the aromatic scent of cedar and pine.

How is it I recognize all of these smells and sounds? I've never been in the forest before.

Do you dream of running? At night, are you a wild creature racing through the woods? All of the others have mentioned dreams—dreams they'd had long before they ever shifted.

Shocked, she stopped dead in her tracks. Ig paused, staring over his shoulder. The dark tip of his long tail whipped the air, but Sunny couldn't move until she thought this through.

She'd always loved her dreams. Only at night had she truly felt free. Though trapped in a body that couldn't respond, at night she'd run through dark forests and crossed rushing creeks, had hunted and raced the wind, free and wild and whole.

She'd always thought her vivid dreams were nothing more than wishful thinking. *I always dream of running. I had no idea . . .*

The others, too. Ask them later. They'll tell you. It seems to be part of an ancient instinct, this knowledge of the wild. He snorted, effectively ending the conversation, and trotted on. They followed a well-established trail. The trees here were fairly small, mostly saplings. She knew they'd had a bad fire here a few years back, which explained the blackened stumps among the small pines and cedars. A few trees, much larger and older, had obviously been survivors.

She sniffed the air and recognized familiar scents of people she knew—Millie and Ric must be running this way tonight, and she thought she picked up Nick and Beth, Stefan, Baylor and Manda as well. Using her mind, she searched for conversations but found only the feral thoughts of hunting wolves.

Somewhere, they'd found game. She wondered what it would be like, to hunt something weaker than herself. To kill. She'd never taken a life of any kind—not even an insect. Tonight at dinner she'd tasted her very first piece of meat.

Thinking of the amazing flavor made her salivate, and some primitive, feral part of her mind suddenly craved the rich taste of warm meat and hot blood.

Now, that was something she'd not expected. Wanting to eat something barely dead, something still warm? Still bleeding? Why didn't it gross her out?

Amazing. That was something she hadn't expected. She wasn't all that aware of her thinking processes as a wolf being all that different from when she was a regular girl, but if the thought of chewing on the haunch of a freshly killed deer could make her drool all over herself, there'd obviously been a huge change in her most basic thinking.

She began paying closer attention to her surroundings, testing the air currents for something that might be considered prey. Ig stayed ahead, moving with that sinuous grace that reminded her of his walk when he was human.

Or did the human remind her of the cat?

At least it was a comfortable pace—slow enough so it was easy for her to keep up and still let her mind wander, absorbing and cataloging all the new experiences. She couldn't have done this if she'd run with the wolves tonight. She'd watched them leave the house in the evenings— they took off at a fast pace and returned hours later, sides heaving from exertion, coats often tangled with burrs and stickers. Adam had told her they easily covered many miles on their nightly runs.

Her body wasn't strong enough for that. Not yet, though it should be soon. She'd merely have to work hard at getting into shape. Logan said her life of inactivity would have left another person's muscles atrophied and useless, but when she'd shifted from human to wolf and back again, her muscles had regained their functional condition as a human, just as they had when she'd first shifted into a wolf.

Suddenly Ig slowed and glanced over his shoulder as if

to assure himself she followed. Then he slipped through a break in the trees. Sunny stayed close behind him.

It was darker here, where the cedars grew thick overhead, an area obviously spared by the fire. Trees towered above and their thick branches added to the gloom. Very little moonlight filtered through. Her night vision was exceptional, but the lower light seemed to heighten her other senses.

A new scent came to Sunny, something that had her ears pricking forward and all her feral instincts coming to the fore.

Game. There was something nearby that her wolven mind recognized as food. Something small and yet as wary of her as she was of this new reality.

Rabbit. In the grass near the creek. Trust your instincts.

Her heart pounded until it was difficult to hear Ig's brief instructions above its thunder. She used her nose, sniffing the air, testing the wind currents. Carefully, moving as quietly as she was able, Sunny crept through the grass until she was downwind of her target.

Her human mind intruded the moment she saw the rabbit. Small and timid, it nibbled at the grass growing near a tiny spring. This late in the year, there was very little water left in the pool, but the damp ground was lush with a thick carpet of fresh grass, and the rabbit probably thought it had found a buffet. Sunny's first thought—entirely human—of how cute and fluffy the creature was disappeared in a haze of primal need.

Her eyes narrowed. She carefully judged the distance she'd have to cover before she could leap, then glanced at Igmutaka waiting patiently nearby. He was leaving the kill to her. Even her wolven mind recognized the lack of threat from a small cottontail, but still she realized the importance of the hunt.

Her very first. She inched forward, all quivering predator until her left paw came down on a twig. The sharp snap echoed across the small meadow. The rabbit jerked its head up, nose twitching, ears swiveling, listening. Sunny held immobile, her right front foot still raised.

After a very long minute, the rabbit went back to nibbling the grass. Sunny carefully planted her right foot, the muscles in her hind legs and hips bunched and tightened. She paused a moment, listening to the thundering of her heart, the rapid beat a powerful rhythm in her head pounding a primal song. Ancient beyond memory, yet a part of her. Who she was. What she was.

She leapt, jaws spread, front paws outstretched.

The rabbit never had a chance, did not know from one second to the next its life was over. The moment she landed, it was caught in her viselike jaws, the life crushed out of it so quickly it didn't even struggle. The taste of blood filled Sunny's mouth—hot and thick, a gamey, tangy flavor unlike anything she'd ever experienced.

She choked the small creature down in a couple of snapping, gulping bites, bones and all. The thought of sharing with Ig never entered her mind—at least, not until she wiped her muzzle on the green grass and caught him staring at her. He licked one big paw, padded across the grass, and shifted.

Sunny did the same, rising to two feet with Ig directly in front of her. He held out a hand to steady her. His touch was electrifying. She wanted more. Now.

Was this what everyone meant when they talked about their powerful Chanku libido? Whether it was the act of running as a wolf, the fact she'd hunted and tasted her first blood, or merely that she could actually feel the air across her skin, the way her nipples tightened into hard little peaks, or the dampness between her legs—for whatever reason, Sunny truly understood what Adam meant, what Logan had tried to tell her.

This was desire. This needy, totally physical yearning for the man standing before her. Whether it was his touch, his kisses, or the connection itself, Sunny needed. She wanted.

And tonight, she fully intended to get what Igmutaka so generously offered.

She reached for him as his arms came around her waist. "I want to know it all," she said. "Show me everything."

He kissed her. Gently, so sweetly she whimpered. "Are you sure?" he asked. "Here, in the cool grass, or back at the house, in the privacy of your room?"

She hadn't realized she had options. She knew, though, that she didn't want to wait. "Here," she said. "Here first." Then she laughed out loud. "Later we can do it in my room. Then maybe in yours."

His soft chuckle sent chills over her spine. "I like the way you think," he said. And gently, with great care, he lifted her in his arms and laid her down in the soft, green grass beneath trees older than time.

Chapter 19

Millie chased Ric through the thick forest, reveling in her strength, in the power of this wolven body, the amazing senses that helped her connect with the well-worn surface of the packed trail beneath her big paws, the scents on the night air, the sounds of creatures scurrying from beneath her feet or flying almost silently overhead.

The others had headed back to the house after a successful hunt, but she and Ric along with Beth and Nick had decided to explore further, to run for just a little longer.

She'd never gotten to know these two kids very well. Certainly not the way she knew Matt and Deacon. All the kids—she would always think of them as kids, though she and Ric looked and felt just as young—had been part of the same pack living in Golden Gate Park with Logan and Jazzy Blue. Then Nick had unexpectedly turned into a wolf and saved Tala from muggers.

Now Nick had turned into a wolf and exposed the Chanku to the world. She almost laughed at the irony—the poor kid was having a terrible time getting past the guilt, even though Anton seemed to think it had been a good thing, something bound to happen eventually. At least Nick had friends in high places—after working directly for the president for the past five years protecting the First Family, both Nick and Beth had gained powerful allies.

Tonight, though, Millie and Ric had thoroughly enjoyed both of them. They'd left all their worldly concerns at the house and ran now with the abandon only Chanku could ever truly experience. Nick's offbeat sense of humor, Beth's sly wit, and the stories they'd told of famous people, of faces most of the world only saw on the news, had kept everyone in stitches.

The run and the hunt, the sight of beautiful bodies streaking through the dark forest, slipping in and out of the moonlight, had all of them aroused and almost drunk on the pleasure of the night—the expectations. Suddenly Nick ran on ahead. He nipped Ric's shoulder in passing and the race was on.

Ric snarled, *smart-ass,* dug his nails into the packed earth, and chased after the dark wolf. Millie and Beth picked up their pace, but there was no point in trying to catch the males.

They'd been teasing and challenging each other all evening, ever since Ric had spotted the old buck first. Nick had moved in on the kill, shouldered Ric aside, and pulled the animal down. There was no animosity between them, but a challenge was a challenge. It wasn't about to go unanswered.

Millie glanced at Beth, running easily beside her. *You know where this is going to end up, don't you?*

Beth's eyes and teeth glimmered in the moonlight. *Oh, yeah. I just wonder if Nick realizes what he's asking for. I was with Ric many years ago, shortly after my first shift. Your man is hung like . . . well . . . ouch!*

Maybe that's why Nick's been flirting so outrageously.

Beth's silent laughter at Millie's dry reply had both of them picking up the pace. This could be entertaining.

Both Nick and her mate were definitely alphas.

It was easy enough to follow the scent of the two wolves. Twenty minutes later they caught up to the men in a high meadow at the very edge of the tree line. The view was amazing, with the lights of Kalispell glowing faintly, far to the west, and moonlight glinting off the high peaks of Glacier National Park well to the north.

The view in the meadow was even better.

What'd I tell you? Beth stopped at the edge of the clearing and glanced at Millie.

Oh. My. Millie sighed. Both men had shifted at some point during whatever battle they'd waged, one where Ric had obviously prevailed. There was nothing quite like the sensual ballet of two beautiful, well-built men together. Nick's lean, dark strength had been no match for Ulrich's power and size, but Nick didn't seem to mind the fact he'd ended up on the bottom.

Millie and Beth glided quietly into the moonlit meadow and lay in the cool grass just a few feet from the men. Nick, all dark shadows and angles, was on his hands and knees, legs spread, head down as Ric took him from behind. Ric's silver hair and fair skin shimmered ghostlike in the moonlight—dark and light, angel and devil—two apparitions locked in sensual battle.

The rhythmic buck and sway of his powerful hips as Ric thrust deep and hard inside Nick had a magical, mesmerizing quality. Nick's soft gasps and moans, the sweep of his dark hair, the look of ecstasy on his face, and the steady slap of flesh against flesh raised the heat in the meadow by several degrees.

Nick grunted with every thrust, sounds of obvious pleasure, not pain. Millie watched, growing more aroused with each second that passed. She almost laughed when she finally tore her gaze away from Nick's beautiful face and recognized the look on Ric's—the man was definitely in the zone.

He could go all night like this. That alone was a challenge. Creeping close, belly almost on the ground, Millie drew close to the men, not as an observer, but as a participant. Sliding beneath Nick's belly, still in wolf form, she used her long, mobile tongue to slowly lick his testicles.

He jerked at her first touch. "Millie? Shit . . . warn a guy, will ya?" Strained laughter faded on a soft whimper of pleasure as Millie licked him again and felt him quiver, running her long tongue over and around his sac and down the length of his cock.

She opened her mind to the others and was almost overwhelmed when she linked to Ric, falling into his sense of the tight passage he plumbed, the way he slid deep inside Nick's hot, wet channel, the powerful clench of muscles rippling the length of his thick shaft.

"Holy fuck!" Ric cursed and jerked, slamming into Nick.

Beth lay on her belly between Ric's bent knees. Her long tongue circled his balls. Ric groaned.

"Nick's right. Warn a guy before you do that!"

Beth's soft yip ended in the slurping sound of her tongue licking between his legs again. Linked to Ric, Millie felt the rough sweep of her long, rough tongue, the way it circled Ric's sac and then followed the crease between his cheeks. He moaned.

Millie felt his concentration slip.

She doubled her assault on Nick. Licking steadily, she practically wrapped her long wolven tongue around his sac. Then she moved a bit and concentrated on the hard length of his shaft.

He jerked again when she rolled to one side for better access, licking and even nibbling at his sensitive flesh. Slipping into his mind notched her own arousal to another level.

She almost lost herself in the exquisite tease of her tongue bathing his testicles, laving his cock, nipping at his sensitive foreskin where it had retracted behind his broad crown. Then she did something that she knew Ric loved—she opened wolven jaws wide and totally engulfed the full length of Nick's erection. Using her tongue, she pressed the thick shaft against the ridges at the roof of her mouth, carefully biting down until the sharp points of her canines teased the sides of his cock.

Nick whimpered. Millie sensed the latent fear any man would have with his penis stuffed in a wolf's mouth—fear that bumped his arousal even higher, made his erection even bigger.

Big enough to scrape harder against her sharp teeth.

He was afraid to climax, so tightly clamped inside her mouth, and she blocked some of her thoughts—she wasn't about to let him know he was totally safe with her. Fear was part of the excitement. Fear and uncertainty made his arousal that much more intense.

She sensed Beth's laughter and Ric's as well. He'd been in the same position as Nick on more than one occasion, but Millie realized he wasn't about to let Nick know he was perfectly safe.

Instead, Ric picked up his pace and drove harder, pounding into Nick with enough force to slide him forward on the soft grass—if only Millie weren't holding him quite so intimately.

She finally took pity on Nick and shifted. Instead of a wolf chewing on his cock, a slim blonde with a very talented mouth and teeth not nearly as sharp sucked him deep. She'd never had a problem swallowing Ulrich's huge erection. She easily took all of Nick. Using her palms to carefully cup his sac, Millie gently worked the hard orbs inside between her fingers. Using teeth and tongue and lips, she took him even higher.

His relief was audible—he moaned now, fighting a battle she was bound and determined to make him lose. While Beth used her tongue on Ric, Millie concentrated everything on Nick. She felt the first pulse of his coming orgasm, but she locked her fingers around the base of his cock and squeezed.

After a few seconds, he managed to back off, and once again she took him almost to the top. This was one race she wanted Ric to win, no matter how much he preferred to hang on.

Whatever Beth did next tipped the scales. Ric's hands tightened on Nick's slim hips, his thighs slammed against the back of Nick's, and he roared a curse with each powerful thrust.

"Fuck. Fuck . . . fuck!"

Millie sucked hard on Nick, ran her tongue across his sensitive crown, and squeezed his balls in her palm.

"Oh . . . fuck!" Nick's cock jerked between her lips and he filled her mouth with his salty release. Still holding his balls, she kept sucking and swallowing until he collapsed, still cursing quietly, and rolled to one side in the grass. Ric went with him, still buried deep inside, groaning from the final spasms of his own climax.

Beth rolled away, entirely human now, laughing.

Millie licked her lips, planted a kiss on Nick's softening penis, and sat up. "Whatever you did, Beth, I want to know the trick. It's not easy to make him lose it."

Ric raised his head, grumbling. "She cheated. That's what she did."

"I did it with one little finger. Just one." Raising her middle finger for Millie's benefit, she leaned over Ric and kissed Nick. "Planted all the way to the third knuckle."

Ric lifted his head again and stared at Millie. "Told you she cheated."

Laughing, Millie crawled over Nick and lay across her mate. "You know the rules. All's fair, and all that stuff."

"True," Ric said. "But payback's a bitch." Then, before Millie had time to react, he'd flipped around and had her flat on her back. "My turn," he said.

She couldn't stop giggling as he loomed over her, especially knowing that Nick had Beth in the same position. Then Ric shifted, held Millie down with two very strong paws, and poked his long, wet nose between her legs.

When the hot length of his tongue swept between her sensitive folds and curled deep inside, Millie decided payback was perfectly okay, as far as she was concerned. Beth's soft moans appeared to agree.

And far, far in the back of her mind, she sensed even more of a healing. The connection with her past, with the ugliness that had haunted all that she'd done for all of her life, was gone. Instead, her pleasure was here, now, with the man she loved, with the packmates who were the family of her heart.

Though she knew the mechanics of sex, Sunny realized she didn't have a clue what the reality was like. Igmutaka was physically huge compared to her, all long, lean muscles on powerful arms and even more powerful legs. His broad chest was smooth, the musculature clearly defined, his long hair a sensual curtain that swept across her suddenly oversensitized skin like the silk sarong she'd worn earlier.

Shivering as much from nerves as from arousal, she lay in the cool grass and watched him as he knelt beside her. She certainly wasn't cold—his body radiated enough heat to warm the entire meadow. His erection was huge—the shaft long and thick, riding high and hard against his flat belly. His testicles hung beneath, closer to his body than they'd been earlier when he'd not been this aroused, but still more than a handful, and nothing at all like the ones she'd seen on the Internet.

No, Igmutaka put all those guys to shame.

She'd not expected the sense of power she felt, knowing that while his shapeshifter libido was generating the energy behind his arousal, she was the focus. He was looking directly at her, seeing her. There was no denying the desire in his eyes, the slight tremor in his hands.

He ran his fingers along her sides, raising shivers wherever he touched. Her body was unfamiliar to touch of any kind. His gentle strokes—his passion so obviously just barely leashed—were absolutely killing her. Her breasts ached. She wanted him to touch them, wanted his mouth on her nipples, his teeth biting her, his huge member filling her . . . his body covering hers.

"Then tell me." His smile glinted white in the moonlight. "Tell me what you want, sweet one. I will do whatever you desire. As much or as little as you wish."

She licked her lips and tried to say the words, but it was just too embarrassing.

He laughed. "Then think them. Open your mind, imagine what you want. It's all the same to me. Only never forget how much I want you. How much I desire you." He said it so matter-of-factly, as if it wasn't really all that important, but she sensed the need in him growing with every moment that passed even as he calmly shrugged and sat back on his heels.

"I will be your fantasy tonight." He almost purred.

She took a long, slow, shuddering breath. *Then come back. Touch me everywhere. Taste me. Make love to me. I've never done any of this, so I don't know what to ask you. I just want you to do it.*

He nodded. His teeth glinted like ivory in the moonlight that filtered through the treetops. He leaned close and wrapped those perfect lips around her left nipple. Tugged, nipped her with the sharp edges of his teeth. Laved the sting with the flat of his tongue.

She arched her back, closed her eyes, and moaned. The ripples of desire were still racing over her body when he switched to her other nipple, sucked and licked, nipped and licked again, and then kissed the very tip.

She felt each touch as if his mouth were between her legs, and he wasn't even close. Shivers raced over her skin, arcs of lightning spreading from one point to the next, wherever his lips touched her. She was burning up, shivering, on fire one moment, ice cold the next. When he kissed her belly, her pussy clenched. He ran his tongue over her belly button and all those muscles inside her sex tightened and rippled, but there was nothing inside her to clench, no one to hold on to.

He kept kissing and licking, never moving below her belly, taking her higher, driving her crazy, but not taking her far enough. Not touching her where she really needed to be touched.

She dug her fingers into the soft earth, ripping grass from its roots. She bucked her hips, wondering why he didn't kiss her there, between her legs where she really, really wanted him.

He laughed, leaned over, and kissed her mouth. His lips moved over hers with a quiet confidence that had her shivering even harder. His tongue tangled with hers. He tasted wild and free, like sin and all those things she'd wondered about and never expected to know. She was enveloped in heat as he moved over her, surrounded her. Covered her with his body.

Once again his lips moved over her flushed skin. Waves of hot and cold undulated across her surface. She was burning, then freezing, then burning again, and still he kissed her, stroked her, touched her.

She felt his fingers on her hips. Felt them slide beneath her butt and he was lifting her—lifting her up until her skinny legs sprawled inelegantly over his forearms. Lifting her to his mouth and kissing her inner thighs, kissing the soft blond curls covering her pubes, nuzzling between her legs, inhaling as if he needed her scent as much as she craved his touch.

She felt his gaze on her and opened her eyes. He stared at her, cat's eyes watching her in the moonlight. When he realized she was looking at him, he winked, smiled, and dipped his head between her upraised thighs.

The first touch of his tongue made her hips jerk and sent fire through her blood. One long, slow lick that separated the swollen folds and found the source of the wetness shimmering on her inner thighs.

He licked steadily, lapping at her like a cat with cream, using his tongue to tease her virgin passage, gently, softly licking deep, curling the tip against the sensitive walls.

She was aware of the pressure, but arousal ruled. She wanted more, needed more, but he continued to lick and probe much too gently with his tongue, teasing the sensitive nerve endings.

Then, after what felt like a lifetime of teasing, he set her back down and sat back on his heels. "You're so small inside. Untried . . . too tight." He sighed, sounding as frustrated as Sunny. "I'm very large and I would hurt you too much. Maybe your first time should be with another man, one not so big. Tonight I will give you pleasure, but anything else?" Again, he shrugged. "I don't want to hurt you."

"No." She shook her head. "I don't want another man. It's going to hurt if you go slow or fast. I want you to do it now, tonight." Breathing hard, panting with the effort of waiting one more minute for something that had eluded her for an entire lifetime, she struggled for calm. Her body thrummed with need, her skin rippled with sensations too new, with arousal simmering over the surface, deep inside. Somehow she had to find enough control to make a sensible argument.

He thought it wasn't going to happen tonight? No way.

He sighed and glanced away, then looked at her again. "Are you sure? Logan can give you a shot to take away the pain. He can remove that part that blocks me, give it a day or two to heal. Then we can do this."

"You're kidding, right?" Frustration rolled over her in dark, angry waves. She dropped her head back on the grass and stared at the dark sky. "He's got to be fucking kidding. Please tell me he's kidding. . . ." She propped herself up on her elbows. That voice she was still getting used to had a gravelly edge to it she'd not heard before, didn't know she was even capable of.

"Tonight, Ig. You, me, the Louisville Slugger. If it hurts, I'll get over it. If you don't do it, I will probably kill you. What'll it be?"

He laughed. Shook his head. Laughed harder. "What happened to my shy little one who was afraid to tell me what she wanted?"

"That was before you went all sensitive gentleman on me. I'm almost twenty years old. I've known about sex for a long time. I never thought I'd get to experience it, and right now I'm waiting for my first orgasm and my first fuck. If it's not you, I'm going to hunt down one of the other guys as soon as we get back. I don't care how big his cock is. I imagine someone there will help me out."

She blinked. Wow . . . was that really her? Going all alpha bitch on the poor guy? Damn, she hoped she didn't get the giggles. That would totally blow it.

Igmutaka ran a finger along her cheek. "Did you know my first time with Adam and Liana was my first sex as a human? I was a virgin that night. And you're right. Some of it hurt, but the pleasure and the pain are . . ." He shrugged. "They're part of the same. The pain makes the pleasure greater. I promise I will be careful, but I can also promise you it will hurt."

She shivered. Somehow, the mention of pain turned her

on even more. Was that because of a lifetime without feeling? She didn't know and certainly didn't intend to worry about it now. Ig lifted her again, only this time he used his tongue on that tiny bundle of nerves she knew had to be her clitoris.

Her legs twitched and shivered with every lick of his tongue as he slowly, carefully brought her back to a fever pitch of arousal. He stroked her with his long fingers, teasing at her opening, pressing one finger as far as the membrane would allow, withdrawing it, pressing again. Her excitement built until she trembled from head to foot. His tongue grew more insistent. She balanced on the edge of something wonderful, but she had no idea how to make that final leap.

He wrapped his lips around her clit, sucking and using his tongue, pressing harder with his finger, until the combination of pressure, of incipient pain, of overwhelming pleasure grew, and grew some more.

Panting, her hips bucking in his grasp, she reached for something, for some unknown something when a shock of lightning struck deep inside. Her body clenched, her lips pulled back in a grimace she couldn't control, and she wrapped her legs around his shoulders, tightened her thighs against his head, and pressed hard against the finger that was almost where it needed to be.

Almost but not quite. Lightning exploded again, her body jerked, and his finger pressed deep, tearing through, sinking deep. Sharp, biting pain, a rush of pleasure, screaming . . . that was her screaming as she went absolutely rigid—rigid and yet pulsing and clenching against his mouth, around his long, thick finger, against the brush of cool night air.

Sobbing, wanting more, aware her body would never be the same, she curled into Ig's warm embrace and let him hold her until the shivering stopped. It seemed to take a long, long time as her body convulsed around that one long, thick finger slowly pressing in, sliding out, then in again. It stung, but it felt so good she didn't want him to stop, and she already knew they were going to do this again, and then again.

But next time, she fully intended to ride this crest of pleasure with Ig's Louisville Slugger buried deep inside.

Chapter 20

Millie raised her head, still half asleep but already instinctively sniffing the cool breeze. The wind had picked up, blowing out of the west and carrying the hint of coming weather . . . and something else. She rose to all four feet and glanced about the meadow.

They'd fallen asleep after all that amazing sex. She'd ended up with Nick, Ric with Beth, and then the four of them had fallen together in a tumble of warm and sticky human bodies before shifting and dozing off as wolves.

But something was wrong. Something that lifted the hackles along her spine and had her nipping at Ric's shoulder, nudging Nick and Beth awake.

What is it? Ric stood and shook himself. *Crap . . . I didn't mean to fall asleep. It's late. The moon's gone down.*

Nick raised his nose and sniffed the air. *I smell smoke. With this wind, it could be a long ways off. . . .*

Or very close, Beth added. She walked to the edge of the meadow where they'd been able to see the lights from town earlier. *Unless there's a power outage, I think there's a fire on the hills below us. It's really smoky. Can't see any lights.*

The others trotted over. Ric shifted, standing tall for a

better view. "Down there, to the south. See that glow? That's fire. Looks like it's near the main road."

Millie stood beside him. "Good Goddess! With the way the wind is blowing, the house is right in the fire's path!"

Ric nodded. "I'm raising Anton now." He waited a moment, then he nodded again. "Stefan's calling it in. Smoke's thicker down there but no one had noticed it—they were all asleep. Anton's checking to see who might still be out running."

They waited, watching as the glow grew brighter. It was still miles away, but with the brisk wind and dryness typical of the fall, the forest was like tinder just waiting for a match.

"Shit." Ric let out a big breath. "Everyone's back but the four of us . . . and Igmutaka and Sunny. They went out hours ago. No one's heard from them since."

"Should we search for them?" Millie grabbed his hand.

Ric shook his head. "No. Anton's going to try and reach them. He wants us back before it's too late. He said the wind's blowing a gale down there. There's no time to evacuate, especially with everyone there. He said he'll contact the Forest Service again and let them know there's no need for rescue, that we've got a safe place to ride it out. Then they'll fight it off as long as they can. If it looks like the house is going to go, they'll head into the caves. Ig knows all the access points on the mountain. Anton will keep trying to reach him, tell them to take cover."

They shifted and hit the ground running. Already the acrid scent of wood smoke was growing stronger, though the air was still clear enough to breathe. Millie sent out a call to Sunny, but there was no answer. Fighting a growing sense of panic, she raced with the others, running down the hill at full speed, heading for Anton's huge home and the growing wall of flames.

*   *   *

Sunny hadn't intended to fall asleep, but she didn't mind a bit, not when she'd been awakened by the slow and sensual massage of Ig's warm hands over her back and butt. Somehow, she'd ended up sprawled on top of him with the thick length of his erection trapped between her thighs.

He had definitely grown in the last few minutes since he'd brought her out of her sound sleep with whisper-light strokes of his fingers. She clamped her thighs around his thick shaft and smiled when he softly moaned.

They still hadn't actually made love, but she knew it was going to happen. Soon. She honestly didn't know where Igmutaka found his patience, though that appeared to be waning quickly. Still, even though she was growing more aware of his tension as the seconds passed, she couldn't help but think that the man's self-control was amazing . . . and it was definitely working.

She trusted him completely and now felt totally relaxed, her muscles almost fluid from his soft strokes and gentle kisses. At the same time, her level of arousal was steadily building. Her pussy no longer hurt at all, but he'd laved her with his tongue, soothed her with his slow and gentle ministrations, until she could think of nothing beyond the two of them connecting on that most primal level.

She was ready. She wanted him—now.

"I don't want to hurt you."

"I don't want you to hurt me, either, but we're going to do this." She leaned close and kissed him. His lips were firm, not nearly as relaxed as they'd been earlier.

"Sunny. We can—"

She pressed her finger to his lips. "No. We can't. Be still." Then she planted her hands on his chest and rose to her knees. His cock rose with her, standing tall, a perfect—but immense—invitation. Slowly, carefully, she lowered herself over the broad head.

She was wet and buttery soft and warm down there, but she used her fingers to open herself wider, clasped his thick shaft, and rolled the tip back and forth between her legs, covering the crown with her fluids. He groaned again and she almost giggled. It appeared the man's composure was fading fast. He clasped her thighs in his big hands, steadying her.

Tilting her hips, Sunny lowered herself, giving her body time to adjust, taking his first inch inside. Then another, and another, working the burn, easing slowly down the full length, well aware she was driving him absolutely insane.

Panting, legs trembling with the effort, she carefully rolled her hips, forcing him deeper. It seemed to take forever, but he held perfectly, rigidly still until, finally, she managed to take all of him. Panting, she rested her hands on his chest, leaned close, and kissed him. "Thank you. And for your information, it doesn't hurt at all, though if you were even a fraction bigger, I don't think this would work."

He laughed, bouncing her up and down. Then he groaned and carefully rolled Sunny to her back. He grabbed her legs and wrapped them around his waist, put his hands beneath her back, and gently lifted her as he sat on his heels. She clung to him, wrapped her arms around his neck, and held him close.

He thrust slowly, carefully, perfectly angled so his thick, slick shaft rubbed over her clit on every penetration. She hadn't expected to come again—this time really was for Ig—but she felt that amazing coil of heat building, growing, taking her closer to the now-familiar precipice.

Only it wasn't the same—not this time. Not with him so deep inside, so deep that she felt his thick, deceptively hard glans bump against the even harder mouth of her cervix on every thrust, then the deep slide as he passed over the hard mouth of her womb and stretched her vaginal channel even further, filling her to her limits. Thick, hard, and hot, touching every nerve inside until her heart pounded and her lungs strained to keep up with the growing level of need, of sensual overload.

He'd taken her to her peak and beyond at least a dozen times already tonight. She couldn't believe he was going to do it again. After a lifetime without sensation, making love with Igmutaka had probably ruined her for anyone else. She wanted to laugh with the joy she felt, with the utter freedom of sex with a man who only wanted to please her.

They were so much alike, and yet not. So similar in so many ways, and yet she knew he wasn't her mate. Would never be her bonded mate. He was a man who loved her, as he loved them all, and for that gift alone, he would always be special.

At this moment, at this perfect time and place, she loved him without reservation. But deep in her heart, even as he filled her, as he made her body sing, Sunny knew she would one day love another. For some odd reason, that knowledge made the sex with Igmutaka even more special—more meaningful.

Another thrust, and another, and she was quivering inside, pulsing around his cock, shivering in his arms, and clutching him to her heart. Holding on to his hard body as he cried out, as his cock jerked inside, filling her with his hot release.

That blast of hot ejaculate against her womb was all it took. Sunny cried out and arched her back, forcing Igmutaka deeper. Her body rippled and clenched around him, her heart stuttered in her chest, and she leaned forward, collapsing loose-limbed and sobbing against his chest.

It was too much. It was perfect. It was—

A shout filled her mind.

But it wasn't Ig's cry of pleasure that caught her on the other side of orgasm. It was Anton's warning. His frantic cry, telling them to hurry, warning them of mortal danger.

Fire burned on the mountain. Wind carried the flames and there was no time to waste. They must escape or die.

He and all the others were going into the caverns. He hoped they were near enough to find refuge in one of the caves that dotted these mountains.

Igmutaka answered. Then he raised his head and sniffed the air. "I'm sorry, sweet one. No time for pillow talk." He stood up and set her on her feet.

Thick streams of his ejaculate spilled down her inner thighs. She smelled his scent on her, the pungent aroma of sex, but there was something else. Something terrifying.

"I smell smoke." She looked around to see where it was coming from, but the night was black. The moon had either set or was lost behind unseen clouds of smoke. The trees hid any sign of flames. "What are we going to do?"

"Shift and follow me. There's a cavern not too far. It leads to the ones that run beneath Anton's home. We have to hurry, before the fire cuts us off from the entrance. The other openings into the system of caverns are much farther away."

They shifted, and with her wolven eyes the night was not so dark, but the stink of smoke was all around. Animals passed them, moving out of harm's way.

She and Ig did exactly the opposite. Running as quickly as she was able, Sunny followed him through the woods with her nose close to the ground where the air was clear.

They could hear the fire now, the roar of flames and the distant crackling of burning wood and falling trees. Sunny's legs already trembled with the effort. She wasn't used to running.

Hell, until yesterday, she couldn't even walk. Hadn't Adam and Logan cautioned her about taking it easy? She had a feeling this wasn't quite what they'd meant—a night of amazing sex and a hard run through a dark forest fleeing for her life didn't sound like the kind of therapy Logan had in mind.

Lungs burning, she followed close on Ig's long, cougar tail. He wasn't built for extended running, but he kept a steady ground-covering pace, leading her over small, drying creeks and through thick tangles of brush. Finally they slowed. The sky was brighter here, the smoke thicker. Burning embers fell around them, but they'd entered a meadow that was still fairly damp, and so far nothing in the immediate vicinity was burning.

Ig leapt straight up and landed on a ledge about six feet overhead. Sunny stared at it, lungs heaving with the effort to breathe, too exhausted to be afraid, practical enough to know what he asked of her was impossible.

There was no way in hell she could jump that high. Instead, she looked for another way around.

Hurry, Sunny. The fire's just over the hill and moving fast. What's wrong?

I can't jump that high. My legs aren't strong enough.

Shift! Suddenly Ig was kneeling on the ledge, leaning over with his hand out.

She shifted and reached for him. Embers blew in a whirlwind gust of hot air, falling all around now as he wrapped his strong fingers around her wrists and tugged. She was on the ledge beside him before she even had time to think about whether or not he could lift her so far.

"Shift," he said. Without waiting to see if she complied, the cougar spun around and headed toward a split in the cliff. Shifting just as quickly, Sunny followed, squeezing through the narrow cleft behind the big cat.

It was easier now, shifting without thinking, acting purely on instincts too long ignored. Physically exhausted, still her body responded. She followed the cat, moving on willpower alone.

Ig kept going, even though the darkness was absolute, but he kept up a steady mental conversation, and his stream of words helped calm her. He told her about the caves, about the times he'd hidden here when the rains came, how he'd found so many of the various tunnels exploring the area when he first returned to his cougar form after eons as a spirit guide.

Sunny followed close behind, hanging on to his tales, ignoring the claustrophobic sense of walls closing in around her. They really were closing in—it wasn't just in her head. The tunnel they followed grew narrower and tighter, until Ig had to crawl forward on his belly. Sunny was thankful for her thick coat—the stone walls were rough and the ground beneath her belly littered with shards of rock.

They seemed to go on this way forever until Ig finally stopped. *Wait here.*

You're not going to leave me! She scrambled closer, until she could touch his tail with the tip of her nose.

Only long enough to find a light. I left a lantern here, ages ago. I know it's somewhere. Matches, too. You're okay.

She waited, counting the seconds. Her heart thundered in her chest and she was positive she could hear the rush of blood in her veins. Her harsh breaths created a steady counterpoint of sound. The scuffs and scrapes of Ig moving around in a cavern beyond echoed and faded, then returned again.

She couldn't hear the forest fire anymore, which was a good thing. It was hard enough knowing the fire already burned the forest outside and most likely blocked the cave entrance.

A sudden glow had her blinking, waiting for her eyes to adjust. Ig stood, tall and confident, about ten feet away at the end of the tunnel she was in. He waited, lantern in hand, in the middle of a large cavern. She became aware of the steady drip of water as she crawled forward. That and the harsh rasp of her labored breathing echoed eerily around her. Finally she reached a wider opening with what looked like about a three-foot drop to the cavern floor.

She could do this. Landing clumsily on legs that would barely hold her, Sunny shifted as soon as she hit the ground.

And collapsed in the cool sand. Immediately, Ig was beside her. He set the Coleman lantern on the ground and ran his hands over her shoulders, touched her face, swept his fingers through her spiky hair.

"You're okay?"

She nodded. Then she laughed.

He cocked an eyebrow and looked at her as though she were nuts. Maybe she was.

"What's funny?"

It took her a minute to catch her breath. "Not quite the way I ever imagined my first time to have sex. You sure know how to show a girl a good time."

He sat down beside her and wrapped his arm around her shoulders. He leaned his cheek against her hair, but he wasn't laughing. Instead, he sounded sad. "You're right. For a first time, I've been told that a woman should have flowers and a soft bed. Not a muddy field with a forest fire on the way."

She leaned against his shoulder and thought of how he'd made her feel. "I wouldn't have it any other way, Ig. And I don't remember mud, just soft, cool grass. Tonight was perfect. More than perfect. It was unique. My life has changed so much in the past few days. And you, my friend, are the best change that's happened yet."

She leaned close and kissed him. He kissed her back, but this time there was no passion. Exactly what she needed—the kiss of a man she could count on. A friend. Her life was too new, her feelings too fresh and fragile to want anything more.

Anton's voice slipped into her mind. *Ig and Sunny? Are you safe?*

We're in the cave near the northern border. Sunny is ex-

*hausted, so we'll rest before we come back to the house. Is
everyone back safely?*

*They are. We're running the sprinklers in the meadow
and Stefan's got more set on the roof. It's burning hot and
fast, though. I don't know if we'll be able to save the
house. We've just about got everyone moved into the caverns.*

*Take care, my friend. Is the Forest Service responding
yet?*

*They are, but the fire's threatening a small community
south of us. More homes and families will take up their re-
sources. We can't expect a lot of help.*

We'll get there as soon as we can. Be careful.

You, too.

"That amazing home could burn?" Sunny had never
seen a house as gorgeous as Anton's, filled with beautiful
furniture, original artwork, and tons of electronic equipment. The high-tech medical equipment in Logan's clinic
had to be worth a fortune.

"A house is merely stone and wood and glass. The people inside are what count. Anton will keep the pack safe.
That's most important."

She knew he was right, but it didn't seem fair. Of
course, wasn't she a prime example that life lacked a sense
of fairness?

"I hope they're able to save it," she said. Then she
yawned and leaned close against Ig. Exhaustion swept
over her as she and Ig stared into the steady glow from the
lantern, both of them lost in their own thoughts.

Keisha stuffed bags full of the kids' favorite things. She
refused to think about the fact her husband was out there,
facing the oncoming flames. That Adam, Oliver, Stefan,
Baylor, and Jake were manning hoses and wetting down
the house and grounds. That Tinker and Luc were moving

vehicles and doing their best to protect the chopper. She couldn't function if she let herself dwell on the danger. It was her job to see that the children were safe, so that was the job she'd do.

The risk of fire here in the mountains was always high this time of year, though they'd dodged the bullet often enough to gain a sense that maybe it wouldn't happen, maybe they were immune to the danger. It appeared their luck had run out.

She tried to remember if they'd grabbed everything important, but how did you choose from a house filled with all the treasures of daily life? "Gabe? Sweetie, did you pack Pooh Bear? Mac . . . what about Eeyore? Did you find him?"

Gabe held up his bedraggled bear as Mac pulled his beloved blue donkey out from under his covers. Both sleepy-eyed boys still wore their pj's, but Keisha'd packed plenty of clothing.

It would only be for a few hours, wouldn't it? She sent a quick prayer to the Goddess. Eve had kept them safe before. She had to trust her to do it now.

Lily ran into the room, already dressed with her backpack bulging. Under one arm she carried her Harry Potter book—the one she'd been reading before taking off on her big adventure.

Keisha gave her a harried smile. "Have you got everything, sweetie?"

Lily nodded. "Mom? Who's Sunny?"

"She's the new Chanku Nick found. You haven't met her yet. She's with Igmutaka, but she'll come meet us in the caves later." Keisha continued to check the boys' room. She couldn't allow herself to think that all of this might be ashes come morning. They'd gotten in the habit of storing irreplaceable items in the cavern, so she didn't need to worry about old photos and keepsakes, but had she grabbed enough clothes for everyone? Did they have plenty of bedding?

"Did you know she's the last one? The one the Ancient Ones told me about. They hoped I could help find her. I'm sure glad she's already here."

Keisha paused with her hand on Mac's dresser. "What did they tell you?" She and Anton had decided not to question Lily right away, but if she offered, they were more than willing to listen.

Lily sat on the floor and made a face at Lucia. The baby grinned, obviously loving the fact she had company in the middle of the night. "They don't know where all the missing Chanku are, either, but they knew about Sunny because she tried to shift when she was too little. They felt a spike in energy when she tried, but then they couldn't find her. It happened with Manda, too, when she got caught, but they've been worried about Sunny. Is she okay?"

Keisha nodded, leaned over, and picked up Lucia. "She is. She was in a wheelchair, but now that she's learned to shift, she can walk again. You'll get to meet her later." Distracted again as she caught the strong odor of smoke, Keisha glanced about the cluttered room. "Okay, guys. Have we got everything important?"

Mac kicked the leg of the bunk bed. "We don't have our bed."

"No, but we have sleeping bags and soft, comfy mattresses in the cavern. You'll be fine. Daddy said ten minutes and it's been nine. We have one minute to get to the stairs. Fast feet, kids. Who's gonna get there first? Don't go down without me!"

Races they understood. Even Lily scrambled to her feet, bag in hand, and raced down the hall. Keisha did a last look as they passed the room she shared with Anton. She had so many wonderful memories in this room. Her eyes filled with tears. Smoke was beginning to swirl around outside the windows. She could hear the big sprinklers running, but the wind had picked up.

Footsteps on the roof told her Stefan was still wetting down the slate tiles. She heard voices as everyone gathered up what they could and headed toward the kitchen. No laughter, though. Not this time. The fire was too close, too angry.

They'd done this drill before. Every single time they'd returned to their own beds, their own things.

Their own home. Why, then, did tonight feel different? Tonight, when the entire pack gathered? She shivered and blinked away incipient tears. This was no time for self-indulgence. Clinging to Lucia, following the other three down the hall to the kitchen, Keisha felt a frisson of fear.

So many changes so quickly. Finding Sunny had been a good one—she was sweet and loving and so very brave. The vote was still out on exposing their secret to the world, but Anton was right—they'd have been outed sooner or later. Better to have done it with the whole world watching as one of their kind performed an act of heroism than to be caught doing something stupid, but it still frightened her.

She met Millie and Ric at the doorway to the cellar. "Is everyone back? Nick and Beth? What about Ig and Sunny? Anton said he contacted them, but they're not here yet, are they?"

Ric shook his head. "Nope. Ig and Sunny took refuge in a cavern on the mountain. Ig says it connects to this one. Nick and Beth are helping Logan move some more of the equipment from the clinic." Ric stepped aside, but he reached for the heavy diaper bag she'd thrown over her shoulder, plucked it off, and looped it over his own.

"Thanks," she said, flashing him a quick smile. She'd always liked Ulrich—Ric, now. Millie'd certainly helped the man relax. Keisha remembered when she'd first met him, shortly after his kidnapping. He'd seemed so much older then, and gruff, not nearly as outgoing and friendly as he was now.

"I'm really glad you've heard from Sunny and Ig. I was so worried about them." She laughed. "Well, about Sunny, anyway. Igmutaka's been taking care of himself for a long, long time. C'mon, kids. Get moving. Everyone else is already down below."

Ric and Millie followed. Keisha heard the sound of many voices, a few babies crying. Anton and the others had promised not to take chances—they'd be joining the rest of them down there before it got too dangerous.

She sent him a quick message—a reminder of his promise. There was no room for heroes tonight. If the fire took the house, so be it. She'd rather have her man safe beside her.

His response, his renewed promise to take care, whispered across her mind. Smiling, she stepped through the door from the cellar and entered the narrow tunnel into the caverns. As long as her family and pack were safe, nothing else really mattered.

Chapter 21

Anton dragged one of the big sprinklers closer to the forest and aimed the spray directly at the tall cedars lining the driveway near the house. So far, the fire was burning through the dry underbrush and debris along the forest floor, but if the flames got into the tops of the trees with this wind blowing, there'd be no stopping it.

Baylor and Jake were farther out in front, setting more sprinklers in the big meadow near the main entrance at the far end of the driveway. Stefan was still wetting down the roof. Slate tiles wouldn't burn, but the water kept the inside cooler and discouraged embers from smoldering on the stones.

Adam and Oliver were inside, making certain everyone had cleared out of the main house and moved into the caverns. With so many people on the property, Anton didn't want to risk missing someone in case the house caught fire.

Tinker and Luc were inside helping to carry more equipment from Logan's clinic into the caverns, but they'd moved all the vehicles to the center of the back meadow—the largest expanse of closely mowed lawn on the property. Everything, including the chopper, was covered in fire-retardant tarps and there were sprinklers all around to keep the grass from burning.

It was the best they could do.

Embers landed in the dry grass near Oliver and Mei's cottage. Anton raced across the driveway and used his shovel to smother the flames.

"Stand back." Stefan leaned over from the roof. "I'll douse that area again. The wind's already dried it out."

Anton stepped out of the way while Stefan shot a steady stream of water over the dry grass. Steam hissed from the small patch that had caught fire.

A deep roar had Anton spinning where he stood. Baylor shouted something he couldn't hear over the noise. In the glow of the fire, Anton saw Jake running toward the house with Baylor on his heels. Anton had first focused on the men, but his eyes were immediately drawn to the nightmare behind them.

The fire was crowning. Pushed higher and hotter by the growing winds, it burst through the treetops and shot straight into the night sky. Flames boiled out of the thick limbs and intense heat quickly raised the temperature of the sap inside nearby trees to explosive levels. A huge pine exploded, sending fiery pitch and burning branches into the sky. The one next to it blew, and the next.

The sound was a roaring freight train, bearing down on all of them. Unstoppable. Deadly. Racing faster than any man or wolf could hope to run.

Burning debris shot through the air, deadly fireworks lighting the night sky, falling to the ground all around Bay and Jake. Despite the water they'd poured on the dry grass, small fires sprang up everywhere, whipped immediately into frenzied whirlwinds. In front of the men, behind them, fed by the wind, swirling tornadoes, spreading more flames wherever they blew.

Anton shouted at Stefan. "Stef! Get down. Off the roof now! It's too late. We need to get into the caves."

Stefan threw the hose off the roof and raced for the ladder. Anton turned again and watched the two men running before a fire that chased them across the burning meadow in a horrible race they couldn't possibly win.

Flames licked up the side of Mei and Oliver's cottage. The heat was intense—the air filled with smoke and swirling, burning embers. There wasn't enough air to breathe—all of it fueled the fire, burning their lungs, stinging their eyes. Anton turned his gaze away from the burning cottage as Stefan raced across the driveway and skidded to a stop at his side.

Baylor was almost to the house when Jake cried out and stumbled forward. He fell, screaming, hit in the back by a burning branch, blown from one of the exploding trees.

Baylor spun around and raced back across the burning grass to help him. Anton and Stef ran full-tilt across the meadow, sidestepping the dozens of small fires that grew even as they leapt over and around them—fires that flared up and spread, all pushed by the wind toward the beautiful house that had stood in this perfect meadow for so many years.

Anton couldn't think of his home. He focused only on the man screaming in pain, rolling in the grass, frantically trying to dislodge the burning pitch from his back.

Bay reached Jake first and ripped the shirt off him, cursing and beating the flames out with his hands. Burned flesh tore away with the fabric, but Jake's screams had stopped. He lurched to his hands and knees and then, with Bay's help, he stood. He stumbled slightly, swaying for a moment from shock and pain. His eyes were glazed, his legs unsteady, but he still managed to move forward.

Anton and Stef reached the two of them as yet another huge pine burst into flames. More debris fell like fiery rain around them. Holding Jake's arms, practically carrying him through the inferno, they reached the main house.

Oliver and Adam flung open the door as Bay, Stef, and

Anton ran up the wide front stairs, holding Jake. Oliver and Mei's cottage was fully engulfed, lighting the night like a torch. Flames licked the walls of the main house, burning hot just outside the kitchen.

They had to pass through the kitchen to access the caverns.

"We were just coming to get you. We don't have much time if we expect to make it to the caves." Adam stepped aside so Anton and the others could get Jake through the door. "How is he?"

"Badly burned," Anton said. "I think he's going into shock." When they reached the kitchen, Baylor took up Anton's hold on Jake, and Anton stepped aside.

Oliver held the door to the cellar open. Flames boiled in a seething storm just outside the kitchen window, and smoke made it difficult to breathe. The generator-powered lights flickered and went out, but the shed was probably in flames by now and light from the fire illuminated the room. Heat in the kitchen was already growing unbearable, though the roar of the fire seemed muted here inside the walls.

At least for now. Anton moved out of the way as Adam leaned over and grabbed Jake's legs. Baylor carefully held Jake's upper body, avoiding the burned and blackened skin on his back and shoulders. The two of them could get him into the cavern faster this way. Jake moaned, barely conscious. Oliver went on ahead, opening doors as Bay and Adam carefully carried Jake down the stairs to safety.

Anton glanced at Stefan. Soot covered his face and there were tears in his eyes. "Stef? What's wrong? Are you hurt?"

A window somewhere in the house exploded. Smoke was getting thicker, filling the once-bright kitchen, but the light wasn't from moonlight or the sun or the emergency lights—it was the angry red of fire boiling just outside the windows.

"It's gone, Anton. Your home will be gone by morning."

Anton shifted his eyes away from the pain in Stefan's. His gaze fell on the refrigerator, on the colorful drawings made by so many of the children—drawings carefully taped to the smooth stainless steel finish.

At first, those wonderful childish drawings filled him with pain, at the thought they would soon be nothing more than ash. Then a calming sense of acceptance washed over him.

All his priorities clicked perfectly into place.

There was nothing they could do. The house was going to burn. The pictures would burn. . . . He raised his head and smiled at Stefan. The children were safe. What else mattered?

He clapped a hand on Stefan's shoulder. "It's just a house, Stef. Wood and glass and steel. All replaceable. You, my friend, are not. Now get your skinny ass down those stairs before I have to carry you myself."

Stefan gave him a crooked grin, turned, and headed down the stairs. Anton paused on the top step for a moment and stared once more around the kitchen where he'd shared so many wonderful times with people he loved. For some reason, he thought of that morning with Eve when she'd left Adam and gone in search of herself. Instead, she'd found Mei Chen. Oliver had found love. Eve had gone on to become their goddess.

Flames burst through the kitchen window. Anton stared at the fire licking up the kitchen wall. It appeared this fire was too much, even for a Goddess.

A piece of the ceiling fell and landed on the kitchen table. The same table where he'd sat one morning and shared coffee with Igmutaka—a man he'd known only as a cougar until then. Thank the Goddess Ig and Sunny were safe.

Fire ran up the walls and the freight train roar grew

louder. Anton shut the kitchen door and ran quickly down the wide stone staircase leading to the cellar. Stefan waited for him, holding the heavy metal door at the bottom of the stairs.

At Keisha's insistence, Anton had installed an expensive fireproof door between the kitchen and the cellar, something he'd teased her about at the time.

Was that woman ever wrong about anything?

Stefan carefully shut the door and led him through the cellar to the far side where a tunnel led to the caverns beyond. He slid the cabinet aside that hid the entrance to the caves.

Anton stopped as a muffled *whump* shook the small room. "Sounds like the propane tank just blew. I've been wondering when it would go."

Pausing, Stef cocked his head. "Sounds like. You ready?"

Anton nodded. He turned and gazed at Stefan, looking for any sign of censure. Then he sighed and looked away, toward the heavy steel door leading to the burning kitchen. "I feel as if this is all my fault."

Again Stef paused. "Why would you say that? When I called the dispatcher at the Forest Service to tell him we wouldn't need rescuing, he said the fire started near the highway when some idiot pulled over to check a bad tire and tossed a cigarette in the grass. Sorry, Anton. You can't take credit for that. It's not your fault."

He bit back an indignant snort. "Actually, I was thinking of that night we got together, when I told you I had a feeling there was change coming. I hope wishing something or thinking about something doesn't make it so."

Laughing, Stefan shoved him through the door into the tunnel and pulled the cabinet across the opening. "My friend, if that were the case, I would have first gotten laid by the time I was twelve instead of having to wait until I was sixteen."

Anton stared at his friend, his lover, the one who always made him laugh—especially when he didn't feel like it.

And he laughed. "Excellent point, my friend. Excellent point."

They stepped into the main cavern, into a room of controlled chaos. A baby cried somewhere in the shadows. Pallets and mattresses for kids and grown-ups, including a couple of portable cribs for the smallest babies, filled the huge chamber. Many of the adults were still getting the older children settled, but most of the little ones already slept soundly, oblivious to the danger just overhead.

Anton paused in the doorway, stopped, and just stared.

"I know," Stefan said.

The man always seemed to know exactly what Anton was thinking. Bemused, he turned to look at Stef.

"Did you ever imagine we'd be this prolific?" Stefan grinned at him as if they didn't have a worry in the world.

Then he thought about what really mattered—he had Lily home. His family and packmates were safe. Stefan was beside him. Everyone who mattered, everything that counted, was all right.

"There're twenty-five little rug rats now," Stef added. "I counted."

Shaking his head, Anton could only smile. The youngest and oldest were his, but that was about to change, with four of their women pregnant and one of them—Daciana—carrying twins. He was still thinking about what mattered, when Keisha found him.

"I'm so glad you're finally here." She wrapped her arms around his waist and laid her cheek against his chest. "I was getting worried, and when they brought Jake in . . ."

"How is he?" Anton brushed her tousled hair back from her eyes. Though she'd tried to hide it, he could tell she'd been crying. "Will he be okay? Will you be okay?"

She nodded. "I'm okay. Jake . . . I don't know. Logan's

got the equipment from the clinic set up in a smaller chamber. Come with me." She stepped away and tugged his hand. "Stef? I'm glad you're finally here. Xandi's been worried sick about you. I think she finally got Alex and Amber down, but now Ariel is awake and she's inconsolable."

Stefan grinned and tipped a brief salute to Anton. "I thought I recognized the sound of that particular shriek." His grin faltered. "Anton? It will all be okay. Whatever happens, we'll make it work."

Anton nodded as Stef headed across the huge cavern toward Xandi. Sound in here echoed. It was amazing so many children slept through the din. Keisha's fingers closed around his forearm. "What did Stef mean, that you'll make it work?"

Anton sighed and wrapped his arms around his beloved wife. "Mei and Oliver's cottage is gone. The main house was almost fully engulfed by the time we came down the stairs. It will be gone by morning. I'm sorry, my love. We did every—"

"No. Damn it, Anton." She cut him off, unaccountably angry. With him? Sometimes he didn't know what she was thinking, this complicated, beautiful, amazing woman he'd mated and married. When she stood on her toes to kiss him, it made even less sense.

"It doesn't matter," she said. She pressed her hand against the side of his face, the way he'd seen her comfort Lily when something had upset her, the same way she soothed their sons, calmed their infant daughter. Her house was burning to the ground and she was comforting him. Go figure.

"Can't you see that, my love? It doesn't matter. None of it." She clutched both his arms and forced him to meet her unwavering gaze. "You're what matters. The children matter. I matter. Our friends, our packmates—they're what matter, and all of them are here, all of them safe. Adam and Logan are healing Jake's burns as we speak. A house is just a thing. We—all of us in this room—we're what make it a home."

He was truly blessed. That was the only thought in his mind as he pulled Keisha into his arms and held her close. Blessed above all others, to have found the perfect woman to stand beside him, to bear his children, to be his mate.

He chuckled as an errant thought entered his mind.

Keisha leaned back and gazed at him with a quizzical lift to her brows. "What? One moment you're almost weeping. Now you're laughing? I'd check to see what's going on in that convoluted mind of yours, but you're blocking me."

"Didn't mean to." He laughed out loud. "Ah, my love, I never mean to hide anything from you, but I was thinking how blessed I am to have you as my mate. And then I realized I truly am a lucky devil—there's not another woman on the face of the earth who would put up with me."

Keisha kissed his nose. "I agree. You're a pain in the butt and a terrible trial and you're damned lucky to have me." Flashing him a saucy wink, she grabbed his hand. "Now that we have that cleared up, we need to check on Jake. Come with me."

She tugged him along, down a tunnel that led to another chamber. This one was much smaller, though it was brightly lit by overhead lights powered by deep-cycle batteries Logan had insisted on installing a couple of years ago. Anton wondered if the solar panels that powered the lights and equipment were far enough above the tree line to avoid the fire.

No matter. The batteries had a full charge, and with any luck, the fire should burn through by morning. There were other issues of more importance—like the man stretched out beneath the glare of the overhead lights.

Jake lay on his stomach on a raised gurney with Shannon sitting on a stool near his head. She held both his hands, and it was obvious they were deeply linked. Sweat and tears rolled down Shannon's face as she shared her mate's pain. Lisa, Tinker, Manda, and Baylor sat off to one side with their hands linked, absorbing even more, and from the extent of Jake's burns, the pain had to be tremendous. Adam and Logan sat on tall stools on either side of Jake, eyes closed, hands resting on unburned skin.

There wasn't much that hadn't been charred. Ugly burns ran from his shoulders to the middle right side of his back. Burning pitch had stuck to his skin, and even rolling in the dirt hadn't dislodged all of it. The wounds were deep and ugly, affecting muscle tissue and tendons, but even as Anton watched, skin began to heal, replacing gray or black with healthy pink.

Keisha turned and linked with Anton. *Go back to the others. Tell them how Jake is doing, that we might need others to take shifts to manage his pain. I'm going to stay.*

He didn't question his mate when she turned his hand loose and joined the others to help with Jake's pain. He merely nodded and left all of them to do what they did best.

As he walked back toward the main chamber, his thoughts were spinning with the amazing talents his people had. Jake had been suffering excruciating pain, but now he slept as their healers repaired his damaged body from the inside out.

Packmates shared his pain, suffering with him so that, shared, it became bearable. All of them—every known Chanku—had gathered here in Montana because they knew Anton might need them in his search for Lily, yet they'd already planned to be here for the birth of Adam and Liana's third child.

Again, to help one of their own. To share her pain as

well as the joy of the entire pack in welcoming a new member.

He'd eavesdropped shamelessly throughout the week, listening to all of them talking among themselves—agreeing that moving here, accepting his leadership for the chance to be together as a family, as a single pack, was worth whatever inconvenience it might mean to any one of them. Each of these people—his people—saw and recognized the importance of family.

A family that had continued to grow and prosper over the past eight years—ever since the night Stefan had rescued Xandi in a raging blizzard, and weeks later, when both of them had rescued Anton from his own, lonely hell.

And, he thought, *Keisha has saved us all.*

She was his heart, and the heart of a strong and powerful family facing its biggest crisis in the days and weeks ahead.

It wasn't merely the loss of his house that worried him. No, it was the growing clamor from human populations across the globe.

Everyone wanted to know more about the shapeshifting Chanku. The White House had put the reporters off for now, delaying the release of information while Nick ostensibly healed from his injuries. They couldn't keep using that excuse forever.

Anton had to believe the time was right for this to happen. All of them were together, and, as Eve had reminded him mere days ago, together they were stronger. Somehow they must figure out a way to explain their existence. To describe their amazing abilities without sending fear throughout the world over a heretofore unknown alien population existing among humans.

A population that had been here first, long before humans had walked the Earth. Now, that would make it difficult for anyone who might want to kick them off the planet!

He stepped into the main chamber. It was quiet now. The babies and children slept. Exhausted, most of the adults had found their pallets and were taking advantage of a chance to rest. Tomorrow loomed with unknown challenges, but dawn was many hours away.

Anton glanced into the shadows. Nick and Beth were curled up asleep beside Matt, Deacon, Daci, and Jazzy Blue. The link the kids had forged on the streets of San Francisco held strong and true, all these years later.

His heart went out to Nick.

No matter what Anton had said to help lift the burden, the young man carried the weight of their newfound celebrity squarely on his shoulders. Before they dealt publicly with the world, he hoped to figure out a way to take some of that weight from Nick, make him realize he'd actually done a good thing for all of them.

Somehow, they'd have to deal with the fallout in a manner that would protect the pack and offer all of them a future without fear. He walked across the shadowed chamber to check on the children. Gabe and Mac slept on either side of baby Lucia's small portable crib, protecting their infant sister. Lily slept at their heads with her body curled around her three siblings.

No wonder they idolized their elder sister—they relied on the knowledge she would do anything to keep them safe. Stefan's three were close beside Anton's little group. In sleep, Alex looked like an angel—proof that appearances could be deceiving. And even in sleep, four-year-old Amber held on to Ariel's hand, assuring that the toddler wouldn't toddle away.

Anton stood there, hands shoved in his pockets, head bowed, watching them sleep. He took great peace in their innocent faces, in the connection his children felt to their siblings and to the other children within the pack—a connection he'd never known as a child. It gave him hope, knowing their children would grow to adulthood fully aware of their heritage. Even more important, they would grow up knowing they were loved.

He could think of no better legacy to give them.

He yawned and checked his watch. It was only a little after one, though it felt much later. He had to get some sleep in case he was needed to relieve the ones helping with Jake's pain. He sent the thought out, that everyone be prepared should Keisha call on them. Soft murmurs in his mind told him they were ready.

Quietly he searched the darkened cavern for the pallet Keisha had pointed out as theirs, but as he moved carefully among his sleeping packmates, he noticed a familiar figure sitting alone in the shadows on the far side of the pond, close to the astral gateway. He skirted the far end of the natural pool and knelt beside Liana. She turned and smiled at him.

Quietly, she whispered, "Anton. Hello. I thought you'd be asleep by now."

"Liana? Is something wrong?"

She leaned against him and sighed. "My timing sucks. My water broke. Contractions haven't really started, but I imagine I'll be going into labor pretty soon. I didn't want to bother anyone yet. Everyone's so exhausted."

He turned, sat beside her, and leaned against the wall. "I'll keep you company," he said. "Adam's doing an amazing job healing Jake, so I imagine he'll be busy for a while."

She leaned her head against his shoulder. "I know. I'm blocking him. He thinks I'm sleeping. I don't want him to worry about me. From past experience, I know this could go on for a long time. Jace took over thirteen hours."

"Your labor with Eve Elizabeth was really short, though as Keisha always reminds me, don't borrow trouble. Rest while you can." He wrapped an arm around her shoulders and felt her tension ease as she allowed herself to relax.

He closed his eyes as well, thinking of the woman beside him, of the way things seemed to come full circle. So many years ago, she'd been their Goddess—a vain and self-serving immortal who'd not only lost track of her ultimate duty to protect her people, she'd lost the ones she'd been charged with protecting.

She'd brought Anton to her for sex—nothing more than sex to recharge her waning powers—but she'd discovered that he was different. He was Chanku. One of those she'd lost.

He quickly became her link to rediscovering others of their kind. Liana's transformation had mirrored Anton's. As he'd learned more about himself and his heritage, she'd helped manipulate lives and events so that more and more Chanku were brought together. Of course, she'd done it more to avoid the wrath of the Mother who watched over all of them, but without Liana's help, the pack as it was today would not exist.

Now Liana was mortal—or as mortal as Chanku could be—carrying Adam's third child. She'd found her place in a world where she truly belonged, while Eve, Adam's first bonded mate, watched over them as the goddess they should have had from the beginning.

And here he sat, while his wife helped heal a packmate, while their children slept, while their house burned. He'd not allowed himself to think about that at all—not since shutting the kitchen door behind him. It was a huge place, though, with a heavy slate roof and solid construction.

It would take many, many hours to burn.

He tightened his hold on Liana, sent a prayer to Eve that he hoped she could come up with a plan for all of them.

The corner of his mouth quirked up, totally involuntarily.

The guys had teased him for years about his plans. The running joke had quickly become "Anton's got a plan," generally followed by a hearty curse.

Not this time. He had no idea what they'd do next. No idea at all. In a way, it was almost a relief to turn his worries over to Eve, close his eyes, and drift into sleep.

Chapter 22

A little girl slipping onto his lap jolted Anton out of a sound sleep. Blinking himself more fully awake, he felt Lily's small body snuggling close against him. Liana slept fitfully beside him, so he used what Lily called his "quiet voice."

What are you doing here, sweetie? I thought you were sleeping with the others.

He felt her sigh against him. *I was, Daddy, but we have work to do.*

We do? With Lily, one never knew. . . .

The Ancient Ones—that's what those men in the funny red robes told me to call them—gave me a very important job, and with everyone together, this is the perfect time to do it.

He was almost afraid to ask, but . . . *What is it, sweetheart? I will help in any way I can.*

I knew you would. I told them you would. She put her arms around him and hugged. Anton's eyes immediately welled with tears. She was home now. He had to relax. He was not going to lose his daughter. Never again.

I have all the memories about our ancestors. The Ancient Ones put them in me. There's a lot of stuff, and I don't understand all of it, but they said you would. I'm supposed to give them all to you, and you are supposed to give them to everyone else. Even the babies.

The babies? He almost laughed. Lily's sense of superiority must be a bit upset about that. She held herself far above anyone younger. But then, Lily'd been a child going on adulthood since the day she was born.

Before she was born, for that matter.

Yes, Daddy. Even the babies. Even Liana's little girl who isn't even borned yet. I think it's stupid, but the Ancient Ones said it was too important not to share with everyone.

Born. Not borned. The automatic correction slipped out before he even thought about it and he smiled against Lily's soft curls. Keisha and Xandi's influence was stronger than he thought. *If the Ancient Ones said it was important, it must be. What else did they tell you?*

She twisted around and sat on his lap, facing him. He looped one arm around her waist so she wouldn't tumble off his legs. *All kinds of things, like the place where they came from, and what it was like before there were other people on this planet. Did you know they saw dinosaurs?*

He'd never imagined such a thing. How long had the Chanku been on this world? He wondered if, during that time, they'd evolved. Were they the same people who had landed here so long ago? He tried to remember the monks—the Ancient Ones—he'd met so long ago. They hadn't struck him as unusual in any way. Slightly built, more along Oliver's lines than his own, but typical human men. *Dinosaurs? I wish I could have seen them.*

You can, Daddy. They're in my memories. All you have to do is open your mind to me and let me share them. The Ancient Ones said I'd do a better job if I'm asleep. This would be a really good time, because I'm very tired. She yawned and curled up against him again, a warm and trusting little bundle holding the history of an entire race of people beneath those dark brown curls.

The idea boggled the mind. He glanced at Liana. She slept soundly now, her body slowly readying for the birth of her daughter. He cast his thoughts out and realized Jake slept, as did the ones who'd been taking his pain. Keisha was with their little ones—she knew Lily was with Anton, knew Anton sat with Liana. All was well.

He wondered how long it would take. Wondered how many secrets he would finally learn.

Wondered if he was truly ready for so much information—he, who had craved knowledge his entire life. *Go to sleep, sweetheart, but be sure to leave your barriers down. I'll see if I can get all those memories tonight, while it's quiet and everyone is asleep.*

G'night, Daddy. I love you.

I love you, too, Lily. Holding her close against his chest, he blinked back tears, thinking of the long days and nights when he'd thought she was lost. Then he opened his thoughts and reached into Lily's amazing mind.

The moment he connected, he felt the pull, as if a great whirlpool sucked him down. His first instinct was to resist, but then he realized that was exactly why they'd chosen a child for this momentous duty. Lily would have opened to them with the trust of the innocent.

But was their intent entirely innocent? He'd not even questioned if there might be danger involved. He'd taken Eve's word, but what if she was wrong?

It was too late. He'd have to trust in the wisdom of their Goddess, in the goodness of the Mother. Caught in the swirling maelstrom of Lily's mind, he forced himself to let go of the struggle, felt his consciousness fading, his thoughts swirling, spinning, melding with the minds of people who'd existed for millions of years.

And then, as if he fully existed in another time and place, Anton stepped out onto the lush and fertile ground of a world long dead, among people who had been gone for millennia. He walked on the world of his ancestors, the birthplace of Chanku.

Sunny rose to all four legs and shook the sand out of her thick coat. Igmutaka slept beside her, a long, tawny cougar with paws the size of dinner plates. The lantern still burned, though much of the cavern they'd taken refuge in was lost in shadow.

She followed the sound of running water and found a small pool. It smelled perfectly fresh, though it wasn't as cold as she'd hoped. Still, her throat was dry and she took a long drink, lapping the water up with her tongue. She'd been drinking for a few seconds before she realized exactly what she was doing—drinking water in her wolven form.

Another first, but then the last hours had been one first after another. First time to shift and walk on four legs, to shift back and walk on two. First meal at a table with other people, first run in the forest.

First orgasm. She sat back on her haunches, gazed across the shadowy cave, and watched the cougar sleep. First orgasm, second, third . . . How many times had Igmutaka brought her to climax in the hours they'd made love?

She felt no residual soreness as a wolf, but imagined she was going to be tender when she switched back. Even so, she wanted more. Her body thrummed with need, even in this form, though she knew they'd not have sex as wolves. Playing around as wolves, using tongues and teeth and cold, wet noses . . . now, that was one thing, but sex with another wolf was serious business.

It didn't get much more serious than the mating bond. No way in hell was she ready for that kind of commitment, not when she finally had a body that moved on four legs or two, and a voice that worked. This freedom was much too exhilarating, whether as a wolf or a woman. To have a body that actually did what she wanted—amazing. It was absolutely amazing.

Ig raised his broad head and stared at her with eyes made demonic in the lantern's reflection. *Is everything okay?*

I was thirsty. The water's not as cold as I hoped, but it tastes good.

These mountains have many hot springs. One must feed this particular cavern. Not so good for drinking, wonderful for bathing.

I don't think I want wet fur. Sounds uncomfortable.

Wet skin sounds sexy.

She hadn't thought of that. Now that he'd put the idea in her mind, however . . . *Shouldn't we go back to the others?*

They're all sleeping. I searched and found no waking minds, though Anton's seems busy. I can't read him, but I don't know that the man is ever totally at rest.

You love him, don't you? She knew he'd been with Adam and Liana as their lover, but there was a certain inflection to Igmutaka's voice when he spoke of the pack's über alpha that made her suspect there was more going on than she'd first assumed. Of course, Adam as much as said they were all intimately acquainted, that sex among packmates was not only accepted, it was expected. She figured she'd get used to the idea at some point—now it was more a fascination than a reality.

The cougar dipped his head, acknowledging her assumption. *It's impossible not to love Anton. Sometimes it's impossible not to hate him, either. He's a man of many sides, many desires. He's pragmatic and spiritual, sensual and practical. The first time he saw me as a human, do you know what he did?*

Mesmerized by the powerful sense of respect in Igmutaka's voice, Sunny slowly shook her head.

I walked into his kitchen early in the morning, long before anyone else was awake. My first morning as a human. He'd never seen me before. He looked up from his laptop computer, smiled, and said good morning to me. Then he poured me a cup of coffee, offered me a seat at the kitchen table, and asked how it felt to walk on two legs instead of four. Never once did he question my right to be there or ask who I was.

He knew who you were? How?

I have no idea. He might have been in my mind even then. His power appears absolute, at times, but what makes all of us love him the way we do is that he is very much, at heart, a simple man. He's not perfect. He makes mistakes. When he succeeds, he does it with great modesty, when he fails—Ig's chuffing snort had to be laughter—*when he fails, he does it magnificently.*

I don't really feel as if I know him very well. He'd been really nice to her. He'd welcomed her so graciously into his home and pack, but it had not been a week conducive to long conversations with people, not with so many things happening.

You will grow to love him as we all do . . . when you're not thinking of ways to murder him.

She blinked. What did Ig just say?

I was only teasing, sweet one. Now shift. I want to bathe with you in that clear spring, and then I want to make love to you once again before we return to the others.

You do? She shifted, amazed once again by the ease of the change, the fact there was no pain in the process of morphing from wolf to girl.

"Not a girl." Ig stood in front of her and palmed her breasts. His bronzed hands were almost red against her fair skin. Both of them studied the contrast. Her nipples peaked and he gently brushed his thumbs over their hard tips. She felt his touch arc from her breasts to that needy spot between her legs, a spike of heat that manifested in an involuntary clenching of her sex and a hot spill of fluids that wet her inner thighs.

He drew in a deep breath. Sunny wondered if he could smell that rush of fluid. If he smelled her arousal.

"When you first arrived, I though you were a child," he said. "I saw you as a young girl, still trapped in your chair. Now that I've seen you naked and watched your face when you come . . ." He shook his head, leaned over, and ran his tongue over her nipples. First one, then the other. "There is no doubt in my mind you are a woman."

He swept her up in his arms as if she didn't weigh anything at all. When he kissed her, she sort of melted into the sensation of his soft lips moving over hers, the tip of his tongue tracing the seam between. When she opened to him, touching her tongue to his, learning of all the things she could do to raise the level of their arousal and the strength of this amazing need already building in her center, she felt as if her world was finally complete.

He stepped into the clear water and waded out to the center where it was deepest. It rippled around his chest, which meant she'd not be able to touch the bottom. It didn't matter. He turned her and she wrapped her legs around his waist. His thick cock pressed against her sex, but she was already pliant and soft, her body ready.

It took only a simple thrust of his hips to gain entrance.

She wriggled against him, sighing with the sense of fullness, the slow stretch and glide as he filled her. Once he was entirely buried inside, he stood perfectly still, holding her steady as he kissed her. One big hand was under her bottom, the other on her back.

She tilted her hips, thrusting against him, pushing him deep, sliding down his thick shaft, then lifting up and away. He moaned against her mouth, and she did it again. There was power here—power in the control she'd suddenly taken, power in the clench of her tight vaginal muscles around his huge cock.

He'd teased her with the words earlier, when she'd hesitated to use what her foster mother had told the other kids were bad words. *Cunt* and *pussy, cock* and *balls* and *fuck*—those were all things the children had never been allowed to say, or, in Sunny's case, write. They were "dirty" words.

Except they didn't sound dirty spilling from Igmutaka's lips. Not when he gazed at her with those gorgeous green eyes and said he wanted to lick her pussy and make her come. Not when he'd begged her to put her lips on his cock and she'd discovered just how much of that huge thing she could get in her mouth—and how quickly she'd learned to love the taste.

Now he was doing something else she'd not experienced. His fingers traced the crease between her bottom cheeks, teasing over her anus. She never dreamed that could be so sensitive!

She clenched her vaginal muscles around his shaft and he pressed against her sphincter, setting off all kinds of shocks and unexpected feelings, needs she couldn't explain.

She tightened her legs around his waist and tilted her hips, taking him deep, opening herself to his fingers, pressing forward to take his erection, pressing back against that teasing fingertip.

When he finally broached the tight entrance, it was more of a relief than anything else. At first.

Then he timed the thrust of his finger to the rhythm she'd established. In and out, dragging against those oversensitized nerves until she knew she couldn't take much more. He added another finger, and then another, until she was going wild on him, her body thrashing, heart pounding, lungs chuffing with each harsh gasp for air.

He took over the thrusts, driving into her until the pool rippled and water sloshed over the edges, until her head was buzzing with the pleasure of so many nerves being stimulated, of so many taboos broken.

He drove deep, changing the pace so that his fingers went deep as his cock pushed up hard against her cervix, and for some reason, she opened her thoughts, opened her mind to the man in an intimate exchange they'd not done before.

And she was there, in Ig's mind, feeling the tight clasp of her pussy around his cock, the hot, tight channel that clenched his fingers. How he felt himself, sliding his fingertips over the thin sheath separating his fingers from his cock deep inside her body. Making that connection each time he filled her.

It was too much. Arching her back, she pressed forward with her hips, leaned back, and screamed. Her cry echoed off the walls and startled a small colony of bats in a nearby chamber. She heard their distant squeaks and the flutter of wings as they raced for an exit, but even the thought of bats couldn't distract her from the ripple of heat, the amazing sense of his cock pumping inside, spilling his seed deep within her body.

Sobbing, she clutched weakly at his shoulders even as he dipped down in the water and floated both of them to a narrow ledge. He sat there with Sunny curled in his lap and held her while she shivered and her tears fell.

So many new experiences. So much she'd not known this body could do, so much pleasure she didn't know if she could bear it, didn't know if she could bear to be without it.

She'd only been with this one man. Had only been touched by him. She'd experienced rapture, a euphoric introduction to her own sensuality unlike anything she could have possibly imagined. She'd never even known to fantasize about some of the things they'd done. This had been one night she would never forget, no matter how many nights she might live.

"You may not forget tonight, sweet one, but you will have other nights filled with even more pleasure. Nights and experiences you can't even begin to imagine."

She shook her head. "How can it possibly get better?"

He laughed. Out loud, as though she'd just made the funniest joke of the year.

Frowning, she rubbed her face against his smooth, hard chest. "Why are you laughing at me? Did I say something stupid?"

"No. Only something innocent. You've had one night with one very average male. Imagine making love with Logan and Adam and maybe even Tia or one of the other women. Think of what three men could do for you, or a man and a woman with your pleasure as their goal. Imagine taking Stefan's cock in that tight little hole where my fingers were, while I fill your pussy and Nick and Beth suck your breasts."

She laughed, but it was definitely a strangled sound. "Is this the spirit guide equivalent of phone sex? Because I think you're going to make me climax just thinking about those things. Though I have to admit, I'm not so sure about putting anyone's cock where you had your fingers."

His laugh bounced her against his chest and set the water rippling around them. "You might be surprised what this body of yours can do. Things that might hurt a human woman will only bring you pleasure. Remember, sweet one. You are Chanku." He tipped her chin up with his fingertips and gently kissed her.

"You were a virgin just a few hours ago. Your body had never been violated in any way, your innocence had never been tested. I've torn through that small membrane that signified your innocence for all these years. We've made love too many times to count. A human woman wouldn't let me near her right now, and yet I can feel your arousal, I sense your body growing ripe. You are ready for me. Again."

He laughed. "Just as I am ready for you. Ah, Sunny . . . what you do to me." He slipped his hand between them and ran a finger over her swollen vaginal lips. Her muscles clenched around him. Her first thought made her want to laugh, that if she'd still thought of herself as human, she'd be embarrassed by her immediate reaction to his touch.

Except she wasn't human. She was something totally different. A creature ruled by her powerful libido. A woman who could become a wolf. And, as she'd proved to Igmutaka only hours ago, not only a wolf but an alpha bitch.

Who'd have thought she had that kind of attitude? She snorted and covered her mouth, and her gaze snapped to Ig's, to the twinkle in his eyes. She let it go, bursting into laughter for the pure joy of the moment. For the wonder of feeling, for all the myriad sensations coursing through a body that had never been able to experience any feelings at all.

He'd made it happen. This man with the patience of a saint and equipment worthy of the devil himself. Sunny's laughter ended on a sigh. She touched her forehead to his.

"Ig? Thank you. For this night, for this moment, for everything. I will treasure every memory of every single thing we've done." Once again she straddled his hips. He didn't complain a bit when she lowered herself, sliding carefully over the full length of his shaft.

She'd think about that other stuff another time, about sex with more than one partner, with another woman, with other men. Right now it was just the two of them—Sunny Daye and Igmutaka—and an almost mystical pool in an even more mystical cave. Reality could wait. She'd lived harsh reality for almost twenty years. It was time to enjoy her fantasy, if only for a little while longer.

Chapter 23

Something startled him awake, some nebulous uneasiness he couldn't identify. Adam raised his head from the pallet next to Jake's and stared through the gloom, but everything looked as normal as it possibly could, considering the circumstances. He'd sent Logan off to get some much-needed sleep, but they'd decided at least one of them should remain close to Jake until he was entirely stable.

Adam focused on his patient. Jake lay on his belly, his body surprisingly relaxed. His back and shoulder were covered with new, pink skin, something that amazed Adam. When he'd first seen Jake's back, the skin was burned away, even muscle and tendons badly charred.

At the time, Logan had exchanged a less-than-encouraging look with Adam—neither of them thought they'd be able to repair the damage. Jake's burns had been so horrible—deep and ugly, beyond anything either healer had dealt with before—but they'd gone in with the idea of fixing as much as they could.

After so many years working together on various members of the pack, he and Logan had developed an unexpected, almost preternatural symbiosis—an ability to function as a single unit, drawing on one another for strength. Often Liana joined them, but her advanced pregnancy made that feel a little too risky, so it had been just the two of them—and wounds unlike anything either man had ever experienced.

With the help of an ever-changing team of packmates selflessly handling Jake's pain, they'd achieved more than they'd dreamed possible.

He'd been horribly disfigured with burns that could have killed an average man. Now, though, he slept soundly. Shannon lay beside Jake on the mattress where they'd moved him, holding tightly to his hand even in sleep. All seemed perfectly okay . . . so what had awakened him?

Sitting up, he realized Shannon watched him with eyes half open. *Is anything wrong? Do you need any help?*

He shook his head. *No. You must be exhausted. Go back to sleep, but call if you need me, if Jake feels pain when he wakes up. I'm going to check on Liana.*

Shannon nodded and closed her eyes. Adam slipped on a pair of sweats and padded silently to the tunnel leading to the main cavern. All was quiet. Even the babies slept soundly.

Battery-powered lamps burned low, throwing just enough light to keep him from tripping over anyone. He detoured to the small cavern set aside as a privy, used the rather rudimentary facilities, and washed his hands and face in a clear waterfall that dropped from the level above into a shallow pool. Feeling more alert now, he cast his thoughts about for Liana.

She was either sleeping soundly or blocking him. Knowing his hardheaded wife, he was almost positive she blocked him.

Which made him equally certain she was in labor.

The last time she'd contacted him, he'd sensed she was being evasive, but he was just getting ready to start working on Jake, and they'd kept their communication brief. Now, though, he wondered at the sense that maybe she wasn't telling him everything that was going on. Sometimes he got so caught up in a project—in this case, healing Jake—that everything else was pushed to the side.

Had he inadvertently pushed his mate aside when she needed him every bit as much as Jake? Shit. He could be such an ass.

His anxiety spiked. Where the hell was Liana? He splashed more water over his tangled hair and finger-combed it back from his face. Then he reentered the main cavern and checked the pallet where their children slept soundly.

Liana'd chosen a spot near a wall beside Mei and Oliver in case she went into labor and they needed someone close to keep an eye on Eve Elizabeth and Jace—all the kids slept together in a tangle of arms and legs, teddy bears, favorite blankies and dolls. Mei and Oliver's four-year-old Leo blocked nine-month-old Emeline on one side while three-year-old Jace fenced her in on the other. Eve Elizabeth had taken up her spot at the foot of the bed, acting as the gateway to keep Emeline corralled against the cavern wall.

Now that she was walking, everyone had taken up "Emeline patrol." Adam stood there a moment, watching the kids. They grew so damned fast, and his two were getting easier by the day—yet he and Liana were doing it again. So why did the thought of a new baby in the pack—his new baby—make him smile like an idiot?

Never in his wildest dreams had Adam ever imagined being a father. But then he'd never imagined life with a woman like Liana. She completed something in him that had always been missing, even when he'd been mated to Eve.

Funny, how things turned out. His first mate now their Goddess, their first Goddess now his mate. How the hell had he ever gotten so lucky? Why had two such amazing women chosen him?

And where the hell was Liana? He yawned and gazed about the shadowed cavern, but there was no sign of her. Anton, for some reason, slept on the far side of the pond with Lily curled up beside him, but they looked like they were sound asleep, and he didn't see any point in disturbing them.

He wandered past all the sprawled, sleeping bodies, but Liana wasn't anywhere in the main cavern. He glanced once again at Anton and Lily—Anton always knew how to find everyone whether they were blocking him or not. Before he could make up his mind whether or not to intrude, he noticed a dim light coming from a tunnel leading to one of the smaller chambers.

Sending out a quest for his mate, he headed toward the tunnel. His anxiety grew the closer he got—the sense that all was not well. By the time he reached the tunnel he was running. He ducked to get through the opening and raced down the short, narrow passage that quickly opened up into a small chamber. A candle burned on a stone ledge against one wall.

Liana knelt in the center, wearing a nightgown but bent over on hands and knees, lungs heaving, panting her way through what had to be a serious contraction. So intent was she on her labor, she didn't appear to notice he'd entered the chamber.

Adam was positive his heart stopped beating as he slid to his knees beside her and grabbed her shoulders. "What the fuck are you doing in here? Why didn't you call me?"

She gasped for air, took another deep breath, slowly expelled it, and glared at him when the contraction finally ended. "Don't curse at me, Adam Wolf. You were busy with Jake. He needs you. I'm okay. I've done this before."

"Not by yourself, you haven't. Damn it, Liana." His voice broke on her name. He sat back on his butt on the dirt floor and drew her into his arms. "I love you. We got you pregnant together, we have this baby together. Don't lock me out."

"I'm sorry." She took a couple of deep breaths. "My water broke about the time they brought Jake in. I knew he needed you and it would be hours before I went into serious labor. I didn't want to distract you."

"This is our baby. You are my wife. You're supposed to distract me for things like this." Damn. His heart thudded against his ribs. He wasn't sure if he wanted to cry or curse.

She leaned her head against his chest. "Adam, I'm so sorry. All I could think of was that I didn't want to worry you. I guess I didn't think. How's Jake?"

Adam pulled her closer. His heart rate finally settled down to some semblance of normal. "Jake is fine. I think Logan and I repaired the damage enough that he won't even have much scarring. He's sleeping comfortably now." He sighed and hugged her closer. "I've been sleeping, too. While you've been in here doing this all by yourself, I've been asleep. I'm the one who's sorry." He kissed the top of her head. "How far apart are your contractions?"

"Between five and eight minutes. Please, don't feel bad. If you'll recall, I stayed this way for hours with Jace." She nuzzled his neck and her arms went around his waist.

"You had others helping you with the pain. There's no need to hurt, sweetheart."

She shook her head slowly against his chest. "Everyone's exhausted. The children are frightened by the fire. Mei's watching ours, but I can't ask anyone to leave their kids. It's all been too traumatic." Her breath sort of jerked and her body tensed.

"Stop blocking me." Adam cupped her face in his hands and forced her to look at him. "I can't help you if you block me. Let me in."

She nodded and immediately began to pant.

Adam's mind flooded with pain, with the tightening of

her womb, the powerful clench of muscle, and he did as he'd watched the women do for one another—he took her pain into himself. Bit back a startled cry as agony coursed from his belly to his balls, as his muscles cramped and strained under unfamiliar impulses.

Liana's breathing evened out and she gazed at him, wide-eyed. "Adam, no." She touched his face as he worked through the pain of her contraction and then took a deep, shuddering breath.

"You don't have to do that. I've heard it's harder for men—you don't have a womb to transfer the pain, so it affects nerves that aren't equipped to handle it. I'll be okay. Women have been doing this for millions of years."

"You're not doing this by yourself. And that was no five to eight minutes. More like two. Do you have any blankets in here, anything clean to lie on? I want to examine you."

"That bag has blankets and some towels." She wouldn't look his way.

He stared at her. Felt anger boiling just beneath the surface. "You were planning to go through delivery by yourself? Risk your life and our child's? Liana, why?"

"What did you expect me to do?"

She was crying, damn it all. He didn't want to make her cry.

Sobbing harder, she said, "Jake needed you. He was dying. I may not be a goddess anymore, but I can feel when someone's life force is fading, and his was almost gone. Adam, I will be okay. The baby is strong, I'm strong. If I needed help, I could call anyone to me and they would come. But I couldn't call you. Not then. Jake needed you more."

He bowed his head and held her close. "You can always call me, Liana. I'm your mate. Your husband. The father of this baby. I need you to call me." He looked at her, gently cupped her face, used his thumbs to brush away the tears, and forced her to look at him. "I need for you to need me as much as I need you. I love you so much it hurts. I know I don't say it enough, and I probably don't show you often enough, but I love you. I will always need you."

"I know." She cupped his cheek with her hand. "I love you. I . . . oh . . . oh, Adam." Her eyes went wide. "You'd better get that blanket ready. Now!"

Anton stirred, vaguely aware of cramped muscles and a dull thudding pain in his head. He lay there, propped uncomfortably against the cavern wall, and catalogued the sensations—the headache, the sense of many bodies around him, the warmth of Lily sleeping beside him.

His mind was filled with something, but he didn't understand what he was thinking. There was a sense he needed to sort through something, but he wasn't certain what.

A soft cry caught his attention. He cast out his thoughts in spite of the pain in his skull and heard a long, low moan. Liana? Getting carefully to his feet, he leaned over and picked up his sleeping daughter. Walking quietly around the edge of the pond, he carried her back to the pallet where Mac, Gabe, and Lucia slept beside their mother.

Keisha blinked sleepily and gazed up at him. *Why are you carrying Lily? Is she okay?*

He knelt beside her and laid the little girl down beside her brothers and sister. *She's fine. I was sitting with Liana and Lily joined us. Go back to sleep. It's barely three in the morning. I'll call if Liana needs you. Her water broke a few hours ago.*

Okay. I'll get what sleep I can. Helping Adam and Logan with Jake took a lot out of me. Keisha smoothed Lily's hair back from her face and lay back on her pallet. Anton stood and searched for the source of the cry he'd heard, then strode quickly across the chamber to one of the smaller rooms.

He moved quickly down the narrow passage, following the dim glow of light. Adam knelt in the middle of the small chamber, barely visible in the light from a single candle. Liana lay on her back, knees raised, fingers twisting the blanket beneath her as she obviously labored.

"Good Goddess, Liana! Adam? Is everything okay?"

Adam didn't answer, but he nodded as Liana cried out. The soft sound belied the pain she must be in. Anton linked, reached for her pain—and cursed as it brought him to his knees.

"Thank you." It hardly sounded like Liana. Harsh breaths exploded as another contraction tightened her body.

Anton felt it grab hold of his middle and squeeze. The power of her pain, the shock of how much she endured shattered his concentration. Clamping down on his thoughts, he took what he could and pulled in even more, holding Liana's agony close as she struggled to push her baby into the world.

The coppery smell of blood was strong, the sour stink of sweat and fear, but Anton recognized Adam's fear for what it was. His wife was in pain, his child not yet born, and he held the terrible responsibility for their lives in his hands.

Only Liana seemed calm. Linked entirely with her, Anton carefully compartmentalized the excruciating pain and allowed himself this amazing opportunity to take an objective view of the entire birthing process.

He'd never entered a woman's mind while she labored. Other than connecting with Keisha on a rudimentary level, he'd done his duty as a male and stayed the hell out of the way while the women gathered and did their thing.

Liana needed him right now. It was just the three of

them—Adam, Liana, and Anton. Each of them had a job to do . . . but would it hurt anything if he took his job a bit further and experienced this amazing process?

With her pain controlled by Anton, with Adam ready to catch their daughter, Liana let out a huge sigh. "Thank you, Anton. I feel like I can finally concentrate on what I'm supposed to be doing."

She touched his hand and smiled at him, and Anton thought she had never looked as beautiful as she did at this moment, with her blond hair darkened with perspiration and her face drawn from exhaustion. Even as a goddess, she'd not glowed with this ethereal beauty nor projected such a powerful sense of purpose.

"Get behind me, Anton. Please? Hold me up so I can push."

He scrambled around behind Liana and raised her shoulders, clasping both her hands in his. Focused solely on holding her pain at bay, he sent it to another place, somewhere else in his mind where it wouldn't distract either of them from this miracle. Then, without any sense of shame at all, he slipped into an alternate reality, one in which he became Liana.

One that allowed him to celebrate firsthand this miracle of a new life.

Once again her body contracted and a sense of peace filled him, filled Liana. Included Adam in a warm cocoon of love and safety. Oblivious to his surroundings, Anton felt every muscle, every breath, every beat of Liana's heart, yet all was muted.

The act of pushing a baby from her womb took on a mystical quality, a timeless effort of heart, mind, and soul, of many minds, many souls. Many hearts, all beating as one, all working toward this amazing act of birth, this show of maternal courage.

He would never, ever grow tired of this—of the birth of a new member of their pack. Her contraction eased and

Liana took a moment to take deep, steady breaths. Pulling himself out of the self-absorption of sharing Liana's experience, Anton focused on her mate. Adam's face was a study in fierce love and tangible fear. He'd assisted Logan in the delivery of almost every single child, yet this was his mate, his child.

The risk was entirely personal, the love and fear profound.

And yet the fear lifted. The pain subsided. Liana cried out; Anton tightened his grasp on her hands and whispered encouraging words. His eyes never left her face—there was something so amazingly beautiful in the struggle to give birth, from the lines of strain bracketing her mouth to the veins standing out, stark and defined across her forehead as she labored to push the child free.

Yet he felt no pain. He was pulling her pain to him, but there was none to take. He was aware of her straining muscles, her laboring heart and lungs. He felt the fullness of the baby's body sliding through the birth canal from womb to world, and yet, even as he experienced the act of giving birth through the link with Liana, there was no pain.

She gave a final, powerful push. Her hands clamped down on his so hard he felt the bones shift in his fingers, but he steadied her, gave her the solid strength of his body for leverage as Adam let out a shout—a sound of joy, of relief. Liana sighed, and their daughter opened her mouth and announced her presence to the world.

Anton closed his eyes against the unexpected rush of his tears, leaned down, and kissed Liana's forehead. "Beautiful. Absolutely beautiful."

"She is, isn't she?" Filled with awe at her own creation, Liana barely raised her voice above a whisper. Adam carefully laid their daughter on her mother. Logan shoved a scalpel into his hands.

Adam's head shot up. "When did you get here?"

Logan laughed. "A few minutes ago. You didn't think you guys were going to do this on your own, did you?"

Anton raised his head and laughed. The room was filled with members of the pack. Not everyone, but at least a dozen had squeezed into the small space. "No wonder the pain went away. Were all of you . . . ?"

Mei knelt beside Liana. "I can't believe you weren't going to tell us. Oliver's with the kids—they're still sleeping, but if Anton hadn't called out, we would have missed this." She laughed and kissed Liana's cheek. "And I never, ever would have forgiven you!"

Liana tilted her head and frowned at Anton. "When did you call them?"

He shrugged. "I don't know. Mei, what did you hear?"

Mei and the others looked at one another. Giggles started in one corner and spread from smile to smile, until everyone was laughing. "I think it was something along the lines of, 'son of a bitch, that hurts!' " She nudged Millie standing beside her. "Is that what you heard, Millie?"

Nodding sagely, Millie agreed. "It was about the time Anton decided to shoulder Liana's labor pain."

Tinker pushed through the crowd and reached for Anton's hand. "Put 'er there, boss. It takes a real man to help a woman in labor. Believe me, I know."

Grinning broadly, too jubilant to be embarrassed, Anton shook Tinker's hand.

Adam finished clamping his daughter's umbilical cord and moved aside so that Logan could finish up with Liana. Then he kissed his wife and stared silently at their little girl, who was already rooting at her mother's breast. "You're right, Tink. I tried it and didn't last very long. Hurts like hell. Damn, Liana. You are amazing . . . and you're absolutely beautiful."

Anton gently shoved a pillow beneath her head and moved out of the way. The rest of the pack members quietly filed out of the chamber behind him. It was time to give the new parents a few moments alone with their daughter.

And though it was still too damned early, probably time to think about facing the new day and the changes in their lives. He watched as everyone quietly returned to their personal space within the large cavern. He didn't know why he was so surprised to see them settling back down for a few more hours of rest.

Everyone was exhausted, both physically and emotionally. He certainly couldn't begrudge anyone time to catch up on sleep. There was nothing they could do until the sun came up. That would be soon enough to face what waited for them above ground.

He stood there for a moment, unsure what to do next. He was way too wound up to sleep with an excess of adrenaline still coursing through his body, his mind spinning and going nowhere fast.

But damn it all . . . what now?

He shook off the odd sense of depression and wandered in to check on Jake. It was quiet in the makeshift clinic, and Shannon and Jake slept soundly. Anton watched them for a while, thinking of the night past, the horrible fear they'd all felt for Jake. The pain he'd suffered, and yet his injuries were healed.

Incredible. Shaking his head in amazement, Anton went back into the main chamber. Keisha had gone back to sleep, and when he checked on Adam and Liana, they were sleeping together on their pallet with their new daughter between them.

He sat in a quiet corner, feeling unaccountably melancholy, watching over his pack. He was still sitting there when Igmutaka and Sunny crept in from one of the side passages. Smiling, he watched the spirit guide lead the young woman to an empty pallet, and the two of them lay down together.

Now, that could be interesting, especially since he knew

that Ig already felt connected to Tala and Mik's little Star. But, as with everything else, things would work out the way they were meant to.

Silence settled over the chamber, and for the first time, he thought of all that he'd learned tonight from Lily. Maybe that was the source of his odd anxiety. He couldn't wait to share his knowledge with the rest of the pack.

Why not now?

The voice in his head was so clear, he twisted his neck looking from one side to the other for the Goddess. She sounded as if she were standing right next to him. *Eve?*

Who else invades your waking dreams?

Her soft laughter teased his nerve endings.

I should have known you'd be here. Did you come for the birth? We have a new pack member. Adam and Liana just had a little girl.

I know. I was watching. Liana's such a wonderful mother. I'm glad you could share the experience.

It was . . . He thought about it a moment, the way Liana had labored to deliver her daughter. How it had felt to be there with her, a part of it. *It was magic. Pure magic.*

As are all of you. Sleep, Anton. Sleep and dream, and share your dreams with the others. Lily's given you everything, but it's not for you alone. The others need to know the truth of their legacy. It's meant to be shared. It must be shared.

He thought of all the information that filled his mind— a history of their kind he'd not even begun to assimilate. So much to try to make sense of. *But what of the children? Are they ready for so much information? I don't want to confuse them.*

They'll only be aware of what they can understand. Sleep. Your body is exhausted, your mind needs a chance to understand what you've learned. It's time to share the burden, along with the knowledge.

With Eve's soft words, exhaustion swept over him, almost as if the last vestiges of adrenaline left his system all at once. He barely made it to the pallet where Keisha slept so soundly. Kicking off his shoes, he didn't even bother with his clothes. Morning was only a couple of hours away. A little sleep would do him good.

Eve was right. This was the perfect time to share what he'd learned. Now, while all was quiet, while they were here, all of them together under a single roof. Who knew what the new day would bring? What they would find outside when the sun rose?

He lay beside Keisha and the children. Gabe and Mac gravitated toward his warmth. Drifting in that dreamlike state between wakefulness and sleep, he felt his sons curling close against him like warm little puppies. As sleep claimed him, he remembered to open his thoughts. Remembered to connect with the other minds.

Strange, the sensation of linking with every mind here, older minds and younger, even to Adam and Liana's brand-new babe. He carefully organized his thoughts and set them free, aware on some level that each mind was unusually receptive, open and inviting. Every soul in the cavern welcomed him as he shared what he'd learned.

A thought filtered through, that it was sort of like sending a group e-mail. . . . Stefan would approve. Wasn't he always harping on Anton to sharpen his computer skills? He'd have to remember to tell Stef his perceptive analogy in the morning.

Sighing, smiling lazily, Anton's eyes drifted shut, and he let his dreams take flight.

Chapter 24

Mei, Oliver, and Jazzy Blue already had the long table at one end of the cavern loaded with fresh fruit, sliced ham, muffins, and scrambled eggs when Anton finally awakened. Groggy after sleeping so soundly, he wandered across the cavern past tangled bedding and a few still-sleeping bodies to the waterfall at the end of the pond, stuck his head under the spray, splashed more water on his face, and finger-combed his hair.

"Wondered when you were going to join the living."

Anton glanced up as Stefan handed him a soft towel. "Thanks. I didn't think to grab one."

"Figured as much. I wanted to let you know that Tinker and Luc went out at dawn to see what was left."

Anton dried his face and straightened up. "And?"

Stef shook his head. "A lot of the forest is still healthy. Looks like it rained some during the night. The fire's out, but the house is gone. Mei and Oliver's cottage burned to the ground, too." He shook his head. "Hell, Anton . . . not a single structure survived. Luc says it looks like Armageddon out there, though all the vehicles and even the chopper made it through unscathed, so at least we've got transportation. Luc contacted the authorities in town, let them know we were all okay. Said he's got some calls in to a few companies that handle RVs. Thought a few big motor homes or trailers might work best for everyone until we figure out what to do next."

Anton wanted to kick himself. He hadn't even thought of what they'd do for housing after the fire. It wasn't like they could stay underground—not with so many little ones. "Good. I'll get in touch with the contractor who built that addition to the house a couple of years ago for Adam and Liana. He did good work. We'll see about getting the house and cottage rebuilt."

Stefan nodded. "Might want to upgrade the plans. Everyone intends to stay." He grinned and raised his eyebrows.

"Everyone? Even after this?"

Stefan nodded again. "Especially after this. And after that little 'dream along with Anton' trip you took us on this morning."

It felt like someone had punched him in the gut. "You remember?"

Laughing, Stefan threw an arm over his shoulders and walked him toward the food and the scent of fresh coffee. "You think we're not going to be aware of a mental download of history that runs like a 3-D sci-fi movie? Good Goddess, man . . . what a rush! I lay there in bed for over an hour after I woke up this morning. Didn't want to get up and disturb the images that were flashing through my head."

Anton shot him a sheepish grin. "Pretty amazing, isn't it? And to think I got all of that out of Lily's hard little head." He chuckled softly. "Blows me away. I still haven't had a chance to think about what I've learned, to sort it all out. I remember setting foot on another planet, seeing people I knew in my dreams but have never seen in real life, but the rest . . ." He poured himself a cup of coffee and nodded to Jazzy as she added more eggs to the warmer. "Did you see the part explaining how we change? How we make the shift from human to wolf so fast that no one can see it?"

Stefan grabbed a plate and started to fill it with food. He tilted his head and grinned at Anton. "You mean that little tidbit about altering time and space? The fact that each time we shift, we manipulate time? Oh yeah, I saw it. I still don't believe it, but I saw it."

Anton stared at Stef's plate and decided it looked pretty good. He grabbed his own and began filling it. "Let's find a seat. I want to talk."

Stef's gaze went serious in a heartbeat. "So do I."

They found a quiet corner away from the growing activity as more of the pack awakened, as more children demanded breakfast. A baby cried, laughter broke out . . . typical morning sounds, with the addition of echoes from the cavern walls and the ever-present trickle of falling water.

"Stef, my biggest concern right now, even more than our housing situation, is how we're going to face the growing furor over our existence. How much of this history do we share?" Anton took a bite of eggs, glanced up, and caught Mei and Jazzy looking their way. He signaled that all was wonderful. The women laughed and went back to their self-imposed breakfast duty.

"As little as possible, as much as we have to." Stef leaned back against the rock wall. "You and I need to go public. Nick already has. Luc will have to as well, since Pack Dynamics will need to be part of this, but I think we're safer if we leave our actual numbers out of it."

"We have to mention Sunny—the fact we didn't know she was one of us. The fact that there could be others out there." Anton hadn't totally thought it through, but he still felt the need to find the others. To save them from lives like the one Sunny had been living. It was what the Ancient Ones wanted—he felt a powerful need to honor their final request.

"Sunny, yes, since she's part of Nick's story. But the rest? Not right away. Can you imagine the nuts that would come out of the woodwork if we did an open call for potential shapeshifters?"

Stef's laughter was too strained for Anton's peace of mind, though he had to agree. "Okay. We hold back on that. I think we need to do this all through official channels—offer DNA samples, maybe even physical exams, but only to a single medical team with the caveat that the information be made public. No secrets. The more open we are, the less chance of any conspiracy theories taking off and gaining credence."

"Good point. Oliver was right. The last thing we need is that Area 51 kind of notoriety." Stef sipped his coffee and stared across the cavern. "I have to agree with you, though. Even though it was unplanned, the way Nick outed us couldn't have been better. The government can't come in under cover of darkness and bundle us up and hide us away, though we're going to have to stay on our toes. There's always the chance they might try. Thing is, when Nick took us public, he did it in an indisputable manner."

Nodding in agreement, Anton said, "The government has no idea how many of us there are. Where we are. I think now that we're out, we need to stay out. We do the talk shows, we go on the nightly news for interviews, we do whatever we can to market ourselves as good citizens of the world." Anton saw Nick and Beth with their plates, walking away from the buffet table.

"Hey, Nick. You and Beth want to join us?"

Nick glanced up, said something to Beth, and they both headed toward Stefan and Anton.

"G'morning." Nick grinned at Anton. "I've been wanting to talk to you. I take it that dream we had this morning was courtesy of either you or Lily. Whoever the source, I want to thank you. Amazing."

Anton nodded his head. "I sent it, so the delivery was mine, but the info came via my most precocious daughter. Glad you liked it. Guys, I'm hoping to get everyone together later today and see what the general consensus is about our unexpected past. For now, though . . . you ready to help plot our coming-out party?"

Nick laughed as he scooted over to make room for Beth. "Personally, I think I've already 'come out,' as you so plainly put it, but as long as it doesn't require my dropping my pants on live TV, sure. Been there, done that."

"That you have," Anton said. He saluted Nick with his coffee cup. "You have definitely done that."

As the others awakened all about them, Igmutaka lay quietly on the pallet beside Sunny and tried to make sense of the amazing dream he'd had. This was obviously what Lily had gone in search of, this most unbelievable history of their kind. He glanced at the woman sleeping beside him and wondered how she was going to feel about the history she now owned—one she'd not known she was part of until just over a week ago.

He had always known. Oh, not the details, but he'd known the fact he was part of an ancient race, though he'd thought at first that his kind had always been cougars, or eagles, great horned owls, foxes, or wolves—they'd been skinwalkers and spirit guides, the creatures who guarded the native peoples in this half of the world.

Now it appeared his ancestors had been among the very first to leave their landing site in Tibet—they were the first among the Chanku to spread out across the world. And in their slow but steady migration around the Earth, they spread the first seeds of legend and the mythology of shapeshifters in almost every culture.

Now he knew that Chanku were the Norse berserkers who turned into wolves and bears during battle, the Mestaclocan of Mayan mythology who could change their appearance to those of the animals around them. They were Native American skinwalkers and Gypsy shapeshifters, the source of all werewolf legends, and the Japanese kitsune, or werefoxes. All of them Chanku. All of them making their homes in ancient lands long before humans walked the Earth. Becoming the things legends were made of, the stories that formed the mythology of cultures around the world.

These were his ancestors, and his was a proud tradition. A powerful tradition. One he would always honor.

"Ig? Are you awake?"

He turned to his right and gazed into Sunny's dark amber eyes. "I am. I'm thinking of the dream Anton gave us. Do you understand everything he's put in your mind?"

She nodded, her eyes still sleepy, her short hair spikier than usual. "I wondered if it was real. Our ancestors came from another world? Really?"

Ig sat up and crossed his legs. He'd donned a loincloth before entering the chamber, but Sunny struggled for a moment, adjusting and tying her sarong to cover herself. They'd made the journey through the dark caverns as wolves, traveling underground from the chamber where they'd made love to this one, where they were surrounded by children, by the other Chanku.

He missed the privacy of that far-away cavern. Waking up hard and needy beside a beautiful woman still discovering how much fun sex could be was not conducive to carrying on a calm conversation.

He would try. "It is all true. Much of it I knew as legend passed down by my own ancestors. I am many thousands of years old, and . . ." Sunny's eyes went so wide he stopped talking and grinned at her. "I take it you did not realize how old I was."

"Well, duh." She giggled. "How was I supposed to know? You look about twenty, if that."

"So do you." He smiled, leaned close, and kissed her.

"Actually, you look about twelve, but since you said you're almost twenty, I'll have to believe you."

"Thanks loads. C'mon. I'm hungry. I smell food."

He stood and pulled Sunny to her feet. Already she walked with more confidence, with more strength in her slender legs. He had a feeling she was going to need that strength. They hadn't been given their history on a whim. The Mother must know something was coming. As Ig followed Sunny to the long table laden with food, he had a good feeling it had something to do with this modern media and the fact the secret of their existence was out.

Knowledge was power. In the coming days, he figured they'd need all the power they could lay their hands on.

Luc, AJ, Mik, and Tinker sat with Tia, Lisa, and Tala. The kids played and tumbled while Lisa nursed eleven-month-old Ricky. Luc watched everyone for a moment and then finally asked the question that wouldn't leave him alone.

"So what do you think? We can go back to San Francisco and wait until Anton gets the house rebuilt with room for all of us, or we can go home, pack up and move back here, tough it out in RVs and trailers, but be closer to the pack. Remember, this is Montana. It gets damned cold in the winter, so this really has to be a group decision."

AJ and Mik both looked at Tala. As with all of them, it would be the woman's choice where they ended up. Her hand immediately covered her flat belly. At three months she wasn't showing yet, but Luc knew her pregnancy would help her decide.

"I think I'd rather be miserable and cold with pack than warm and comfortable without them." She blinked back tears and focused on each of them. "I love you guys, but I'll be honest. I'm scared. I know what it's like to be hunted." She grabbed Lisa's hand. "We all do, but the idea of being here with everyone else makes me a lot more comfortable. I can handle roughing it for as long as it takes, as long as we're together."

She laughed. "It's not just the fact that the whole world is going to be checking us out and all the nutcases are going to be after us now that we're public. It's the kids. Living here in such a beautiful, isolated area gives them a chance to grow up in the kind of country wolves or cougars or whatever they turn into need. It's not going to be all that long before they're shifting. I'd much rather they do it here than in downtown San Francisco."

Tia laughed. "I know. I can't stop thinking about that . . . all those worst-case scenarios. I'm already afraid to take the girls to the zoo. What if they see an animal and decide they want to be one?"

Tinker doubled over, laughing.

Tia punched his arm. "Okay, big guy. What's so funny?"

"Stay away from the elephant house. Shay and Cami would never fit in the car. You couldn't get 'em home."

"Funny boy. I'm with Tala, though. I'd rather rough it among packmates than be comfortable in our place in the Marina District and scared to death."

She sighed and Luc wrapped an arm around her. Two sets of twins, and Tia was still as gorgeous as the day he'd first seen her—all grown-up, coming down the escalator at the airport, looking over the sea of people in the baggage claims area in search of her father.

She'd never expected Luc, and not in his wildest dreams had he imagined how he'd feel about her, the once-skinny teenager he'd last seen. It felt like a lifetime ago.

"Lisa? What about you?"

Tinker's wife glanced at her sister and then at Tia. "No questions in my mind. I've missed the mountains ever since I left Colorado. I know Bay and Jake are planning to make the move west with their families, and I really miss big brother Baylor, so I'm all for it. What about you, Luc?

Can you run Pack Dynamics from Montana? If Millie and Ric move there, will it be a problem having Ric in the same place? I mean, he started the company. Will he get in your way?"

"It's a good point, Lisa. I can run PD from just about anywhere, and Ulrich and I have never had any alpha issues over how I do it. He trained me, so I think I operate the same way he did for years." He shrugged and hugged Tia close. "If it ain't broke, don't fix it, right?"

Tia kissed Luc's chin in obvious agreement. "Tinker?" She touched Tink's knee with her fingertips. His eyes snapped in her direction.

"What, sweetie?"

"You haven't said how you feel. Are you okay with leaving the city?"

Though he held tightly to Lisa's hand, Tinker's eyes rested steadily on Tia. He'd been up front with Luc about loving Tia from the very beginning, so many years ago. He would have wanted her as his mate if things had been different. Not that he didn't love Lisa, because he adored her.

That didn't mean he couldn't love Tia just as much, and it was there right now, in his dark eyes, in the serious smile on his face. There wasn't a hint of the teasing they always expected from Tinker. Not now.

"Wherever you and Luc go, wherever AJ, Mik, and Tala go, Lisa and I will be there with you. You don't even have to ask. San Francisco is just a place. Wherever this little pack is . . ." He sighed. "Well, that's where home is. That's where we'll be."

Mik slung an arm around Tinker's shoulders and hugged him close. "What he says. Right, AJ?"

Always the quiet one, AJ nodded. "We're family." His voice was soft, almost hesitant. "Wherever we go . . ." He shook his head. "Doesn't really matter. Not as long as we do it together. Not as long as we keep our families safe." His gaze fell on Tala. She was only three months pregnant, but they already knew she carried his daughter. He smiled at Tala and squeezed her hand. Then he sort of shook himself and turned to Luc. "Luc? How about you? You're our alpha. What do you want?"

He looked at AJ but couldn't speak. He hadn't expected to feel this way after merely asking such basic questions—where they wanted to live, where they preferred to run the business. Sometimes, the simplest things affected a guy the most.

Something as basic as choosing where to move reminded him of what was really important in his life. And it was all right here, with these people he loved. This pack of strong men and women who openly acknowledged him as their alpha.

They were his family. The only family he'd known for more years than he could count. He finally got his emotions under control and grinned at Tia. "Well, sweetie. It looks like we're moving to Montana."

Bay looped his arm around Manda while they sat with Liana and Adam. Liana nursed her newborn daughter and Manda fed Donovan, but Bay wasn't giving either their new niece or his son their due attention. No, his thoughts were in the other room with Jake, where Logan was once again checking the healing burns on his back before turning him loose.

Shannon was with Jake, but she'd been updating Bay on her mate's progress all morning long. Jake was damned lucky to be alive. Even luckier that he wouldn't be horribly disfigured or even maimed by the burns he'd gotten.

They'd come too damned close last night. Bay kept thinking how easily this could have happened in Maine, thousands of miles from Adam and Logan, the only ones capable of healing such horrific injuries. He thought how he and Jake had talked about making the move to Montana, but they'd not discussed details.

It was time for details. Time to get their butts in gear and sell the property in Maine. Time to make the move.

He glanced up as Millie and Ulrich wandered over with fresh cups of coffee and sat with them. Four-year-old Keegan clung to his Grampa Ric like a limpet while Jake and Shannon's triplets trailed along behind.

They'd been unusually quiet since their father's injury, though the entire pack had rallied around to keep them occupied and unafraid. That was another reason to make the move. Grandparents, packmates—the security of loving, caring friends and family. An amazing support system they all needed.

He glanced up and caught Adam smiling at him. "Admit it, Bay. You're gonna do it, aren't you? You're going to leave that gorgeous piece of Maine you and Jake guard like feudal lords and move to Montana, right?"

Baylor nodded, and caught Manda studying him. "It's up to Manda and Shannon, of course, but yeah. I'm ready. Jake's injury reminds me how vulnerable we are by ourselves. If you and Logan hadn't been here to help him . . ." He glanced to his right. All three of Jake and Shannon's four-year-olds hung on every word he was saying. He shut up and smiled at the kids. "I'm just really glad your daddy's okay."

He caught Shannon's soft mental comment and grinned at her kids. "Do you know where Daddy is? Where the clinic is?"

Two little redheaded, green-eyed girls and one amber-eyed blond boy who could have been Jake's clone nodded in unison.

"You can go see Daddy now. Mom just said so."

They scrambled and ran for the clinic. Manda laughed softly, but Bay noticed tears in her eyes. "You okay?"

She nodded. "I am." She reached for his hand and held on. "I know you and Jake have been hoping to stay in Maine, but it's time. The kids are loving being around so many others. I'm getting a chance to see my brother and sister-in-law . . . and the new baby." She leaned close and ran her fingers over the baby's soft cheek. Then she raised her head and smiled at Millie.

"Most of all, I've missed time with my mom." She shrugged and stared at little Donovan, who was almost asleep in her arms. "I think we're meant to live together, the way wolves do. In a pack, with all our children and our siblings. You'll have Lisa and Tala nearby, I'll have Adam and Mom. Our kids will know their family so much better. And now that the world knows we exist, we'll be safer. We're always safer together."

Bay nodded. He had to agree with everything she said, though even if he didn't, he would defer to her wishes and do it gladly. She asked for so little and gave so much.

The sound of laughter caught him, had him gazing toward the clinic. Jake walked out under his own power with Shannon beside him, the triplets crowding all around. Logan stood off to one side with a pleased smile on his face.

Bay didn't even realize he'd risen, but he was crossing the small distance between them, reaching Jake, stopping and standing in front of him.

And he couldn't stop grinning. Not for anything could he wipe the stupid smile off his face. He'd come so close to losing this man he'd grown to love so very much. "You okay?"

Jake nodded. "I am. I understand I'm in debt to a lot of people, though." He glanced at Logan standing beside him, then at Adam. He gazed around the chamber at the suddenly quiet gathering and blinked rapidly. Shannon moved close and slipped her arm around his waist. Bay stood at his other side and gave him another shoulder to lean on.

"I'm going to say this now," Jake said. Then he cleared his throat. "Because if I wait, I probably won't be able to do it. You all know how good I am at screwing up the simplest things."

Soft laughter, a few murmured words, but everyone waited. Each one had a stake in what he wanted to say. Jake looked at every person in the big chamber, and his eyes shimmered with tears.

Bay knew Shannon had told Jake how almost every adult here had helped the night before, taking shifts to carry away his pain. They'd suffered so he wouldn't have to. It hadn't been easy. Bay had taken a shift, and it had been agonizing, but he'd done it. They all had, because Jake was hurting and he was one of their own.

Jake took a deep breath and got himself under control. "I can never thank all of you, any of you, enough. I know what it felt like when my back was burning. I will never forget the agony, the fact that I wanted to die because I couldn't bear the pain. Nor will I ever forgot the fact that you willingly shared that pain so I wouldn't suffer."

He swallowed, and the sound was overloud in the quiet chamber, his voice hoarse from screaming when his back and shoulder had been on fire. "I owe each of you more than I can possibly repay," he said. "You've given me a gift without measure, one no man can put a price on. And you've reminded me once again what an amazing family this is."

The tears were running freely down his cheeks. He gave Bay a sheepish grin and then turned to Shannon. She was weeping openly, but her smile lit up the room. "C'mon," she said, helping him to move forward. "You're still wobbly. Let's go sit down."

She helped him to the pallet where Bay had been sitting moments ago. Jake glanced at his mate and something passed between them. Then he turned to Bay and said, "It appears the decision has been made. We're selling the place in Maine. Moving here. That okay with you?"

Grinning, Bay nodded. "Works for me," he said. Then he lifted Donovan out of Manda's arms and settled the sleeping baby against his shoulder. So many changes were coming.

He liked the idea of meeting them with a united front. Surrounded by his packmates.

Chapter 25

Anton glanced at his watch. He'd called a meeting of the ones he considered his top alphas, but it was still half an hour away. He stood in the shadows, away from the others. He really needed a few minutes to regroup before sitting down with the men.

He thought he had it all together, was almost sure he knew what to say, but did he really? And where was this self-doubt coming from? Why was he so unsure of himself? Why couldn't he get it together?

He held out his hands, amazed to see them trembling. Shit. He never doubted himself. He was legendary for always knowing he was right—even when he was wrong.

And that, he decided, was the problem. He'd made too many mistakes in the past. A lot of mistakes, but in every case his packmates had bailed him out, had made things work in spite of his screwups. They all thought he was such a master at getting things done. Didn't they realize they were the ones?

It was the pack that kept it all together, yet now they were looking to him for answers, and he had none. Not a damned thing. What the hell was he going to say when they sat down to make decisions that would affect the future of the pack forever?

"My love? What is it?"

Blinking in surprise, he realized Keisha stood mere inches from him, gazing at him with nothing but love and understanding. She wasn't looking at him to solve everyone's problems. No, she was looking at him like a woman who loved him in spite of his many faults.

He took a deep breath and rested his hands on her shoulders. Glanced around to reassure himself they were entirely alone, out of the hearing of the others. Gazed into amber eyes so filled with love that it shook him to his core.

How could this woman possibly love so completely? So selflessly? Even knowing him as well as she did?

Which was the only reason he could speak his heart. "Keisha . . ." He sighed. "Sweetheart, I don't know how to say this, but I'm scared to death. For once in my life, I honestly don't know what to do."

She smiled, rose up on her toes, and kissed him. Her soft lips moved over his with a confidence he wished was his.

"Come with me."

She took his hand in hers and tugged. He followed, willingly. He couldn't imagine any situation where Keisha wanted to lead that he wouldn't follow.

"Watch your head," she said, ducking through a low opening that led to a narrow tunnel.

"Where are we going?" He couldn't recall coming this way before, though there was so much of this underground system of caves and tunnels he'd never explored.

"Mei showed this to me last week when we were restocking supplies. There's something I want you to see."

"Not more hieroglyphs, I hope."

She merely laughed.

"Don't we need a flashlight?"

"Nope. It's dark but you won't get lost. This tunnel only goes one way."

"I have a meeting in half an hour."

Her laughter sent tingles down his spine. He loved to hear her laugh. "I'll get you back in time for your meeting. Now just shut up and follow me."

"Yes, ma'am." She always managed to make him laugh, no matter what kind of mood he was in. They only walked for a couple of minutes before he noticed light shining up ahead. It got brighter and the air smelled fresh, though there was a hint of smoke—a remnant of last night's fire.

They rounded a slight curve, and Anton could only stand there with his mouth hanging open. "How did you find this?"

Keisha gazed up at him with twinkling eyes. "Mei found it. She actually found it one night when she was hunting in leopard form. It's difficult to access from outside—we're under that big rocky outcropping southeast of the house. I know it doesn't seem as if we've come that far, but the entrance is at the top. See?"

She pointed to a slash of blue sky that was at least a hundred feet above them. "That rocky dome we see from the house is partially hollow. We're inside it. It's all volcanic, so Mei and I were thinking it must have been a huge gas bubble at one time."

They stood before a massive, natural bowl that looked as if it had been carved into the rock by eons of water wearing at the surface. Or even, as Keisha had said, a bubble of gas from some long-ago volcanic eruption. However it had formed, the walls curved and narrowed at the top. The sides appeared to be fairly smooth, with ferns growing from every tiny crevice, nook, and cranny. A thin stream of water fell from a tiny cleft high overhead.

Beneath it was absolute magic—a beautiful pool almost hidden in shadow, with only a narrow shaft of sunlight cutting across one end. It was hard to judge how deep the water was—bands of colored rock were visible through the crystal-clear water almost to the center, where it appeared much deeper.

A few birds had made their nests in the clumps of ferns growing on the walls, and their chattering and chirping echoed against the curved bowl with acoustics like an amphitheater.

A narrow ledge ran along one side of the pool and a small opening drained water into the caverns below, but there was truly a sense of magic about the place. Of timeless beauty, almost as if peace and eternity were kept here on hold.

"It's almost impossible to get to from above, thank goodness, because that would be quite a drop for anyone who fell in." Keisha took both his hands in hers. "I wanted to share this with you. It's so peaceful here. I thought maybe you could take a few minutes, relax, maybe prepare yourself for the day ahead."

She leaned against him and Anton held her close, slowly stroking her back, absorbing the quiet of this magical place, the warmth and life of the one he loved. She was wrong on one count, though. The soft pressure of her body clinging to his didn't do a thing to lower his heart rate. Instead, his heart pounded and he felt his body's insistent clamor for more.

More of her taste, her soft lips, her even softer breasts. The scent of her, the sound of her heart thundering against his. He leaned close and kissed her, but this wasn't a soft and gentle sharing. No, this time he took what she so willingly offered. Her hands slipped inside his shirt and her fingers left trails of fire across his back. Her hips thrust hard against him and he felt his cock rise and swell, felt the rush of blood to his groin and the need coiling deep and hard for Keisha.

For his mate, for the only one who could truly ease this

need. His breath hitched in his throat as she stepped back and slowly untied the knot holding the silky sarong at her shoulder. He watched as the fabric practically floated to the ground. One edge landed in the still pool, and the teal blue of the silk was almost the same color as the water beneath it.

Naked, she flashed him a quick, knowing smile and slipped the top metal button of his jeans free. He cupped her full breasts in his palms, loving their weight, their firm shape, so filled with milk for their daughter. He thumbed her nipples as she carefully released the second and the third buttons, slowly working her way along the thick bulge of his cock forcing the closures forward.

When she'd undone the final one, she slipped her hands inside the open fly. He felt her fingers sliding down his shaft and groaned when she cupped his balls and the fat length of his cock. Gently fondling, lightly rubbing, until he lost focus and tilted his hips forward, wanting more, needing what only Keisha could give him.

She went to her knees on the sandy floor and freed his entire package. His pants slipped low on his hips, almost falling off but for the wide stance of his legs holding them in place. The waistband teased him, cutting across the middle of his butt, just low enough for the coarse fabric to tickle the back side of his sac.

Keisha blew a soft breath of air over his cock and he jerked. His balls drew up close between his legs, and when she wrapped her lips around the fat head, he groaned and tangled his fingers in her hair.

Forcing himself not to force her, he stood perfectly still as she licked the velvety skin of his glans, tongued the sensitive slit, and then swallowed him down, working her throat muscles with long practice, sucking him deeper still until her lips brushed the thick patch of hair at his groin.

He felt the quiver of muscles straining against the need to thrust and fought his own nature. Fought the growing desire to tighten his hold on her tousled hair and use her mouth, use her to assuage this growing need, this almost mind-shattering need to find release.

Her throat muscles worked over his length, her lips teased him, and she pulled away, then took him deep again, moving so slowly he wanted to scream, making it so good he could easily weep. She took him out of himself, out of the day, away from the nightmares and the worries, away from the pressures and the fire and the fact they'd lost everything.

She reminded him they still had what mattered.

Reminded him once again of what counted and what didn't.

Then she was releasing him, backing away, and standing up. Lifting one leg to rest on the bony ridge of his hip, looping her arms around his neck, pulling herself up his body, and wrapping her other leg around his waist. Climbing him so easily, and then lowering herself over his straining erection, clinging to him, connecting to him, becoming one with him. Her mind opened and he felt the amazing joy Keisha shared, the sense that no matter what happened, they would always have each other.

Not for a month or a year. Not for many years, but forever, on this plane or the next, there would be no end to their love. This was what Keisha had taken from the memories the Ancient Ones shared. Not the fact they'd come from another world or could take shapes other than wolves. Not the manipulation of time and space when they shifted, or the various types of shapeshifters around the world.

No, Keisha, being Keisha, had taken the deeper story, the important story of the Ancient Ones themselves. The fact they'd waited all these eons, all this time, to share their history with their people. And yet, while they'd waited, they'd yearned for the ones they loved, the ones who'd left them behind.

The ones they were finally free to return to as soon as Lily's job was done.

The temple was no more, the records long gone to dust, and the Ancient Ones had joined their mates on the other side of the veil, following them into that next adventure beyond.

"Don't you see, my love? No matter what happens, should we live or die on this plane, we'll have each other forever. When we cross over, we'll still be together. Still able to share what we have now. No matter what happens, everything that counts, your family, your pack, your wonderful, brilliant, convoluted mind—all of us, all of this, will eventually be together. Love is forever. It is eternal, so you don't have to worry about what happens over the next few days. It will all work out. It has to, because you will make it work."

Her hips rose and fell with her words, with the rhythm of the promises she made. And he believed. He would always believe whatever Keisha said. She had the wisdom of the ages in her soul, the heart of an angel, and she loved him.

How could any man fail with a woman like Keisha Rialto Cheval beside him? He held her close and picked up the pace, rocking and thrusting, filling her, taking her higher, climbing right along with her.

But it wasn't until she looked into his eyes, gazed at him with amber eyes gone dark with lust, and softly said, "I love you," that he felt the final push that took him over the top.

Off the precipice, flying as if he could fly forever, rushing into whatever the day might bring. Fearless, prepared, ready to welcome change. Thrusting into her soft body, his passion knew no bounds—no earthly bounds could hold him.

Lightning raced from spine to balls to freedom.

Keisha screamed, a long, low howl of pure ecstasy. Her

fingernails found purchase in the hard muscles of his back, her hips thrust forward, and her legs clamped tightly around his hips. It was all he could do to stay upright as the final tremors of orgasm slowly faded away.

He held her for a moment, legs trembling, lungs heaving with each labored breath. Held her close until, shivering in the aftermath of orgasm, Keisha slid her legs down his sides, pulled free of his rapidly softening cock, and leaned her head against his chest. "Each time we do this," she gasped, still struggling to draw enough air, "I think it can't get any better. And then we do it again and it does. It is. Good Goddess, how I love you!" She tightened her hands around his waist and held him close. "But now I need to go back. Mei's got the kids and I told her I wouldn't be gone long."

"Ah." Laughing, he tilted her chin up. "So you planned this ahead of time?"

She snorted and he felt the tremors where their bodies met as she laughed. "Honey, we've got four kids under seven. All our spontaneous sex is planned ahead of time." She leaned back in his embrace. "You haven't figured that out yet?"

He merely raised one eyebrow as she slipped out of his arms, turned, and dove into the crystal-clear pool. Coming to the surface, she treaded water for a moment. "It's not as warm as the pool inside, but it's not bad. Want to join me?"

He was out of his clothes in a heartbeat, swimming beside her in the cool, clear water, and miracle of miracles— or should he say, miracle of Keisha, his mind was as clear as this hidden pool, his vision wide open, and his heart at rest.

He swam close and, treading water, stared into her dark eyes. "Thank you."

"'S okay. You needed to unwind."

He shook his head, still lazily treading water. "No, not

just for this. For everything. Thank you for who you are, for never giving up on me. For loving me."

"My pleasure," she said. "It works both ways."

Then she swam to the edge and lifted herself up on surprisingly strong arms. Slowly, sensuously, she wrapped the teal silk around her dark, wet body. It clung to her like a second skin. She glanced over her shoulder and shot him a quick grin. "My breasts ache. Lucia must be hungry. Good luck at your meeting. Remember, we follow your lead because you're a good leader. You've never asked for that position, but you've honored the pack's trust in every way. You'll make the right decisions because you make them for the right reasons. Trust yourself the way we trust you."

Then she turned and walked away, her hips swaying gently with each step, the wet silk not hiding a thing, merely emphasizing the perfect body of the beautiful woman he loved.

Chapter 26

Anton took over the small chamber Logan had set up as their clinic. The ones he considered his generals–those who quietly led without any overt show of dominance— began to arrive. Luc, Ulrich, Adam, and Baylor, and this time, at Ric's suggestion, Matt Rodgers. The young man had matured over the past couple of years, and all of them respected his opinion.

Nick joined them as well because he was the one who'd started this, and therefore he had a part in whatever happened. Anton respected the young man's opinion. Politically he was a lot more savvy than the rest of them, familiar with the ins and outs of Washington because of his job.

And, as always, there was Stefan.

Anton's other half.

The one who balanced his faults and made them strengths.

Normally Liana, Xandi, and Keisha would have been included as well, but they'd begged off. Liana was still recovering from giving birth, while because of the trauma of the fire, Xandi and Keisha felt the children needed them more than their mates did.

Anton had calmly informed Keisha that he always needed

her the most—until she reminded him he'd just had her, quite profoundly, thank you very much, in that beautiful grotto she'd led him to, and he'd have to take his turn.

Laughing, she'd kissed him thoroughly enough to make his blood pressure rise—among other things—and told him she'd be in contact with him should an *overwhelming* need arise.

And while the group meeting here was small, every member of the pack was linked with them, listening, able to comment should the need arise, aware of everything that was going on, whatever decisions were made.

Sensing the powerful but respectful links from his pack-mates, Anton glanced up and made eye contact with Stefan. *I've never really thought about it before,* he said, *but we have achieved democracy in its purest form.*

Stefan winked. *I wondered when you'd figure that out.*

Anton kept his comments to himself while the others arrived for the meeting and found places to sit. Tinker, AJ, and Mik were up above, clearing away the smoldering debris to make the area where the house had once stood safe for everyone when it was time to climb out of the caverns.

The others who'd remained below were keeping the children busy, which, from the sounds of laughter and splashing and the occasional squeal, had something to do with swimming in the warm, shallow pond that filled one side of the main chamber.

Here, though, it was quiet. It appeared there were enough chairs and stools for everyone to sit, and Jazzy had set up a large pot of fresh coffee. They'd each grabbed a cup and sat quietly, waiting for Anton to begin. He glanced about the room, comforted by the quiet strength emanating from every man there.

There was no struggle for leadership—every person fell naturally into his role—yet each of them looked to Anton for guidance. Not to make decisions for them, but merely to discuss the current situation with them, to offer his opinion.

An opinion with no more weight than any of theirs.

It was a good system, and it worked well. It was time to get things going, though he knew, in his heart, he was putting off that walk outside, the first view of his destroyed home. He didn't want to think about it—what it would feel like to see all they'd built over the years reduced to ash.

Forcing a smile he didn't really feel, Anton began with the one who'd set so much in motion. "Well, Nick. Are you feeling completely healed yet?"

Since he'd been fine within a day or two of the bombing, Nick ducked his head and shrugged. "Physically, yes. Mentally? I'm still feeling like an ass."

"I figured as much, but please don't. That's generally my job, and I've had a lot more practice at it than you have." Anton chuckled. "I know you all probably think I'm nuts, but I truly believe what Nick did was a good thing. I also don't think he had any other choice, and I'm not referring to his method of disposing of the bomb. I'm talking about fate and those things that are going to happen no matter what we do to avoid them."

Stefan laughed. "I already conceded, Anton. We're not going back to that coincidence versus fate argument, are we?"

Shaking his head, smiling, Anton agreed. "No need to. Look at the events leading up to what happened before Nick saved those kids. First sign that something was off? Lily suddenly decided to go for a walk on the astral plane. Now, I'll admit I have a precocious kid, but as Millie said, even for Lily that was a bit much. Then we discovered our oldest kids, Lily and Alex, are already shifting. Not only that, they're powerful enough to hide that knowledge from their parents."

He glanced at each of the others. "It's not the shifting itself that concerns me, or even hiding it from their parents. The important question becomes, do they understand the consequences of their acts enough to hide their powers from the rest of the world?"

"Probably not, and that's scary." Adam leaned against one wall with his arms folded across his chest. "But I agree with Anton on that—young children able to shift is something we weren't expecting. It makes it imperative we deal with the public learning of our existence sooner rather than later. I'd hate for it to happen because one of my kids decided to turn into a wolf in the middle of Walmart."

Nodding, Anton focused on Nick. "Now that fear is a moot point. Nick, events have been leading up to what you did and how you did it. Lily told me the Ancient Ones only knew of one missing Chanku—Sunny Daye. They'd felt the energy spike when she attempted her shift over seventeen years ago, knew she was suffering because of it, but hadn't been able to find her. You found her. Knowing she was out there is all that has kept them locked on the astral."

Nick frowned and stared at him. "Sunny? They've hung around for her?"

"Yep." Anton shrugged. Now it seemed almost unreal, the way it had all come together, but . . . "Once Liana found me and directed me to find others—with Oliver and Stefan among the first—the Ancient Ones figured they finally could move on across the veil and join the loved ones who'd gone before them so many years before. Except they didn't feel free to leave—they knew of three Chanku caught in the midst of a shift who suffered, who were in pain. Manda was the first, almost thirty years ago, then seventeen years ago, Sunny was trapped. Stefan was the last to get caught in mid-shift, but the first one freed. Manda was next, but they knew Sunny was still out there, suffering and in pain. She's not the only Chanku still missing, but she was the last one they knew of who was hurting because of her attempt to shift.

"If any of you've had time to work through those memories I uploaded to your hard heads this morning, you'll know that the Ancient Ones have been existing as quasi-corporeal bodies for millions of years. They're tired. Ready to go home, and home to men who should have died eons ago is the other side of the veil. The Ancient Ones were damned old—among the first settlers who came to Earth during the age of the dinosaurs."

"I still find that hard to believe." Ulrich shot a glance at Luc. "And here I've always felt like such an old fart in this group. I'm a veritable kid."

"We all are." Anton stood up and folded his arms across his chest. He was buzzing with energy, too much to sit on a stool and stay in one place. "I think everything that's happened had to happen now. We can't stop our children from shifting while they're still kids. The parts of their bodies that control their Chanku abilities were forming while they were in the womb, exposed to the nutrients through their mothers. They got more when they nursed—essentially, they've been getting those nutrients since conception, and there's no going back. They're going to shift, and before long, one of them was going to get caught. Everyone's got a camera phone or other recording device. It was only a matter of time."

Again he focused on Nick. "You shifted on the national news with worldwide coverage, doing something truly heroic. You saved lives at risk of your own."

Nick ducked his head, obviously embarrassed at being singled out. Anton rested a hand on his shoulder. "Don't hide from it, Nick. Be proud of what you did. You didn't hesitate, and for that, our nation is as grateful as I am. As far as exposing our existence, along with your very ample package, to legions of admiring fans—" He broke off laughing as the rest of the group cracked up, including Nick.

"Hey, it's good PR. Personally, I'm willing to take what we can get!" Anton patted his back. "Nick, you could not have picked a better time or place. It's hard to look vicious or scary when you're protecting a room filled with good kids, especially when two of them are the president's daughters. Whatever you do, don't feel guilty. I've been wondering for the past couple of years how we could possibly go public. You took the decision out of my hands, and I couldn't be happier."

Then he focused on the rest of them. "The next step is to determine how much we make public. What do average citizens need to know about us that won't scare them, that won't make us targets of their fear? You know what's going to happen. You know that some parts of the media will try and whip up anger and hatred against us using society's natural fear of the unknown. There's going to be a huge push at first to find out whatever they can to hold over us, so we need to be united in what we disclose."

Anton took his seat on a stool beside Stefan. Stef glanced at him, silently asking permission before he spoke.

You don't need to ask before speaking, Stef. None of you do. Your voice is every bit as important as mine or any other member of the pack.

Thanks, but you just looked so commanding, I couldn't help myself.

Anton snorted as Stef teasingly punched his shoulder. "Someone mentioned that we need to hide the fact we're telepathic," Stef said. "I think that's a good idea. Some of our abilities make us more frightening to the average human, and being able to communicate with our minds might be a bit much for people to accept right away. The shifting? Not so hard. Shifting has been covered, often favorably, in popular literature for years. It's part of legends in every culture in the world."

He shrugged and laughed. "Of course, now we know that those legends are based on our ancestors, and I think that's something we can go public with. The fact that skin-walkers, shapeshifters . . . even the legends surrounding the Gypsy Rom and the pertinent Greek and Roman mythology that deals with shapeshifters are all directly related to our ancestors. All of it gives us a legitimacy we might not otherwise be able to claim."

"Which is why I think Nick's act of courage was preordained," Anton said. "It happened when all of this knowledge—our knowledge of our own history—started coming together. That history gives us the tools we need to take our story to the world, to do it in such a way that—if we work it right—should help us hold on to the heroic 'good guy' image Nick established."

Matt spoke up, quietly, but with the confidence of a born leader. "We still have to protect our children. We have to protect the women, too. Not because they're not powerful in their own right, but because they need the freedom to concentrate on raising the kids, on holding the pack together." He sat with his hands hanging loosely between his knees, a big kid with a serious, thoughtful demeanor.

"No matter how tough we think we are, the women are the strength behind the pack. They're the ones that make it work. They make us—all of the males—better people. We have to protect them from those nuts you're talking about, Anton. Because we know they're out there. They'll think our women are weaker, and that's who they'll target. The women and the children."

Everyone nodded. No matter how any of them felt about their roles within the pack, their nature as Chanku couldn't be denied. The women were physically as strong as the men in their wolven form, but their instincts were always to protect their young. As more and more babies were born, that gender-specific division had become even more pronounced.

As Matt pointed out, the women were the heart of the pack, the ones who kept the wheels greased, who held it together when faced with adversity. They balanced the needs of the men with the needs of the children and the overall needs of the pack. And they were the ones who would be targeted. It was something they all had to be aware of.

"I'm glad you brought it up, Matt. I hate to think of the risk, but you're right. Maybe we should emphasize how powerful our women are, the fact we're a matriarchal society."

He sensed laughter—Keisha and Mei, Daci, Xandi, and Millie and the rest. There might be seven men in this room, but the entire pack was mentally linked with them, free to weigh in on any part of the discussion. They knew their ideas and concerns would be taken seriously.

And it was more than obvious they were seriously enjoying a discussion admitting the strength of women.

Anton ignored the mental cheering section and focused on Matt. "The point is, I agree, Matt. This is exactly why I've called you together. I think we're going to have to go public in a big way. Stef and I talked about options—interviews, talk shows, whatever. We're going to be asked to shift in public, and people will want to know how we do it."

He laughed and slowly shook his head. "After getting the history from Lily, I know how it happens. I'm just not sure I believe it yet."

"I don't get it either." Ulrich looked as perplexed as Anton felt. "We're manipulating time whenever we shift? How the fuck do we do that?"

Anton shrugged and glanced at Stefan. "You're the brains of this operation, Stef. You explain it."

Stef grinned at Ric. "It's an entirely individual anomaly, from what I can figure out. A time shift that affects only the individual and the immediate space and time they occupy. I think scientists will have a wonderful time trying to figure it out. I know that there have been times when Anton and I tried to film it and we couldn't slow the film down enough to find the point between one form and the next. It's like one winked out and the other appeared. I know that there have been times when I was sure I saw the shift, the visible morphing from man to wolf, but I think it's because I wanted to see that. My mind gave me a visual that wasn't really there."

Interrupting him, Anton said, "There was one time when I was very close to a man who had hurt Keisha. He'd been stalking her—this was right after she and I first met. I wanted so badly to kill him that I was actually fighting with my wolf, forcing it not to appear and rip out the bastard's throat. I remember my body shaking with the need to shift as I followed him up the stairs to her house. I saw the fur on the backs of my hands, the claws. Now I wonder if I actually saw that or if it was what I wanted to see. Possibly the intense emotion I felt overcame the time shift. I just don't know."

"You all know I was trapped mid-shift for years," Stefan said. "So was Manda, and now, as we've just learned, so was Sunny. That proves there's a gradual morphing from one form to the next, but it's essentially happening in another dimension, one that we must slip in and out of during the process. I'm thinking it works the same as time on the astral does. Lily was gone for a couple of weeks for us, but it felt like less than a day to her. I think we can explain shifting to the public as we understand it, but since none of us understands it that well, it will give them a mystery to work with."

"That's not a bad idea." Luc hadn't said much, though he'd obviously been paying close attention. "Diverting at-

312 / *Kate Douglas*

tention is an effective way to get folks not to look at the bigger picture, the fact that we're an alien species, not even human, living and breeding among them. Give scientists a puzzle to keep them busy."

"I want to give them medical data, too." Adam gazed around the room. "I think we should allow ourselves to be examined, poked and prodded as much as a chosen medical team wants. Anton mentioned this to me, and it's a great idea. One team of the government's choice, with the caveat that all data be made public. The fewer our secrets, the less of a threat we become. Logan and I have talked about our healing abilities, too. We want to offer our insight to the medical community as a whole. See if we can train other physicians to do what we do."

Nick interrupted Adam. "Won't that give away our telepathic abilities?"

"Not if we let them think it's limited to our healers." Adam's frustration was obvious. "Nick, I can help people. So can Logan. Hell, I can help animals as well, so I know it's not limited to Chanku. Humans could benefit from what we've learned to do, and if we can find others with the ability to do the same, we have to share this. I think that could be our greatest asset to humanity—our ability to integrate ourselves within a person's body, to fix things from within. You know some humans are better able to mindspeak than others. We've all run across the ones whose minds are wide open. I think they may be able to learn to do what Logan and I can do. I'd like permission to give it a try."

"Adam, you don't ever need permission to help people." Anton gazed at the man who had fascinated him from the beginning. So much power inside him, so much they still didn't understand. That ability to separate himself from his body and move about at will . . . where the hell had that come from?

Even the Ancient Ones hadn't touched on that . . . or at

least, he'd not found it in the new memories filling his head.

Adam nodded. "Thanks. That's good to know."

"Another thing." Anton grinned. "I understand everyone is taking up my invitation to settle here in Montana. You realize it's going to be a trailer park until we get some houses built. I've recently purchased more property, so we don't all need to live in one place, but we'll get together with the whole pack before we build anything and figure out exactly what we need. I'm really pleased you've all decided to join us. We're stronger together. Healthier. I think we're going to need whatever strength we can find in the coming months."

He paused for a moment as Mik's voice slipped into his mind. *There's a big chopper coming in low over the trees. Not U.S. Forest Service. Looks official, maybe military. You might want to come up.*

On our way.

He stood up and clapped his hands together. "I just heard from Mik. We've got company. It appears it's show time."

Chapter 27

Stefan stopped Anton with a soft touch on his arm. "I don't have a good feeling about this. The only Chanku anyone knows of is Nick. Why would the military come here? Nick lives in Washington—there's no way to connect him with us. What's bringing them here?"

Anton cocked his head and stared at Stef. "I have no idea, but you've made an excellent point." His mind was suddenly spinning with an entirely new set of problems. "Get some of the guys. Shift. Use the tunnel in the woods and come in from the far side of the meadow. Hold back and keep an eye on things. See what happens, but stay out of sight."

He fingered the cell phone in his pocket. Freshly charged, without any numbers to dial, it gave him a direct link to the president. He fully intended not to use it, but it was nice having it. Very nice. "Stef, I trust you to know if and when you're needed."

"Got it." Stef glanced quickly at the small group. "Matt? Get Deacon and Oliver. Ric? Can you come with us, too? We're going as backup. Four-legged backup." He tipped an imaginary hat to Anton and headed for the main cavern with Matt and Ric close behind him.

Anton nodded to Luc, Adam, and Nick. "We'll go as

men. Only shift if you have to. Mik says the chopper's landing now. He and AJ will meet it. Tinker's staying back, out of sight in wolf form." He made eye contact with each of them. "Are you ready? Good. Let's go."

Anton led Nick, Adam, and Luc out of the main cavern, with each step trying not to think of the fact this was the first time for him to leave the cavern since fleeing the fire the night before. The first time to see what, if anything, remained.

Mik, Tinker, and AJ had shoved the heavy cabinet hiding the caverns from the cellar back in place, but it slid aside easily on oiled tracks.

The cellar was intact, protected by the concrete foundation overhead, the natural rock walls, and the steel door that led to the fire-resistant stairwell. The steel door stood open. The wide stone steps had been swept clean, but instead of leading into the kitchen, the stairwell opened to the blue sky above.

That incongruous patch of blue stopped Anton for a moment. Though he knew his house was gone, he'd not really contemplated the reality of it. How it would look . . . what it would feel like to have everything so changed. The stink of fire was everywhere—burned wood, burned plastic, melted metal.

He wished he could stand here for a little longer and absorb the changes, experience the scents and sights—even the sounds of smoldering wood—in order to deal with them later. But now was not the time. There were matters to attend to, and he would grieve another day.

He climbed the stairs quickly and was the first of their group to step out into the gray wasteland—all that was left of his home. He paused in what had once been the kitchen and gazed out at a moonscape—what had just yesterday been the truly magnificent, naturally landscaped grounds Keisha had labored over for years. Everything was gone. The fire had burned so hot that not even twigs remained. Nothing but soot-stained boulders and a few broken pieces of once-priceless metal and stone artwork that had graced the beautiful gardens around the house.

Nothing of the structure remained but the stone foundations, and what little metal hadn't melted entirely. Piles of broken and charred slate, once the roof, lay all over the ground. It was difficult to imagine the heat that must have been generated to destroy everything so thoroughly. Anton moved quickly past the burned-out hulk of what had once been a refrigerator covered with childish drawings, stepped carefully through shards of broken, blackened tiles where kids had played underfoot while parents fixed their meals.

Nothing. None of it was left.

He couldn't think about that now. Couldn't look at it. Couldn't consider his financial and personal loss, the work lying ahead of all of them, the changes in their lives.

The terrible, unstoppable changes. Not with a Sikorsky Black Hawk helicopter squatting like a giant bug in the middle of what had only yesterday been a beautiful meadow. Not with armed men marching toward the ruin that had once been his home. Anger welled up in him, anger that these men should come here now, at a time when he wanted to mourn what was lost. Anger that they would defile a place that had been almost sacred to him, to his family. His pack.

He glared at the helicopter, unaccountably angry at the machine. Except it wasn't just a machine. It was an abomination, sitting there in what had been a living meadow mere hours ago. The way it blended in with the blackened earth beneath, the slow, deliberate spin of the huge rotors overhead, the sunlight glinting off darkened, bulletproof windows—all of it adding a sense of malevolence.

Three men in uniform with heavy rifles held at an identical angle across their chests took up positions outside the open door of the Black Hawk.

Mik and AJ waited in front of what had once been the broad redwood staircase leading to the intricately carved front doors of Anton's home. Not even the door frame remained. The wide front deck, the huge house—all of it was gone. Only ash and metal, stone and broken glass and a few smoldering timbers marked what once had been.

His men were covered in soot, obviously unhappy their work had been interrupted. Anton noted how much they'd already accomplished. Four huge piles—one of broken glass, another of twisted metal, a third of smoldering timbers, and the fourth of indescribable refuse—filled what had been the parking area between the house and Mei and Oliver's cottage.

He thought of the effort it had taken to move so much and realized they'd needed the physical labor. They'd wanted to work off some of the anger at what couldn't be changed. He understood that drive. He felt it himself, even now. He felt pride, too. Pride in the ones who stood beside him, pride in the men who'd been out here trying to put this outrageous mess right.

There was no fixing it this time. There was only moving forward. He turned his attention from what was lost to what he had. There was no price to be put on loyalty, no way to measure the love of good people.

AJ, looking gorgeous even when he was dressed in torn jeans and covered in soot, stood slightly behind Mik. Backing him up, always. As deceptively relaxed as a snake preparing to strike.

Mik merely looked pissed. He made it perfectly obvious he'd been busy, that he resented the interruption, and he didn't give a rat's ass how many stars the man walking toward him wore on his beret or how many armed men walked beside him.

Anton bit back a smile. It was hard to imagine a more imposing force than Miguel Fuentes. Unusually tall and broad shouldered, with skin the color of burnished bronze emphasizing his sharply drawn Native American features, he looked like a man from another century. His waist-length black hair was pulled back in two long braids, and he had a stained strip of leather tied as a sweat band around his forehead. He stood proudly, impassively, with his thick, muscular arms folded across a powerful chest.

No shirt.

Not for Mik, who rarely wore one. With faded jeans slung low on his narrow hips, heavy work boots firmly planted on the scorched ground, his chest bare and ripped with muscle honed by hard work, he put every man walking toward him to shame.

Anton recognized the army officer leading the four heavily armed men dressed in army field uniforms—the general was the favorite son of a number of radical organizations, a dangerous adversary who was constantly at odds with the president and his cabinet and all of the liberal media.

Stay close. Follow your instincts. Anton's warning went to all of his men. *This could get ugly.*

"General." Anton stepped forward, moved smoothly between Mik and AJ, and held out his hand. The general stared disdainfully at him, ignored his outstretched hand, and stood at parade rest with his own hands folded behind his back. "No time for pleasantries, Mr. Cheval. We're here for the freak." He nodded toward Nick. "Get your things, boy. You're going with us."

"I think not." Anton slowly folded his arms across his chest. "First of all, unless you have a warrant, you're trespassing. You do have a warrant, don't you?"

The man straightened to his full height, which was still several inches less than Anton's, though what he lacked in height, he made up in sheer bulk. He wasn't fat, but he was built like a bulldog. "I come with the full authority of Congress and the U.S. military. If we have to remove Nick

Barden by force, we will. I would suggest you stand aside."

"General . . ." Anton made a show of leaning forward in order to read the man's nametag. "Schmidt," he said, drawing out the sound. "Well, General Schmidt, as I said, you are trespassing. You have no right to be on my property, nor do you have any right to arrest anyone here without due cause, up to and including Nicholas Barden. I would suggest you leave. Now."

Be ready, but be careful.

The general glanced at the soldiers on his left. "Take him."

Anton never moved. He didn't have to. As the first soldier stepped forward, a huge black wolf with golden highlights in his fur leapt out from behind a stone wall. He knocked the rifle from the man's grasp and took him down, snarling and snapping his long canines in the terrified soldier's face.

Luc moved just as quickly and caught the second soldier with a knee to the groin and a quick karate chop to the neck, disarming him and holding him immobile with the man's arm twisted high between his shoulder blades.

At the same time, Adam and Nick grabbed the two on the general's right, taking their weapons and forcing both men to the ground before either one had a chance to react.

It was over within seconds. Anton hadn't moved at all while his Chanku disarmed the group. Even in human form, their Chanku speed made them a superior force over mere humans. Anton stared at Schmidt. "You were saying, General?"

The general spun around, but the three soldiers behind him stood with hands raised. The pilot jumped down from the open door of the helicopter with both hands in the air. Matt had shifted back to his human form, but as large as he was, even naked, he made an imposing figure holding an M14 rifle trained squarely on the soldier in the middle—especially when there were two large wolves covering a soldier on either side.

The rest of their weapons lay in a pile on the ground.

"Anton?" Matt glanced over his shoulder. "The pilot says there are a couple of reporters in the chopper. They've got their cameras rolling now. Do you want them to remain inside, or should we bring them out? And what about the camera gear?"

Anton bit back a grin. Knowing the general's politics and the news programs he regularly appeared on, he couldn't have asked for anything better than this. *Thank you, Eve.* She had to have a hand in this. It was too perfect for her not to.

"They're free to get out, Matt. My argument isn't with the press, though you might want to put some pants on if they're filming." He chuckled. "On the other hand, you make a rather imposing figure standing there bare-ass. It's up to you."

Matt's laughter obviously added insult to injury, especially when he ignored Anton's suggestion to cover up. The general glowered at Anton as a man and a woman climbed quickly out of the helicopter and carefully skirted the four huge wolves. The man carried a camera on his shoulder, obviously recording everything, while the woman couldn't seem to take her eyes off Matt.

Anton waved them over. He recognized the woman, a popular but opinionated reporter. She was the one mainly responsible for creating the public image of the pompous idiot standing there with stars marching across his beret.

Anton wondered how she felt about bringing the man down.

She approached Anton, obviously prepared for a fight. He quickly assessed her—attractive but, up close, definitely older than she appeared on television. Hard edged but not stupid. And definitely interested in the tall, gorgeous men guarding the soldiers. Anton picked up her scent and smelled her arousal.

It was really hard for him not to smile.

"What's going on? General Schmidt? What's happened here?"

The general glared at her, but he didn't speak.

Probably the smartest thing he'd done all day, as far as Anton was concerned. Nodding politely to the woman and her cameraman, he said, "You're more than welcome to record what's taking place. We have nothing to hide from the press."

He glanced down, reached for her arm, and carefully moved her to one side, away from a large slab of broken glass sticking out of the rubble near her ankle. "Be careful, though. There are some hot spots, lots of broken glass. It's dangerous."

Startled, the reporter looked where he pointed and realized she could have easily sliced her leg open. "Thank you. I didn't see that."

The cameraman continued to film.

"You're welcome." Anton shrugged and gazed about them. "It was a beautiful home until yesterday. We had a heck of a fire last night. I'm Anton Cheval. And you are?" He held his hand out to the well-known reporter as if he hadn't a clue who she was. And he was still treating her like visiting royalty.

Looking more than a little shell-shocked, she stared around at the burned-out home for a moment before responding. "Melissa Carole. ALN News, Mr. Cheval." They shook hands; the cameraman nodded, but he kept the lens focused on Anton, the now-disarmed soldiers, and the large black wolf sitting over one of them.

"Is that one a . . ." The reporter pointed at Tinker.

"Chanku? Yes, he is. Go ahead and shift, Tink. I imagine Ms. Carole's seen a naked man before."

Not one like me she hasn't. The wolf snorted.

And shifted, standing taller and broader than Anton, taller even than AJ or Mik. And wider. Much wider.

And very well endowed. And, as often happened after shifting, he was magnificently erect. Anton bit back a bark of laughter.

Melissa Carole dropped her tape recorder. Anton deftly caught it before it hit the ground. She took it from him without even looking as Tinker dipped his head in a polite greeting and held out his hand. "Ms. Carole," he said. "I'm Martin McClintock. Folks call me Tinker."

Dazed, she shook hands. Her eyes went wide as her hand was completely engulfed in Tinker's huge mitt. He grinned at Anton. "I'm gonna go grab my pants. Excuse me, please, but I hate to make my debut on national TV the way Nicky did—bare-ass and buck-naked." Laughing, he turned away and, walking like a king reviewing his subjects, headed into the burned-out rubble of the house where he'd hidden his clothes.

Anton turned his attention to the general once again, well aware Ms. Carole was still watching Tinker walk away, but even Anton had to admit, the man did have a magnificent butt.

The cameraman continued to record everything that happened.

"Okay, General Schmidt. So exactly what do we have here? You show up on private property with armed soldiers, prepared to take a private citizen into custody. You've brought your own TV crew, so I imagine the purpose of having the press on hand is to record the entire incident."

He smiled at Melissa Carole. She smiled back. "As I said, I'm fine with the media's involvement. Obviously, our secret is out, so there's no point in hiding who and what we are, but we certainly haven't broken any laws. Since you haven't presented me with a warrant, I can only assume you have absolutely no authorization to take Nick into custody. That makes your action blatantly illegal by anyone's standards and quite specifically illegal according to the Constitution you're sworn to defend."

He turned and gave the reporter his most ingratiating smile. "Ms. Carole? Can you tell me what pretenses the general used to get you to come out here today? I can't imagine a woman of your integrity being involved in anything like an illegal arrest, which is nothing more than a kidnapping. What did General Schmidt say he was planning to do?"

Melissa Carole straightened her spine and smiled at Anton. "He told me there was a nest of criminals living out here, that he was making an authorized raid on a compound where a group of illegal aliens were plotting to overthrow the government. He promised us an exclusive." She glared at the general. "We had no idea he was after Chanku or we never would have become involved. Especially after this young man saved the lives of all those children in Washington. He's a hero, not a criminal. General Schmidt, you should be ashamed of yourself!"

"Goddamned son of a—"

"Now, General. There's a lady present." Anton held up a hand. "Watch your language. I'm going to make a quick call." He smiled again at the reporter and the cameraman. "If you'll excuse me for just a moment." Anton pulled the black phone out of his pocket and hit the red button.

The general's eyes went wide.

Obviously, he recognized the significance of the special phone, but it was just as obvious the reporter didn't. Anton turned his back on the general but made sure the cameraman could get a clear shot of him calling, along with the audio.

It only rang twice before the call was taken. "Yes, Mr. President. Anton Cheval here. Nick's fine, thank you, but we do have a bit of an incident here in Montana. Yes, unexpected, but I thought you should be aware of what's

going on. Yes, sir. It has to do with a General Schmidt . . .
Yes, that's the one. General Schmidt, seven heavily armed
soldiers, and a rather large Sikorsky Black Hawk parked
in what used to be my front yard. Oh, and the press. A
Ms. Melissa Carole and her cameraman. Correct. ALN.
I'll be sure and tell her."

He flashed a quick smile at the reporter and nodded.
"Yes, sorry to say, the fire took the house, but we're all
fine. Nick and Beth are okay. Nick's with me now. Thank
you for asking. An hour? I believe we can convince the
general to remain here until your people arrive. Thank
you, sir. Good day to you, too."

He ended the call and grinned at the reporter. "The
president said to tell you hello and hopes you get your
story." Then he turned toward General Schmidt and held
out his hand. "Your weapons, General. I've been authorized to hold you and your men under citizen's arrest until
members of the president's special ops team arrive."

"You have no right . . ."

"I have every right." Gone was the polite façade. Anton
turned his anger free and stepped forward until he towered over the man. "You have come onto my property,
threatened my family, and put my people at risk. You've
done it without any authorization beyond your own self-
righteous belief that you can do as you wish because the
media has so easily manipulated your already bloated ego.
You, sir, are an ass. You're lucky we didn't kill every single
one of you, but we, unlike you and those who follow you,
believe in treating one another with the honor and dignity
each of us deserve. Though, in my opinion, you, General
Schmidt, deserve none. Your men, however, are merely
taking orders. They do not merit punishment for following a horse's ass with more stars on his cap than brains beneath it."

The general's jaw was working and his face had gone

beet red. He glanced at the reporter, at the camera that continued to record as Anton stood there with his hand out and a look of grim determination on his face. Anton was outwardly furious as the general slapped a 9mm automatic pistol into his hand.

Inside, it was all he could do to contain his elation.

Every bit of this was being covered. Film of Anton in his burned-out house, surrounded by an overzealous military officer stomping all over his constitutional rights.

Film of his companions protecting him, standing bravely in the face of overwhelming military might. Of the scorched earth and the obscenity of the Black Hawk helicopter on private land.

Visuals tell stories, and his was being told beautifully. There was no way this story could come off as anything other than favorable to the Chanku. They were the victims here. Brave citizens standing up to the more powerful foe, a man obviously misusing his military power.

People were going to love it. He couldn't have hired a publicist and gotten a better shot at swaying public opinion in their direction.

Best of all, everything was happening in full view of one of the most opinionated news reporters in the nation—a woman whose voice made nuts and fanatics all across the country stand up and take notice. And he had her in the palm of his hand.

Once her story aired, no one could accuse the Chanku of being less than good citizens. No one would dare call them dangerous aliens or subversives.

Tinker, fully dressed now in heavy work boots, worn jeans, and a red flannel shirt, looking even more powerful than he had before, appeared beside Anton. Anton glanced at him without smiling and handed over the general's sidearm. "Hang on to this for me, would you? You can turn it over to the special ops guys when they get here." Then he nodded to Luc and Adam, Mik and AJ. "See if you can find a spot out of the sun where the general and his men can wait comfortably."

He made a point of gazing around the burned-out landscape and shrugged. "Maybe in the shade of the helicopter? The president's men are going to have to push it to make it here in an hour. Tink? Why don't you go down and grab a case of bottled water. Don't want anyone getting dehydrated. I'm going to take Ms. Carole around and introduce her to Matt and his crew."

Tinker stuck the handgun in his waistband and then headed for the cavern. Adam grinned. AJ flashed his most charming smile. Anton caught another strong burst of feminine pheromones.

So far, so good.

"Ms. Carole," he said, ever the gentleman. "After you."

Chapter 28

Adam touched his fingers to his forelock in a quick salute. "Anton, I'm going back in. I really need to check on Liana and the baby."

Melissa Carole's eyes lit up. "You've got a baby?"

Adam nodded. "Yes, ma'am. Born during the night while we were all hunkered down in the shelter, knowing the house was burning over our heads. She came a bit early, but everything's fine. Liana—she's my wife—is a real trouper."

His eyes burned, but he didn't even try to stop the tears. No point in wasting anything that would garner more sympathy, but the tears were real. The emotions were real.

Liana amazed him. And he really didn't want to waste time explaining more to this woman, but he appreciated Anton's concerns.

"Could we come down? Get a shot of your wife and the baby?"

Adam shook his head. No need to check with Anton on this. "No, ma'am. Our families are private. You know what's out there, the people who don't think anyone who's different should be allowed to exist. Personally, I want to keep my children safe, and that means keeping the media and cameras out of our private lives as much as possible."

When the reporter opened her mouth to protest, Adam held up a hand, though he managed a smile. "This is only my opinion. I'll ask my wife how she feels about showing off our new daughter. If she's all right with it, we'll be back before you leave, but it's entirely up to Liana. I would never think to make decisions for her. That's not our way."

Surprise had the reporter opening her mouth, then shutting it. Adam thought she looked like a rather overly made-up carp.

"But I got the feeling the men were in charge," she said. "Don't men make the important decisions among... among your kind? Aren't the women just..." She shrugged dismissively and stuck her microphone under his nose.

Adam chuckled. "You must have misunderstood. The ladies let us think we're in charge, but we all know differently." He grinned at Anton. "You're gonna have to tell her how it really works, who's calling the shots. I need to check on my family."

As he walked away, Adam listened to Anton setting the reporter straight. He was still laughing over the woman's astonished gasp at the words, "... are a matriarchal society. In our pack, among our kind, the alpha bitch is in control ... and believe me, every last woman I know, including my six-year-old daughter, is an alpha."

Doc Logan, Igmutaka, and Sunny were sitting with Liana when Adam reached the cavern. Four-year-old Eve Elizabeth was curled up in Ig's lap, and three-year-old Jace cuddled with Sunny.

"Adam!" Liana reached for him with her free hand and tugged him down to sit beside her. "I'm glad you're back. We've been listening in on everything. What do you think of that reporter? She's usually so judgmental and opinionated. Is she going to hurt us? Do you think she'll turn public opinion against us?"

He leaned over and ruffled Jace's hair, laughing out loud. "I think Melissa Carole's met her match in Anton Cheval. She really doesn't want to approve of us, but he's being so damned charming he makes your teeth itch. I've never seen Anton pour it on quite so thick, but she's eating it up. She has no idea we can scent her interest, and believe me, you could cut the pheromones with a dull knife."

Still grinning, he ran his fingers over the baby's soft blond wisps of hair. "How's our girl?"

"She's perfect, just like our other two." Liana smiled at both of the older kids. "Adam, I think I want to take her topside to meet your reporter."

"Are you sure?" He really hated the thought of using his family to make a point, but if this was what Liana really wanted . . .

"I am. But I don't want you with me."

He jerked his head up and stared at her. "Why not?"

"Because you, Logan, Ig, and Sunny are going out to check for injured wildlife. You should have been out there hours ago. And I'm going to tell that reporter where you are and what you're doing, that you're healing suffering animals that couldn't flee the fire in time. Not only will you be doing what you should have been doing already, but you'll make a lot of good karma points with the public."

Logan snorted. Really loudly.

Adam glanced at Logan, who was obviously trying as hard as Adam not to laugh. Finally he lost it. "Your point, Logan?"

"Hell, man . . . she should have been in marketing."

Liana added, "It will also emphasize the fact that I am an alpha and I can be a bitch at times. And that my man understands his position in the family hierarchy."

Adam winked at Liana. She sent him a smile that would put the Madonna to shame.

Ig grinned. "I'm not all that sure what Logan means,

but such a decision will help sway public opinion. And the animals do suffer. I was about to leave with Sunny to see what we could do to help when Liana made her suggestion. I would add one thing—that we shift and go with Liana so that she can show us off to the reporter before we leave."

He turned and nodded to Logan. "Of course, the good doctor will have his medical bag slung around his neck."

"Hadn't thought of that." Logan picked up the ever-present bag. "Ig, maybe you and Liana should go into public relations together. Sunny? Are you sure you're up to this? You had a busy night and I really don't want to exhaust you."

Adam caught Sunny's soft glance in Ig's direction. "Oh, Ig, you didn't?"

The spirit guide shot him an innocent look. Sunny blushed all the way to the roots of her short blond hair.

Liana frowned. "What did Ig do?" She turned and stared at him.

Adam sighed. "I think he gave Sunny a taste of the Louisville Slugger."

Sunny burst into laughter and covered her face with both hands. "He did. Oh Lordy, he did, and it was absolutely delicious. But I didn't realize everyone would find out!"

Even Igmutaka laughed at that one. Adam cocked one eyebrow at Logan and nodded sagely. "I think Sunny's going to do just fine in this madhouse, don't you, Doc?"

"Definitely. Most definitely." Then Logan lost it all over again.

The laughter ended the moment they stepped out of the unburned stairwell and into hell. Liana fought tears as she crossed the scorched meadow carrying her newborn daughter in her arms. Adam had tried to prepare her for the utter devastation, but she hadn't expected this. She glanced down at the beautiful dark wolf on her left. "I hope you don't burn your paws. This is horrible, Adam. It's absolutely horrible. How did Anton handle seeing his beautiful home . . ."

Better than I did. And don't worry about our paws. It rained during the night. Only a few of the heavier logs are still smoldering. The ground's fairly cool—it's merely warmed by the sun.

Sunny's fair wolf and Logan's solid black were at Liana's right. Igmutaka's big cougar followed along behind. Surrounding Liana and her baby. Protecting both of them. They reached the shadow beside the huge helicopter and Liana smiled at the camera. In her dark blue sarong with her blond hair unbound and falling in graceful waves to her hips and a beautiful newborn in her arms, she knew she made an impressive picture.

But wasn't that what Anton wanted? Pictures to capture a world's attention? Faces the people would remember? Anton turned away from a conversation with Mik and AJ and rushed toward her.

"Liana? Are you sure you should be up? Why . . . ?" He gestured at the others.

She nodded. "Thank you, Anton. I'm fine." Though her words were directed at Anton, she spoke to the reporter and the dark eye of the camera.

"Adam, Logan, Ig, and Sunny are going into the forest to check on the wildlife. While a lot of the animals escaped the fire, there'll be many who need care to heal from their burns. Adam and Logan are healers and Igmutaka can communicate with the various species. Sunny's going along for the experience. She's new, you know."

This time she smiled directly at the reporter and tried to ignore the microphone shoved in her face. Goddesses never had to deal with nosy reporters.

"You met Adam earlier . . . my husband." It was so hard to say *husband* when she generally thought of him as her mate, but they were legally married, and if she could only remember to wear her plain gold band, she would show it off.

Then she realized she couldn't. It was somewhere in the burned-out rubble—probably melted back into a nugget by now.

"Yes, we did. Where is he? I thought he'd be coming with you."

"Oh." Liana smiled. "He did. That's him." She pointed at the gorgeous russet wolf with the striking gold streaks running through his coat. He really was a beautiful animal. "And that's Logan Pierce, our doctor, and the big cat is Igmutaka. He's Lakota Sioux . . . a spirit guide. Beside him, that beautiful blond wolf? That's Sunny Daye. She was the girl in the wheelchair, the one the bomb was attached to. She's the only reason Nick was able to save everyone."

"You're Sunny?" The reporter stared at the blond wolf and looked about ready to pass out. "But . . . but . . . how did she save people? How can she be walking? She was paralyzed!"

They'd discussed this already. No telepathy. "It was the fear in her eyes that led Nick to her. Her fear was a palpable thing. As Chanku, we're close enough to our feral selves that we sense it the way animals do. It didn't fit the occasion. Nick is very perceptive and he was drawn to her. Once his curiosity took him close enough, he smelled the explosive in the bag, and you know the rest.

"As far as her paralysis—once Nick got close, he recognized that Sunny was like us. He knew she was Chanku, but she couldn't shift. There are certain nutrients the body needs in order for that to happen, and Sunny had never had them. Now she has. When she shifted, her body was able to heal itself."

Liana adjusted her daughter's slight weight in her arms and spoke to the wolves and the big cat. "I'm okay. Animals are out there hurting. You guys really need to get out there and help them."

Logan yipped and spun about. The others followed, though Adam paused long enough to rise up on his hind legs and swipe his tongue over his daughter. Then he dropped back to all four big paws and licked Liana's hand before racing across the burned-out meadow toward the equally devastated forest.

"Oh. How sweet!"

The reporter's soft exclamation mirrored Liana's thoughts. He was sweet. There was so much of Adam that most people never saw. She might once have been a goddess, but Adam was by far the better person. She loved him. Loved him so much her heart ached.

So many years searching for something. She hadn't realized what she looked for until she found him. She smiled as Adam caught up to the others and disappeared into the thick undergrowth at the edge of the burned forest. At least here, where the fire had crowned, there was still greenery at the base of the trees.

Already, she knew the forest was beginning to recover. It would take time, but last night's rain would bring new growth. The coming winter would allow the land to heal. Spring would once more bring rebirth.

She stared at the waving branches where Adam and the others had passed. Any other time, she'd be running beside all of them. Not this time. Not for a while—until her daughter was older, her body strong again. Logan and Adam had healed the minor tears from birthing this little one, but it would take a while to regain her Chanku strength.

"May I see your baby? What's her name?"

Snapped out of her musings, Liana pulled the soft blanket back from her daughter's face.

"Oh. She's absolutely gorgeous. And so new!"

Nothing like a new baby to get everyone's attention.

Even the cameraman was smiling, but this little one really was beautiful. Her eyes opened. Now they were as blue as could be, like a newborn pup. But, as with wolves in the wild, that would change as she got older.

"Thank you. We think she's pretty special. We haven't named her yet," Liana said, though in her heart, she already knew what this one would be called. She hadn't said a word to Adam yet. Liana already thought of her as Phoenix. It seemed perfect for this little one, born on the night their world burned.

She was the child who would help all of them rise from the ashes—of the fire, of their discovery by the world. She was the key. *Phoenix Olivia Wolf.*

"Why not? Do you have some sort of naming ceremony?"

Liana frowned at the reporter. "No, but naming a baby means you have to discuss it with the baby's father, and this little one's father has been just a bit busy since she was born. As our healer, he was up most of the night with a badly burned packmate before helping me with her birth."

It was time to go back. Liana turned and focused on Anton. "Is everything okay out here? Do you need anyone else to help keep an eye on these men?"

Grinning broadly, most likely at the sound of authority in her voice, Anton shook his head. "No. We've got it covered. Thanks for bringing this little angel out." He brushed his finger across the baby's cheek and she instinctively turned toward his touch. "She's as beautiful as her mother."

"I think Adam's been practicing your line of BS, Anton, but thank you." Liana turned again to the camera and the reporter. "Did Anton tell you how we handle labor pain during delivery?"

Ms. Carole's eyes lit up. "No. He didn't mention it."

"Our packmates are able to absorb the laboring mother's pain, which makes childbirth entirely pain free, without need of any drugs. Anton was one of those with me last night while I was in labor. You might ask him how it felt from his point of view."

She sensed rather than heard Anton's snort. *I can't believe you told her that.*

Tell her all about it. Be very descriptive. Maybe even whimper a little. Women across the world will love you. Having a spouse experience labor pains is every woman's wet dream. Trust me on this.

As if on cue, the baby let out a little cry. Liana nodded to the reporter. "It's time for me to feed her. It was very nice meeting you." And then she turned and walked away, leaving Anton to explain childbirth from the newly enlightened male point of view. His silent laughter followed her all the way back to the stairs.

Sunny couldn't believe how much stronger her legs felt today. Each time she shifted, her wolf form was more powerful, her coordination better, her senses more attuned to the world around her.

The downside was that the stink of the fire was almost overwhelming.

They'd been out for hours now. She'd seen miracles she might never have imagined if she'd not been invited along. Logan and Adam sitting quietly beside a badly burned sow bear, healing her with the touch of their hands and that weird thing they did where Adam said they actually went inside the injured animal.

Igmutaka was just as amazing. He talked to bears and deer, calmed a frightened fox, helped an eagle down from a branch so Adam and Logan could repair badly singed feathers. Watching the cat as he stared intently at the regal bird, holding it immobile with the force of his mind, was something she'd never forget.

They'd found death today, but they'd saved lives as well. The powers the Chanku had amazed her. The fact she was one of them was hard to accept. That she ran beside them, had a voice, a chance to live like a normal person was so far beyond anything she'd ever dreamed. Never had she imagined actually living the dreams she'd had for most of her life.

The sun was beginning to set when Logan paused along the trail. *I'm going back. I want to check on Jake, see what's going on with logistics. I'm wondering how long we're going to stay in the caverns, what Anton's got planned for our living situation. And I haven't seen Jazzy all day. I miss her.*

Adam shot a glance at Ig and Sunny. *And after he gets laid, because we all know what "missing Jazzy" means, he really wants to see the evening news.*

Logan's tail wagged in silent agreement.

Record it, okay? Not the sex, the news. I want to catch it later. Right now, though, I want to check that rocky area at the tree line. Last time we had a fire, there were a bunch of bighorn sheep that got caught in a blind canyon up there, one they couldn't climb out of.

Sunny? What about you? Do you want to come back with me?

I'm not tired, Logan. I'll go with Ig and Adam.

Good. Don't overdo it. You're still new at this whole walking thing, so be careful. Logan turned and headed back along the trail. Sunny followed Ig and Adam up the mountain, toward the distant tree line.

This was real. This was happening to her, and it still felt like a dream come true.

The foul odor of burned meat lay heavy on the air. Adam paused at the narrow entrance to the canyon. *I know it smells awful, but just in case someone's still alive, I want to check it out. You okay with that?*

Without waiting for an answer, he slipped through the opening—little more than a crevice between two solid walls of granite. Ig and Sunny followed close behind, all of them dreading what they might find.

The stench of death was even stronger inside this narrow path where the air lay heavy and still. They trotted along a meandering stream between two sheer cliff faces, following a gap barely wide enough to pass through in single file. Adam glanced over his shoulder. He'd been keeping a close eye on Sunny—she amazed him with her stamina. He hadn't expected her to keep up as well as she had.

Instead, she'd been an asset throughout the entire day, instinctively calming many of the injured animals, holding them still so that he and Logan could work.

They made a good team—Ig able to talk to most of the creatures, he and Logan with their healing skills, Sunny taking on the role of surgical nurse. If Liana had been able to join them, they could have done even more, but at least they'd saved more today than they'd had to put down.

That, too, was a mercy, though he hated the way it felt to go inside an animal and stop its heart from beating. It was painless and a better death than days of suffering and death from infection or the pure shock of such terrible burns, but he was a healer. Giving an animal a merciful death was still a failure, no matter how he looked at it.

He squeezed through the last narrow spot in the canyon and paused at the opening leading to the meadow. A thick stand of aspen, already turning gold this late in September, grew along one side, and water still pooled in the northern end of the meadow. The grass was thick here. Muddy prints showed evidence that mountain goats and sheep had recently grazed.

The fire hadn't burned this section, and in the falling light he couldn't pinpoint the source of the odor. The stench was overwhelming now that they were in the enclosed canyon, but where was it coming from?

There was no wind here—sheer walls rose well over a

hundred feet on all sides. Only the narrow cleft along the stream gave access. *Let's fan out. See if we can find out what happened. The fire didn't burn here, so I can't figure out why I'm smelling burned flesh.*

Adam took off toward the creek and the grove of aspens while Sunny trotted straight through the middle of the meadow. Igmutaka headed right, toward a jumble of rock piled along the eastern edge of the canyon.

The smell grew stronger as Adam moved through the belly-high grass. He found one dead ram, the body badly burned, the belly torn out, as if a large animal had recently fed on the carcass. Nearby he came across a second animal, and then a third. The second two were dead as well, showing some burns, but their bodies were intact. He stared at them for a moment. They hadn't died from their burns, not from the fire.

Their necks were broken. All three of them.

They'd come here, injured and hurting, seeking a safe place with food and water nearby, but something had killed them. Something huge. He sniffed around, but there was no sign of cougar, and while the ground was trampled, he couldn't find any recognizable prints in the mud. The passageway was too narrow for a bear to slip through, but something had broken their necks. Something had eaten half of a large bighorn ram.

Adam's hackles went up. He raised his head and sniffed the air. The stench of burnt flesh was so overpowering he couldn't pick out any other smells. Looking across the meadow, he spotted movement. Sunny was barely visible in the shadows, though her pale coat glimmered with the last of the day's light. He couldn't see Ig at all. Of course, the cat had a way of blending into his surroundings that was absolutely surreal.

Adam searched along the stream bank, sniffing in thick brambles and checking sheltered spots among the stunted willows. The sheep had been strong enough to come here, even though they'd been burned, obviously seeking sanctuary where there was plenty of food and water. What had killed them? Something big enough to bring down a bighorn sheep with a single blow.

The entrance was much too narrow for a bear. Beyond the broken necks, the amount of damage to the one carcass was pretty excessive for even a large flock of vultures or a single cougar in so short a time. The bighorn sheep had been injured just last night. Since then, many pounds of the carcass had been consumed.

Ig would have noticed if there were cougars about. He was notoriously territorial in his cougar form.

A loud shriek split the night air. *Ig? What's going on?*

Grizzly! He's a big one. Has me cornered in the rocks. East side. He shrieked again, a loud cry of feline anger that ripped open the night.

Sunny? Be careful. Stay back. I'll help Ig.

Except Sunny didn't answer. Adam raced across the darkening meadow. *Sunny? Sunny, where the fuck are you?*

There was no answer. No sound at all. Nothing but the heavy chuffing sound of a large grizzly. Then a deep-throated roar. Ig screamed again, but there was fear in his panther's cry as well as anger. Adam ran faster, searching for Sunny's mental voice even as he raced toward Igmutaka.

The cougar snarled. The bear roared again.

How the hell could a bear have gotten in here? It made no sense—the canyon they'd followed was too narrow for an animal that large to pass. He heard a low growl, another low snarl from Ig.

He's big, Adam. And he really wants a piece of my ass. Any ideas?

Not a one. Where the hell is Sunny?

I don't know. Shit. That was close.

Ig, can the bear get to you?

If he wants me bad enough . . . and I think he wants me. I'm between two boulders against the cliff face. No way out, nowhere to go. There's a twisted pine growing out of the cliff just above me.

I see it. Hang on. Damn. I wish I knew where Sunny was.

Adam saw the bear, a huge monster of a beast barely visible in the fading light. It stared at a dark area between two boulders. Ig's glowing eyes were shining out of the shadows.

Adam slipped around behind the huge beast, looking for anything he could use as a weapon, but damn, there was no escape. Even if Ig could get out from under the rock, they'd have to make a run for the narrow canyon, and grizzlies were fast. Plus, they couldn't leave without Sunny, but he had no idea where she'd gone. Could the grizzly have gotten her?

One thing for sure—the bear couldn't get out of the canyon. He was too damned big to fit between the canyon walls.

And there was no way in hell a wolf was going to kill a full-grown male grizzly. A really pissed-off grizzly. Even with the help of a cougar, odds were the two of them would end up badly injured or worse.

But he had to try. Adam lunged at the bear's hindquarters, latched onto thick fur and loose skin. The bear swung around, moving so quickly he slammed Adam against the side of the boulder.

Shaken, he lost his grip and rolled out of the way of the big paw that slammed the ground beside him. Yipping, he scampered to his feet and lunged out of the way.

His attention divided now, the bear stood in front of the opening to Ig's hideout, swinging his huge head back and forth. His growl split the night. Adam skulked just out of the bear's reach, his belly low to the ground, ears flat to his head.

Snarling, he tried to draw it away from Ig, but the animal seemed confused by two such diverse adversaries. Growling, it rose up on hind legs and glared at the cliff walls. Then it dropped back on all fours and lunged at Adam.

He spun out of the way just a hair's breadth from the animal's deadly claws. Standing just out of reach again, Adam kept his head low and snarled at the grizzly.

A low growl echoed out of the darkness off to Adam's right. Startled, he spun around, hackles flaring along his spine.

No. Absolutely not.

Holy shit, Ig. We've got company. It's another grizzly.

Chapter 29

The second bear was smaller, not nearly as monstrous as the big male. It chuffed and growled, but showed no fear of the larger bear. Adam backed off. *I think it's a female, Ig.*

Great. Maybe they're planning a dinner party.

I don't think so. He stared at the second bear. There was something oddly familiar about the creature. Had he seen this one before? Grizzlies weren't all that common—one had attacked Eve years ago, and they'd had run-ins with a couple of others since, but the big brutes tended to keep to themselves.

Finding two here in this small, blind canyon made no sense at all, especially when the entrance was much too tight for either of them to come in that way. Had they both fallen over the cliff?

He glanced up and tried to judge the distance, but to his wolven eyes it was hard to tell. At least a hundred feet up. The fall would probably kill any animal that had the misfortune to tumble over the cliff.

Holy fuck. Will you look at that.

Ig's soft expletive had Adam spinning around and focusing once again on the pair of bears. The small one was staring intently at the large male, growling and making irritated chuffing noises, almost as if she was reading him the riot act. Then she turned away and headed back across the meadow, lumbering toward the burned carcasses on the far side.

The male swung his big head, growled, and stared after her. Then he took a final swipe at Ig, ignored Adam entirely, and followed the female.

Ig scrambled out from under the rocks. *Figured it out yet?*

Figured what out?

Who the bear is?

Who? Adam stared at the two huge beasts as they crossed the meadow. *Are you saying that's Sunny? Shit . . . it can't be.*

You see her anywhere else? Adam, I understand the grizzly language. The she-bear is Sunny.

They stood there, speechless, watching as the big male followed the female across the meadow. The freshly killed ram caught the male's attention and he squatted down beside the partially eaten bighorn. The female stood beside him for a moment, then she turned away and ambled through the tall grass, directly toward Adam and Ig.

Even though she was smaller than the male, she still made a formidable adversary. Both men stood their ground. Adam swung his head around and stared at the cat for a long moment. Finally he huffed out a deep breath of air. *Ig, I sure as hell hope you know what you're talking about, because if that's not Sunny, we're in trouble.*

So do I, Adam. So do I.

Sunny lumbered through the tall grass toward the wolf and the cougar. This body wasn't nearly as easy a shift as the wolf, but the ability to communicate with the big bear made it worth the discomfort.

Just the fact she'd been able to take this form totally blew her away. She stopped in front of Adam and Igmutaka and shifted. This time she went to human, though, standing tall and way too proud of herself in front of them.

Both men immediately shifted. "How the hell did you do that?" Adam was laughing, but there was definite admiration in his eyes.

Sunny couldn't have wiped the grin off her face if she'd tried. She didn't try at all. "I just thought bear. I could sense his distress. That poor guy didn't really want to hurt you, Ig, but he's scared and mad at everything."

Adam glanced at the bear. The hulking beast was barely visible, but the sound of crunching bones echoed off the high walls as he fed on the ram. "You could have fooled me. Did you see the claws on that thing? You could understand him okay?"

Sunny shrugged, but she turned and watched the bear, too. "A little. Enough to know that he fell off the cliff about two months ago, and it's been feast or famine ever since. He can't get out and the only food he gets is what he can catch that comes in through the narrow canyon. When those three injured sheep showed up this morning, he hadn't eaten for many days. He knows the seasons are changing and he hasn't built up enough fat reserves to make it through the winter."

She smiled at Ig. "He thought you were here to steal his food. I told him you were here to help him get out."

Ig smiled at her. "Okay, sweet one. And how do you expect us to do that?"

"Well, I thought maybe Tinker could use his helicopter to lift him out. Can it carry something as heavy as a bear?"

Adam made a funny choking noise. Ig glanced at him and lost it. Sunny flattened her hands on her hips and glared at both of them. "Want to tell me what's so funny?"

"Just trying to figure out how we're going to explain all this to Tinker. He's a bit protective about the chopper."

Adam slung an arm around her shoulders. "Let's head home. Your buddy has plenty of food for now. We'll see if we can get him out of here in a day or two."

"Well, okay. But I need to tell him we're going." She stepped away, but Adam wrapped his fingers around her arm before she had time to shift.

"He's eating. He's a bear. He's already forgotten the conversation. We'll come back as soon as we can. Trust me."

She wondered if Adam was just patronizing her, but she looked into his dark eyes and realized he was deadly serious. Both of them were. They were also both heavily aroused.

Not nearly as much as she was.

This need for sex after shifting was no joke. Last night Ig had been there to take the edge off for her, but tonight . . . she found herself imagining all sorts of combinations that included the three of them. Felt her body growing damp and needy.

The idea of both of them joining her for . . . well, crap. Adam had a wife and new baby waiting, so that was probably out. Sighing, Sunny dragged her thoughts away from the desire growing in every cell of her body. "Okay. As long as you promise not to forget him." She gazed at the bear for a moment. "I feel sorry for him. He's all alone here and he's afraid."

Adam looped an arm over her shoulders. "He's okay. He's got plenty of food and water, and I promise you we'll come back for him."

"Okay." She glanced from Ig to Adam. "What now?"

"Now we hunt," Adam said. "Though actually, I think we can just look for something that didn't survive the fire. No need to kill when there's so much food available. I'm hungry and I'm tired, and it's late. The people food will all be put away at the cavern. C'mon."

Sunny trusted him completely. She shifted.

Adam headed across the meadow and out through the narrow canyon. Sunny and Igmutaka followed close behind. It amazed her, how well she could see in what had appeared almost total darkness to her human eyes.

The sound of the bear's noisy meal, his growls and the crunching of massive teeth against fresh bones eventually faded as they traveled along the small creek. Once they popped out of the cleft in the rocky hillside, the night opened up to millions of stars and a cool breeze blowing.

They'd left the stench of burned meat behind them, and the smell of the fire wasn't as strong here. It got worse as they dropped lower. Rain had stopped the flames' progression up the mountain, but Sunny, Ig, and Adam were moving downhill toward the main cavern and the ruins of Anton's house.

Adam continuously sniffed the air for other predators. The animals were all on edge, frightened, disoriented, many of them suffering burns and other injuries from the fire. Creatures in pain often acted totally out of character, which made the forest a dangerous place tonight.

It didn't take long after they'd reached scorched trees and blackened shrubs to come across a dead doe lying near a shallow pool of clear water. The animal was fresh, the body untouched, though badly burned. Adam sniffed the air, searching for other predators before settling down to eat. All he could smell was burned wood and partially cooked deer. The smell of the meat made him salivate. Sunny didn't hesitate. She attacked the animal's haunch, while Ig tore at the belly.

Adam ate slowly, savoring the taste of a fresh kill, though he'd had no part in the hunt. He watched Sunny, fascinated by the girl, by her willingness to accept so much change in her life. He still couldn't believe she'd been able to shift into a bear when she'd only been taught to become a wolf.

It made him wonder if they'd all locked themselves into the wolven form. Could he become a bear? An eagle, like Alex? Was there no limit to the Chanku ability to shape-shift?

He'd think about it another time. Exhaustion was beginning to set in. He'd gone most of the night without sleep, had depleted his energy healing Jake, helping Liana. Healing the animals today had taken more out of him.

He checked in with Liana, linking to her sleepy mind. She was just lying down, preparing to sleep. The kids were fine. The baby was sleeping but she'd nursed well. All was as it should be. Then she added a postscript to her sleepy message.

She thought he should spend some quality time with Igmutaka while he had the chance. And Sunny, too . . . if the poor girl was up to the chore of dealing with the two of them. Liana's soft laughter faded from Adam's mind as, belly full, he backed away from the body of the deer and shifted. The blood and dirt fell away from his human skin, but he still felt hot and sticky. The woodland pool beckoned.

He left Ig and Sunny still feeding and waded into the water. It was cold and invigorating and surprisingly deep in the center, coming almost to his waist. He dipped down, dunked his head, and then scrubbed the sweat from his face. When he stood up, Sunny was wading in beside Igmutaka.

She laughed, a nervous sound that surprised him.

"What's the matter?"

"I was just thinking of watching a movie about people swimming in a pool in the mountains. They got out of the water and had leeches all over their legs. Yuck."

Adam threw back his head and laughed.

"What's so funny?" She leaned over and splashed her hands in the water, though she'd only waded out deep enough for it to reach her knees.

"You faced down a full-grown male grizzly today and you're afraid of leeches? Think about it, Sunny."

She stared off in the distance, almost as if unwilling to meet his eyes. Her silence unnerved him. "Sunny? What's wrong?"

"Just that. I turned into a bear today. I didn't know I could do that, but I wanted to and I did. I've been a wolf. I'm walking." She glanced at Ig as he stepped into the pool beside her. "I've had sex for the first time, so I'm not a virgin anymore. I can feel things. Eat things. Everything's different. I think . . . I think . . ." She covered her face and sobbed.

Ig wrapped his arms around her. Adam lurched up out of the water and stood in front of her. He pulled her hands away from her face and forced her to look at him. Her eyes stared at him out of a pale oval in the dim moonlight; her tears sparkled like diamonds on her cheeks.

"It's okay, Sunny. Don't be embarrassed. You're such a natural at all this, we forget it's entirely new to you. Do you have any idea how amazing you are? How terribly brave you've been? Good Goddess . . . you arrived just when we as a species were going through so many unexpected changes. You've been caught up in this mess and you've just rolled with it, changed with it, adjusted to it. Don't cry, please. Don't be afraid, don't be uncomfortable. Don't let it overwhelm you. Just keep doing what you're doing, because we're all pretty damned impressed with you."

She sniffed. Blinked back tears. Sniffed again and shivered.

"Are you cold?"

She shook her head and took a deep, shuddering breath. "No. You nailed it. Overwhelmed. And horny." She choked on her laughter. "I had no idea what sex felt like until last night, and now it's all I can think about. I feel as if my body is ready to explode, as if all my nerve endings are on fire. Is it always like this? Do you guys feel it, too?"

Adam glanced at Ig. The spirit guide stared at him.

They both exploded into laughter.

Sunny frowned and then stared at both men. Adam felt his cock rise even higher. Still laughing, he said, "Hey. The guy likes an appreciative audience."

"What?" Sunny barely spit out the word. She slapped a hand over her mouth.

Ig didn't say anything, though he dunked down in the water and washed himself off with his hands. Then he waded out of the pond. "Follow me." He shifted and stared impatiently at them.

Adam shrugged. "The man says we need to follow him. C'mon."

He and Sunny both quickly rinsed off and shifted as soon as they reached the edge of the pond. Ig was already trotting along the trail, heading at an oblique angle from the house.

Sunny turned and sent a questioning glance in Adam's direction. *I haven't got a clue,* he said.

He merely followed the cat.

Anton shut off the flat-screen TV the guys had carted into the caverns during their rush to salvage whatever belongings they could from the fire. He'd thought it fairly frivolous when Mik and AJ had carried the big thing down the stairs, but now he was truly thankful to have this link to the outside world.

The guys had set it up in one of the smaller caves away from the main room, but no one had had time to get it hooked up and running until this afternoon when Tinker and Oliver had gotten the satellite receiver set up in the ruins above. With the solar panels still generating power, they'd gotten a terrific signal.

And what a signal it was.

He took a deep breath and carefully set the remote on the table beside the screen. It took all his willpower to keep from doing a handstand and making an absolute fool of himself, but damn.

Just . . . damn.

Though many in the pack had already gone to bed, Anton had more than a dozen stalwart souls grinning back at him—his packmates who'd stayed awake for the late-night news. He'd been worried about Melissa Carole's coverage. She could be a real bitch.

It appeared the bitch was on their side.

Hallelujah!

He'd turned on the TV set with his heart pounding in his chest, and fear for all of them clamoring against his sense of reason and hope for a fair shot.

Now he stood in front of his packmates with a stupid grin on his face. ALN reporter Melissa Carole had managed to scoop all the other networks with her story on the Chanku from their "undisclosed location in the wilds of Montana."

She'd caught the pompous general trying to arrest Nick without a warrant, Anton's private call directly to the president, the short yet dramatic tussle as wolves and men disarmed the soldiers.

She'd painted them as heroes, as good citizens who were unique and amazing, but still people. Still just like everyone else, with their love of family, their sense of fair play, their kindness, their good manners.

She'd not come right out and said anything about how good looking the men were, but the fact that the camera had lingered on Mik's proud profile, on Tinker's broad chest, on AJ's beautiful smile spoke volumes.

She'd captured Liana's comments about the men sharing labor and Anton's humorous account of discovering just how hard it was to give birth.

She'd managed to show their respect for each other,

their love of country, their fears for the future now that their existence was public knowledge. And then she'd done her best to assure the rest of the world that, other than the fact these were people who could shift into animals, they were still people, just like everyone else.

The same needs, the same desires, the same hopes for a safe and prosperous future.

Her interview with Luc had been fairly brief, but she'd found some old clippings of stories where Pack Dynamics had made daring rescues, found missing children, and saved lives.

Again, the Chanku were heroes. Good people. Neighbors. She'd ended her lengthy coverage with an open invitation to Anton or any of the others to come on her program, to tell the world about themselves. To bring their families if they wanted. And then she'd thanked them for giving her access to what she called "the most important story in the world today. Not only proof there are people from another world living among humans, but proof that they are good and decent people."

Anton laced his fingers behind his back. "I think this calls for a toast," he said. "Unfortunately, my bottle of Hennessey didn't make it through the fire." He sent a chagrined glance in Stef's direction.

"Actually, it did." Stef reached under his chair, stood up, and raised the bottle high. "The brandy snifters didn't make it, but the bottle is just fine." He pulled out the stopper and took a big swallow. Then he passed the bottle on to Anton. "Here's to raising our children in a world that knows of us but doesn't fear us."

Anton took the bottle and stared into its amber depths. "I'll drink to that, Stef. This is just one reporter with one opinion, but she's preaching to those whose response we feared the most. Here's hoping they're listening to what she said."

He took a sip and passed the bottle on to Oliver, and on

it went. To Keisha and Xandi, to Mei and then to Luc, AJ, and Mik. Tala, pregnant with AJ's daughter, passed on the toast and handed the bottle to Tinker, who shared it with Lisa. She gave it to Nick, who looked more relaxed than he had since the entire incident began. He took a drink and passed the bottle to Beth.

She gave it to Ric. Ulrich stared at the bottle for a long moment, took a swallow, and handed it back to Anton. "I never thought this day would come," he said. "When I first met Tianna's mother, I never dreamed there were more shapeshifters. After Camille's sister's death, we thought she was the last of her kind. After Camille died, I had no intention of telling our daughter of her heritage. It was too frightening."

He turned to Luc and sighed. "Then I met Luc. And Tia had the nerve to grow up and fall in love with the bastard." His harsh burst of laughter had all of them grinning. "Of course, by then I'd collected Mik and AJ, and Jake and Tinker and I finally figured out maybe we weren't alone, that maybe there were a few more shapeshifters out there."

He stood up and brushed the dust from the floor off his pants. "Then I met you, Anton, and there was no disputing the fact there were many more Chanku than I ever dreamed. There are still more out there. Finding Sunny is proof of that, but I can still remember that feeling, of Tia and me being the only ones left when Tia's mother died. You are all my family now. I hope you appreciate how thrilled I was to discover I was wrong."

He nodded to Anton and grinned at the others. "And now I have a lovely woman, a shapeshifter, actually, waiting for me in a quiet corner of the cavern with more on her mind than the nightly news." He tipped an imaginary hat. "I bid each of you adieu."

Anton watched Ulrich as he walked through the low opening toward the main cavern. "He's right, you know.

There are still more out there, and somehow, we're going to find them. But for now we need to concentrate on getting our lives in order."

Stefan stood up and yawned. "Personally, I'm going to opt for a good night's sleep, first." He reached down, grabbed Xandi's hand, and pulled her to her feet. "Congratulations, Anton. I think today's coverage might be exactly what we needed to stem negative press."

Anton shook his head, aware of a sense of another presence close by. "Don't thank me," he said. "Thank Eve. If anyone had a hand in things, I'd say it was our Goddess."

The air around them shimmered, though she didn't appear. She didn't have to. He knew she was close by. Knew she protected them still. With that in mind, he helped Keisha to her feet and headed out to the main cavern and the soft pallet where their children slept.

Chapter 30

Igmutaka struck a match to the old-style kerosene lantern, and light filled the small space. Sunny's gasp of wonder echoed off the walls as she stood up, staring wide-eyed at the rainbow of colors cascading from what appeared to be amethyst crystals embedded in the walls and ceiling of the cavern.

"How did you ever find this place?" It was unbelievable, as if they'd stepped inside a giant geode. The predominant color seemed to be a deep purple. Even the small pool of water reflected shades of soft lavender.

"When I first manifested as a human, I was still confused by my new body, the way it worked, the way my mind seemed to function on a level so far removed from my cat. I found a few caverns, hidden from everyone, deep inside the mountain where I could come and consider the new side of myself." Ig nodded at Sunny. "You and I stayed in one of them last night."

She felt herself blushing, but she wasn't sure if it was from Ig mentioning what she couldn't stop thinking about, or the fact Adam was grinning so knowingly at her.

Then he cocked his head and smiled at Ig. "Liana and I used to worry about you when you'd take off in the snow.

We wondered where you went at night, how you stayed warm. We had no idea you were spending time away from us as a man. We pictured you as a cat, holed up in a rough den beneath a fallen tree, shivering in the cold."

Igmutaka laughed, reached into a dark corner, and pulled out a bedroll. "And all the time I was here, surrounded by beauty, sleeping on a comfortable bed." He spread the bedding out on the ground. Sunny knelt and helped him smooth out the thick blankets.

"I can't believe we didn't know about this place." Adam gazed at the crystals in the ceiling and walls. "Oliver and I've explored almost all of Anton's property. We've been mapping all the entrances to the cave system, but we never found anything like this. Does it connect to the one beneath the house?"

Ig nodded. "It does, though it's a fairly difficult route to get there. We're actually on the new property Anton bought. You wouldn't have had a reason to look for this one."

Adam scooted over and sat on the bedding, tugging Sunny down beside him. She shivered, just from the firm grasp of his fingers around hers. The simplest touch had her going wet with arousal. Her vaginal muscles clenched and the breath hitched in her throat.

Both men were heavily aroused, but they just ignored those huge erections that were standing so high and proud. How'd they do that? She couldn't even ignore the taut little peaks of her nipples. If she had something that big banging against her belly, she wouldn't be able to think of anything else.

Shamelessly, she stared at both men, making comparisons in which neither suffered. They were both perfect in their own ways—Adam bronzed from the sun with his sun-bleached tangle of chin-length hair and the darker mat of hair on his chest. As always there was stubble on his chin, a few cuts and scratches on his hands, and a twinkle in his eyes. His cock was long and thick, the tip smooth and broad.

Igmutaka's skin was darker, his chest smooth, his long, silky hair almost black. His eyes were a clear emerald green. There was no way to describe his beauty—he would have made a gorgeous woman, but there was no doubting his masculinity. Unlike Adam, he was uncircumcised. The broad head of his cock was framed with the soft folds of foreskin.

As large as Adam was, Ig's package was even larger; as beautiful as Ig was, Adam was just as enticing. And Sunny suddenly realized both of them were well aware of her perusal.

They each studied her just as closely. But what did they see, these men who were used to such perfect women? Adam's mate had been a goddess—she was still unbelievably beautiful. Ig could have any woman he wanted—why had he aligned himself with a skinny nineteen-year-old who knew absolutely nothing about the ways of men, of sex, of anything?

And then their thoughts spilled into her head. How they saw her as courageous and beautiful, as strong and as brave as any woman they knew. She'd battled adversity her entire life and yet it had never beaten her down. She still had her spirit, her joy for life, her amazingly open personality.

She was tough—a fighter, yet she'd not lost her femininity. She had the look of a true minx about her, a beautiful, tough, adventuresome spirit that had her taking on the form of a she-bear and going up against a rampaging grizzly to protect her friends.

She'd never seen herself as any of those things. Never imagined any man could look at her and see anything beyond a crippled girl with eyes too big for her face, and withered legs that would never carry her upright.

"Not true." Adam reached for her and pulled her into his lap. "Try seeing yourself as we see you, Sunny. You're sweet and innocent and sexy as hell, and yet you never show fear. No fear of anyone." He ran his fingers along her side, gently cupped her breast, and then slipped them lower, down her flat belly, between her thighs. Slowly, he stroked her as he held her. She whimpered as his fingertip slipped gently over her swollen clit and circled her vaginal opening.

Her body actually hungered. "That's not enough," she said, and her voice sounded rough, almost hoarse with need. She grabbed his wrist with both hands and forced him against her, harder. Damn, she was practically breaking his wrist, she held him so tightly.

Adam chuckled. "I know it's not. C'mon, Ig. The girl needs help here."

Igmutaka was grinning when he crawled close to the two of them. "You think I don't? What about me?" Laughing, he wrapped his fist around his own shaft and stroked up and then down, sliding the foreskin back behind the broad head. Then he leaned over Sunny and planted a kiss on first one nipple and then the other. She cried out and bucked her hips, forcing Adam's fingers deep inside. Shoved her breast close against Ig's mouth. Made a strangled noise that seemed to come from somewhere deep inside.

Ig rolled over on his back and reached for her. As if she weighed nothing at all, Adam handed her over; Igmutaka grabbed her waist and lowered her over his erection.

She felt the pressure, the burn from his thickness as he entered her, and then her sex rippled around the broad crown and she settled slowly over his full length. She was wet and slippery and he went all the way in, sliding across the hard mouth of her cervix, stretching her, making room for his massive size.

She settled herself more fully and felt the brush of his

pubic hair against her vaginal lips. He was all the way in. Every last inch of the Louisville Slugger was buried deep inside her body. She giggled, remembering the first time she saw him naked and knew there was absolutely no way any woman could ever fit that much man inside herself.

Thank goodness this body was pliable, because he fit perfectly. Rising up on her knees, she leaned forward and brushed the tips of her breasts across his chest. Kissed that beautiful mouth, running her tongue over his perfect lips.

The contact sent bursts of fire spiraling straight down between her legs.

Adam knelt behind her. His lips teased the soft globes of her bottom as he kissed her. Then she felt his fingers stroking the narrow cleft between her cheeks and one fingertip softly pressing against her anus.

Dear Goddess . . . she'd not expected such sensitivity there, but maybe it was everywhere, the arousal that seemed to consume her, the sensations exploding from wherever she connected with either Ig or Adam. Adam pressed against that tiny opening again, and this time she pressed back.

Again and again, and her arousal grew and the feelings blossomed, taking her higher, closer to that amazing edge that Ig had introduced her to just a few hours ago.

Two men, both intent on her pleasure, each uniquely different and yet with the same goal. Completion. Fulfillment. Climax.

She shivered, reaching for the finish. Her body burned with the force of her passion. Trembled with growing need. Sensations expanded, desire blossomed and grew, engulfing her, swallowing her in unbelievable lust until she opened her mind and set herself free.

Adam was there, and Ig, too. Both waiting for her to join them, wanting to share what they felt, what they needed. She saw the thick tip of Adam's finger pressing and retreating, then pressing harder against the tiny wrinkled orifice in her bottom. Her first thought was to pull away. It was too much, too intimate, too . . . too good to stop.

She pressed against his finger and softly groaned when he slipped through the tight opening. Sawing in and out, slowly stretching the opening wider, softening that taut ring of muscle. He added another finger and she tensed at the intrusion, but Ig was stroking her clit with the soft pad of his fingertip and his big cock was slipping in and out of her sex. She was wet and soft and swollen, and what Adam did just made all of it feel even better.

She closed her eyes and gave in to the sensation, the amazing fullness of Ig's slow and steady thrusts, the sensual slide of Adam's fingers. There was something so wicked about this, so amazingly, wonderfully wrong about two men working toward nothing more than her pleasure.

Giving, not taking. Concentrating on her needs, her desire.

So why did it feel so amazingly right?

"Relax, Sunny. This might hurt a little at first, but not if you relax."

Okay, so Adam was telling her something sort of scary, but she could do this. She could totally relax while he teased that amazingly sensitive spot that she'd never once thought of as an erogenous zone. She let her body go and fell forward against Igmutaka's chest, presenting herself to Adam. Ig stroked her back and murmured in her ear—soft sexy words in a language she didn't understand, but they relaxed her even more.

Adam pulled his fingers out of her bottom, but something else took their place. She slipped into his thoughts once again and watched in utter amazement as he placed the broad head of his cock against that little—*tiny*—little puckered hole.

Now this was going to be interesting. She separated herself from that person and became Adam, slipping so completely into his mind that she was barely aware of anything Sunny experienced. She felt Adam's growing arousal, his struggle to be gentle, to take her higher, to show her a level of eroticism she'd never even imagined.

Fascinated, she watched as he dipped his fingers inside her sex, right alongside Ig's thick shaft. They were wet with her fluids when he rubbed them over her sphincter and easily slipped one finger inside. Just one. She'd done that easily.

Then he rubbed the broad head of his cock over the taut opening, pressed the tip against her, and slowly pushed forward. Some instinct had her pushing back against him. His soft instructions had her relaxing even though he stretched her impossibly wide, even though it burned.

Through Adam's eyes she watched as his glans seemed to reform, to narrow enough to fit through, to pass beyond that tight ring and into the wider channel beyond. Once he'd breached that small barrier, the rest of his cock slid all the way in.

Sunny let out a long, low sigh.

"You okay, sweetie?" Adam's lips brushed her shoulder.

"I am. I can't believe you're both in me."

"How does it feel?" Adam kissed the back of her ear.

She moaned dramatically, and thought about it a moment. How did it feel? Ig held perfectly still. So did Adam. "Full. Very full." Then she tilted her hips. "Move. I want to feel you sliding against each other."

Ig groaned and raised his hips as Adam pulled out. In, out, in and out again. Both men going impossibly deep, her body adjusting completely, taking them both. She sensed their control, how difficult it was for each man as he held back, making it good for her. Building her arousal to a fever pitch, touching where she needed to be touched, thrusting when she had to have them deep inside.

They'd linked with her, become her, and Sunny let go of

whatever inhibitions she might have clung to. Let go of her fears, of her need for anything beyond the here and now, reaching instead for the fulfillment that came from two men loving her, two men who loved each other.

She felt cherished beyond belief, a part of something so profound it was almost impossible to wrap her thoughts around it. Adam moved faster. So did Ig, the two of them thrusting in and out while they bathed her in feelings of love, in a connection unlike anything she'd ever experienced.

Rising high on a tide of passion, her body screaming for release even as her heart and soul clung to the moment, to the men who loved her, she set herself free.

Free to fly. Orgasm slammed into her. A release so powerful she took both men with her. Igmutaka's shout, Adam's deep-throated howl, her own powerful scream as their voices blended, their bodies shuddered and clenched in an impossible climax.

One that seemed to go on forever. On and on, bodies trembling in the aftermath, hearts pounding, lungs heaving with each deep gasp for air. Sunny fell forward against Igmutaka. Adam collapsed over her back, and they lay there, gasping for air, each caught in the thoughts of the other.

Sunny broke first. She giggled. Laughed harder until she felt the answering tremors in Ig's chest, heard the laugher in her ear as Adam joined them both. "Shit," she said. Then she giggled again. "You guys do this often? Because if you do, I'm not sure how much I can handle."

"All the time," Adam said. He kissed her neck. "We're Chanku, Sunny. Get used to it. This is just the way things are."

Anton lay beside Keisha as the last stragglers settled in to sleep. It was odd, really, to lie here beside his sleeping wife after watching his family discussed so openly on the eleven o'clock news, and actually feel good about the day.

Very odd, that he could be preparing to sleep on a rough pallet in an underground cavern, surrounded by his packmates and their young while the remains of his home smoldered overhead, and still feel entirely positive about his future.

But Luc and Stefan had been busy all afternoon, arranging for temporary housing for everyone here on the property. Motor homes and travel trailers would begin arriving in the morning and an architect was due by afternoon.

They would rebuild. Not the same house, and probably not just one house. He owned more than enough property now for them to live close, but not on top of each other. The separate packs could retain their autonomy, but they'd still be together.

Still be connected. Best of all, their children would have the chance to grow up surrounded by others like them. They would know only love, and if everything continued as it had begun tonight, the fears of discovery were a worry of the past.

It wouldn't happen right away, but one day Chanku would be accepted as just another race among many, part of the soup that made up all of humanity.

A low moan and then an exultant scream of pleasure filled his head. He chuckled softly. Ig and Adam were obviously helping Sunny feel more connected to the pack. He'd have to suggest she learn the difference between sharing thoughts with her partners and broadcasting to all of them.

At least she learned quickly.

The girl was amazing. Adam had sent him a private message earlier, one he still had trouble believing. She'd become a bear, talked to a rampaging grizzly, and convinced the animal they would help him escape the canyon where he was trapped.

Never in his wildest dreams . . . and they were pretty wild.

There was still so much to learn. Still so much of their history to understand. Even now with that knowledge in the minds of all of them, it was difficult to make sense of everything.

He almost rubbed his hands with glee.

There was nothing he loved more than a challenge.

But the day had been long, and it was time to rest. He cast out his thoughts and found Mei and Oliver quietly making love with their two little ones sound asleep on the pallet beside them. Sunny's sexy little outburst obviously hadn't gone unnoticed. Xandi and Stefan slept close beside one another with their three kids sprawled next to them. His two boys and Lily slept there tonight as well.

At least Lily was still a little girl.

He wondered what Xandi would say when she awoke to find Alex sleeping as a wolf beside her. That was a new one. So far Anton had only seen him as an eagle and a cougar, but the child had an amazing imagination. He was truly his father's son.

Anton's thoughts moved on, past Ulrich and Millie and Deacon, Matt, and Daci. He hovered a moment by Lisa and Tinker and their three, all sleeping soundly, and moved on to Tala, Mik, and AJ.

Tala was out like a light, while Mik and AJ made slow, quiet love to one another. They were alone tonight—the twins were curled up on the other side of the cavern with Luc and Tia and their two sets of twins, and Adam and Liana's two oldest kids.

Liana quietly nursed the new baby a few pallets away. *Anton? Are you out roving tonight?*

Of all of them, Liana was the most often aware of

Anton's nightly bed check, as she called it. *I am,* he said. *You know me. Just checking. How are you? How's Phoenix?*

She's hungry. This little one loves to eat.

That's a good sign. Sleep well, Liana.

Thank you, Anton. You, too.

He heard Logan and Jazzy's soft laughter, sensed their gentle touches and growing intimacy, and quickly moved away. He found the pack from Maine and eavesdropped for a moment, listening to Baylor's soft whispers as he quieted baby Donovan so Manda could sleep. Then he moved on to Shannon and Jake.

The triplets slept along one side of their father, along with Baylor's four-year-old, Keegan. They'd already picked up the nickname of the Irish pack, and it fit them perfectly.

Shannon clung to Jake even in sleep. She among all of them realized how close she'd come to losing her beloved mate. What Adam and Logan had done was nothing short of miraculous, but the entire pack had a hand in Jake's healing.

Thank the Goddess they'd not lost him. Jake had always fascinated Anton—he was a man of many faces, many sides that very few people really knew.

Only his mate and his closest packmates, Bay and Manda really understood the depth of the man. Anton wondered if Jake realized how much he was loved and admired. Sometimes he feared Jake believed his own press— the bad-boy image he'd cultivated for so long.

Of course, after this brush with death, maybe he finally realized how the rest of the pack felt about him. They'd shouldered unbelievable pain, and they'd done it without hesitation. Every adult member of the pack had waited in line to take a turn carrying Jake's pain while Adam and Logan healed his horrible burns. Thank the Goddess they'd all succeeded.

Anton moved on. Nick and Beth were both asleep. He paused a moment to make certain Nick slept without guilt. At least tonight's newscast should reassure the poor kid. After watching the program, Anton had a good feeling about things. Besides, if there was any trouble, he trusted Eve to watch over them.

He spread his thoughts beyond the cavern and touched on Sunny, Adam, and Igmutaka. Only Ig was still awake and aware of Anton's subtle contact.

There's no need to worry about this little one, Anton. I think she's going to bring one surprise after another.

He smiled, picturing the cougar, the wolf, and the bear. *She's already surprised us. I understand Tinker needs to take the chopper into the back country.*

That he does. It should be an adventure. Good night, Anton.

Good night, Igmutaka. Anton stretched and yawned. Settled in to sleep. All was well, the pack safe.

Daddy? Are you still awake?

Smiling, he answered his daughter. *I am. But what are you doing awake, Lily?*

Waiting for you.

He was almost afraid to ask. *Why, Lily? I already told you good night. It's very late.*

I know, Daddy. But I forgot to tell you about the book we have to write.

A book?

A history book. All about the Chanku and the world we came from and the things we can do. I'm supposed to write it, but you're supposed to help me.

He thought about that for a moment. It was going to be a long winter. They wouldn't be able to start construction on any of the houses until the snow melted in the spring. The memories were fresh, and Lily was always happier with a project.

So are you, my love.

Keisha? He rolled his head to one side and looked into her deep amber eyes. *What are you doing awake?*

Listening to you and Lily. You're thinking too loud. Lily? Go to sleep. You and Daddy can work on the book tomorrow.

G'night, Mommy. G'night, Daddy. I love you.

Like a switch going off, Lily slipped out of Anton's thoughts. *How does she do that?* He leaned close and kissed his wife. Keisha was smiling as their lips met, melded, clung far longer than two old married people usually kissed. *I love you,* he said. *More than I ever imagined loving anyone. Ever.*

Then make love to me. I think I'd like to show you how I feel. Again, and again, and again.

Forever, my love.

He pulled Keisha close. Held her tight and thought about his words as he filled her. Forever. They were Chanku. Forever wasn't just a word. It was a promise.

If you enjoy Kate Douglas's super-erotic
WOLF TALES novels, you're in for a different
but equally delicious treat with her paranormal
romance series, the DemonSlayers!
Turn the page for a special early preview
of the newest book . . .

CrystalFire

Don't miss it!

Chapter 1

The steady *slap, slap, slap* of Taron's sandals echoed off the rough stone walls. He checked his sword, made sure his tunic and pants were properly fastened, and wondered if he'd ever get used to this absurd style of clothing.

After a lifetime in scholarly robes, it was difficult to believe these new designs were more practical, though he had to admit that the pants didn't tangle around his legs the way his robes often had. Of course, he'd rarely had to rush as he rushed now, hurrying down the dark and empty utility tunnel toward the training grounds.

Any other time he would have taken the main passage, but these narrow tunnels, used mostly by the Lemurian Guard, were more practical when one was in a hurry. Besides, there was little risk of being waylaid by any of his fellow scholars. He didn't want to have to explain why he, a well-known scholar and philosopher, was now training some of Lemuria's new Paladins.

He still wasn't quite certain himself.

"Who the nine hells do they think they're kidding?" He would have laughed if it didn't sound so pathetic. Though well trained in battle strategy and swordsmanship, he was a man who won battles with words, not a sword.

Gods be damned, but his own so-called sentient blade

still didn't think enough of his fighting skills to speak to him, but times were changing.

He did have the skills, and he had, after all, volunteered.

After Roland, the new Captain of the Guard, twisted his arm.

A flash of blue caught his eye as he rounded a curve in the passage. He jerked to a stop.

It couldn't be . . . could it?

"Willow?" His heart pounded as he flattened his palm against the wall and searched for the elusive blue sparkle. He'd never thought to see that amazing little will-o'-the-wisp again.

He drew his sword and used the light from the crystal blade. "Willow . . . are you there?"

Carefully he searched the narrow passage. She couldn't be . . . but there was always a chance, always. . . . A small chip—a bit of crystal embedded in the tunnel wall—reflected swordlight with a flash of blue. *Gods be damned.*

He let out a big breath and sheathed his weapon. "Of course you're not here, are you?" What the nine hells was he thinking? Willow was gone, nothing more than consciousness now—that amazing mind, that beautiful little sprite, stuck inside the body of a stupid dog.

Sighing, remembering Willow, wishing the impossible and feeling like a fool, he continued down the tunnel to the training field.

"Nine hells, woman. Be careful!"

Blinded by sweat, Taron lunged to one side. His foot slipped out from under him on the slick stone floor; he ducked his head and rolled to the left. Shoulder first, he hit the ground hard, a hairsbreadth ahead of the sharp edge of the Paladin's sword. The shimmering crystal blade sliced much too close to his throat.

Lying on his back, gasping for air and absolutely livid, he glared at his opponent. "This is a training exercise, Isra! You're not supposed to try to kill me!"

Isra held out her hand in immediate apology. "I am sorry, Taron. Thank the gods you're so quick! I guess I got a bit caught up in our battle."

"Mock battle, Isra. And gods be damned, but quick had nothing to do with it. I fell on my ass or I'd be a dead man. Please, try to remember I'm one of the good guys." Shaking off his unexpected anger, he took her offered hand.

She tugged and he stood, but she didn't turn him loose. Her full lips lifted into a sexy smile. "That you are, Taron of Libernus." Her voice had gone low and rather husky, and she cocked one dark eyebrow as she studied him with unabashed interest. "You are most definitely one of the good guys."

He glanced at their hands—still linked—and back at her face. She continued to assess him in a most forthright manner. He wasn't quite sure how to react—the average Lemurian woman was not so bold.

Isra, though, was a Paladin. Once a slave in the crystal mines, now a soldier in Lemuria's new army of woman warriors.

Paladins knew no fear, nor did they lack confidence.

Taron could use a little of that confidence himself, he thought, staring uncomfortably at their linked hands. He'd learned long ago that women were not for him, and he wasn't about to let this one distract him from his scholarly goals.

Isra glanced at their clasped fingers and then raised her head. "Would you, by any chance, be interested in . . ."

Gods be damned, no! Taron quickly extricated his hand from her grasp. "I'm flattered, Isra, but I'm a scholar. My interests lie elsewhere."

Frowning, she stepped back a pace and stared at him like he had two heads. What? Didn't the woman believe him when he said he wasn't interested?

Obviously not.

Still staring, she said, "You're well formed and powerful. You move with a soldier's grace and speed. You're here, training women to fight. Not a very scholarly occupation, is it?"

He shrugged. "We do what we must in times such as these. Once the Paladins are fully trained, I will return to my studies and my solitude."

Laughing softly, she shook her head. Why would she look so confused? It was only the truth, after all. "Are you a celibate?" she asked. "Is it possible you prefer the company of men?"

His laughter surprised him as much as her question. "No, Isra. I do not prefer the company of men. I am celibate by choice. It's not unusual for a man to choose a life of quiet study over the constant turmoil of politics and warfare—or love."

She grinned at him, still shaking her head.

"Do you think I make light of you?" He honestly didn't know what she thought. He didn't really care, though he did not want her to think him rude. Women had always been, and probably always would be, a mystery to him.

One he had absolutely no interest in solving.

Still smiling, Isra was the one to shrug this time. "I know better, Taron. You are not one to make light of an honest question. I guess it's just not the answer I expected."

"Well, I certainly didn't intend to confuse you, though I'm pleased you realize I would never play you false." Truth be told, she was a lovely young woman, and if he were so inclined, he might be showing interest in Isra the female rather than merely dodging her crystal blade in training.

Isra reached for a cup of water while he turned away and grabbed a towel. Wiping the sweat from his face, he tried to think of Isra as a woman, as someone with whom he might want to form a relationship.

He couldn't do it. He saw her as a Paladin and nothing more. It wasn't the Lemurian way to lust after women, and it certainly wasn't his way. Control of what he thought of as his baser instincts, that wild creature buried deep inside, was more than a matter of honor—it was the way he had chosen to live.

It was a choice many of his peers had made, though that so-called "Lemurian way," like many other things in their society, was undergoing a rapid change. For one thing, these strong-willed, intelligent women now training as warriors were not quiet and soft-spoken like their aristocratic counterparts.

No, they were bold beyond measure.

Taron found their attitude refreshing. Invigorating, even, though he had no intention of pursuing any of them for romance.

They were much too distracting.

This was different, though, this position as a trainer for the women who'd once been slaves. This was a role that had essentially chosen him—one he found he enjoyed in spite of the risk to life and limb.

Of course, Isra's sentient sword never would have allowed her to actually harm him, which was the only reason they were able to train with their crystal blades. Nor could he blame her powerful strike on demon influence. His people—for now, at least—were free of the bastards. None remained who were possessed by demonkind.

Isra—an average-sized woman fully a foot shorter than he and with only a fraction of his reach—had almost taken him down, proving once again that women had the ability to stand as equals beside their men.

One more long-standing Lemurian tradition that had

quickly been erased. Like the one that said a woman waited all her life to be chosen by an interested male, so she might then focus her life on making his easier.

Taron had a feeling that that particular tradition was already gone. But just as women were now free to flirt, Taron was free to ignore that flirtation. Setting his towel aside and smiling ruefully, he did exactly that, shaking his head over Isra's skill and his own clumsiness.

"You've learned quickly, Isra. I'm going to need more work with Roland if I expect to best any of you in battle, mock or otherwise." He bowed his head in respect. "You have done well. All of the Paladins are doing an amazing job, but you have truly excelled."

A brilliant flash of blue light set him back a step. Again, the image of Willow and her trail of blue crystals entered his thoughts, but only for a split second. A strange voice— a woman's voice—echoed from everywhere, yet from nowhere in particular.

"Taron is right. You have done extremely well, Isra."

Taron was almost certain his heart stood still. He stared at Isra's glowing sword, unwilling to believe what he'd just heard, but there was no denying truth.

Impossible. Absolutely impossible. How could this be? It was too soon—Isra was too new a warrior. He swallowed back a curse, raised his head, and focused on the wide-eyed woman.

"Isra. Your blade. It speaks."

Ginny Jones redialed her cousin's number, but the call didn't go through. She stared at her cell phone long enough to register Markus's panic and the blinking icon telling her the battery was going dead. Then she shoved the phone in her pocket, turned around, and walked right into the solid wall of red rock.

In seconds she'd passed through the portal at Red Rock

Crossing, in Sedona, Arizona, and entered the vortex. She bypassed the tunnel to Bell Rock, where the main entrance to Lemuria was located, and took the small portal leading directly from this vortex to the Council of Nine's chancellor's office.

It took mere seconds to step out of Earth's dimension and enter Lemuria's, something that never ceased to amaze her.

She'd have to save the amazement for later. Ready or not, there was another crisis looming, but where the hell was her team? The damned chancellor's office was empty.

"Shit. Where is everyone?" Ginny brushed her hand over her crystal sword, as much from habit as the need to connect to her ever-present companion. After another quick glance about the empty chamber and adjoining rooms, she slipped through the doorway and took off at a full run, heading for the great plaza with her cousin Markus's panic-stricken words echoing in her ears.

Ginny! Something bad is going on. Animals are acting really weird. I mean really, really weird. Tom the cat's got all those teeth again and he just ate the neighbor's dog. Like chewed him up and swallowed him. And the dog's a Rottweiler. Uh . . . he was a Rottweiler. Ginny? Answer the phone! Where are you?

Skidding as she rounded a jeweled column, Ginny collided with Alton. Her mate grabbed her arms, steadying her as she gasped for breath.

"Ginny? Sweetheart . . . what's wrong?"

Blowing so hard she couldn't speak, Ginny linked and telepathically shared Markus's message.

Hanging on to her arm, Alton spun around and looked out across the great plaza. He called out to a familiar figure near the dais. "Dax! Grab Eddy. See if you can find Daws and Selyn. We need to go to Sedona. Now."

Eddy Marks popped out of one of the council chamber

rooms. "What's going on? We were just headed back to Evergreen to check in with Dad and see how BumperWillow's doing."

Ginny shook her head. "There's no time. I just got a message from Markus. It sounds like a full-scale invasion in Sedona. I tried calling him back. He didn't answer, but my battery's really low. I barely got a signal."

Dax, Selyn, and Dawson Buck trotted across the plaza. Ginny waved them over. "Can you guys leave now? We really need to hurry."

Dawson nodded. "We're ready. I need to check on the clinic, anyway, make sure my assistant's got everything under control. He's a good vet. Esteban's used to running the place, so if animals are affected again, he'll have heard." He checked his blade and then glanced toward the plaza filled with citizens. "Should we tell anyone we're going?"

Alton nodded. "I've contacted Taron. Told him we've got a new demon outbreak in Earth's dimension. I wonder if this is the group Isra saw the demon king sending toward Sedona?"

"It has to be." Ginny took off at a trot toward the council office and the small portal. "We couldn't find any sign of them when we were there a couple days ago, though. Makes me wonder what they've been up to."

Alton shook his head as he pushed the pace. "Nothing good, that's for sure."

He and Ginny led Dax, Eddy, Daws, and Selyn through the door into the chancellor's office. Dawson paused by the portal—the one that led directly to the small vortex at Red Rock Crossing.

"Let's go to my place first," he said. His home was close to the portal. "We can charge our cell phones while you use the landline to try and reach Markus. I'll get in touch with my clinic, see if they've heard anything, but we might want to fan out, cover as much area as we can."

Ginny nodded. "Works for me. Let's go."

They slipped through the portal and entered the vortex at Red Rock Crossing. The entire chamber reeked of sulfur, and Dax stopped everyone with a wave of his hand. "Look. The portal to Abyss. It's open again."

Ginny drew DarkFire. "I've got it." Anxiety rippled across her shoulders as she pointed her sword at the pulsing gateway to hell. A beam of dark light shot from the end of her amethyst blade. Silently she willed DarkFire to hurry. In less than a minute, the small portal was once again sealed. Ginny slipped her sword into the scabbard and set a glamour over the blade.

The brilliant amethyst sword faded from sight.

Dawson was the first to step through the portal out of the vortex and into the waning light of a late October afternoon. The area was empty, the blue sky a welcome change after the caverns of Lemuria.

Ginny took a deep breath of the clean, desert air. No sulfuric stench of demon here, no sense of danger, but Markus had sounded absolutely terrified.

Alert and moving quickly, she followed the others—this amazing band of demonslayers—along the well-marked trail. It led to a shortcut that ran cross-country for a short distance before eventually dropping them into the back side of Dawson's property.

It would be night soon. The perfect time to hunt demons.

Visibly trembling, Isra clutched the hilt of her crystal sword and stared at the shimmering blade. "Why, Taron? I heard her voice, but . . ." Slowly raising her head, Isra stared at him. "I've done nothing to deserve her praise. How can this be?"

The other women in the training room gathered close as Isra's sword shimmered, diamond bright and pulsing with life.

Once again the blade flashed and the sentience within

spoke. The voice was soft and melodic, definitely a woman. "You will call me FrostFire, Isra. My name will forever be a reminder of the cold that once encased your heart. I speak because I wish to, because it is time. You had more personal demons to overcome than most, Isra, once a Forgotten One. You turned away from evil. You saved Nica's life. You have fought your own demons to become a stronger, better woman. You've done this not for personal glory but for Lemuria. We will make a formidable team, you and I."

The glow faded; the blade was once again merely faceted crystal. Isra raised her head and stared at Taron, not as a man she wanted to bed, but as a friend, one who might understand what had just happened. All sense of her earlier flirtation was gone. Tears coursed down her cheeks, but she didn't say a word. Her rapt expression spoke volumes.

Isra's silence was not unexpected. Taron figured if his gods-be-damned sword ever condescended to speak to him, he'd not know what to say, either.

He bowed low to Isra, a heartfelt show of respect,

Respect tainted by his own unfathomable jealousy—a foolish and unwelcome response he quickly buried. "Your sword is correct, Isra. You will make a formidable team. Congratulations to you, and to FrostFire. May your partnership be long and successful."

She nodded, but her attention shifted quickly from Taron to the crystal sword clutched in her hand. Taron turned and walked away as Isra's sisters gathered around her . . . walked away, clasping his own mute weapon in his right hand.

The proof of a warrior's value was in the sentience of his blade. Isra, who'd partnered with a crystal sword for mere days, had already been validated as a warrior, while he, a Lemurian aristocrat who'd carried crystal for millennia, who'd wielded his blade in battle, had not heard a word from his weapon.

If he'd proven himself, his sword would have spoken by now. Would have at least acknowledged him as a demon fighter. What did he lack? What did he need to do? He'd fought demonkind, and fought them bravely, yet obviously it wasn't enough.

Even if he had wanted to romance a woman—and he knew he could choose any of the Forgotten Ones with the odds of a successful outcome—he didn't feel worthy.

His sword had been the one chosen to replicate the crystal blades that now armed those same women; he'd killed demons in battle, had stood bravely against powerful odds.

Still, it had not been enough.

No matter what he did, it was never enough.

He knew he should not be so beholden to anyone or anything for affirmation of his own value, but the truth hurt. He needed to know his blade found him worthy, that he'd earned the respect of the sentience within his crystal sword.

There was no one else. He was a man without family. His parents were long gone. Alton had been the closest thing to a brother he'd ever known.

Now, Alton had Ginny and a sword that spoke to him. Taron was truly alone for the first time in his life.

Head down, heart heavy, he walked slowly back to his quarters, much too aware of the disconsolate sound of his footsteps as he headed down the long tunnel. His shadow, the dark shape of a powerful warrior bearing a sword, mocked him.

The melodramatic thoughts in his head mocked him even more. Why did this bother him so? Why couldn't he just let it go and get on with his life? *Fool*, he thought. *You act the fool.*

Yet once inside his apartment, he set the sword down on the low table in front of his couch, sat back in the comfortable chair and stared with unabashed bitterness at the blade.

So much had occurred over the past month, and through it all, he'd expected the sentience in his crystal sword to finally make itself known. He'd felt as if he paused on the precipice of history when he and Alton made the decision to free the demonslayers from their cell. He'd risked death, and yet he still believed the choice they'd made that night to defy the Council of Nine's edict would bring about change.

Change for the better of his world and his people. And, in many ways, it had, even though the demon king still lived.

Artigos the Just, a leader they'd long thought dead, had been freed from captivity and now governed Lemuria with his son beside him. The new Council of Nine—one untainted by demonic possession—would be seated in a couple of days. This would be the first council including both women and common folk since the great move to this dimension in the depths of Mount Shasta. The women, those brave Forgotten Ones, were no longer slaves. Now Paladins, they had become honored guardians of Lemuria, ready to usher in a renewed age of strong women warriors.

So many amazing changes in such a short time—unheard of in a world that was slow to embrace change of any kind. But where was Taron of Libernus's place in the new order? What role would he be called upon to play?

If he were called to play any future role at all.

He stared at the sword, running through all that had occurred since that moment just four weeks ago when he and Alton had first spied what they thought were normal humans sitting forlornly in their Lemurian prison cell.

Dax and Eddy had looked absolutely pathetic, and the silly dog hadn't been much better.

And Willow. Dear, beautiful little Willow. Unexpected tears stung his eyes at the thought of her. He'd been fascinated with the sprite from the very first moment he saw her. Not even as tall as his smallest finger, she'd stood there in the palm of his hand and actually flirted with him.

The others hadn't noticed, thank the gods, or he'd still be getting teased, but the little flirt had spoken mind to mind with him, and every word had been loaded with teasing innuendo. It should have sounded ridiculous, coming from such a tiny creature, but there'd been something special about the sprite. Something that tugged at his soul and made him smile even now, though, inexplicably, his heart was breaking.

How could he grieve so for a creature he hardly knew, one that could never be more to him than a friend? Still, the thought of that perfect little body being eaten by the demon king as the tiny sprite bravely battled evil made Taron's failings even more painfully obvious.

Ginny said Willow was handling it well. Just one more change among many—new life for Willow, new leader for Lemuria, new way of life for a people who preferred to debate a subject to death rather than deal with it.

Taron wished he was as good at dealing with change as Willow appeared to be, but there were just so many changes, so much to do . . . it made his head spin.

He closed his eyes and leaned back against the sofa. Consciously, he slowed his breathing, eased the taut muscles in his shoulders, and hoped the knot in his gut would finally settle.

Nine hells, but what a long month this had been . . . and yet it felt as if all that was familiar had been upended in the blink of an eye—which was quite close to reality for a man with a near-immortal span of years. What was one month in thousands of months? One year in millennia? He drifted, falling deeper and deeper into a sea of calm, relishing the sense of utter relaxation, if only for a moment.

A thought flittered through his mind, that it was probably not the smartest thing, to steal this time for himself . . . sort of like inviting chaos or tempting the gods.

As if merely giving freedom to that thought had opened a door, a brilliant blast of light flashed brightly across his closed lids.

Nine hells . . . Blinking, Taron opened his eyes. Shut them tightly, opened them again, and stared.

The entire room glowed. His crystal sword flashed again—blue fire almost blinded him. He blinked and jerked away from the shimmering light, then slowly leaned forward. Heart racing, he gazed, transfixed by the glowing blade. There was a sense of portent about the moment, a feeling that power gathered.

Tempting the gods, indeed!

Chills ran along his arms. He rubbed them, barely aware of the act, at least until a voice filled the room. A man's voice, speaking with strength and conviction.

His gods-be-damned crystal blade was actually speaking.

"Nine hells and then some . . ." Taron swallowed back another curse as the voice rang out.

"Taron of Libernus? Prepare. The final battle draws nigh. It is time."

Holy shit, as Ginny would say . . . time for what?

He took a deep breath. "I'm listening. What should I do?"

"Go now to Evergreen. Posthaste. Time is short."

The glow faded. The blade went silent.

Evergreen? It wants me to go to Earth's dimension?

He thought of Alton's brief message, received a short time ago. His friend was probably there now, slipping into Earth's dimension as if it were no big deal. He'd done it often enough over the past few weeks as one of the soldiers on the front lines of the battle against demonkind.

But not Taron. His work had all been here, in Lemuria. Until now. *Time is short.* How short? And why?

Still in shock, Taron ran his fingers over the faceted surface. The crystal felt cool to his touch, though it pulsed with a new sense of life.

His fingers trembled as he stroked the blade. His throat felt tight. He gazed at the crystal he'd carried for thousands of years, lost in wonder.

He couldn't wait to tell Alton, but his friend was already out of reach, already in Earth's dimension. Well, if Taron followed his blade's orders, he'd be seeing Alton soon. He couldn't wait to tell him his sword had . . . "Nine hells and then some."

Taron burst into laughter. Shoulders shaking, he laughed like a veritable madman until the tears ran down his cheeks and he knew he looked and sounded like an idiot.

Finally he got himself under control. Wiping his eyes, he stared ruefully at the silent sword. "The least you could have done after all these years," he said, "was tell me your name."

Wolf Tales / Sexy Beast Time Line

Title	Date	Introduces / About
Wolf Tales	Nov.–Dec. 2005	Stefan, Xandi, Anton, & Keisha
Sexy Beast: Chanku Rising	Late May– early June 2006	Ulrich Mason, kills off Keisha's stalker
Wolf Tales II	August 2006	Tia & Luc Stone and Pack Dynamics / packs' first time to work together
Wild Nights: Camille's Dawn	Halloween	Camille Mason's story/Keisha's pregnancy
Wolf Tales III	Aug.–mid-Sept. 2006	Jake & Shannon's story/Baylor Quinn added
Sexy Beast II: Chanku Fallen	Apr. 2007	Tala Quinn/AJ & Mik
Wolf Tales IV	End of Apr. 2007	Tinker & Lisa Quinn
Sexy Beast III: Chanku Journey	May 2007	All characters/Lily is born / Tia & Luc married
Wolf Tales V	May 30–end of June 2007	Ulrich Mason & Millie West/ Baylor Quinn & Manda Smith
Sexy Beast IV: Chanku Destiny	June 2007	Adam Wolf, Oliver, & Eve Reynolds
Wolf Tales VI	July 1–20, 2007	Adam & Eve/Oliver & Mei Chen
Sexy Beast V: Chanku Wild	Aug. 2007	Oliver & Mei Chen/Igmutaka
Wolf Tales VII	Aug.–Sept. 2007	All Characters/Tia pregnant

Title	Date	Introduces/About
Sexy Beast VI: Chanku Honor	Mid-Oct. 2007	Introduces (Rupert) Logan Pierce, Jazzy Blue, Elizabeth Ann Garner, Matthew James Rodgers, Christopher Andrew March (Deacon), Nicholas Robert Barden
Wolf Tales VIII	Oct. 2007	Daciana Lupei & Montana/pack Millie West and Matt/Beth, Tala, & Ulrich
Sexy Beast VII: Chanku Challenge	Late Oct. 2007	Beth & Nick/Tala and Keisha
Wolf Tales 9	Apr.–May 2008	Babies a year old/Tia gives birth to twins/characters tell life stories/Lisa & Tinker pregnant/Tala pregnant with AJ & Mik's twins
Sexy Beast VIII: Chanku Spirit	Sept. 2008	Matt & Anton kidnapped by Goddess Liana/Daci, Matt, & Deacon bond/Nick & Beth to SF to work for Pack Dynamics
Wolf Tales 10	Late Sept. 2008	Eve dies/Tala & Lisa's pregnancies five months along
Wolf Tales 11	Late Nov.–Winter solstice 2008	Lisa & Tala kidnapped/attempted presidential assassination/Anton has a plan
Wolf Tales 12	Aug.–Sept. 2013	Five years have passed and change is coming

Montana Pack

Anton Cheval 2/1/1955 (58)
Keisha Rialto Cheval 8/3/1971 (42)
    Daughter: Lily Milina 6/4/2007 (6½)
    Son: Gabriel Fane Cheval 10/31/2009 (4)
    Son: Marius Nicolai Cheval 10/31/2009 (4)
    Daughter: Lucia Camille Cheval 4/28/2013 (5 mos.)

Stefan Aragat 7/20/1963 (50)
Alexandria Olanet Aragat 4/29/1975 (38)
    Son: Alexander Anton Aragat 5/29/2007 (6½)
    Daughter: Amber Leigh Aragat 9/15/2009 (4)
    Daughter: Ariel Mei Aragat 11/1/2011 (22 mos.)

Oliver Cheval 11/3/1965 (47)
Mei Chen: 6/23/1981 (32)
    Son: Leonard Adam Cheval 12/5/2009 (4)
    Daughter: Emeline Isobelle Cheval 1/18/2013
    (9 mos.)

Adam Leyton Wolf 7/10/71 (42)
Liana Wolf ageless/once a goddess
    Daughter: Eve Elizabeth Wolf 7/14/2009 (born
    a month early) (4)
    Son: John Charles/Jace Wolf 6/14/2010 (named
    after Adam's father) (3)
    Daughter: Phoenix Olivia Wolf 9/25/2013

Logan (Rupert Logan Pierce) 2/12/1977 (36)
Jazzy Blue Pierce 1/1/1987 (26)
    5 months pregnant with daughter

San Francisco Pack

Lucien (Luc) Stone 8/20/1965 (48)
Tianna Mason Stone 3/3/1980 (33)
    Daughter: Camille Rose Stone (Cami) 4/7/2008 ($5\frac{1}{2}$)
    Daughter: Shannon Olivia Stone (Shay) 4/7/2008 ($5\frac{1}{2}$)
    Son: Mason Andrew Stone 11/20/2010
    Son: Eric Michael Stone 11/20/2010

Andrew Jackson (AJ) Temple 2/7/1967 (46)
Miguel (Mik) Fuentes 4/18/1971 (42)
Tala, aka Mary Ellen Quinn Temple-Fuentes:
born 3/15/77 (36)
    Daughter: Mikaela Star Fuentes (Star) 12/21/2008 ($4\frac{1}{2}$)
    Son: Jackson Miguel Temple (Jack) 12/21/2008 ($4\frac{1}{2}$)
    3 months pregnant with AJ's daughter (no more twins!)

Igmutaka ageless spirit guide (looks about 25)

Martin (Tinker) McClintock 8/27/1979 (34)
Lisa Marie Quinn McClintock 8/27/72 (41)
    Daughter: Anna Marie McClintock 12/21/2008 ($4\frac{1}{2}$)
    Son: Michael Baylor McClintock 6/27/2010 (3)
    Son: Richard Lucien McClintock 10/15/2012 (11 months)

Maine Pack

Baylor Quinn 6/17/1964 (49)
Amanda (Manda) Jane Smith Quinn 7/10/71 (42)
    Son: Keegan Adam Quinn 8/4/2009 (4)
    Son: Donovan Patrick Quinn 3/17/2013 (6 months)

Jacob Trent 5/10/1969 (44)
Shannon Murphy Trent born April 17, 1979 (34)
    Daughter: Kiera Lianne 7/28/2009 (4)
    Daughter: Rowan Tianna 7/28/2009 (4)
    Son: Jacob Connor (goes by Connor) 7/28/2009 (4)

White House/Washington, DC

Nicholas (Nicky) Robert Barden 3/5/1985 (28)
Elizabeth Ann (Beth) Garner-Barden 6/24/1988 (25)

Sunny Daye 2/7/1994 (19)

Colorado Pack

Ulrich Mason 1/5/1943 (70)
Millie West-Mason: 4/12/51 (62)

Christopher Andrew (Deacon) March 8/20/1987 (26)
Matthew James Rodgers 2/11/1984 (29)
Daciana Rodica Lupei Rodgers-March (Daci) 5/12/1984
(29)
    6 months pregnant with twin girls

On the Astral Plane

Eve Reynolds September 13, 1976 (deceased/now their
Goddess)